THE QUEEN'S CONFESSION

The Queen's Confession

Victoria Holt

1968

Doubleday & Company, Inc.

Garden City, New York

Design by Raymond Davidson
Library of Congress Catalog Card Number 68–10586
Copyright © 1968 by Victoria Holt
All Rights Reserved
Printed in the United States of America
First Edition

For

Naomi Burton

Guide, Counselor and Friend

Contents

Louis XVI meant to write his own memoirs; the manner in which his private papers were arranged pointed out this design. The Queen, also, had the same intention; she long preserved a large correspondence, and a great number of minute reports, made in the spirit and upon the event of the moment.

Madame Campan's Memoirs.

THE QUEEN'S CONFESSION

1

"The only real happiness in this world comes from a happy marriage. I can say this from experience. And all depends on the woman, on her being gentle, amusing, quick to please . . ."

From a letter to Marie Antoinette from Maria Theresa

THE FRENCH MARRIAGE

It was said that I was born "with the vision of a throne and a French executioner" over my cradle; but this was long after and it is a habit to remember prophetic signs and symbols when time has shown the course of events. In fact my birth caused my mother little inconvenience, for it happened just as the Seven Years' War was about to break out and she was more concerned with this threat than with her baby daughter. Almost as soon as I was born she was carrying on with state affairs, and I am sure scarcely gave me a thought. She was accustomed to bearing children; I was her fifteenth child.

She had wanted a boy, of course, although she had four, because rulers always want boys; and she had seven daughters left to her, three having died before I was born, either at birth or in infancy. I liked to hear how she had made a bet with the old Duke of Tarouka as to what my sex would be. She had wagered that the child would be a girl. So Tarouka had to pay up.

While she was awaiting my birth, my mother decided that my sponsors should be the King and Queen of Portugal. In later years this was considered to be another evil omen, for on the day I was born a terrific earthquake shattered Lisbon, wrecking the town and killing forty thousand people. Afterward, long afterward, it was said that all children born on that day were unlucky.

But few Princesses can have had a happier childhood than mine. During those long sunny days when my sister Caroline and I used to play together in the gardens of the Schönbrunn Palace, neither of us gave a thought to the future; it never seemed to occur to me that life could not go on in this way forever. We were Archduchesses, our mother was the Empress of Austria, and it was the nature of custom and tradition that our childhoods should inevitably be cut short and that we, being girls, would be sent away from home to be wives to strangers. It was different for our brothers—Ferdinand who came between Caroline and me, and Max who was a year younger than I and the baby of the family. They were safe. They would marry and bring their brides to Austria. But we never discussed this during these summers at Schönbrunn and winters at the Hofburg in Vienna. We were two happy carefree children—our only anxieties being which of the bitches would have her litter first and what the little darlings would be like. We loved dogs, both of us.

There were lessons but we knew how to manage our Aja, as we called her. To everyone else she was Countess von Brandeiss—outwardly stern and fond of ceremony, but she doted on us and we could always get what we wanted. I remember sitting in the schoolroom looking out on the gardens and thinking how lovely it was out there while I was trying to copy Aja's writing. There were blots on the page and I could never keep the lines straight. She came to me and clicking her tongue said I would never learn and she would be sent away because of it. Then I put my arms about her neck and said I loved her—which was true—and that I should never allow her to be sent away—which was absurd, because if my mother said she was to go away she would go without delay. But she softened and drew me to her; then she made me sit beside her while she drew for me in fine pencil so that all I had to do to produce an excellent drawing was go over her pencil lines in ink. After that it became a habit; and she would even write out my exercises in pencil and I would go over them with my pen, so that in the end it seemed as though I had written a very fair essay.

I was called Maria Antonia—Antonia in the family; it was not until later, when it was decided that I should go to France, that my name was changed to Marie Antoinette and I had to learn to forget I was Austrian and become French.

Our mother was the center of our lives although we did not see her very often; but she was always there, a presence, someone whose word and wish were law. We were all terrified of her.

How well I remember the cold of the Hofburg in winter, where all the windows had to be kept wide open because our mother believed that fresh air was good for everyone. The bitterly cold wind would whistle through the palace. I have never known anything so cold as those Viennese winters and I used to pity her attendants, particularly the poor little hairdresser who had to get up at five in the morning to dress my mother's hair and stand in that cold room near the open window. She was so proud when my mother had selected her to do her hair on account of her special talents, but I asked her—for I was always friendly with the attendants—if she did not sometimes wish she had not been so good, then she would not have been chosen.

"Oh, Madame Antonia," she replied, "it's *glorious* slavery."

That was how everyone felt about my mother. We all had to obey her but it seemed right and natural that we should, and we should never have thought of doing anything else. We all knew that she was the supreme ruler because she was the daughter of our grandfather Charles VI who had had no son, and although our father was known as the Emperor, he was second to her.

Dear Father! How I loved him! He was lighthearted and careless, and I imagine I took after him. Perhaps that was why I was his favorite. Mother had no favorites and we were such a large family that I scarcely knew some of my elder brothers and sisters. There had been sixteen of us, but five I never knew because they died before I was able to be aware of them. Mother was proud of us and used to bring foreign visitors to see us.

"My family is not small," she would say and her manner showed how pleased she was to have so many children.

Once a week the doctors used to examine us to see that we were in good health and their reports were sent to our mother who studied them carefully. When we were summoned to her presence we were all subdued and unlike ourselves; she would question us and we had to have the right answers. It was easy for me being the youngest but one; but some of the elder ones were terrified—even Joseph, my eldest brother, who was fourteen years older than I and seemed so important because he would one day be Emperor. Everyone saluted him wherever he went and in fact, when he was not in my mother's presence, he was treated as though he were already the Emperor. Once when he wanted to ride his sleigh out of season, his servants brought snow down from the mountains so that he could do so. He was very obstinate and inclined to be haughty and Ferdinand told me that our mother had reproved him because of his "wild desire to have his own way."

I believe our father was in awe of her too. He took little part in affairs of state, but we saw a great deal of him. He was not always happy and once said rather sadly, and a little resentfully: "The Empress and the children are the Court. Here I am simply an individual."

Long afterward when I was lonely and in my prison, I thought of those early days and I understood my family much better than I had when I was surrounded by them. It was like standing back and looking at a painting. Everything fell into focus and what I had been scarcely aware of at the time became very clear to me.

I saw my mother—a good woman, eager to do the best for her children and her country, loving my father dearly, but determined not to give up one bit of her power to him. I saw her, not as the martinet, whom I had feared too much to love, but as the wise, shrewd mother, who was constantly concerned for me. How she must have suffered when I went to my new country! I was like a child walking a tightrope, not realizing the danger I was in; but she, though miles away, was deeply aware.

Then my father. How could any man be expected to live contentedly under the domination of such a woman! I know now that the whisperings I heard meant that he was not faithful to her and that this was something which wounded her deeply. Yet, although she would have done a great deal for him, she would not give him what he wanted—a little of her power.

As for myself, I was featherbrained. I know I had the excuse of youth but I was naturally like this. I was full of high spirits, very healthy, and loved being out of doors, playing . . . always playing. I could not sit still for five minutes at a time. I could never concentrate for a moment; my mind would fly off at a tangent; I just wanted to laugh and chatter and play all the time. Looking back I can see what great dramas were going on in our household—and there was I playing with my dogs, whispering my little-girl secrets with Caroline and not being aware of them.

I must have been seven when my brother Joseph married for he was twenty-one. He did not want to get married and said: "I am more afraid of marriage than of battle."

That surprised me for I had not thought marriage was something to fear. But like everything else I heard it went in at one ear and out of the other; I never concerned myself about anything or wondered very much. I was absorbed by what ribbons Aja would put out for me and whether I could change mine for Caroline's if I did not like the color.

Now I can visualize the drama clearly. His bride was quite the loveliest creature we had ever seen. We were all so fair and she was dark. Our mother loved Isabella, and Caroline confided to me that she was sure our mother wished we were all like her. Perhaps she did, for Isabella was not only beautiful, she was very clever—which none of us was. But she had one other characteristic which we lacked. She was melancholy. I might have been frivolous; I might have known little about books; but there was one thing I did know and that was how to enjoy life; and this was something which, for all her learning, was beyond Isabella's powers. The only time I ever saw her laugh was with our sister Maria Christina who was a year younger than Joseph.

Isabella would go into the gardens when Maria Christina was there; they would walk together arm in arm, and then Isabella looked as nearly happy as she ever could. I was glad that she liked one of us, but it was a pity it was not Joseph for he had fallen deeply in love with her.

There was a great deal of excitement when she was going to have a baby; but when the child was born it was a weakling, and it did not live long. She had two children and they both died.

Caroline and I were too busy with our own affairs to think much about Joseph and his. I must have noticed that he looked very sad always and it certainly made some impression on me even then because it comes back so clearly all these years later. What a dark tragedy that was! And there was I living under the same roof with it.

Isabella was constantly talking about death and how she longed for it. That seemed strange to me. Death was something which happened to old people—or little babies whom one did not really know. It had little to do with us.

Caroline and I, hiding ourselves behind a clipped hedge in the gardens, once heard Isabella and Maria Christina talking together.

"What right have I in this world?" Isabella was saying. "I am no good. If it were not sinful I would kill myself. I should already have done so."

Maria Christina laughed at her. Maria Christina was not the kindest of our sisters and on the rare occasions when she did notice us she would say something spiteful, so we avoided her.

"You suffer from a desire to seem heroic," she retorted. "It's utter selfishness."

Then she walked away and left Isabella looking after her, stricken.

I thought about that scene for five whole minutes which was a long time for me.

And Isabella did die—just as she had said she wanted to. She was in Vienna for only two years altogether. Poor Joseph was heartbroken. He was constantly writing letters to Isabella's father in Parma and they were all about Isabella, how wonderful she had been, how there was no one like her.

"I have lost everything," he told my brother Leopold. "My beloved wife . . . my love . . . has gone. How can I survive this terrible separation."

One day I saw Joseph with Maria Christina. Her eyes were flashing with hatred and she was saying: "It's true. I will show you her letters. They will tell you all you want to know. You will see that I . . . not you . . . was the one she loved."

It falls into place now. Poor Joseph! Poor Isabella! I understand why Isabella was so sad and wished for death, ashamed of her love and yet unable to suppress it; and Maria Christina, who would always want her revenge, had betrayed her to poor Joseph.

Immersed as I was then in my own affairs I saw this tragedy as through a misted glass, but because my own suffering has now made of me a different person from the careless creature I was in my youth, I understand so much and I have sympathy to give to others who suffer. I brood on their sufferings—perhaps because I cannot bear to contemplate my own.

Joseph was very unhappy for a long time but because he was the eldest and more important than any of us he must have a wife. He was so angry when a new wife was selected for him by our mother and Prince Wenzel Anton Kaunitz that when she arrived in Vienna he scarcely spoke to her. She was very different from Isabella, being small and fat, with brown uneven teeth and red spots on her face. Joseph told Leopold, in whom he used to confide more than in anyone else at our mother's Court, that he was wretched and he was not going to pretend to be anything else for it was not in his nature to pretend. Her name was Josepha and she must have been unhappy too, for he had a barrier built across the balcony onto which their separate rooms opened so that he would never meet her if she stepped from her room at the same time as he stepped from his.

Maria Christina said: "If I were Joseph's wife, I'd go and hang myself on a tree in the Schönbrunn gardens."

When I was ten years old I was aware of tragedy which was real even to me because it concerned me deeply.

Leopold was going to be married. There was nothing very exciting to Caroline and me about this, because with so many brothers and sisters there were other weddings; and it was only one which was held in Vienna which would have interested us; but Leopold was being married in Innsbruck. Father was going to the wedding, but Mother could not leave Vienna as her state duties kept her there.

I was in the schoolroom tracing a picture when one of my father's pages came to say that my father wanted to say goodbye to me at once. I was surprised because I had said goodbye to him half an hour earlier and I had seen him ride off with his attendants.

Aja was in a fluster. "Something has happened," she said. "Go at once."

So I went with the servants. My father was on his horse looking back at the Palace and when he saw me coming his eyes lit up and he seemed very pleased. He did not dismount but I was lifted up and he held me against him so tightly that it was painful. I felt he was trying to say something and did not know how to, that he hated to let me go. I thought he was going to take me to Innsbruck with him, but that could not be, for my mother would have arranged that if it were so.

His hold loosened and he looked at me tenderly. I threw my arms about his neck and cried: "Dear, dear Papa." There were tears in his eyes and he gripped me with his right arm while he touched my hair with his left. He had always liked to touch my hair which was thick and light in color— auburn, some called it, though my brothers Ferdinand and Max called me "Carrots." His servants were watching and abruptly he signed to one of them to take me from him.

He turned to the friends who were beside him and said in a voice shaken with emotion: "Gentlemen, God knows how much I desired to kiss that child."

That was all. Father smiled goodbye and I went back to the school-room, puzzled for a few minutes and then characteristically forgot the incident.

That was the last I saw of him. In Innsbruck, he felt rather ill and his friends begged him to be bled, but he had arranged to go to the opera with Leopold that afternoon and he knew that if he were bled he would have to rest and cancel the opera which would worry Leopold who, like all his children, loved him dearly. It was better, he said, to go to the opera and be quietly bled afterward without disturbing his son.

So he went to the opera and was taken ill there. He had a stroke and died in Leopold's arms.

It was naturally said afterward that he, being near death, had had a terrible premonition of my future and that was why he had sent for me in that unusual manner.

We were all desolate because we had lost our father. I was sad for several weeks and then it began to seem as though I had never known him. But my mother was heartbroken. She embraced my father's dead body when it was brought home and she was only removed from it by force. Then she shut herself into her apartments and gave herself up to grief which was so violent that the doctors were forced to open one of her veins in order to give her relief from her terrible emotion. She cut off her hair—of which she had been so proud—and she wore a widow's somber costume which made her look more severe than ever. In the years which followed I never saw her differently dressed.

After my father's death, my mother seemed to become more aware of me. Before, I had been just one of the children; now I would often find her attention focused on me during those occasions when we all had to wait on her. This was alarming, but I soon discovered that if I smiled I could soften her, just as I could dear old Aja, though not so easily and not always; and of course I tried to cover up my shortcomings by using this gift of mine for making people indulgent toward me.

It was soon after Father's death that I began to hear talk of "The French Marriage." Couriers were constantly going back and forth with letters between Kaunitz and my mother and my mother's Ambassador in France.

Kaunitz was the most important man in Austria. A dandy, he was nevertheless one of the shrewdest politicians in Europe and my mother thought very highly of him and trusted him more than she trusted anyone else. Before he became her chief adviser he had been her Ambassador at Versailles where he had become a great friend of Madame de Pompadour which had meant that he was well received by the King of France, and it was while he was in Paris that he had conceived the idea of an alliance between Austria and France which would be through a marriage between the Houses of Hapsburg and Bourbon. Living in France had given him the manners of a Frenchman and, as he also dressed like one, in Austria he was considered rather eccentric. But he was very much a German in some ways—calm, disciplined, and precise. Ferdinand told us that he used egg yolks for his complexion, smearing them over his face to keep his skin fresh; and to preserve his teeth he used to clean them with a sponge and a scraper after every meal—at the table. He was so determined that his wig should be powdered all over that he ordered his valets to form two rows between which he walked while they used their bellows. He was enveloped in a cloud of powder, but this insured that his wig was evenly powdered.

We used to laugh at him. I did not realize then that while we were laughing together about his odd habits, he was deciding my future, and but for him I should not be where I am at this moment.

Caroline discovered that there was a possibility that either she or I might marry the King of France which set us giggling at the incongruity of this, for he was an old man nearly sixty and we thought it would be funny to have a husband who was older than our mother. But when the Dauphin of France—the son of that King who might have been a husband to one of us—died and *his* son became Dauphin, there was great excitement because the new Dauphin was only a boy, about a year older than I was.

Sometimes Caroline and I talked about "The French Marriage" and then we would forget about it for weeks; but all the time we were growing farther and farther away from childhood. Ferdinand tried seriously to discuss it with us—how good it would be for Austria if there was an alliance between Hapsburg and Bourbon.

The widow of the recently dead Dauphin, who had great influence with the King, was against it and wanted a Princess from her own House to marry her son; but she died suddenly of consumption which she had probably caught when nursing her husband, and my mother was very pleased.

My brother Joseph's poor unhappy wife died of the smallpox and my sister Maria Josepha, who was four years older than I, caught it and died. She was on the point of going to Naples to marry the King and our mother decided that an alliance with Naples was necessary so Caroline should be the bride instead.

This was the biggest tragedy of all so far. I had loved my father and had been sad, in my way, when he had died, but Caroline had been my constant companion and I could not imagine what it would be like without her. Caroline, who felt everything more deeply than I, was heartbroken.

I was twelve; Caroline was fifteen; and as Caroline had been selected for Naples, my mother at this time decided to train me to be ready to go to France. She announced that I should no longer be called Antonia. I should be Antoinette—or Marie Antoinette. That in itself made me seem like a different person. I was now brought into my mother's *salon* and made to answer the questions important men put to me; I had to have the right answers and was primed beforehand, but it was so easy for me to forget.

The comfortable life was over. I was watched; I was talked about; and I fancied that my mother and her ministers were trying to represent me as a very different person from the one I was—rather the person they wanted me to be, or the French would like me to be. I was always hearing stories about my goodness, my charm and cleverness which astonished me.

When I was younger, Mozart the musician had come to the Court; he was only a child then, but brilliant and my mother was encouraging him. When he came into the great *salon* to play to the company he was so overawed that he slipped and fell and everyone laughed. But I ran out to see if he was hurt and to tell him that it did not matter, after that we became friends and he played for me specially. He said once that he would like to marry me and as I thought that would be pleasant, I agreed to his proposal. This was remembered and told about me. It was supposed to be one of the "charming" stories.

On one occasion my mother told me that the French Ambassador would probably talk to me when I visited her *salon* and if he were to ask me which nation I should most like to rule I must say "the French"; and if he were to ask why, I was to reply: "Because they had Henri Quatre the Good and Louis Quatorze the Great." I learned it off by heart and was afraid I should get it wrong because I was not very sure who these people were; but I managed it and that was another story which was told about me. I was supposed to learn about the French; I was to practise speaking French; everything was changing.

As for Caroline she was always weeping and was no longer the pleasant companion she had been. She was very frightened of marriage and knew she was going to hate the King of Naples.

Our mother came to the schoolroom and talked to her very severely.

"You are no longer a child," she said, "and I have heard that you have been very bad tempered."

I wanted to explain that Caroline was only bad tempered because she was frightened; but it was impossible to explain to my mother.

Then she looked at me and went on: "I am going to separate you from Antoinette. You spend your time in stupid chattering and there is to be no more of this useless gossip. It will stop at once. I warn you that you will be watched and you, Caroline, as the elder, will be held responsible."

Then my mother dismissed me and kept Caroline there to lecture her further on how she should behave.

I went away with a heavy heart. I should miss Caroline so much. Strangely enough I did not think of my own fate. France was too far off to be real and I had perfected my natural inclination to forget what it was not pleasant to remember.

Caroline left at last—pale-faced, silent, and not in the least like my gay little sister. Joseph accompanied her and I believe he was quite sorry for her; there was something good about Joseph although he was so haughty and pompous.

There was trouble with another of my sisters but this seemed more remote for Maria Amalia was nine years older than I was. Caroline and I had known for a long time that she was in love with a young man of the Court, Prince Zweibrücken, and hoped that she would be able to marry him, which was perhaps foolish of her, for she should have known that we had to marry heads of States for the good of Austria. But Maria Amalia was like me in that she was apt to believe what she wanted to, so she went on believing that she would be allowed to marry Prince Zweibrücken.

Caroline's fears were fully realized. She was very unhappy in Naples and wrote home that her husband was very ugly, but because she remembered what my mother had told her, she tried to be brave, and added that she was growing quite accustomed to him. She wrote to Countess von Lerchenfeld, who helped Aja as governess:

> "One suffers martyrdom, and it is all the greater because one must pretend to be happy. How I pity Antoinette who has to face this. I would rather die than suffer it again. But for my religion I should have killed myself rather than live as I did for eight days. It was like hell and I wished to die. When my little sister has to face this I shall weep for her."

The Countess had not wanted to show me this but I begged and pleaded and she gave way as she always did; and when I read it I wished I hadn't. Was it really so bad? My sister-in-law Isabella had talked about killing herself. I, who loved life so much, could not understand this attitude; yet it seemed strange that those two who had had so much more experience of life than I should have both talked like that.

I thought about Caroline's letter for some hours and then it slipped to the back of my mind and I forgot it—perhaps because my mother was now turning her attention more and more on me.

She came to the schoolroom to investigate my progress and was horrified when she realized how little I knew. My handwriting was untidy and laborious. As for speaking French, I was hopeless, although I could chatter in Italian; but I could not write even German really grammatically.

My mother was not angry with me; she was merely pained. She drew me to her, held me in the crook of her arm and explained to me about the great honor which might be done to me. It would be the most wonderful thing in the world if this plan which Prince von Kaunitz here in Vienna and the Duc de Choiseul in France were trying to work out could come to fruition. It was the first time I had heard the Duc de Choiseul's name mentioned and I asked my mother who he was. She told me that he was a brilliant statesman, adviser to the King of France and, most important of all, A Friend to Austria. So much depended on him and we must do nothing to offend him. What he would say if he knew what a little ignoramus I was, she could not imagine. The whole plan would probably founder.

She looked at me so severely that I was momentarily downcast. It seemed such a great responsibility; then I felt my mouth turning up at the corners because I could not believe I was all that important. And as I laughed I saw that my mother was trying not to smile, so I put my arms about her neck and said I was sure Monsieur de Choiseul would not mind very much that I was not clever.

She held me tightly against her and then, putting me from her, looked severe again. She told me about the mighty Sun King who had built Versailles which, she said, was the greatest palace in the world, and the French Court was the most cultured and elegant, and that I was the luckiest girl in the world to have a chance of going there. I listened for a while to her accounts of the wonderful gardens and the beautiful *salons* which were far more splendid than anything we had in Vienna but soon, although I was nodding and smiling, I was not really listening.

I suddenly realized that she was saying my governesses were not suitable and I must have other teachers. She wanted me, in a few months' time, to be talking in French, *thinking* in French, so that it would be as though I *were* French.

"But never forget that you are a good German."

I nodded, smiling.

"But you must speak good French. Monsieur de Choiseul writes that the King of France has a very sensitive ear for the French language, and that you should have an accent of grace and purity which will not offend him. You understand?"

"Yes, Mamma."

"So you will have to work very very hard."

"Oh yes, Mamma."

"Antoinette, are you listening?"

"Oh yes, Mamma." I smiled widely to show her I was taking in every word and giving it serious consideration—at least as serious as I was able to manage. She sighed. I knew she was concerned for me, but she was far less severe with me than she had been with Caroline.

"Now there is a theatrical company in Vienna—a *French* theatrical company, and I have commanded that two actors shall come here and teach you to speak French as they do at the French Court, and French manners and customs . . ."

"Actors!" I cried ecstatically, thinking of the fun we used to have during winters in the Hofburg when my elder brothers and sisters acted plays and danced ballets and sang in opera. Caroline, Ferdinand, Max, and I were only allowed to watch, being, as our elder sisters and brothers told us, too young to take part. But how I had longed to! When I had a chance I would leap onto the stage and dance, until they turned me off with the constant cry of: "Go away, Antonia. You are too young to play in this. You must watch." If it was a play or a ballet I could scarcely stop myself from joining in, in spite of them. I loved dancing more than anything. So when my mother told me actors were coming I was excited.

"They are not here to play with you, Antoinette," she said severely. "They will be here to teach you French. You must study hard. Monsieur Aufresne will advise you on your pronunciation and Monsieur Sainville will take you in French singing."

"Yes, Mamma." My mind was far away—on the amateur stages when Maria Christina was so angry because she was not the heroine of the play, or Maria Amalia was watching the Prince Zweibrücken all the time she was saying her lines; and Max and I were jumping up and down in our seats with excitement.

"And Monsieur Noverre will come to teach you to dance."

"Oh . . . Mamma!"

"You have never heard of Monsieur Noverre but he is the finest dancing master in Europe."

"I shall love him!" I cried.

"You must not be so impulsive, my child. Think before you speak. One does not love a dancing master. But you should be grateful that you have the finest teacher in Europe and you must follow his instructions."

That was a happy time. It helped me to stop thinking of poor Caroline in Naples and that other family crisis when Maria Amalia was sent off to Parma to marry Isabella's brother. She was twenty-three and he was only a boy—not much more than fourteen—and Maria Amalia had to say good-bye to the Prince Zweibrücken. She was not meek like Caroline; she stormed and raged, and I thought she was going to do what no one had dared do before—defy my mother. But she went, because it was good for Austria, and we continued our alliance with Parma, so stormy Maria Amalia had this little boy for a husband while Caroline who was only fifteen had the old man from Naples.

But so much was happening to me that I had only time to think of what was expected of me. My mother was in despair because I could not learn. My actor teachers never forced me to study; and when I spoke French—as

I was obliged to all the time—they would smile tenderly and say: "It is charming, charming, Madame Antoinette. Not French, but charming!" Then we would all laugh together, so the lessons were not unpleasant. But what I enjoyed most were the dancing lessons. Noverre was delighted with me. I could learn the steps easily and he would applaud me almost ecstatically. Sometimes I made a false step and he would stop me and then cry: "No. We will leave it just like that. It is more charming the way you do it." My teachers were all so kind. They were constantly paying compliments and never scolding and I thought the French must be the most delightful people in the world.

My complacency did not last. I was closely watched and the Marquis de Durfort, the French Ambassador at our Court, reported everything to Versailles, so it was soon known there that I was being taught by Monsieur Aufresne and Monsieur Sainville. The Dauphine of France to be taught by strolling players! That was unthinkable. Monsieur de Choiseul would see that a *suitable* tutor was sent without delay. I had my lessons one day and the next my friends were gone. I felt very sad for a while; but I was growing accustomed to having people to whom I had become familiar suddenly whisked away from me.

My mother sent for me and told me that Monsieur de Choiseul was sending me a new tutor. I must forget my old ones and never mention them. I was being greatly honored because the Bishop of Orléans had found a French tutor for me. He was the Abbé Vermond.

I grimaced. An Abbé was going to be very different from my gay actors. My mother pretended not to see the grimace and gave me one of those homilies about the importance of learning the language and customs of my new country. I was not looking forward to the arrival of the Abbé Vermond.

I need not have worried, because from the moment I saw him I knew that I could cajole him as I had my governesses; and when I was young I had an insight into character which was astonishing in one of my superficial nature. I do not mean that I could probe deeply into the motives of those about me. If I had been blessed with that quality I might have saved myself a good deal of trouble; but I could see little quirks of behavior which I could reproduce rather amusingly (I think I could have been a tolerably good actress) and this enabled me to get what I wanted from people. Most of my sisters and brothers were cleverer than I, but they did not know how to lure my mother from a scolding mood to one of affection, as I did. It may have been because of my childishness, my innocence as they called it; and then, of course, my appearance helped. I was small and fairylike; in fact the French Ambassador who was constantly commenting on my appearance to his masters at Versailles referred to me as "A dainty morsel." But I don't think it was entirely this. I do believe that I could, in an extremely superficial way, of course, assess those little traits of character which would enable me to know how far I could go in my dealings with a person. So as soon as I saw the Abbé Vermond I was relieved.

He was learned, naturally, so he was going to be appalled by my ignorance; and he was. What could I do? I could speak Italian and French after a fashion—with a great many German expressions to help me along— my handwriting was disgraceful; I knew little of history and nothing of French literature which Monsieur de Choiseul had said was so necessary. I could sing fairly well; I loved music; and I could dance *"comme un ange,"* as Noverre had said. I also had been an Archduchess from my birth and when I was in my mother's *salon* I seemed to know instinctively which people I should speak to and to whom I should merely incline my head. This was inherent. It was true that in the privacy of my own apartments I was sometimes too familiar with my servants and if any of them had any young children I liked to play with them, for I adored children and when Caroline had said that marriage was hateful, I did remind her that marriage meant having children; and it must be worth a lot of discomfort to have them. Although I was more friendly with the servants than the rest of my family were, because I had this inherent royal demeanor, they rarely took advantage of it. My mother was aware of it, and I believe she thought it better not to try to change it.

The Abbé Vermond was by no means handsome. He seemed old to me but now I would say he was middle-aged when he came to Vienna. He had been a librarian and it quickly became clear to me that he was delighted to have been selected for this appointment to teach me. I was beginning to be aware of how important I was becoming. I was being trained to become the Dauphine of France who could very quickly become the Queen and this was one of the most elevated positions any woman in the world could hold. It was very different from being Archduchess of Austria. Sometimes it was too alarming to be thought of—so in accordance with my usual practice, I did not think of it.

Although the Abbé was astonished by my ignorance, he desperately wanted to please me. The actors and my dancing master had wanted to please me because I was an attractive girl; but the Abbé Vermond wanted to please me because one day I might well be Queen of France. I knew the difference.

It became clear soon that he was quite unaccustomed to living in palaces and although our Schönbrunn and Hofburg would not compare with Versailles, or the other châteaux and palaces of France, he betrayed quite clearly that it was very grand in his eyes. He had been brought up in a village where his father had been a doctor and his brother an *accoucheur*; he himself had become a priest and would never have reached his present position but for the patronage of the Archbishop.

Aware of this desire to please not only my mother but me, I was quite content to study with the Abbé. We read together and studied for an hour each day which he said was enough because he knew that was all I could endure without becoming bored and irritated. Much later when I talked about those days with Madame Campan, who by then was more than first lady of the bedchamber and had become a friend, she pointed out the harm Vermond had done. But she disliked him and she thought he had a share of the blame for everything that happened to us. Instead of reading together in our lighthearted way, and his allowing me to break off and give imitations of various people of the Court of whom some remark would remind me, I should have been given a thorough grounding not only in French literature but in the manners and customs of that land. I should, she said, have been made ready for the Court of which I was to be a part. I should have been made to study throughout the day if necessary (no matter how unpopular that made Monsieur Vermond); I should have been taught something of French history and of the people of France; I should have learned something about the rumbling dissatisfaction which long before I went there was making itself felt. But dear Campan was a natural *bas bleu* and she hated Vermond and loved me; moreover, she was desperately anxious for me at that time.

So although I had to substitute a priest for my actors, the exchange was not so bad after all; and the daily hour with Vermond went pleasantly enough.

But I was not left alone. My appearance was under continual discussion. Why? I wondered, thinking of Joseph's wife with the dumpy figure and the red spots. I had a good complexion, fine and delicately colored; my hair was abundant; some said it was golden, some russet, some red. *Blond cendré*, the French were to call it; and in the shops of Paris they would display gold-colored silk and call it *cheveux de la Reine*. But my high forehead caused a great deal of consternation. My mother was disturbed because Prince Starhemburg, our Ambassador in France, reported that: "This trifling imperfection might appear considerable at a time when high foreheads are no longer in fashion."

I would sit before the mirror contemplating this offending forehead which I had not before noticed was different from other people's; and very soon Monsieur Larsenneur arrived from Paris. He clucked over my hair, frowned at my forehead and went to work. He tried all sorts of styles and eventually decided that if my hair were dressed in a high pile straight up from my forehead, the latter would appear to be low in comparison with the hair. So it was pulled up so tightly that it hurt, and was held in place by false hair, my own color. To my disgust I was obliged to wear it like that, and as soon as Monsieur Larsenneur had gone I used to loosen the pins. Some of my mother's courtiers thought it unbecoming, but old Baron Neny said that when I reached Versailles all the ladies would dress their hair "à la Dauphine." Remarks like that always gave me an uneasy twinge because they implied that the great change was coming nearer and nearer; and I was trying hard to forget this in all the excitement of new hair styles and dancing steps, and luring Abbé Vermond from the book we were reading to give imitations of people at Court.

My teeth gave cause for concern too because they were uneven. A dentist was sent from France and he looked at them and frowned, as Monsieur Larsenneur had over my hair. He was always pushing my teeth about but I don't think he made much difference and eventually he gave up. They were a little prominent which as they said made my lower lip look "disdainful." I tried smiling which, although it exposed the uneven teeth, did abolish the disdain.

I had to wear stays which I hated and to grow accustomed to high heels, which prevented my running about the gardens with my dogs. When I thought of leaving the dogs I would burst into tears and the Abbé would comfort me by saying that when I was Dauphine I should have as many *French* dogs as I desired.

As my fourteenth birthday approached my mother decided that there should be a *fête* over which I should preside. The whole Court was going to attend, and it was to be a test to discover whether I was capable of being the center of such an occasion.

This did not greatly alarm me. It was lessons which I could not endure. So without a qualm I received the guests and danced as Noverre had taught me. I knew I was a success because even Kaunitz, who had come solely to watch me and not to be entertained, said so. My mother told me afterward that he had remarked: "The Archduchess will do well in spite of her childishness, providing no one spoils her."

The words my mother emphasized were *childishness* and *spoils*. I must grow up quickly, she insisted. I must not believe that everyone would do as I wished merely because I smiled.

The time was passing. In two months, providing all the arrangements had been made and all the disagreements between the French and the Austrians settled, I was to leave for France. My mother was deeply disturbed. I was so unprepared, she said. I was summoned to her *salon* and told that I should sleep in her bedroom so that she could find spare moments now and then to give me her attention. I was far more horrified by this immediate prospect than by the all-important one of starting a new life in a new country—which was an indication of my character.

I still remember—nostalgically now—those days and nights of utter discomfort and apprehension. The big state bedroom was icy; all windows were wide open to let in the fresh air; the snow fluttered into the room but that was not so bad as the bitter wind. We were all supposed to have our windows open but in my room I would persuade my servants to close them. They were willing enough—as long as they were opened again before it could be discovered that they had been shut. But there was no such comfort in my mother's bedroom. The only warm place was in bed; and sometimes I would pretend to be asleep when she stood over me, pulling the clothes from my face, and it was all I could do to stop myself wincing from the icy draft. With cold fingers she would move the hair out of my eyes, and she would kiss me very tenderly so that I almost forgot I was pretending to be asleep and would want to jump up and throw my arms about her neck.

Only now can I understand how anxious she was for me. I believe I became her favorite daughter not only because I had been my father's, but because I was small, naïve, impossible to educate and . . . vulnerable. I realized later that she was continually asking herself what would become of me. I thank God that she did not live long enough to find out.

I could not always pretend to be asleep, and there were long dialogues or rather monologues—in which I was instructed what I must do. I remember one of them.

"Don't be too curious. This is a matter on which I am very concerned for you. Avoid familiarities with subordinates."

"Yes, Mamma."

"Monsieur and Madame de Noailles have been chosen by the King of France to be your guardians. You will always ask them if you are in any doubt as to what you should do. Insist that they warn you of what you should know. And don't be ashamed to ask for advice."

"No, Mamma."

"Do nothing without consulting those in authority first . . ."

I found my thoughts straying. Monsieur and Madame de Noailles. What were they like? I started building up incongruous images in my mind which would make me want to smile. My mother saw the smile and was half exasperated, half tender. She took me in her arms and held me against her.

"Oh, my darling child, what will become of you?"

It would all be so different there, she said. There was a vast difference between the French and the Austrians. The French believed that everyone who was not French was a barbarian. "You must be as a Frenchwoman, for you will *be* a Frenchwoman. You will be the Dauphine of France and in time Queen. But do not show eagerness for that. The King would detect it and naturally be displeased."

She said nothing about the Dauphin who was to be my husband, so I did not think of him either. It was all the King, the Duc de Choiseul, the Marquis de Durfort, Prince Starhemburg, and the Comte de Mercy-Argenteau—all those important men who had taken their minds from state affairs to think about Me. But then *I* had become a matter of state—the most important they had ever had to deal with. It was so incongruous that I wanted to laugh at it.

"At the beginning of every month," said my mother, "I shall send a messenger to Paris. In the meantime you can prepare your letters so that they can be given to the messengers and brought to me *at once*. Destroy my letters. This will enable me to write to you more frankly."

I nodded earnestly. It seemed so very exciting—like one of the games Ferdinand and Max used to like to play. I saw myself receiving my mother's letters, reading them and hiding them in some secret place until I could burn them.

"Antoinette, you are not attending!" My mother sighed. It was a reproach I constantly heard.

"Say nothing about domestic affairs here."

I nodded again. No! I must not tell them how Caroline had cried, how she had declared the King of Naples to be ugly; what Maria Amalia had said about the boy she had been sent out to marry; how Joseph had hated his second wife and how his first had loved Maria Christina. I must forget all that.

"Speak of your family with truth and moderation."

Should I speak of these matters if I were asked? I was pondering this but my mother went on: "Always say your prayers on rising and say them on your knees. Read from a spiritual book every day. Hear Mass every day and withdraw for meditation when you are able."

"Yes, Mamma." I was determined to try to do all she said.

"Do not read any book or pamphlet without the consent of your confessor. Don't listen to gossip, and don't favor anyone."

One had one's friends, of course. I could not help liking some people better than others and when I liked them I wanted to give them things.

It went on endlessly. You must do this. You must not do that. And I shivered as I listened for although the weather was improving as we came nearer to April it was still cold in the bedroom.

"You must learn how to *refuse* favors—that is very important. Always answer gracefully if you have to refuse something. But most of all never be ashamed to ask for advice."

"No, Mamma."

Then I would escape perhaps to the Abbé Vermond for my lesson, which was not so bad, or to the hairdresser who pulled my hair, or to my dancing lesson which was sheer joy. There was an understanding between Monsieur Noverre and me that we would forget the time; we would be surprised when a servant came to tell us that Monsieur l'Abbé was waiting for me, or the hairdresser, or that I must be ready for my interview with Prince von Kaunitz in ten minutes' time.

"We were absorbed in the lesson," he would say, as though by referring to that delightful exercise as a lesson he excused us.

"You are fond of dancing, my child," my mother said in the cold bedroom.

"Yes, Mamma."

"And Monsieur Noverre tells me you make excellent progress. Ah, if only you were as well advanced in *all* your studies." I would show her a new step and she would smile and say I did it prettily. "Dancing is after all a necessary accomplishment. But do not forget that we are not here for our own pleasure. Pleasures are given by God as a relief."

A relief? A relief from what? Here was another suggestion that life was a tragedy. I started thinking about poor Caroline but my mother brought me out of my reverie with: "Do nothing contrary to the customs of France, and never quote what is done here."

"No, Mamma."

"And never imply that we do something better in Vienna than they do in France. Never suggest that anything we do here should be imitated there. Nothing can exasperate more. You must learn to *admire* everything French."

I knew I should never remember all the things I was to do and not to do. I should trust to my luck, to my ability to smile my way out of my mistakes.

During those two months I was sleeping in my mother's bedroom she was in a state of tension because she feared there might be no marriage at all. She and Kaunitz were constantly closeted together and the Marquis de Durfort was always coming to see them.

This was a respite for me because I was spared those lectures which had become a part of my life in the drafty state bedroom. It was all a matter of who should take precedence over whom—whether my mother's and brother's names or that of the King of France should be first on the documents.

Kaunitz was calm but anxious. "The whole question of a marriage could be dropped," he told my mother. "It's ridiculous that so much should hang on such insignificant details." They were arguing about the formal reception of handing me over. Should it take place on French or Austrian soil? One or the other had to be chosen. The French said it must be on French; the Austrians said it must be Austrian. My mother sometimes told me snatches of these matters. "Because it is good for you to know."

So much prestige was involved. It was a matter of the greatest importance how many servants I took with me and how many of these should accompany me into France. There came a time when I was certain there would be no marriage and I was not sure whether I was pleased or sorry. I should be disappointed if all the attention stopped, but on the other hand I thought it would be comforting to stay at home until I was twenty-three as Maria Amalia had.

I have often, during the last months, thought of those wrangles and wondered how different my life would have been if the statesmen had failed to come to an agreement.

But fate decided differently and at last agreement was reached.

The Marquis de Durfort returned to France to receive instructions from his master; there were hasty reconstructions to enlarge the French Embassy because there must be fifteen hundred guests and it would be a breach of etiquette to leave one out. Etiquette! That was a word I heard repeatedly.

News reached us that since there was to be rebuilding in Vienna, King Louis had decided that an opera house be erected at Versailles so that the wedding could be celebrated there.

My mother was determined that I should be provided with clothes as grand as anything the French could produce. I could not help showing

my delight with all this fuss surrounding me and sometimes I saw my
mother watching me quizzically. I wonder now whether she was glad of
my frivolity which prevented my being too concerned at the prospect of
leaving home. After the suicidal attitude of Caroline it must have been
a relief.

When the Marquis de Durfort returned to Vienna it really did seem
like a wonderful game in which I had been selected to play the biggest
and most exciting role, for this was the beginning of the official ceremonies. April had come and the weather was benign. On the seventeenth
of that month the Ceremony of Renunciation took place, when I was
called upon to renounce the hereditary Austrian Succession. It all seemed
rather meaningless to me as I stood in the hall of the Burgplatz and
signed the Act, which was in Latin, and took the Oath before the Bishop
of Laylach. I found the ceremony tedious but I enjoyed the banquet and
ball which followed.

The huge ballroom was brilliantly lighted with three thousand five
hundred candles and I was told that eight hundred firemen had to work
continuously with damp sponges because of the sparks which fell from
the candles. When I danced I was oblivious of everything but the joy of
dancing. I even forgot that this would be one of the last balls I should
attend in my own country.

The very next day the Marquis de Durfort entertained the Austrian
Court on behalf of the King of France, and of course this occasion must
be as grand—if not grander—than that of the previous evening, so he
hired the Lichtenstein Palace in which to hold it. That was a wonderful
evening too. I remember driving there—it was in the suburb of Rosseau—
and all along the road the trees had been illuminated, and between each
tree a dolphin had been set up, each dolphin carrying a lantern. It was
enchanting and we were exclaiming with wonder as we rode along.

In the ballroom the Marquis de Durfort had ordered that beautiful
pictures be hung, symbolic of the occasion, and I particularly remember
one of myself on the road to France. Spread out before me was a carpet
of flowers which were being thrown by a nymph representing Love.

There were fireworks and music; and the splendor on that evening did
in fact exceed ours in spite of those three thousand five hundred candles.

On the nineteenth I was married by proxy. This was all part of a game
to me for Ferdinand played the part of bridegroom, and because my
brother was standing proxy for the Dauphin of France, it seemed exactly
like one of those plays I used to watch my brothers and sisters perform,
only now I was old enough to join in. Ferdinand and I knelt together at

the altar and I kept saying to myself "*Volo et ita promitto*" so that I should get it right when the moment came to say it aloud.

After the ceremony guns were fired at the Spitalplatz and then . . . the banquet.

I was to leave my home two days later, and suddenly I began to realize what this was going to mean. It struck me that I might never see my mother again. She called me to her room and again gave me many instructions. I listened fearfully; I was beginning to feel apprehensive.

She told me to be seated at a desk and take up my pen. I was to write a letter to my grandfather, for the King of France would now be that. I must remember it. I must seek to please him. I must obey him and never offend him. And now I must write to him. I was glad I was not expected to compose the letter. That would, indeed, have been beyond my powers; it was bad enough to have to write to my mother's dictation. She watched me. I can imagine her fears. There I sat, my head on one side, frowning in concentration, biting my tongue, the tip of which protruded slightly, making the utmost effort, but only managing to produce a childish scrawl with crooked lines. I remember asking the King of France to be indulgent to me and begging him to ask the indulgence of the Dauphin on my behalf.

I paused to think of the Dauphin . . . the other important player in this . . . farce, comedy, or tragedy? How could I know which it was to be? Later I came to think of it as all three. What of the Dauphin? No one spoke much of him. Sometimes my attendants referred to him as though he were a handsome hero . . . as all Princes should be. Of course he would be handsome. We should dance together and we should have babies. How I longed for babies! Little golden-haired children who would adore me. When I became a mother I should cease to be a child. Then I thought of Caroline—those poor pathetic letters of hers. "He is very ugly . . . but one grows accustomed to that . . ." My mother had talked to me of everything that I might encounter at the Court of France . . . except my bridegroom.

My mother then put her arm about me and held me to her while she wrote to the King of France. I looked at her quick pen admiring the skill with which it traveled over the paper. She was begging the King of France to care for her "very dear child." "I pray you be indulgent toward any thoughtless act of my dear child's. She has a good heart, but she is impulsive and a little wild . . ." I felt the tears coming to my eyes because I was sorry for her. That seemed strange, but she was so worried because she knew me so well and she could guess at the sort of world into which I was being thrust.

The Marquis de Durfort had brought with him to Austria two carriages which the King of France had had made for the sole purpose of taking me to France. We had heard of these carriages in advance. They had been made by Francien, the leading carriagemaker in Paris, and the King of France had ordered that no expense should be spared in the making. Francien had lived up to his reputation and they were quite magnificent, lined with satin and decorated with paintings in delicate colors, with gold crowns on the outside to proclaim them royal carriages. I was to discover that they were not only the most beautiful I had ever traveled in but the most comfortable.

The Marquis came with a hundred and seventeen bodyguards, all in colored uniforms; and it was boasted that the cost of this merry little cavalcade was about three hundred and fifty thousand ducats.

On the twenty-first of April my journey to France began. During the last few years I have often thought of my mother when she said goodbye to me. She knew it was the last time she would hold me in her arms, the last time she would kiss me. No doubt words came into her mind. Remember this. Don't do that. Surely she had said it all to me in her icy bedroom; but knowing me she would realize that I had forgotten half of it by now. In any case I should have heard little of what she said to me. Now I knew she was praying silently to God and the Saints asking them to guard me. She saw me as a helpless child wandering in the jungle.

"My dearest child," she whispered; and suddenly I did not want to leave her. This was my home. I wanted to stay in it—even if it did mean lessons and painful hair styles and lectures in a cold bedroom. I should not be fifteen until November and suddenly I felt very young and inexperienced. I wanted to plead to be allowed to stay at home for a little longer, but Monsieur de Durfort's magnificent carriages were waiting; Kaunitz was looking impatient and relieved that all the bargaining was over. Only my mother was sad and I wondered if I could be alone with her and beg to be allowed to stay. But of course I could not. Much as she loved me she would never allow my whims to interfere with state affairs. I was a state affair. The thought made me want to laugh—and it pleased me too. I really was a very important person.

"Goodbye, my dearest child. I shall write to you regularly. It will be as though I am with you."

"Yes, Mamma."

"We shall be apart but I shall never cease to think of you until I die. Love me always. It is the only thing that can console me."

And then I was getting into the carriage with Joseph who was to accompany me for the first day. I had had little to do with Joseph who was so much older and had become so important now that he was Emperor and co-ruler with my mother. He was kind but because of my mood I found his pomposity irritating, and all the time he gave me advice to which I did not want to listen. I wanted to think about my little dogs, which the servants had assured me they would care for. When we passed the Schönbrunn Palace I looked at the yellow walls and the green shutters and remembered how Caroline, Ferdinand, Max, and I used to watch the older ones perform their plays, operas, and ballets. I remembered how the servants used to bring refreshments to us in the gardens—lemonade, which my mother thought was good for us, and little Viennese cakes covered with cream.

Before I left my mother had given me a packet of papers which she said I was to read regularly. I had glanced at them and saw that they contained rules and regulations which she had already given me during our talks. I would read them later, I promised myself. I wanted now to think about the old times—the pleasantness of the days before Caroline and Maria Amalia had been so unhappy. I glanced at Joseph who had had his own tragedies and thought he seemed to have recovered as he sat there so serenely against the gorgeous satin upholstery.

"Always remember you are a German . . ."

I wanted to yawn. Joseph in his labored way was trying to impress upon me the importance of my marriage. Did I realize that my retinue consisted of one hundred and thirty-two persons? Yes, Joseph, I had heard it all before.

"Ladies in waiting, your servants, your hairdressers, dressmakers, secretaries, surgeons, pages, furriers, chaplains, cooks, and so on. Your grand postmaster the Prince de Paar has thirty-four subordinates."

"Yes, Joseph, it is a great number."

"It is not to be supposed that we should allow the French to think that we cannot send you off in a style to match their own. Did you know that we are using three hundred and seventy-six horses and that these horses have to be changed four or five times a day?"

"No, Joseph. But now you have told me."

"You should know these things. Twenty thousand horses have been placed along the road from Vienna to Strasbourg to convey you and your retinue there."

"It is a great number."

I wished that he had talked to me more of his marriage and had warned me what to expect of mine. I was bored by these figures, and all the time I was fighting my desire to cry.

At Mölck, which we reached after eight hours' driving, we stayed at the Benedictine convent where the scholars performed an opera for us. It was a bore. I felt very sleepy and as I kept thinking of the previous night which I had spent in my mother's bedroom in the Hofburg, I felt I wanted to cry for the comfort she could give me. For oddly enough, in spite of the lectures, she had comforted me; without knowing it I had felt that while she was there—omnipotent and omniscient—I was safe because all her care was for me.

Joseph left me the next day and I was not sorry. He was a good brother who loved me but his conversation made me so tired and I always found it difficult to concentrate at the best of times.

What a long journey! The Princess de Paar shared my carriage and tried to comfort me by talking of the wonders of Versailles and what a brilliant future lay before me. To Enns, to Lambach, on to Nymphenburg. At Günsburg we rested for two days with my father's sister, Princess Charlotte. I had vague memories of her at Schönbrunn for she had at one time been a member of our household. My father had been very fond of her and they used to take long walks together but my mother resented her presence. Perhaps she resented anyone of whom my father was fond; and eventually Charlotte retired to Remiremont where she became the Abbess. She talked lovingly of my father and I went with her to distribute food to the poor, which was a change from all the banquets and balls.

We crossed the Black Forest and came to the Abbey of Schüttern where I was visited by the Comte de Noailles who was to be my guardian. He was old and very proud of the duty which had been entrusted to him by his friend, the Duc de Choiseul. I thought he was a vain old fellow and I was not sure whether I liked him. He did not stay long with me for there arose a difficulty about the ceremony which lay before me. It was again a matter of whose names should come first on a document. Prince Starhemburg, who was going to hand me formally over to the French, was in a great passion about this; and so was the Duc de Noailles.

I felt very sad that night because I knew it was going to be my last on German soil. I suddenly found myself crying bitterly in the arms of the Princess de Paar and saying over and over again: "I shall never see my mother again."

That day a letter had reached me from her. She must have sat down and written as soon as I left; and I knew that she had written it in tears. Snatches of it come back to me now:

> "My dear child, you are now where Providence has placed you. Even if one were to think no more of the greatness of your position, you are the happiest of your brothers and sisters. You will find a tender father who will be at the same time your friend. Have every confidence in him. Love him and be submissive to him. I do not speak of the Dauphin. You know my delicacy on that subject. A wife is subject to her husband in all things and you should have no other aim than to please him and do his will. The only real happiness in the world comes through a happy marriage. I can say this from experience. And all depends on the woman, who should be willing, gentle and able to amuse . . ."

I read and reread that letter. That night it was my greatest comfort. The next day I would pass into my new country; I would say goodbye to so many of the people who had accompanied me so far. There was so much I had to learn, so much which would be expected of me; and all I could do was cry for my mother.

"I shall never see her again," I murmured into my pillow.

2

"The Golden Age will be born from such a union and under the happy rule of Marie Antoinette and Louis-Auguste our nephews will see the continuation of the happiness we enjoy under Louis the Well-Beloved."

Prince de Rohan at Strasbourg

THE BEWILDERED BRIDE

On the no-man's land of a sandbank in the middle of the Rhine, a building had been erected and in this was to take place the ceremony of the Remise. The Princess de Paar had impressed on me that this was the most important ceremony so far, for during it I should cease to become Austrian. I was to walk into that building on one side as an Austrian Archduchess and emerge on the other as a French Dauphine.

It was not a very impressive building for it had been hastily constructed; it would be used for this purpose only and that would be an end of it. Once on the island I was led into a kind of antechamber where my women stripped me of all my clothes, and I felt so wretched standing there naked before them all that I had to think of my mother at her most stern to prevent myself breaking into sobs. I put my hand up to the chain necklace which I had worn for so many years, as though I were trying to hide it. But I could not save it. The poor thing was Austrian and therefore had to come off.

I was shivering as they dressed me in my French clothes, but I could not help noticing that they were finer than anything I had had in Austria and this lifted my spirits. Clothes meant a great deal to me and I never lost my excitement for a new material, a new fashion or a diamond. When I was dressed I was taken to the Prince Starhemburg who was waiting for me; he held my hand firmly and led me into the hall which formed

the center of this building. It seemed large after the little antechamber
and in the center was a table which was covered with a crimson velvet
cloth. Prince Starhemburg referred to this room as the Salon de Remise,
and he pointed out that the table symbolized the frontier between my
old country and my new. The walls of the room were hung with tapestries
which were beautiful though the scenes depicted on them were horrible,
for they represented the story of Jason and Medea. I found my eyes straying to them during the short ceremony and when I should have been
listening to what was being said I was thinking of Jason's murdered children and the Furies' flaming chariot. Years later I heard that, before the
ceremony, the poet Goethe, then a young law student at the Strasbourg
University, had come to look at the hall and had expressed his horror at
the tapestries, adding that he could not believe anyone could have put
them where a young bride was to enter her husband's country. They
were pictures, he said, of "the most horrible marriage that could be
imagined." People would see that as an omen, too.

The ceremony was fortunately short. I was led to the other side of the
table, a few words were spoken and I had become French.

I was then relinquished by Prince Starhemburg and given into the hands
of the Comte de Noailles who led me into the antechamber on the French
side of the building where he presented me to his wife who, with him, was
to share the guardianship. I felt bewildered and scarcely glanced at her.
All I knew was that I felt lonely and frightened, and that this woman
was to look after me, and, without thinking, I threw myself into her arms,
subconsciously feeling sure that this childish and impulsive gesture would
charm her.

When I felt her stiffen, I looked up into her face. She seemed old . . .
very old; her face was wrinkled and set into lines of severity. For a second
or so my behavior had startled her; and then gently, but firmly, she
withdrew herself and said:

"I beg leave of Madame la Dauphine to present to her her Mistress
of the Robes, the Duchesse de Villars."

I was too surprised to show that I was hurt. In any case dignity had
been stressed in my upbringing and my mother's instructions to such an
extent that it was almost intuitive, so accepting the fact that I could hope
for small comfort from Madame de Noailles, I turned to the Duchesse
de Villars to find that she too was old, cold, and remote.

"And Madame la Dauphine's maids of honor." There they stood: the
Duchesse de Picquigny, the Marquise de Duras, the Comtesse de Saulx-

Tavannes, and the Comtesse de Mailly—and all old. A band of severe old ladies!

I found myself coolly acknowledging their greeting.

From no-man's island the brilliant cavalcade made its way to Strasbourg, the Alsace possession which had gone to France at the conclusion of the Peace of Ryswick nearly a hundred years before. The people of Strasbourg were delighted with the wedding because they were so dangerously near the frontier, and they were anxious to show their pleasure. The greeting I received in that town took away the flavor of the chilly reception in the Salon de Remise and my introduction to the ladies who had been chosen for me. This was the sort of occasion in which I reveled. In the streets of the city children, dressed as shepherds and shepherdesses, brought flowers to me and I loved the pretty little creatures and wished that all the solemn men and women would leave me with the children. The people of Strasbourg had had the happy idea of lining the route with small boys dressed as Swiss Guards; they looked adorable; and when I arrived at the Bishop's Palace, where I was to stay that night, I asked if these little boys might be my guard for the night. When the little boys heard this they jumped about and laughed with pleasure; and next morning I peeped out of my window and saw them there. They saw me and cheered me. That was my most pleasant memory of Strasbourg.

At the Cathedral I was met by Cardinal de Rohan, an ancient man who moved as though he suffered acutely from the gout. There followed a grand banquet and a visit to the theater. From a balcony of the Palace we watched the decorated barges on the river, and the firework display was very exciting, particularly when I saw my initials entwined with those of the Dauphin, high in the sky. After that—to bed, to be guarded by my little Swiss Guards.

The next morning I went to the Cathedral to hear Mass, expecting to see the old Cardinal again; but on this occasion he was too unwell to attend and in his place was his nephew, a very handsome young man, Bishop Coadjutor of the Diocese, Prince Louis de Rohan, who would most certainly become a Cardinal when his uncle died which from the look of the old man could not be long.

He had one of the most beautiful voices I had ever heard—but perhaps I thought this because I was unaccustomed to the French love of the gracefully spoken word. In a few days time I was to think that the King of France had the most beautiful voice in the world. But on this occasion I was charmed by that of Prince Louis. He was very respectful, but there was a gleam in his eyes which disturbed me. He made me feel very young and inexperienced even though his words were all that even my mother could have wished for.

"For us, Madame," he said, "you will be the living image of that dear Empress who for so long has been the admiration of Europe, as she will be in the ages to come. The soul of Maria Theresa will be united with that of the Bourbons."

That sounded very fine, and I was happy to hear that they thought so highly of my mother.

"The golden age will be born from such a union and under the happy rule of Marie Antoinette and Louis-Auguste our nephews will see the continuation of the happiness we enjoy under Louis the Well-Beloved."

I caught a fleeting expression on the faces of several people when the Prince said those words—almost a sneer, it seemed. I wondered briefly what it meant; then I was bending my head to receive the blessing.

I was to remember that man later—my enemy. My dearest Campan believed that his follies and his license played a great part in bringing me where I am today. But on that occasion he was merely a handsome young man who had taken the place of a gouty old one, and I thought no more of him as we left Strasbourg and made our way across France.

Our progress was *fête* after *fête*. I grew tired of passing under triumphal arches, of listening to my praises sung, except when they were sung by children; then I enjoyed them. It was all very strange and I was often lonely in spite of being surrounded by crowds. The only people with me whom I had known during my life in Vienna were the Abbé Vermond, whom they had decided should stay with me for a while, Prince Starhemburg, and the Comte de Mercy-Argenteau—all serious old men, and I longed for companions of my own age. My ladies-in-waiting I could well have done without. There was no one, simply no one, to chat with, to laugh with.

On went the cavalcade with two wagons in front which contained my bedroom furniture. In each place where we stayed the night they would unload and the bed and stools and armchairs would be taken out and put into a room which had been prepared for me. Through Saverne, Nancy, Commercy to Rheims, the town where the French crowned their Kings and Queens.

"I hope," I said with great feeling, "that it will be long before I come to this town again."

Being at Rheims had reminded me that I could at any time be Queen of France for my new grandfather was an old man of sixty. I felt alarmed at the thought. Many times during that journey a cold shiver would creep over me; but I dismissed my apprehensions and it all seemed like a game once more.

From Rheims to Châlons and on . . . to the forest of Compiègne.

It was the fourteenth of May when I first saw my husband. I had been traveling for nearly three weeks and my mother's Court seemed remote. I wished now that I knew a little more about my new family. I tried to find out, but I could discover nothing from Madame de Noailles, nor from any of my ladies-in-waiting. Their replies were always conventional and a little chilling as though they were reminding me that it was not etiquette to ask questions. Etiquette! It was a word which was already beginning to weary me.

It was a brilliant day; the budding trees were breaking into leaf, the birds were in full song, and the glories of nature seemed as though they were trying in vain to compete with the extravagance of the court scene.

I was aware that the King of France—and with him my bridegroom— could not be far away for the trumpets had started and the musketeers were beating their drums. It was a tremendously exciting moment. We were on the edge of the forest and the trees were like a beautiful back- cloth; there ahead of me I saw the gay uniform of guards and the bright livery of servants. I saw men and women more gorgeously attired than I had ever seen before. And I was aware of the most magnificent figure of them all, standing there . . . waiting for *me*. I knew immediately by his clothes, but chiefly by his bearing, that he was the King of France. He had that dignity, that grace, that complete kingliness which he must have inherited from his great-grandfather, le Roi Soleil.

My carriage had stopped and I alighted immediately which shocked Madame de Noailles who, I knew, was undoubtedly thinking that eti- quette demanded I wait until someone came forward to conduct me to the King. It simply did not occur to me to wait. For three weeks I had been starved of affection and this was my dear grandfather who, my mother had assured me, would care for me and love me and be my friend. I believed that, and I wanted nothing so much as to throw myself into his arms and tell him how lonely I was.

A man was coming toward me—a very elegant man with a rosy laughing face which reminded me of a pug dog I had once had. I smiled at him as I ran past him. He seemed astonished but he was smiling too; and I discovered almost immediately afterward that he was the much-talked-of Duc de Choiseul whom the King had sent to bring me to him.

But I needed no one to take me to the King. I went straight to him and knelt.

He raised me up and kissed me on either cheek. He said: "But . . . you are beautiful, my child." His voice was melodious, far more beautiful than that of the Prince de Rohan; and his eyes were warm and friendly.

"Your Majesty is gracious . . ."

He laughed and held me against his magnificent coat which was decorated with the most beautiful gems I had ever seen.

"We are happy that you have come to us at last," he went on.

When we looked into each other's faces and he smiled, I lost my fear and that hateful sense of loneliness. He was old but one did not think of age in his presence. Regal yet kind, his manners were perfect. I flushed remembering my own imperfect French. I so wanted to please him.

He embraced me again as though he really felt affectionate toward me. His eyes studied me intently from head to foot. I did not know then of his penchant for young girls of my age but thought all this kindness, all this interest and flattering attention was because he had taken a particular fancy to *me*. Then he turned his head slightly and a boy came forward. He was tall and ungainly; he shifted his gaze from my face as though he were not the least bit interested in me, and his indifference, after the warmth of the King's greeting, struck me almost like a blow. The feelings he roused in me were so mixed that I could not attempt to analyze them, for this was my husband. He was gorgeously dressed but how different he looked from his grandfather! He did not seem to know what to do with his hands.

The King said: "Madame la Dauphine honors and delights us with her presence."

The boy looked sheepish and stood there saying nothing, doing nothing except look at the tips of his boots. I thought I would break through his indifference so I took a step closer to him and held my face up to be kissed for since the King had kissed me, why should I not kiss my bridegroom? He looked startled, recoiled, then made a move toward me as though he were forcing himself to some distasteful task. I felt his cheek against mine, but his lips did not touch my skin as the King's had.

I turned to the King and although he gave no sign that he thought the Dauphin's conduct strange, I had always been quick to grasp people's reactions, and I knew he was exasperated. I thought blankly: The Dauphin does not like me. Then I remembered Caroline who had cried so much because they had married her to an ugly old man. But I was neither old nor ugly. The King himself thought me charming; most people thought me charming. Even old Kaunitz had thought there was nothing in my appearance to spoil the match.

The King had slipped his arm through mine and was presenting me to three of the strangest old ladies I had ever seen. These were my aunts, he told me: Adelaide, Victoire, and Sophie. I thought them all very ugly indeed, but more than that—strange. They reminded me of the old witches in a play I had once seen. The eldest of them, who was obviously the leader, stood half a pace in front of the others; the second was plump and had the kindest face of the three; and the third was the ugliest. But they were my aunts and I must try to love them, so I went first to Madame Adelaide and kissed her. She then made a sign for Madame Victoire to step half a pace forward which she did, and I kissed her. Then it was Madame Sophie's turn. They looked like two soldiers on parade, Adelaide being the commanding officer. I wanted to laugh but I knew I dared not. Then I thought what fun it would have been if I could have gone to my room in the Hofburg with Caroline and told her about these new relations of mine, imitating them all in turn. I could have acted each of the three weird sisters—and the Dauphin.

The King said I should meet the rest of the family later and, taking my hand, he himself helped me into his carriage where I sat between him and the Dauphin. The trumpets blew and the drums rolled and we started on the road toward the town of Compiègne where we were to stay the night before we continued our journey to Versailles.

The King talked to me as we rode along and his soft voice was like a caress. He did caress me too, patting my hand and stroking it. He told me he loved me already, and that I was his dear granddaughter and he counted this one of the happiest days he had ever known because it had brought me into the family.

I felt the laughter bubbling up inside me. I had been dreading this meeting for I had always heard this man spoken of with awe. He was the greatest monarch in Europe, my mother had said. I had imagined him stern and forbidding and here he was, holding my hand, behaving almost like a lover, saying such charming things as though I had done him a great honor by coming to marry his grandson—not, as my mother had impressed on me, that a great honor had been done to me. While the King chatted and behaved as though *he* were my bridegroom, the Dauphin sat beside me sullenly silent.

Later I was to learn a great deal about this King who was always charmed by youth and innocence, qualities which I undoubtedly possessed. He might have been wishing I was his bride for he could never see a pretty young girl without contemplating seducing her. As for the Dauphin he could never see a young girl without wanting to run away from her; but my imagination was adding drama and producing a situation which did not exist. It was not, as I wildly believed, that the King had fallen in love with me; nor that the Dauphin hated me. It was nothing so dramatic. I had a great deal to learn of the ways of the French in general, and in particular of the family of which I was now a member.

When we arrived at Compiègne the King told me he wished to present me to some of his cousins, the Princes of the Blood Royal. I replied that I enjoyed meeting all people and that the members of my new family were of particular interest to me.

"And you will be of particular interest to them," he replied with a smile. "They will be charmed and delighted and we shall have them all envying poor Berry here."

The Dauphin, who was the Duc de Berry, half-turned away from us as though to say there were welcome to me; at which the King pressed my hand gently and whispered: "He is overcome by his good fortune, poor Berry!"

I was taken to the King's apartments and there I met the Princes, the first of whom was the Duc d'Orléans, a grandson of the King's uncle; then there was the Duc de Penthièvre, grandson of Louis XIV (I later heard that his grandmother was Madame de Montespan, who had been that King's mistress) and after that the Princes of Condé and Conti. They all seemed very old and uninteresting; but there were some young members of the family who were presented to me that day and one of these was the Princesse de Lamballe. She was twenty-one, which seemed old to me, but I was immediately interested in her and felt I could be fond of her for I was desperately looking for a friend in whom I could confide. She was already a widow and had had a very unhappy marriage, which fortunately for her lasted only two years. Her husband had become "ill" after a love affair, I was told, for he had led a very wild life and he subsequently died. Poor Marie Thérèse! At the time of our meeting she was obliged to be the constant companion of her father-in-law who was eccentric and mourned all the time for his son; all he cared about besides that was his collection of watches, and when he was not in a state of melancholy over the death of his son, he was clucking over his watches, winding them, displaying them to anyone whom he could bore with them. At least if I was apprehensive I was excited. The Princesse

de Lamballe's life was just one morbid journey from castle to castle with
her peculiar father-in-law and his watches. Yet I found comfort in our
meeting and the moment when she was presented to me stands out
clearly in my mind even now, among all those introductions which seemed
to go on for hours and hours.

Everything was done with the utmost ceremony—even the trying on
of my wedding ring. They had to be sure that they had one which would
fit so the Master of Ceremonies came to my apartment accompanied by
the King. With them came the Princes of the Blood Royal and the aunts,
although the sole purpose of this little ceremony was that I should try
on twelve rings to see which fitted me. When it had been found it was
taken from me to be put on my finger by the Dauphin. The King embraced me and took his leave; and then, one by one, in order of precedence, the others did the same.

I was tired out and longing for my bed and as my women prepared me
I began to think of the Dauphin who seemed so different from everyone
else. He had scarcely spoken to me; he had scarcely looked at me; and I
could hardly remember what he looked like. Yet I could remember the
face of the King and that of the Princesse de Lamballe perfectly.

"Madame is thoughtful," said one of my women.

"She is thinking of the Dauphin," whispered another coyly.

I smiled at the two girls; they looked gay, as though they were rather
pleased to escape from the supervision of Madame de Noailles and my
severe ladies-in-waiting.

"Yes," I admitted. "I was." And as I spoke I seemed to hear my mother's
voice: "Do not be too familiar with subordinates." But I must talk to someone. I longed for a little conversation which was not governed by
etiquette.

"It's natural for a bride to think of her bridegroom."

I smiled encouragingly.

"He will sleep under a different roof tonight." The girl's voice rose
on a giggle.

"Why?"

They smiled at me in the indulgent way people did at home in Vienna.

"Because he could not be under the same roof as the bride until the
wedding night. He will stay in the house of the Comte de Saint-Florentin,
the Minister and Secretary of State of the King's Household."

"It's interesting," I said suppressing a yawn.

I lay in my bed and went on thinking about the Dauphin. I wondered
whether he was thinking about me and if so what his thoughts might be.

Years later when I came to know him very well I saw what he had written in his journal on that night. It was characteristic of him and it told nothing (but by that time I had learned his secret and I knew the reason for his strange conduct toward me). It simply said: *"Interview with Madame la Dauphine."*

The next day we were to leave for the Château de la Muette where we were to spend one night before going to Versailles the next day.

As we set out I was immediately aware that something was wrong. In the first place the King did not accompany us. He had gone on ahead. I wondered why. I learned later that it was because the road to Versailles from La Muette passed Paris and the King never rode in state near or through his capital if he could help it. He had no intention, on an occasion like this, of receiving the hostile silence of the people. This is why I had seen those cynical looks on the people's faces in the Strasbourg Cathedral when the Prince de Rohan referred to him as Louis the Well-Beloved. When he was a young man he had been called that; but it was a different matter now. The people of Paris hated their King. They were poor, often short of bread and they were furious because he squandered large sums of money on his palaces and his mistresses while they went hungry.

But this was not the matter which was causing great uneasiness among my friends. Mercy was in a state of uncertainty and had despatched couriers to Vienna. The Abbé looked worried and so did Starhemburg. I wished they would tell me what was wrong but of course they did not. I had noticed, however, the looks of sly amusement on the faces of some of my women. Something was going to happen at La Muette.

On the way we called at the Carmelite Convent of St. Denis where I was to be presented to Louise, the fourth aunt—youngest sister of Adelaide, Victoire, and Sophie. I was interested in Louise; she was different from the other three, and although I should have been sorry for her because she limped painfully and was pitiably deformed with one shoulder higher than the other, I wasn't, because she seemed so much happier than her three sisters. Dignified and, in spite of her Abbess's habit, behaving like a royal personage, she was very friendly and seemed to sense that I wanted to talk to somebody, so she asked me many questions and talked about herself too, telling me how much happier she was at the convent than in the royal palaces, and that treasures on Earth were not found in palaces. She had known this for a long time and had made up her mind that she wished to live her life in seclusion as an expiation of Sin.

I could not imagine that she had been very sinful and my expression must have conveyed this for she said rather fiercely: "My own sins and those of another."

Questions trembled on my lips. What other? But whenever I was about to ask some indiscreet question which would no doubt bring an interesting answer, I would see my mother's face warning me against any light-hearted indiscretions and pause. Then it would be too late.

As we came nearer to La Muette, Mercy's preoccupation grew deeper. I heard him whisper to Starhemburg: "There is nothing . . . nothing we can do. That he should have chosen this time . . . it is inconceivable."

My attention was caught by the people who lined the route, particularly as we grew nearer to Paris. We did not enter the city but wound our way round it and the cheers were deafening. So I smiled and inclined my head as I had been taught to do; and the people shouted that I was *"mignonne"* and I forgot all about Mercy's worries because I always enjoyed this kind of applause so much.

I was rather sorry when we came to La Muette. The King was already there and waiting to present my brothers-in-law to me. The Comte de Provence was fourteen years old—in fact he was sixteen days younger than I was and much more handsome than the Dauphin, but inclined to be a little plump, like his elder brother. He was more lively though and he seemed very interested in me. His brother, the Comte d'Artois, was about a year or so younger than I but there was a lively knowledgeable look in his eyes which made him seem older than his two brothers—more worldly wise, I mean. He took my hand and kissed it lingeringly, while his bold eyes were very admiring and as I was always responsive to admiration I preferred Artois of the two brothers—perhaps of the three. But I was not going to bring the Dauphin into the comparison. In fact I was trying not to think of the Dauphin because to do so bewildered me a great deal and depressed me a little. In fact I did not know what to think of him and I was certainly afraid to think too deeply; so I successfully managed to put him from my mind. I could always live in the present and there was plenty to occupy my thoughts.

Meanwhile, having met my two brothers-in-law, I must be prepared for the banquet which was to be eaten in private—a family affair and therefore much more intimate than all the others I had attended. Now I should be in the very heart of my new family.

The King came to my apartments and told me he had a gift for me which was a casket of jewels. These delighted me, and he in turn was delighted to see my pleasure, and kept saying how enchanting it was to be young and so excited over trifles. Then he took from the casket a pearl necklace and held it up. Each pearl was the size of a hazel nut and they were all of perfect matching color.

"It was brought to France by Anne of Austria," he told me. "So how fitting that it should be worn by another Princess from Austria! This necklace was worn by my mother and by my wife. It is the property of all the Dauphines and Queens of France."

As he ceremoniously fastened it himself, his fingers lingered on my neck and he said the pearls had never been shown to greater perfection. I had beautiful shoulders and when I grew up I would be a beautiful woman, an ornament to the throne of France.

I thanked him demurely, and then I looked up at him and flung my arms about his neck. This was wrong I saw immediately from Madame de Noailles who was standing by nearly fainting with horror at my presumption; but I did not care and nor did he.

He murmured: "Charming . . . charming. I am writing to your mother to tell her that we are all enchanted by her daughter."

He was smiling as he left.

I then received a long lecture from Madame de Noailles as to how I should conduct myself in the presence of the King of France; but I was not listening. I was thinking that if they had married me to *him*—as they had once thought of doing—I should have been far less apprehensive than I was when I remembered that the next day was my wedding day.

At the intimate supper I saw all my new relations. Wearing the pearl necklace which the King had placed round my neck, I sat next to the Dauphin who said nothing to me and did not look my way; but his brother Artois smiled at me and whispered that I looked very pretty.

I was immediately aware of the tense atmosphere, and my attention was caught by a young woman who was seated at the table talking rather more loudly than the rest. I had not been introduced to her and, as this was a family party, I could not imagine who she was. She was very beautiful—the most beautiful woman at the table. Her hair was fair, very thick and curling; her complexion was one of the loveliest I had ever seen; her blue eyes were enormous being slightly prominent; and she lisped slightly which made a contrast to her bold looks. She was magnificently dressed and glittered with jewels; in fact she wore more jewels than anyone present. One could not help watching her, and even the King, at the head of the table, kept glancing her way; he seemed very pleased to see her there and once or twice I saw them exchange a look and a smile which made me feel they were very great friends indeed. But, I wondered, if the King was so fond of her, why is she not wanted here? The aunts were whispering together and when she was not observed I noticed Adelaide throw a glance in the woman's direction which could only be described as venomous. Every now and then the King would turn to me and address me and when I answered in my quaint French he would smile, and so would everyone else. He said my French was charming; and so everyone was saying it. I felt it was a successful evening and I could not imagine why Mercy had been so anxious.

At last my curiosity was too much to be borne and I said to the lady who was seated next to me: "Who is the pretty lady with the blue eyes and the lisp?"

There was a brief silence as though I had said something embarrassing. Had Madame de Noailles been there I should have known how much so by her expression.

I waited for the answer which seemed a long time in coming and then: "She is Madame du Barry, Madame La Dauphine."

"Madame du Barry! She has not been presented to me."

Everyone seemed to be studying their plates and some were trying not to smile.

Then someone said: "Madame . . . what do you think of her?"

"She is charming. What are her functions at Court?"

Again that pause, that slight heightening of color in one or two faces, the tendency to smile. "Oh, Madame, it is her function to amuse the King."

"To amuse the King!" I smiled at him across the table. "Then I want to be her rival."

What had I said? I had merely made a loyal statement. Why was it received in such a manner? I saw the mingling of horror and amusement.

We left La Muette the following morning and in due course arrived at the Palace of Versailles. I sat bolt upright in my carriage for my companion was the Comtesse de Noailles and during the journey I had to hear another lecture. My behavior had disturbed her; I would have to learn that the Court of France was very different from that of Austria. I must never forget that my grandfather was the King of France and although etiquette might forbid even him to show his displeasure, it could nevertheless be there. I half-listened and all the time I was wondering what my wedding dress would be like and whether the Dauphin was dis-appointed in me; and I thought fleetingly of my sister Caroline who would be praying for me on this day—and crying for me too.

At last we came to Versailles.

It was an impressive moment. I had heard the name throughout my childhood spoken in hushed tones. "This is how it is done at Versailles." That meant it was absolutely right. Versailles was the talk and envy of every Court in Europe.

At the gates of the palace, vendors of swords and hats were gathered. I have heard it said since that Versailles was a great theatre where the play of Royalty at Home was presented. There was a great deal of truth in this, for anyone could come to the Salon d'Hercules except dogs, mendi-cant friars and those newly marked with the smallpox—providing they had a hat and sword. It was amusing to see those who had never carried a sword before they took one of those for hire at the gates, swaggering into the château. Even prostitutes were allowed in, providing they did not ply their trade there or seek clients. But in order to enter the more inti-mate apartments it was necessary to have been presented at Court. There was, naturally, very little privacy at Versailles. In our Court at Vienna, where everything was conducted in a far simpler manner, I had been ac-customed to a certain amount of supervision; but here I was to be on show for most of my day.

The palace gates opened to let us in and we drove through the line of Guards—Swiss and French—standing there to do me special honor. I had a strange feeling of excitement mingling with apprehension. I was not given to introspection but in those moments I had an uneasy notion that I was being carried on to fulfill a strange destiny which, had I wanted to, I could do nothing to avert.

In the royal courtyard the equipages of the princes and nobles were already drawn up. I exclaimed in delight at the horses with their red plumes and blue cockades for I loved horses almost as much as I loved dogs; they pranced excitedly and they looked very fine, their dancing manes plaited with colored ribbons.

Before us lay the château, the sun shining on its countless windows so that it seemed aglitter with diamonds—a vast world of its own. And so I entered the Palace of Versailles which was to be my home for so many years—in fact until those dark days when I was driven from it.

On my arrival I was taken to a temporary apartment in the ground floor because those apartments usually assigned to the Queens of France were not ready. When I think of Versailles now I remember in detail the rooms I was to occupy after those first six months—those beautiful rooms on the first floor which open out of the Galerie des Glaces. My bedchamber had been used by Marie Thérèse, wife of Louis XIV, and Marie Laczinska, wife of Louis XV; and from the windows I looked out on the lake—Pièce d'eau des Swisses—and the parterre with the two staircases which were called Les Escaliers des Cent Marches, leading to the orangery which contained twelve hundred orange trees.

But on that first occasion I was taken to my ground floor apartment and there ready for me were those grim ladies-in-waiting with my wedding dress. I gasped with pleasure and my gloomy thoughts were all chased away by the sight of it. I had never before seen such a lovely dress and I was enchanted by its panniers of white brocade.

As soon as I reached my apartment the King came to welcome me to Versailles. What charming manners he had! And with him were two little girls; my sisters-in-law, Clothilde and Elisabeth. Clothilde, the elder, was about eleven, inclined to be too plump but very friendly; as for little Elisabeth, I found her delightful; I kissed her and said we should be friends. The King was pleased and whispered to me that the more he saw me the more he fell under my spell. Then he and the little girls left and the ladies-in-waiting fell on me and prepared me for my wedding.

It was one o'clock in the afternoon when the Dauphin came to lead me to the chapel. It was very hot and although he sparkled in gold spangled net, the brilliance of his clothes only made him look more dour. He did not glance at me as he took my hand and led me into the King's Council Chamber where the procession was forming. I remember noticing the red marble mantelpiece and the smell of pomade; there was a haze of powder in the air from freshly powdered wigs and a frou-frou of silks and brocades as the ladies in their voluminous and elaborate skirts moved across the floor.

The Grand Master of the Ceremonies led the procession followed by the Dauphin and myself, he holding my hand; his was warm, clammy, and, I knew, reluctant. I tried to smile at him but he avoided my glance and immediately behind me walked Madame de Noailles so I could not whisper to him. Behind her came the Princes of the Blood Royal with their attendants, followed by my young brothers-in-law and the King; and after them the little Princesses, whom I had met for the first time that day, with the aunts and other Princesses of the Court.

Through the Galerie des Glaces and the Grand Apartments we went to the chapel where the Swiss Guards were lined up and as the King entered they blew their fifes and beat their drums to herald his arrival.

It did not seem like our chapel at home because it was elegantly decorated. I was sure my mother would have thought the décor irreverent for although the white and gold were lovely the angels looked more voluptuous than holy.

The Dauphin and I knelt on the red velvet edged with gold fringe and the Grand Almoner of France, Monseigneur de la Roche-Aymon, came forward to perform the ceremony.

My bridegroom appeared to be growing more and more bored; he fumbled as he put the ring on my finger and I thought he was going to drop the pieces of gold, blessed by the Grand Almoner, which he presented to me as part of the ceremony.

So we were married. The Archbishop gave us his blessing; Mass followed; then the organ pealed out and the marriage contract was handed to the King for his signature. After the Dauphin signed his name, it was my turn. As I took the pen my hand was trembling and I wrote my name in an untidy scrawl: *Marie Antoinette Josèphe Jeanne.* A jet of ink shot onto the paper and I felt that everyone was staring at the blot I had made.

Later this too became an "omen." If blots were omens I had been scattering them rather freely over my exercises for many years. But this was different. This was my marriage contract.

One would have thought that that was enough ceremony for one day. But no! I was now in truth Dauphine of France and Madame de Noailles conducted me to my apartments where my first duty was to receive the members of my household and accept the oath of fidelity. So many of them: my ladies-in-waiting, my first maître d'hôtel, my almoner, my equerries, my doctors—I even had apothecaries and surgeons—two of the former and four of the latter; although why I, who was in perfect health, should need so many I could not imagine. I had a clockmaker and a tapestry-maker as well as a wigmaker who was also an attendant of the bath. It was wearying to consider how many people had assembled to wait on me; one hundred and sixty-eight persons were concerned with feeding me alone.

As I accepted the oaths of my cellarmen, master cooks, my butlers, pantlers and winebearers, I was half-laughing half-yawning because it all seemed so absurd. I did not know then that my attitude would be resented. I did not understand the French at all. I was to offend so many before I realized the mistakes I made in those early days—and when I did understand, much damage had been done. What might have been obvious to a wiser person was hidden from me; and that was that this etiquette which I had seen so rigorously regarded in higher circles was carried right through to humbler strata. My attitude of *légèreté* toward them and their customs was regarded with as much dismay as Madame de Noailles herself had shown me.

I was really longing for it to be over because the next activity was the opening of the King's wedding present, and having already been made aware of the King's generosity, my expectations were high. Nor was I disappointed. The King's present was a toilet set in blue enamel, a needle case, a box and a fan all set with diamonds. How I loved those cold stones which could suddenly flash with red, green, and blue fire!

I picked up the needle case and said: "My first task shall be to make something for the King. I will embroider him a waistcoat."

Madame de Noailles reminded me that I should have to ask His Majesty's permission first. I laughed at that and said that it was to be a surprise. Then I added that it would take me years to finish it so perhaps I had better tell him what I was doing or he would not know of my gratitude and my plan to use his exquisite present.

She looked exasperated. Poor old Madame de Noailles! I had already christened her Madame l'Etiquette, and when I mentioned this to one of my women she had laughed aloud. I was pleased and made up my mind that I was going to make fun of their etiquette whenever I had an opportunity to do so because it was the only way I could endure it.

The King had also given me various beautifully wrought articles for my entourage, and while I was admiring these I heard a rumble of thunder. The brilliant sky had become overcast and I immediately thought of all the poor people whom I had seen on the road from Paris to Versailles and who had come to see the wedding celebrations for there was to have been a firework display for them as soon as it was dusk; and now, I thought, it is going to rain and it will all be spoilt.

During the storm I was given a little insight into the peculiarities of the aunts. As I went into my apartment I saw Madame Sophie talking to one of my women eagerly and in the most friendly fashion. This was strange because when I had been presented to her she had scarcely spoken to me and I had heard that she rarely uttered a word and that some of her servants had never heard her speak. Yet, there she was talking intimately to the poor woman who seemed quite bewildered and uncertain how to act. As I came forward Madame Sophie took the woman's hands and squeezed them tenderly. When she saw me she cried: How was I? How did I feel? Was I fatigued? There was going to be a horrid storm and she hated them. The words came tumbling out. Just then a clap of thunder seemed to shake the palace and Sophie put her arms about the woman to whom she had been talking so affectionately and embraced her. It was a most extraordinary scene.

It was Madame Campan who told me later that Madame Sophie was terrified of thunderstorms and when they came her entire personality changed. Instead of walking everywhere at great speed, leering at everyone from side to side—"like a hare," Madame Campan described it—in order to recognize people without looking at them, she talked to everyone, even the humblest, squeezing their hands and even embracing them when her terror was at its greatest pitch. I was to learn a great deal about my aunts, but like everything else, I learned it too late.

As soon as the storm was over, Sophie behaved as before, speaking to no one, running through the apartments in her odd way. Madame Campan, in whom Aunt Victoire had confided freely over many years, told me that Victoire and Sophie had undergone such terrors in the Abbey of Fontevrault to which they had been sent as children to be educated, that it had made them very nervous and they retained this nervousness even in maturity. They had been shut in the vaults where the nuns were buried and left there to pray, as a penance; and on one occasion they had been sent to the chapel to pray for one of the gardeners who had gone raving mad. His cottage was next to the chapel and while they were there alone praying, they had to listen to his bloodcurdling screams. "We have been given to paroxysms of terror ever since," Madame Victoire explained.

Although the thunder died away, the rain continued and as I had feared the people of Paris who had come to Versailles to see the fireworks were disappointed. There would be no firework display in such weather. Another bad omen!

In the Galerie des Glaces the King was holding a reception and there we were all assembled. The magnificence of the Galerie on that occasion was breathtaking; later I became accustomed to its splendor. I remember the candelabra—gilded and glittering—each of which carried thirty candles so that in spite of the darkness it was as light as day. With the King, my husband and I sat at a table which was covered with green velvet and decorated with gold braid and fringe, and we played a card game which fortunately, with great foresight, I had been taught to play, and I could play this silly sort of game far better than I could write. The King and I smiled at each other over the table while the Dauphin sat sullenly playing as though he despised the game—which of course he did.

While we played people filed past to watch us, and I wondered whether we ought to smile at them, but as the King behaved as though they did not exist I took my cue from him. There were among the spectators several uninvited guests, for only those who had received special invitations should have been there, but some of those who had not been driven home by the storm, determined to compensate themselves for the loss of the firework display, broke the barriers and forced their way in to mingle with the guests. The ushers and guards found it quite impossible to restrain them and as no one wanted any unfortunate displays of anger on this occasion, nothing was done.

When the reception in the Galerie des Glaces was over we went for supper to the new opera house which the King had had built to celebrate my arrival in France. As we crossed to the opera house the Swiss Guards, splendid in starched ruffs and plumed caps, together with the bodyguards, equally colorful in their silver-braided coats, red breeches, and stockings, made a guard for us.

The real function of this beautiful opera house had been disguised. A false floor had been set up to cover the seats and on this was a table decorated with flowers and gleaming glass. With great ceremony we took our places: the King at the head of the table, myself on one side of him, my husband on the other, and next to me—and for this I was thankful—my mischievous younger brother-in-law, the Comte d'Artois, who was very attentive to me and proclaimed himself to be my squire, implying in his outrageous way that he would uphold the honor of France in the place of the Dauphin at any time I wished. He was bold, but I had liked him from the moment we met.

On the other side of Artois was Madame Adelaide, clearly reveling in an occasion like this, keeping an eye on her sisters—Sophie next to her, Victoire opposite, next to Clothilde—and trying to talk to me over Artois, her sharp eyes everywhere. She hoped that she and I would be able to talk together in her apartments, *intimately*. It was imperative. Artois, listening, raising his eyebrows to me when Adelaide could not see, and I felt that we were allies. At the extreme end of the table—for she was of the lowest rank of the twenty-one members of the royal family—was the young woman who had interested me so much when I had first been presented to my new relations: the Princesse de Lamballe. She smiled at me very charmingly and I felt that with her and the King and my new champion Artois as my friends I need not be apprehensive about my future.

I was far too excited to eat but I noticed that my husband had a good appetite. I had never known anyone who could appear so oblivious of his surroundings. While the King's Meat (as the numerous dishes were called) was being brought in with the utmost ceremony, he might have been sitting alone for his one interest was the food, on which he fell as though he had just returned from a hard day's hunting.

Noticing his grandson's voracious appetite the King said to him quite audibly: "You are eating too heartily, Berry. You should not overload your stomach tonight of all nights."

My husband spoke then, and everyone listened—I suppose because they heard his voice so rarely.

"I always sleep better after a good supper," he said.

I was aware of Artois beside me suppressing his amusement, and many of the guests seemed suddenly intent on their plates; others had turned and were in deep conversation with their neighbors, faces turned away from the head of the table.

The King looked at me rather sadly; then he began to talk over the Dauphin to the Comte de Provence.

The next part of the proceedings was so embarrassing that even now I do not care to think about it. The night had come. When I looked across the table and caught my husband's eye he looked uneasy and turned away. I knew then that he was as disturbed as I was. I was aware of what was expected of me that night, and although I did not look forward to it with any great pleasure, I was certain that, however distasteful it was, the result of what would happen would give me my dearest wish. I should have a child—and any discomfort was worth while if I could become a mother.

Back to the palace he went and the ceremony of putting the bride and groom to bed began. The Duchesse de Chartres, as the married lady of highest rank, handed me my nightgown; and I was led to the bedchamber where my husband, who had been helped into his nightshirt by the King, was waiting for me. We sat up in bed side by side, and all the time my husband had not looked at me. I was not sure whether he thought the whole affair incredibly silly or was just sleepy after all the food he had eaten.

The curtains were drawn back so that everyone could see us and the Archbishop of Rheims as he blessed the bed and sprinkled it with holy water. We must have appeared to be a strange little couple—both so young, little more than children; myself flushed and apprehensive, my husband bored. In truth we were two frightened children.

The King smiled at me wistfully as though he longed to be in the Dauphin's place and then turned away to leave us together. Everyone bowed and followed him out and my attendants drew the bedcurtains shutting me in—alone with my bridegroom.

We lay in bed looking at the hangings. I felt lonely—shut in with a stranger. He did not attempt to touch me; he did not even speak to me. There I lay listening to my heartbeats—or were they his? . . . waiting . . . waiting.

This was what all the fuss of preparation had been about; the solemn ceremony in the chapel, the glittering banquet, the public's peepshow. I was to be the mother of the Enfants de France; from my activities in this bed I was to produce the future King of France.

But nothing happened . . . nothing. I lay awake. It must be soon, I said to myself; but still I lay and so did he . . . in silence, making no move to touch me, speaking no word.

After a long while I could tell by his breathing that he was asleep.

I was bewildered and, in a way, disappointed.

I know now that he suffered even as I did. The next day he wrote one word in his journal. It was *"Rien."*

3

OMENS

I am not sure now when I began to understand that nothing was as I had first believed it to be. The frivolous young girl I was, knowing little of life, formed quick conclusions from what she saw on the surface without understanding, not realizing that her new countrymen, with their love of etiquette, their determination to preserve exquisite manners in all circumstances, were adepts at deception.

I had believed that my husband and I would be lovers, that we would wander hand in hand through the splendid gardens of Versailles, that I would be gloriously happy, and before a year of marriage had passed, would have my own little son who would give me far more pleasure than all my little dogs put together. But I had a husband who was apparently indifferent to me.

I was bewildered; and everyone was watching us slyly, almost furtively: the King with detached resignation, the aunts with hysterical excitement, my brothers-in-law with suppressed amusement; but Mercy, Starhemburg, and the Abbé Vermond were deeply concerned.

Something was wrong. The Dauphin did not like me—and I was to blame.

This did not occur to me during the first days. All I knew was that the marriage was not what I had believed it would be. The day after that of the wedding was full of ceremonies and I had little time for thought as I was hustled from one to another. In the evening an opera was performed in the new opera house. It was *Perseus* which might have been tolerable if someone had not tried to modernize it by inserting a new ballet. Everything went wrong. The director broke his leg at the dress rehearsal and was on a stretcher the whole evening. None of the properties on the stage worked as they should. In compliment to me it had been arranged that a great Eagle—the symbol of my House—should be set high above the altar of Hymen, and this, instead of remaining perched high above the altar, slumped onto it. Perseus slipped and fell at the feet of Andromeda at the very moment of rescue. The only interesting moments were those of disaster—and the director had to be prevented from killing himself.

I was so bored by this performance that I kept yawning and I knew that I was being closely watched, so I wondered in alarm whether my conduct would be reported to my mother. I was sure it would be.

I went to bed with my husband and it was exactly the same as the night before—only this time I did not lie awake, being too tired out from the previous wakeful night and the boredom of *Perseus*.

When I awoke I was alone in the bed. I learned that my husband had risen as soon as it was light to go hunting. Everyone knew this and thought it strange that he should prefer to hunt rather than be with me since we were so newly married.

When he came home from hunting he spoke to me and as he did so so rarely I remember his words and the tone in which he spoke them.

It was simply and coolly: "Have you slept well?"

I answered: "Yes."

Then he gave me a brief half smile and turned away.

The Abbé Vermond, who was with me, looked very grave so I picked up one of the two little dogs which had been given to me on my arrival in France, and started to play with him, but when I heard the Abbé murmur: "It wrings my heart!" I could no longer doubt that there was something very wrong. I, who everyone had said was so pretty and dainty, had failed to attract the Dauphin. He could not love me.

Comte Florimond Claude de Mercy-Argenteau came to see me and asked a great many embarrassing questions. Ever since I had left my mother he had been hovering about me. My mother had said I was to trust him in everything, that I was to listen to his advice, that he would be the bridge which kept us together. I was sure she was right but he was so old and stern—a small man rather bent, and I was sure very clever; but I was

uneasy to be so obviously spied on for one never really likes spies however worthy and for whatever cause they spy.

He was Belgian, coming from Liège, and he seemed to have something akin to the French; but he was entirely my mother's servant. His
one thought, I am sure, was to carry out the mission she had set for
him, and I was all the more uneasy because I was fully aware of his effi-
ciency. He had worked under Kaunitz and I believed I might just as well
have had the latter at my elbow continually as Mercy was to be during
the next years.

He asked questions in a roundabout way, but I knew exactly what he
was trying to discover; he wanted to know what had taken place in the
bed which I shared with my husband when we had been left to ourselves.

I told him that I believed my husband was indifferent to me. He did not
touch me; he seemed to want to sleep as soon as he was in bed; and this
morning he had risen long before I was awake to go hunting.

"You will be thinking that this is strange behavior for a bridegroom," he
said gravely.

I agreed that I did—although I was not sure what I should have expected
from a husband.

"I have studied medicine," he went on, "and I believe the Dauphin's
development to be late because his constitution has been weakened by
his sudden and rapid growth."

So that was it! I had not liked the Duc de la Vauguyon, who had been
my husband's tutor and who, I had noticed, had great influence with
him. Without thinking, I burst out: "My husband's timidity and coldness
is due to the kind of education he has received. I am sure the Dauphin
has a good disposition, but I believe Monsieur de la Vauguyon has led him
by habit and fear . . ."

I stopped. I was trying to find a reason for my husband's coolness
toward me other than the fact that I did not appeal to him.

Mercy looked at me coldly. He had a penetrating stare which made
me uncomfortable.

"I am sure the Empress will be most uneasy when she knows of this
state of affairs. I will tell her that it is early yet and I will give her my
opinion of what ails the Dauphin."

I pictured my mother at home in Schönbrunn and shivered for she had
the power to overawe me even at that distance. I knew I was failing her
for she would be waiting to hear news of my pregnancy as soon as possible. Yet how could I become pregnant when my husband ignored me!

Mercy changed the subject and told me that I must be more discreet in my behavior toward the King. Did I not feel that I was being too free and easy? I replied that there was no doubt that the King liked me. *He* was not cold. He had said that he loved me from the moment I came, that the whole family was enchanted with me.

Mercy replied: "I will tell you what the King of France has written to your mother. 'I find the Dauphine lively, though very childish. But she is young and doubtless will grow out of this.'"

I felt my face flush scarlet. I did blush easily. So . . . he had said *that*, after all the charming things he had whispered to me, all the caresses, all the compliments!

Mercy smiled at my discomfiture, and the implication was that it was good for me to feel foolish for it was the only way in which I could learn the lessons which it was so important for me to master.

He left me depressed. My husband did not like me; nor did the King; the only difference was that one made a secret of his true feelings and the other did not.

I had a great deal to learn.

The aunts had been kind to me; they had implied they wanted to be my friends, so when I had an invitation to visit Madame Adelaide during that day I gladly accepted it.

When I reached her apartment she embraced me warmly; then she held me at arms' length and said: "Berry's wife!" and went off into titters of laughter. She said: "I will summon Victoire whose apartments adjoin these; she will send for Sophie and we will have a cozy party . . . the four of us, eh?"

I noticed a young woman sitting at a small table, a book before her. I smiled at her. I thought her extremely dowdy yet I took an immediate liking to her. Seeing herself noticed she immediately rose and dropped a curtsey, flushing a little.

"This is our lectrice Jeanne Louise Henriette Genet," said Madame Adelaide. "She is a good reader and we are pleased with her."

I told her to sit down and realized immediately that perhaps I was wrong either to speak to her or to give that permission. I should never straighten out this complicated etiquette. At least at the moment Adelaide was friendly enough to overlook it. Victoire arrived.

"Did you ring for Sophie?" asked Adelaide.

"Yes, before leaving," her sister replied.

Adelaide bowed her head. Then she turned haughtily to the young lectrice and told her that she had permission to retire; the young woman slipped out as quietly as a mouse—in fact she reminded me of a mouse, small, gray, and timid.

But I had no time to think of her for Sophie had arrived.

"Berry's wife is here," said Adelaide; and Sophie forced herself to look at me. I smiled and going to her kissed her. I hated doing it because she was so ugly; she did not return my kiss but stood with her hands hanging down at her sides and her gaze turned away from me.

Adelaide laughed a loud braying laugh and said she thought they might sit, although in the presence of the Dauphine; at which I laughed; then Adelaide laughed; Victoire looked at her sister and joined in; and when Adelaide nudged Sophie she laughed too. It was rather horrible laughter, and in view of what Mercy had told me of the King of France I felt uneasy.

"So," said Adelaide, "you are Berry's wife. A strange boy, Berry." She nodded her head and watched her sisters who nodded with her and tried to ape her expression—poor Sophie always coming in late.

"Not like other boys," went on Adelaide slowly, putting her mouth close to my ear.

I looked startled and all the sisters started to nod again.

"He has a good appetite," said Victoire.

Adelaide laughed. "She thinks that a point in his favor. You should see *her* eat. She has the Bourbon appetite."

"But I cannot abide pastry crust," Victoire put in conspiratorially.

"All she thinks of is sitting in her armchair and eating."

"I like my comforts," Victoire admitted.

Sophie looked at her sisters as though marveling at this brilliant conversation. I liked them. They were dears, I thought, though simple. I was looking for friends on that day.

"Poor Berry! He never laughed and played tricks," said Adelaide.

"Like Artois!" added Victoire.

"That boy!" Adelaide was indulgent. She whispered: "He has a mistress already. At his age! Fancy!"

"He is very young," I agreed.

"Now, Berry . . ." She looked at Victoire and they began to laugh. Sophie was some time before she joined in. "*He* was never interested in the girls."

"He likes his food though." Victoire was kindly putting in a good word for him.

Adelaide looked impatiently at her sister and Victoire was alarmed. Adelaide went on: "When he came to see me as a little boy I would say to him: 'Come, Berry. Here you can be at your ease. Talk. Shout. Make a noise. My poor Berry, I give you carte blanche.'"

"And did he?" I asked.

Adelaide shook her head and they stood there like three wise monkeys all shaking their heads.

"He was not like other boys," went on Adelaide mournfully; then her eyes gleamed mischievously. "But now he is a husband. Is he a husband, Madame la Dauphine?"

She laughed shrilly and the others joined in. I said with dignity: "Yes, he is my husband."

"I hope he is a *good* husband," said Adelaide.

"I think he is a good husband."

Victoire began to laugh but she was silenced with a look from her sister who decided to change the subject.

"What did you think of the stranger who came to supper at the Château de la Muette?"

"Oh . . . the beautiful woman with the blue eyes . . ."

"And the lisp."

"I thought she was charming."

Victoire and Sophie were looking to Adelaide for their cue. Adelaide's eyes flashed and she looked militant. "She is leading the King to perdition."

I was startled. "But how . . . ? I heard her duty was to amuse him."

Adelaide burst into loud cackling laughter. I waited for the others to join in, Victoire just ahead of Sophie.

"She is a *putain*. Do you know what that is?"

"I do not remember hearing that word before."

"She is his mistress. Does that explain?" I nodded and she came close to me, her eyes gleaming. "She worked in brothels before she came here. They say she pleases him because she is full of new tricks . . . all learned in the brothels where she was an expert performer."

I was flushing with embarrassment. "It cannot be so . . ."

"Oh, you are young, my dear. You are innocent. You do not know this Court. You need friends . . . you need someone who understands this wickedness . . . you need someone to guide you, to help you." She had gripped my arm and her face was very close to mine. The other two moved in on me, nodding, and I wanted to run away, to go to the King to ask him if this were true. But I did not know the King. He was not the man I had believed him to be. I could trust Mercy; that was one person of whom I could be sure. And he had told me so.

Adelaide was talking in a low monotone. "It was wrong of the King to bring her to supper . . . at such a time particularly. It was an insult . . . to *you*. Your first *intime* supper . . . and he chose that moment to bring her in as she has never been brought in before."

I understood then why Mercy and the others had been disturbed; they knew that this woman, this prostitute, was going to be present and it was an insult to me. I was deeply wounded, for nothing could show me more clearly that the King had little regard for me. I had thought he loved me and all the time he was laughing at me for being childish, and he had brought his mistress to supper to insult me. It was all an elaborate piece of play-acting to hide something underneath, which was sinister and frightening.

"You should not be disturbed," said Adelaide. "*We* are your friends." She looked at her sisters who all began to nod.

"You shall come to us when you wish. You shall use your own key to these apartments. There! Does that not show you how we love you! We are your friends. Trust us. We will teach you how to make Berry a good husband. But always come to us and we will help you."

Adelaide made coffee in her apartments. She was rather proud of this achievement and would allow no servant to do it.

"The King taught me," she said. "He used to make it in his apartments and bring it here when we were younger. Then I would ring for Victoire and before she came she would ring for Sophie, and before Sophie came she would ring for Louise . . . this was before she went into her convent. She went there, you know, not only to save her own soul, but the King's. She prays for him constantly, because she fears he may die with all his sins upon him. What if he died in bed with that *putain* beside him! Louise had a long way to come and by the time she arrived the King would be ready to leave, so there was often only time for her to kiss him before he went. Those were happy days . . . before that woman came here. Of course there was the Pompadour before her. The King has always been the prey of women. But there was a time . . ." Her eyes became dreamy. "One grows old. I was his favorite daughter, you know. He used to call me Loque then. It was meant to be a pet name. He still calls me by it; and Victoire is Coche."

"Because I am so fond of eating," put in Victoire. "It has made me a little fat . . . but not like a pig."

"Sophie was Graille and Louise Chiffe. Our father likes to give people names. He always called our brother's wife 'Poor Pepa.' She was Marie

Josèphe, you see. I have rarely heard him refer to your husband other than 'Poor Berry'."

"Why were these two poor?"

"Pepa because when she came here her husband did not want her. He had been married before and loved his first wife, and on his second wedding night he cried in his new wife's arms for the first one. But she was patient and he loved her in time and then he died. So she was Poor Pepa. And Poor Berry . . . Well, he is different from most young men . . . so he is Poor Berry for that reason."

"I wonder if he minds."

"Poor Berry! He doesn't care about anything but hunting, reading, playing with locks and building . . ."

"And eating," said Victoire.

"Poor Berry!" sighed Adelaide; and they all sighed with her.

When I left them I seemed to have learned a great deal about the royal family which I had not known before. I had the key to the aunts' apartments. I would use it often for at least with them I could escape the rigid etiquette of Madame de Noailles.

At the ball which was given a few days later there was trouble on a point of etiquette. It was all due to the fact that on this occasion—because the ball was being given in honor of me—the Princes of Lorraine had asked that their House should take precedence over all others for my father had been François of Lorraine and they claimed kinship with me. Thus Mademoiselle de Lorraine, who was a distant cousin, believed she should—for this occasion only—take the floor in a minuet ahead of all the other ladies. The Duchesses of the Royal House were outraged and there was a great deal of activity throughout the palace. I heard that the King was pacing up and down his apartment deeply disturbed by his dilemma. To refuse the Lorraines' request would be an insult to the House of Austria; to agree to it would be an insult to the Houses of Orléans, Condé, and Conti.

Never had their etiquette seemed to me so silly. The King had allowed Madame du Barry to sit at table with me and yet he appeared to think I should be offended if a distant cousin did not take precedence over his near relations! I made up my mind that as far as possible I should not be a slave to their foolish etiquette.

However, the controversy continued and finally the King decided in favor of the Lorraines at which the Royal Duchesses declined to attend, pleading indisposition.

I scarcely noticed their absence. I danced—and how I loved to dance! I felt happier dancing than doing anything else. I danced with my husband, who was very clumsy and constantly turning to the right when he should have gone to the left; I laughed aloud and he gave me his slow smile and said: "I am no good at this!" and that seemed a great advance in our relationship. Dancing with my youngest brother-in-law was different. He was a natural dancer. He told me I looked beautiful, that Berry was the luckiest man at Court and he hoped he realized it. That seemed like a question. I parried it, but I found myself growing lighthearted in his company. It was wonderful to be with someone of my own age with whom I had something in common. Artois laughed at everything, as I wanted to, and I was certain we were going to be friends. Then I danced with young Chartres, the son of the Duc d'Orléans, whom I did not like at all. He was gracious but his cold eyes reminded me of a snake. It was my first close contact with him, and I wondered whether I had a premonition on that night, and that something warned me that he was going to be our enemy.

These people were so different from my own and however much they dressed me in French clothes, whatever French manners and customs I adopted, I would always be Austrian. We were unsubtle, more natural, uncultured perhaps; we might seem crude in comparison; we were not witty; but we were easy to understand. We said what we meant and we did not hide our true feelings under a mound of etiquette. Everywhere there was etiquette. I was being suffocated by it. I wanted to scream out that I was tired of it; I wanted to kick it aside, to laugh at it; and to tell them that if they wanted it they could have it, but to leave me out of it.

How could I know that that ball where I had enjoyed dancing so much with Artois and even with my own awkward husband, was a dismal failure, and that I was blamed for it. My relations had spoilt it. Little Lorraine was more important than Orléans and Condé because of me. They had been mortally insulted and I should never be forgiven. They made up their minds on that night that they would be no friends to me, although whenever we met afterward they gave no sign. But they were not showing affection to me; they were only paying homage to the Dauphine of France. What a little fool I was! And there was no one to help me except Mercy whom I tried to avoid, and my mother who was miles away. I was alone and walking blindly into danger, only like everything French it did not seem like danger at this stage; and I did not know that what looked like soft green grass was really a quagmire . . . not until I was deep in it and could not extricate myself. A clever woman might have found it difficult to act wisely in such a Court. What hope had a frivolous, ignorant young girl?

It was some weeks after my wedding, and in all that time my husband had only spoken a few sentences to me. Whenever I saw the King he was so charming to me that I forgot what Mercy and the aunts had told me. I believed that he loved me; I even called him Papa, for I said that Grandfather sounded too old for him. There had been so many *fêtes* and balls that I had forgotten my fears. My brother-in-law Artois was constantly in my company; I had paid several visits to the aunts; I had forgotten my previous uneasiness; perhaps I did not want to think of it. It was much more fun to be gay and believe everyone loved me and that I was a great success.

Madame Adelaide was taking me to see the fireworks, and I was going incognito to Paris because my official entry into the capital must, of course, be a ceremonious one. I had so longed to see the fireworks and Adelaide, always ready to enter into a conspiracy, declared she would take me. I thought wistfully that my husband might have taken me. What fun it would have been if he were as gay as Artois and we had disguised ourselves and driven there together. But he was either hunting or with the locksmith; the King was at Bellevue with Madame du Barry; and so why should I not go, said Adelaide; and we set off in her carriage.

She seemed less strange when her sisters were not present. I believed she imagined she must appear stranger than she actually was in order to impress them and keep her supremacy over them; and she was very friendly as we rode along together toward Paris.

It was a great function, she told me. She had been informed of all that was being done to honor me. All along the Champs-Elysées, the trees were decorated with lamps which would be delightful when it was dusk. The center of activities would be the Place Louis XV where a Corinthian temple had been erected close to the King's statue and there were also figures of dolphins and a great picture of myself and the Dauphin in a medallion. Bergamot had been poured on the banks of the Seine to disguise the foul odors which sometimes arose from that river, and the fountains were flowing with wine.

"All in your honor, my dear, and that of your husband."

"Then I should certainly be there to see it," I replied.

"But unrecognized." She laughed that odd braying laugh.

"It would not be in accordance with etiquette for the people to see me before I am formally introduced to them."

"It would certainly not be. So tonight we are two noblewomen come to see the people enjoy themselves."

As we came nearer to the city the sky was suddenly illuminated with fireworks for it was not dark. I exclaimed in wonder for I had never seen such a beautiful display.

We were almost at the Place Louis XV—which I did not know then—when our escort stopped abruptly. Our carriage pulled up with a jerk. I was aware of screams and shouting; I vaguely saw a mass of people and I had no idea what this meant. The driver turned our carriage; and, the bodyguard surrounding us, we started back with great speed the way we had come.

"What is it?" I asked.

Madame Adelaide did not answer. She was very frightened and she did not say a word as we raced back to Versailles.

The next day I learned what had happened. Some of the fireworks had exploded and started a fire; a fireman's cart coming into the square met a crowd of people and carriages hurrying from the fire; another crowd was rushing into the square to see what was happening; nothing could move; the congestion was complete. Forty thousand people were held up in the Rue Royale, the Rue de la Bonne-Morue, and the Rue Saint-Florentin. There was a panic. Many people fell and were trampled on; carriages toppled over; horses tried to break free. People were climbing over the bodies of those who had fallen in a vain endeavor to escape, and many were trampled to death. There were terrible stories of that night.

Everyone was talking about the disaster. The Dauphin came into our bedchamber; he was deeply shocked and this made him seem older, more alive. He told me that one hundred and thirty-two people had been killed on the previous night.

I felt the tears in my eyes and he looked at me and did not turn away quickly as he always had before.

"It's my fault," I said. "If I had not come here it would not have happened."

He continued to look at me. "I must do what I can to help," he said.

"Oh yes," I answered fervently. "Please do."

He sat down at a table and began to write and I went and looked over his shoulder.

"I have learned of the disaster," he wrote, and I noticed how swiftly his pen glided over the paper, "which came to Paris on my account. I am deeply distressed and I send you the sum which the King gives me each month for my private expenses. It is all I have to give. I want it to help those who have been most badly hurt."

He lifted his eyes to my face and touched my hand—just for a moment. "It is the least I can do," he said.

"I should like to give what I have," I told him.

He nodded and looked down at the table. I knew then that he did not really dislike me. There was some other reason why he neglected me.

The disaster was talked of long afterward. It was another of those omens. There was the storm which had spoilt the wedding day celebrations; the blot I had made when signing my name; and then this great calamity when the people of Paris had come in their thousands to celebrate the wedding and had met death and disaster.

4

"Don't meddle in politics or interfere in other people's affairs."

"You must not take this disappointment too much to heart. Never be peevish. Be tender but by no means demanding. If you caress your husband, do so in moderation. If you show impatience you could make matters worse."

"Listen to no secrets and have no curiosity. I am sorry to have to say Confide nothing—even to your aunts."

Maria Theresa to Marie Antoinette

"To refrain from showing civility towards persons whom the King has chosen as members of his circle is derogatory to that circle; and all persons must be regarded as members of it whom the monarch looks upon as his confidants, no one being entitled to ask whether he is right or wrong in doing so."

Kaunitz to Marie Antoinette

"The dread and embarrassment you are showing about speaking to persons you are advised to speak to is both ridiculous and childish . . . What a storm about saying a quick word. You have allowed yourself to become enslaved and your duty can no longer persuade you."

Maria Theresa to Marie Antoinette

"I trust you will be satisfied. You may be sure that I will always sacrifice my personal prejudices as long as nothing is asked which goes against my honor."

Marie Antoinette to Maria Theresa

THE BATTLE OF WORDS

Choisy

Madame, my very dear Mother,

I cannot express how much I am affected by Your Majesty's kindness and I assure you that I have not yet received one of your dear letters without tears of regret filling my eyes at being parted from such a kind mother; and although I am very happy here, I should earnestly wish to return to see my dear, very dear, family, if only for a short time.

We have been here since yesterday and from one o'clock in the afternoon, when we dine, until one in the morning we cannot return to our apartments, which is very disagreeable to me. After dinner we have cards till six; then we go to the play till half-past nine; then supper; then cards again until one o'clock, sometimes even half-past one. Only yesterday the King, seeing that I was tired out, kindly dismissed me at eleven to my great satisfaction, and I slept very well till half-past ten.

Your Majesty is very kind to show interest in me even to the extent of how I spend my time habitually when at Versailles. I will say, therefore, that I rise at ten o'clock or nine, and after dressing, I say my prayers; then I breakfast after which I go to my aunts where I usually meet the King. This lasts till half-past ten. At eleven I go to have my hair dressed. At noon the *Chambre* is called and anyone of sufficient rank may come in. I put on my rouge and wash my hands before everyone; then the gentlemen go out; the ladies stay and I dress before them all. At twelve is Mass; and when the King is at Versailles I go to Mass with him and my husband and the aunts; if he is not there I go with Monsieur le Dauphin, but always at the same hour. After Mass we dine together but it is over by half-past one, as we both eat quickly. I then go to Monsieur le Dauphin. If he is busy, I return to my own apartments where I read, write, or work, for I am embroidering a vest for the King, which does not get on very quickly, but I trust that, with God's help, it will be finished in a few years. At three I go to my aunts' where the King usually comes at that time. At four the Abbé comes to me; at five the master for the harpsichord, or the singing master till six. You must know that my husband frequently comes with me to the aunts'. At seven, card playing till nine; and when the weather is fine I go out, and then the card playing takes place in my aunts' apartment instead of mine. At nine, supper; when the King is absent my aunts come to take supper with us; if the King is there we go to them after supper, and we wait for the King who usually comes at a quarter to eleven; but I lie on a sofa and sleep till his arrival; when he is not expected we go to bed at eleven. Such is my day. I entreat you, my dear Mother, to forgive me if this letter is too long; but my greatest pleasure is to be this in communication with Your Majesty. I ask pardon also for this blotted letter, I have had to write two days running at my toilet, having no other time at my disposal; and if I do not answer all the questions exactly, I trust Your Majesty will make allowances for my having too obediently burned your letter. I must finish this, as I have to dress and go to the King's Mass. I have the honor to be Your Majesty's most submissive daughter.

Marie Antoinette

This letter, which I wrote from Choisy, one of the royal palaces which we visited now and then, gives a picture of the monotony of my days at this time. I had thought that life in France would be exciting, full of novelty, and I found it more dull than it had ever been at Schönbrunn.

During those first months of my life at the French Court, I was often sick with longing for home and for my mother, although when I received her letters I would shiver with apprehension, wondering what they contained. I did not then realize the extent to which Mercy was observing the intimate details of my life. He had always appeared to be a stern old statesman and the fact that he could be interested in what a young girl wore or how many times she laughed with a certain servant seemed incongruous. That was where I was so foolish. I had scarcely changed from the child who had romped in the gardens of Schönbrunn with her dogs; I was as inconsequential, as unaware. I did not realize then—to my misfortune—that the Dauphine of France, who would one day be Queen, was not so much a girl or woman as a symbol. War and peace could hang on her actions; her follies could make a throne tremble. When I wrote to my mother and asked how she knew so much of my silly little actions she replied that "A little bird told her"; and she never mentioned that the little bird was Mercy. I should have known, of course. But at least Mercy was my friend, although an uncomfortable one; and I should have been grateful to him.

During that time there was of course one great matter which over-shadowed my life: the unusual relationship between myself and my husband. I knew that everyone at Court was talking about it—some gravely, but most with sniggering amusement. Provence, whom I could never like although his conduct was extremely correct, was pleased, I knew, because the last thing he wanted was for me to produce a son. He was jealous because he was not the eldest and believed—and many agreed with him —that he would have made a better Dauphin than my husband Louis. Artois was gay and amusing, very flirtatious, constantly gazing at me with a wistful expression behind which mischief lurked. Mercy was always dropping hints that I should be wary of Artois. Then there were the aunts, throwing out a hundred suggestions, always trying to discover what was happening between "Poor Berry" and myself.

But when my mother wrote that perhaps it was best that things were as they were because we "were both so young," I felt I could put the matter out of my mind for a while and try to enjoy life as well as I could.

There was one man who was my friend at Court and this was the Duc de Choiseul. He was eager that my marriage should be a success because he had arranged it. It was my misfortune that I should have come to France when his power was on the wane, for he would have been as helpful to me as Mercy was—and far more powerful since he was the King's chief minister. He was rather an ugly man, but it was a charming ugliness; he was fascinating and I was fond of him from the moment we met. My mother had told me that I could trust him because he was a friend of Austria, and that drew me to him. But he was in disgrace. Mademoiselle Genet told me that he had made friends with Madame de Pompadour to their mutual advantage, but had underrated the power of Madame du Barry and that was one of the reasons why he fell.

Although I had at first found Madame du Barry fascinating, I now child-ishly loathed her because the King had allowed her to come to that first intimate supper, and, according to Mercy, that was an insult to me. I wrote to my mother "She is a silly and impertinent woman," believing that, knowing her function at Court, my mother would consider my attitude toward the woman the correct one.

"Don't meddle in politics or interfere in other people's affairs," was my mother's reply but I did not realize she was referring to Madame du Barry, and like so many other important matters it went right over my head. I did not want to meddle in politics. It was as much as I could manage to do my lessons. I wanted to enjoy my life. I wanted to see Paris— but I was not allowed to until I did so officially, and that was a matter which had to be considered in all sorts of ways before it could be put into action. "Etiquette!" I groaned.

"At least," I said to Mercy, "I could have two of my dogs brought from Vienna."

"You already have two dogs," he answered sternly.

"Yes, I know, but I love them and they'll be pining for me in Vienna. Little Mops will, I know. Please ask them to send him."

He wanted to refuse but could not very well go so blatantly against my wishes. I had my four dogs. When puppies arrived I should have more and I would not be parted from them, although Mercy was hinting at unclean habits which would be frowned on in the elaborate Versailles apartments.

During those first weeks the Duc de Choiseul visited me frequently and he too told me how I should behave to the King.

"Be earnest and natural," he said, "and not too childish, although His Majesty does not expect you to have a knowledge of politics."

I said I was glad of that and told him of my dislike of Madame du Barry.

"I cannot bear to hear her silly lisp, and she seems to think she is the most important lady of the Court. I always look straight through her when I see her as though she does not exist. Yet she always looks hopefully my way as though she is imploring me to speak to her."

Monsieur de Choiseul laughed and said that naturally she wanted a show of friendship from the Dauphine.

"She will not get it," I retorted, and since this was exactly what Monsieur de Choiseul wanted me to say I made up my mind that I would keep to it.

Dear Monsieur de Choiseul! He was so charming and at the same time so sincere . . . where I was concerned. I am sure that if he could have stayed near me I should have been saved from many follies.

When I arrived in France the odious du Barry had already become the center of a party which called itself the Barriens, and in this were some of the most powerful ministers, such as the Duc d'Aiguillon, the Duc de Vauguyon, and the Duc de Richelieu—and these men were all enemies of Choiseul and sought to bring him down. This they were managing very successfully, blaming him for the disaster of the Seven Years' War— which had broken out the year I was born and in which my country was involved—and the loss of the French Colonies to England. He was blamed for everything; and I understood afterward that the Austrian marriage was a plan of his to attempt to reinstate himself. He must have been a very worried man when I met him, but he gave no sign of this; he was one of the gayest people I had ever met.

It was a great blow to me when he received his *lettre de cachet* from the King banishing him to his château at Chanteloup. It happened suddenly—on Christmas Eve. He simply disappeared and I could not believe he had gone. It was sad to lose a friend and at the same time it alarmed me that such a fate could befall someone so rapidly. I was particularly hurt by Mercy's attitude toward the Duc.

"He has hastened his disgrace by his indiscretions," he said. "It would have surprised me if he had stayed in office much longer. Let us hope that he may not be replaced by someone who is an even greater muddler than he."

"He is our friend!" I cried aghast.

"He is of no use to us now," replied Mercy cynically.

I was very hurt and sorry; but we did hear of him now and then. He was living very grandly at Chanteloup and sending out chansons about Madame du Barry whom he regarded as his enemy in chief. She was constantly finding scraps of paper covered with obscene rhymes in her apartments, but she always laughed at them and they seemed to lose their impact.

Letters continued to flow from Vienna, and every time a letter from my mother was put into my hands I would shiver. What had I done now? I had not worn my stays—my hateful *corps de baleine* which made me sit bolt upright or in discomfort. It was necessary for me to wear them at this stage of my growth, I was warned. I must always be aware of my appearance. The French were very susceptible to appearance and I must always think of pleasing my husband. Always there were hints about my relationship with my husband.

> "You must not be in too much of a hurry for increasing his uneasiness will only make matters worse."

On one occasion she wrote:

> "You must not take this disappointment too much to heart. You must never show it. Never be peevish. Be tender but by no means demanding. If you caress your husband do so in moderation. If you show impatience you could make matters worse."

Not only the court of France but all the courts of Europe seemed to be discussing the inability of the Dauphin to consummate our marriage. They were saying he was impotent and that if a girl as attractive as I was could not rouse him, the case was hopeless.

It was tremendously embarrassing for us both. I clung to my childishness, trying not to understand even when I did, playing with my dogs, dancing when I could, trying to pretend I did not know there was anything strange about our marriage. My husband's method was to feign indifference—which I knew he did not feel. His defense was to pretend to be bored, to shut himself up with his locksmith and builder friends; he hunted whenever possible and would eat heartily—as though all he cared about were these things. But I did discover that he was as uneasy as I was— more so, because he was more serious and the fault was his; and during the past months he had begun to show me in a hundred little ways how sorry he was that he was not a good husband. He was anxious to please me, and although his tastes were in exact opposition to my own he never tried to stop my doing what I liked.

I was growing quite fond of him and I believed he was of me. But this hateful situation was between us. Had we been two lusty lovers we should have been smiled at indulgently; as it was the secrets of our bedchamber were the concern of Europe. Envoys were going back and forth from Versailles to Sardinia and Prussia as well as to Austria. In the streets songs were being sung about us. "Can he or can't he?" "Has he or hasn't he?" If my husband's infirmity were due to some mental conflict this was enough to prevent his ever overcoming it.

My mother reiterated that I was to keep her informed of *every detail*. I was to report everything the Dauphin said or did. I was to read her letters and burn them when I had done so. I knew that I was surrounded by spies and the chief of these was my husband's tutor, the Duc de Vauguyon, who was a friend of Madame du Barry. Once when I was alone with my husband one of the servants, who was in the room, suddenly opened the door and there was the Duc bending down; his ear had obviously been at the keyhole. I think the servant may have been trying to warn us. I remarked to Louis how inconvenient it was having people listening at our doors. The Duc de Vauguyon was very embarrassed and muttered some excuse; but I don't think Louis ever had such a high opinion of him again.

It was not in my nature to brood on my position. I wanted to enjoy myself. There was nothing I liked so much as riding, but horses had been forbidden, because my mother thought that violent riding might make me sterile. As if I had a chance to be otherwise! And she and Mercy had decided that they would ask the King to give an order that I should not ride.

This was a great blow to me. I wanted to shout that I was bored at the

French Court, that when I was riding with the wind in my face and my hair free from those pins with which the hairdresser tortured me, I was happy.

I went to the King; I was my most appealing; I called him Dear Papa and I told him how unhappy I was because I was being prevented from riding.

He was perplexed. I should have known that he found this kind of situation irritating and hated to be asked to make a decision which was going to offend anyone, particularly a pretty girl. But he gave no sign of this. He was all smiles and sympathy. How was I to know that he was inwardly yawning at my childish problems and wishing me far away? He laid his hand on my shoulder and explained very tenderly that my mother did not wish me to ride horses. Did I not wish to please my mother?

"Oh yes, dear Papa, I do indeed . . . but I cannot *bear* not to ride."

"They consider that horses are too dangerous, and I have agreed that you shall not ride them." He lifted his hands and his face was illumined by that charming smile which in spite of the pouches under his eyes and the countless wrinkles made him still handsome. "They did not mention donkeys." He had the solution. "No horses . . . but ride a donkey for a while."

So I rode donkeys which I found humiliating.

Nevertheless once I fell from the saddle. It was a foolish incident really. The donkey was stationary and I was sitting loosely; he turned sharply and the next thing I knew was that I was on the ground. I was not in the least hurt but my attendants were very concerned and they all hurried to me; but I lay there laughing at them.

"Do not touch me," I cried. "I am not hurt in the least. I am not even shaken. It was the silliest tumble."

"Will you not allow us to help you rise then?"

"Certainly not. You must call Madame l'Etiquette. You see, I am not quite sure what ceremonies should be observed when a Dauphine falls from a donkey."

They all laughed and we resumed our ride very gaily; but of course the incident was reported. My mother heard of it. She was very hurt that I was riding—even donkeys—and I know now that she feared she was losing her influence over me. This was no wish for power on her part; it was due to a deep understanding of her daughter's character and a terrible fear as to what would become of her. She saw me as an innocent lamb among the wolves of France—and she was, as usual, right.

She wrote to me:

"I hear you are riding a donkey. I have told you I do not care for this equestrian activity. It will do more harm even than spoiling your complexion and your figure."

When I read the letter I was sorry I had displeased her and I vowed I would not ride again until I had her permission to do so—which would be when I was a little older, when I was a true wife, when I had shown that I could bear children. (How it all came back to this!) But I soon forgot and a few days later I was out on my donkey again.

I was seeing a great deal of the aunts, who made much of me. Adelaide was always angry about something. She had to have a cause to fight for and she would take up the least little thing. Madame du Barry was her great target; but when she heard that I had been forbidden to ride a horse she turned her attention to this.

"It is ridiculous!" she declared. "Not ride a horse! Everyone must ride a horse. A donkey for the Dauphine of France! It is an insult."

Victoire nodded and Sophie joined in a few seconds later.

"It is our enemies who have arranged this," said Adelaide darkly.

I was going to point out that it was my mother who had forbidden it and that Mercy and the King supported her. I could hardly call these my enemies. But Adelaide never listened when she had a cause to fight for. I was not going to be ill-used. I was not going to be humiliated. She and her sisters were my champions and she had a plan.

The plan was that I should ride out on my donkey as usual. An equerry with a horse would have been sent out and I should meet them at a spot to be decided on. Then I should dismount from the donkey, mount the horse, go for my ride, and then come back to the spot where the donkey would be waiting for me, mount the donkey and trot back to the Palace. It was very simple.

"And it will outwit them all," cried Adelaide triumphantly.

I hesitated. "It would displease my mother."

"How should she know?"

"All the same, I do not want to go against her wishes."

"She is far off in Vienna. She does not know that you are a figure of fun here . . . riding your donkey."

They persuaded me and there was a great deal of conspiratorial whispering; and in due course I rode out with some of my attendants and met the equerry who had the horse waiting for me. They were all rather afraid because they knew that the King himself as well as my mother had said that I should not ride a horse, and I was suddenly ashamed. I agreed that

I would not canter or gallop and I would allow the equerry to hold the bridle while I walked the horse. But what joy it was to be really on horseback once more! I forgot how disobedient I was being and I found the tears of laughter in my eyes when I thought of what Mercy's face would be like if he could see me.

I mentioned this to one of my attendants and they all joined in my laughter. It was such fun—and then we went back to where one of the attendants was waiting with the donkey and I rode it solemnly back to the palace while the equerry galloped off with the horse.

One of those attendants who had accompanied me and laughed with me hastened to tell Mercy what had happened and when he presented himself at my apartments I knew from his stern looks that he had discovered my deception. He was pained and grieved. I blurted out: "So you know I have been riding a horse?"

"Yes," he said.

"I was going to tell you," I said, and added defensively: "Those who saw me were pleased that I had had such pleasure."

"I should be mortified," he replied in his solemn way, "if you believed that I should join those who were delighted. As I am deeply concerned with your affairs I can only be grieved that something should have happened which could be injurious to you and would give great displeasure to the Empress."

I was frightened as always at the thought of my mother. I said quickly: "I should be desolate if I thought I had grieved the Empress. But as you know riding is the Dauphin's favorite exercise. Should I not therefore follow something which gives him such pleasure?"

Mercy did not reply to this, but merely remarked that he would retire and leave me to contemplate what I had done.

I wished I hadn't done it and I was sorry; then I grew angry. It was all so silly. Why should I not ride a horse if I wanted to?

But I was very upset. One thing remained clear in my giddy mind and that was that my mother cared for my well being as no one else on earth did; and she had as much power to alarm me here in France as she had in Vienna. She was, of course, informed of what I had done; she wrote back, pained that I had acted so. She conceded that the King and the Dauphin had both given their consent to my riding and that they must "dispose of all concerning you," but she was very displeased.

"I shall say no more," she finished her letter, "and shall try not to think about it."

She must have heard what part the aunts played in this because she was soon afterward warning me against them.

> "Keep a neutral position in everything. I desire you to be more reserved than ever as regards what is going on. Listen to no secrets and have no curiosity. I am sorry to have to say confide nothing . . . even to your aunts whom I esteem so much. I have my reasons for saying this."

She had very good reason. Probably more than she at that time realized.

A year after I was married my brother-in-law Provence was given a wife. She arrived at Versailles in May—as I had—Marie Josèphe of Savoy. I disliked her on sight; she was very ugly and completely lacking in charm; and this was not only my opinion. Provence was very disappointed in her; and everyone made comparisons between her and myself which came to her ears and enraged her. I knew that she hated me although she was always anxious to pretend that she did not, for she was rather clever.

I was indifferent to her attitude toward me because I had made a friend of the Princesse de Lamballe whom I found kind and gentle; though the Abbé Vermond said she was stupid because he did not want me to be too friendly with anyone other than himself. I defended the Princesse to him.

"She has a good reputation," I said, "which cannot be said for everyone at this Court."

"She could lose *that* reputation tomorrow," he retorted, "but her reputation for stupidity grows every day!"

I laughed with him, for we were on very friendly terms.

There was another friend I made and although he did not like her either, he could not complain of her stupidity. This was Jeanne Louise Henriette Genet, the lectrice who worked for my aunts. I had seen her often in my aunts' apartments and I had been attracted by her quiet ways and her rather severe looks. It was the attraction of opposites. I sensed that although she had a great respect for my aunts, and for me too, in addition she liked me.

I asked the King if I might share my aunts' lectrice and he said yes, immediately. So I used to have Mademoiselle Genet in my apartments so that she might read to me; but I preferred to talk to her for she had such stories to tell of the Court that I do believe I learned more from her than I had so far from anyone else.

She was only three years older than I but she seemed at least ten, so demure so *sérieuse* was she. I was sure my mother would have approved of her. Sometimes I used to think that nice sensible Jeanne Louise would have been a much better daughter for my mother than I was. Her father had been employed by the Foreign Office and so had come to the notice of the Duc de Choiseul; and thus Jeanne Louise had been given her place at Court. She had been a studious child who had astonished everyone by her learning; and one of her greatest assets was her voice which was clear; and another was her ability to read aloud for hours at a time. Thus she became lectrice to my aunts.

She was fifteen when she came to Court and I loved to hear of her first impressions. I would lure her away from the book and say: "Come now, Mademoiselle Lectrice, I would have you talk to me."

She would demurely shut the book and look very guilty; but I knew she liked to talk as much as I did.

"Tell me about the first day you came to Court," I said one day, and she told me how she went into her father's study to say goodbye to him and how he wept to see her in her Court attire.

"I was wearing tight stays for the first time and a long dress with panniers. My pale face was smeared with rouge and powder which was necessary as part of Court custom even for one as humble as I."

"Etiquette," I murmured; and I laughed at her for my free and easy manners shocked her.

"My father is a very wise man. I realize that now more than I did before. He said to me: 'The Princesses will make full use of your talents. Great people know how to bestow praise graciously, but do not allow their compliments to elate you too much. Be on your guard. Whenever you receive flattering attentions, you may be sure you will gain an enemy. I swear that if I had been able to find another profession for you, I would never have abandoned you to the dangers of Court life.'"

She had a way with words which I found fascinating. She talked of the day of her arrival when the Court was in mourning for Queen Marie Leczinska, and how in the courtyard were coaches with horses waving their great black plumes, and pages and footmen with their spangled black shoulder knots. The state apartments were hung with black cloth and canopies decorated with sable plumes had been placed over the armchairs.

She made me see a new picture of the King. "He was the most imposing figure I had ever seen and his eyes remained fixed on you all the time he was speaking."

I nodded, agreeing with her.

"Notwithstanding the beauty of his features he inspired a sort of fear."

"I felt no fear," I said impulsively.

She smiled her slow calm smile. "You are the Dauphine, Madame. I am the lectrice."

"Did he speak to you?"

"Yes, on two occasions. One morning when he was going out to the hunt I was in Mesdames' apartments and he came to see Madame Victoire and asked me where Coche was. I was bewildered, for I did not know of the nicknames he used for Mesdames. Then he asked my name and when I told him, he said: 'Oh, you are the lectrice. I am assured you are learned and understand five languages.' 'Only two, Sire,' I answered. 'Which?' he asked. 'English and Italian, Sire.' 'Fluently?' 'Yes, Sire.' Then he burst out laughing and said: 'It is enough to drive a husband mad.' All his retinue laughed at me and I was overcome with confusion."

"It was not very kind of him," I said. I studied her. She could scarcely be called pretty in her plain dress; and I supposed he had not found her attractive.

On another day when she was reading to the aunts he came to see them. She retired hastily and went to wait in an anteroom and having nothing to do there she amused herself by twirling in her court hoop and suddenly kneeling for the sheer pleasure of seeing her rose-colored silk petticoat swirl round her. In the midst of this the King entered and he was very amused to see the erudite little lectrice behaving like a child. "I advise you to send back to school a lectrice who makes cheeses," he said. And once more poor Jeanne Louise was overcome with confusion. She had not seen the King at his best, as I had; and I fancied she was a little critical of him; naturally she was anxious not to betray her feelings to me—and how right she was! She doubtless knew I would chatter, so she was careful. Long afterward, when he was dead, she told me how he had set up the *trébuchet,* the bird snare, close to his apartments in Versailles and later contented himself with the pleasures of his little seraglio in the Parc aux Cerfs where young girls of my age and hers were brought to him for his pleasure by Madame de Pompadour; and later Madame du Barry performed the same duty. If I had known of these matters then I might have understood him better.

And there was something else she told me much later which it would have been useful for me to know at that time. But would I have made use of the knowledge? I doubt it. This is what she told me and what, she explained, she had written in her journal, for she had always felt the urge to write and set down the events of the days as they passed:

"I heard my father compare the Monarchy of France to a beautiful antique statue; he agreed that the pedestal which supported it was mouldering away and the contours of the statue were disappearing in the parasitic plants which were gradually covering it. 'But,' he explained, 'where is the artist skillful enough to repair the base without shattering the statue?'"

But had she told me at this time I should not have understood what she was talking about. Years later, when the terror was upon us, I understood too well.

I was very interested in Madame Louise, the aunt whom I had seen before I arrived at Versailles when I stopped at the Carmelite Convent of St. Denis to see her.

Mademoiselle Genet told me: "I used to read to her for five hours a day and my voice frequently betrayed the exhaustion of my lungs. The Princesse would then prepare for me *eau sucré*, place it before me and apologize for making me read so long. She did it, she said, because she had prescribed a course of reading for herself. She wanted to read the histories of countries for she believed that when she entered her convent she would only be allowed to read religious works. One morning she disappeared and I learned she had gone to the Convent of St. Denis."

"Were you sad, Mademoiselle?"

"I was very sad, Madame. I loved Madame Louise. She was . . ."

I looked at her slyly. I knew she was on the point of saying Madame Louise was the most reasonable, the most sane of the aunts; but of course she stopped herself in time.

"Go on," I commanded.

"Madame Adelaide was angry. When I told her Madame Louise had gone she said 'With whom has she gone?' She thought she had run away with a lover."

"Madame Adelaide would. She likes everything to be dramatic; and it is far more dramatic to run away with a lover than to a convent. It was less work for you, though."

"I was afraid that Madame Victoire would follow her example." I nodded. Already my little lectrice had made it clear to me that of all the three aunts Victoire was her favorite.

"I told her I feared it and she laughed and said she would never leave Versailles. She was too fond of food and her couch."

It was tiresome that Mademoiselle Genet and the Abbé Vermond took a dislike to each other. Still, I determined to keep her with me, and perhaps one day snatch her away from the aunts altogether and make her entirely my servant. But that was for later.

And so life went on during those months at Versailles. My friendship with the Princesse de Lamballe was strengthening; letters from my mother arrived regularly. My hours with the Abbé when he tried to improve my mind; my interviews with Mercy when he tried to improve my conduct; my intimacy with my aunts; my friendship with the King; my coquetries with Artois; all this continued and in addition there was a growing affection for my husband. But we were so much in the public eye, and so aware of being watched at every turn that our situation did not have much chance of changing.

Even meals were taken in public—a custom I hated; but no one else seemed to mind, and of course the people expected it. They would come in from Paris to watch us at our meals. We were like animals in highly gilded cages.

When it was time for dinner the people would come to watch my husband and me take our soup and then hurry away to see the Princes eat their *bouilli*; and after that they had to run until they were out of breath to witness Mesdames at their dessert. We were a peepshow for the people.

The King's special feat at table was the clever way in which he could knock the top off an egg with one stroke of his fork; and this was talked about throughout Versailles and Paris. He was therefore condemned to eating eggs constantly so that those who had come to see him perform this feat should not be disappointed. Although he refused to go to Paris to see his people they came to Versailles to see him—or perhaps it was merely his trick with the egg they came to see. He performed so dexterously; but to me the amazing part of the performance was that he behaved as though he were entirely alone—like an actor on a stage totally unaware of the spectators.

There was a rumor in the Court that Adelaide had once had a child who appeared in the Princesses' apartments and was made much of by the royal sisters and reminded people of Louis XV in his youth. This affair, the loss of her good looks, and the King's contempt for her which had replaced his affection, had no doubt had their effect on Adelaide's character and turned her into the eccentric she had become. There was an even uglier rumor that the King had loved her incestuously. Perhaps this was why she put on an air of great knowledge and wanted me to know that she could advise me as to how I should behave toward my husband.

I did not need their advice. I knew that my husband did not dislike me; in fact he was pleased with me. I was admired for my appearance, my grace and my charm; and these qualities were constantly referred to. My husband liked to see Artois in attendance on me; the only trouble was that he could not caress me or pay me compliments without acute embarrassment. When he was in his hunting clothes or workshop overalls he appeared to be a man; he looked tall and upright then, unconscious of himself; but as soon as he put on the clothes of the court gallant he became awkward and shuffling. I tried to understand the things he was interested in. Though I loved to ride I hated to see animals suffer so I had never cared for hunting; in any case I was still not allowed to ride a horse. I went into his workshop and he tried to explain to me what he was doing with the lathe there, but I could not understand and I found it difficult to stifle my yawns.

When he became ill with a slight indisposition—he had overeaten at table, a habit of his for he would come in very hungry from the hunt or the workshop—he had slept in a separate room in order not to disturb me. This had caused amusement in some quarters and consternation in others, for it was well known what was happening. The most embarrassing part of the whole affair was that everyone was watching and all our actions were commented on, interpreted and often misconstrued. For a sensitive boy, aware of his affliction, this was a very delicate situation indeed.

But our affection was growing. He no longer looked away from me. Sometimes he would take my hand and kiss it—or even kiss my cheek. I asked him if he were disappointed in me and he said that he was very content.

Then one day he said: "Do not imagine that I am ignorant of the duties of marriage. I will prove it to you . . . soon."

I was excited. Everything was going to be all right. I only had to wait. It was true that we were both too young.

Waiting was rewarded for when we were alone in our apartments—it was just as I was going to visit my aunts—he whispered to me: "Tonight I shall come back to our bed."

I looked at him in astonishment and he took my hand in his clumsy way and kissed it with real affection. I said to him: "Louis . . . do you rather like me?"

"How can you doubt it?" he asked. "I love you sincerely, and I esteem you more."

It was hardly the impassioned declaration of a lover but it was the nearest he had ever come to it; and I went to the aunts in a state of great excitement, which was foolish of me for they recognized at once that something had happened.

"You have just left Poor Berry," said Adelaide. "Has something happened?"

"He is going to sleep with me tonight."

Adelaide embraced me and Victoire and Sophie looked at me in a startled fashion.

"Yes," I announced triumphantly, "he has told me so."

"In a very short time you will be telling us some exciting news," said Adelaide archly. "I am sure of it."

"I hope so. Oh, how I hope so."

How foolish I was! Before the day was out the whole Court was buzzing with the news: "The Dauphin is going to sleep with the Dauphine. Tonight is the night." Those cynical courtiers like Richelieu—that old roué—were laying bets on the success of our encounter. "Will he? Won't he?" There was whispering everywhere. Worst of all Adelaide summoned Louis to her apartments because she wanted to "Advise" him.

That night I lay waiting for my husband. He did not appear. I should not have been surprised. My reckless talk had spoilt it.

Although the matter was now causing the gravest concern, I doubt that the King would have bestirred himself but for my mother. She was constantly writing to the King and begging him to do something. The truth about the Dauphin must be disclosed, and if there was a remedy it must be found.

Because of my mother's importuning, the King sent for my husband and there was a long consultation; as a result Louis agreed to submit to an examination by the King's physician, Monsieur Lassone, who reported that the Dauphin's inability to consummate our marriage was due to nothing else but a physical defect which the knife could rectify. If the Dauphin would submit to this operation all would be well.

Everyone was discussing the operation but Louis did not say whether he would submit to it. We slept in the same bed and he behaved like a lover; but our lovemaking always failed to reach that climax which we both so earnestly sought; and after a while we both found this state exhausting and humiliating.

There was no more talk of the operation. The King shrugged his shoulders; it was left to Louis to decide and it became clear to me that he had decided against it. He was desperately trying to prove that he did not need it; but he did.

I cannot imagine why he would not submit to the operation at this time. He was no coward; but I suppose the whole business sickened him as it did me. If we had been an ordinary couple we should have settled the matter in a very short time; but we were not; we were Dauphin and Dauphine of France. His impotence was discussed in the Court and in the Army. Our most intimate servants were constantly questioned and when we discovered that the Spanish Ambassador had bribed one of the bedroom servants to examine the sheets and let him know the state of them, it seemed the last straw. Although we continued to occupy the same bed, Louis would retire early and be fast asleep by the time I went there; and when I awoke in the morning it would be to find him already gone.

This state of affairs continued while I received angry letters from my mother who cared much more than I did about the humiliation of my position.

And as I entered the second year of my marriage another controversy arose which made everyone forget the tragedy of our bedchamber.

My quarrel with Madame du Barry had been brewing ever since the aunts had told me of her true position at Court. I did not understand then that I should have been wiser to form an alliance with her than with the aunts. They, unknown to me, had resented my coming from the first. They had been strongly against the Austrian alliance and were no real friends to me, whereas this woman of the people, vulgar as she might have been, had a good heart, and although Choiseul had arranged the marriage, and he was her enemy, she bore no animus toward me. Had I shown her the slightest friendliness she would have returned it doubly. But I was foolish. Egged on by the aunts, I continued to ignore her; I used my gift of mimicry and gave little imitations of her which caused a great deal of amusement and which, naturally, were reported to her. I could imitate her mannerisms, her vulgar laughter, her silly lisp—and I did, exaggerating them ever so slightly to increase the amusement.

It did not occur to me that she must be wiser than I to have climbed to the top place at Court from the streets of Paris. The King doted on her; he allowed her to perch on the arm of his chair at a council meeting, to snatch papers from him when she wanted his attention, to call him "France" in an insolently familiar way. All this he found amusing and if anyone criticized her he would say "She is so pretty and she pleases me—and that ought to be enough for you." So everyone realized that if they wished to remain in the King's good graces they must please Madame du Barry. But I *was* in his good graces. I did not have to conform to ordinary standards . . . so I thought . . . and I made up my mind that I would never seek the friendship of a street woman, no matter if she were the King's mistress. So I behaved as though I could not see her. Often she would seek the opportunity to present herself before me but she could not speak to me until I spoke to her—etiquette forbade it, and even she had to bow the knee to etiquette. So every time I ignored her.

Although she was not a woman to bear rancor she was no respecter of persons either. She gave me the nickname of Little Austrian Carrots, and as this was taken up by others I grew very angry, and increased my imitations of her crudities and continued to look through her every time we met. This snubbing became so obvious that soon the whole Court was talking of it, and Madame du Barry became so incensed that she told the King she could endure it no longer and that Little Carrots should be ordered to speak to her.

The King, hating trouble, was annoyed, and I lacked the sense to realize that he was angry with me for making it. His first action was to send for Madame de Noailles and naturally he did not come straight to the point. Madame de Noailles, in a state of fluster reported to me immediately the King dismissed her. He had begun, she said, by saying one or two complimentary things about me and then he had criticized me.

"Criticized!" cried Madame de Noailles in horror. "You have evidently displeased him greatly. You are talking too freely and such chatter can have a bad effect on family life, he says. In ridiculing members of the King's household you displease him."

"Which members?"

"His Majesty named no specific one, but I think that if you would say a few words to Madame du Barry you would please her, and she would report her pleasure to the King."

I pressed my lips firmly together. Never! I thought. I'll not allow that streetwoman to dictate to me.

Foolishly I went at once to the aunts and told them what had happened. What excitement there was in their apartments. Adelaide clucked and clicked her tongue. "The insolence of that *putain!* So the Dauphine of France must be dictated to by prostitutes!" She believed the woman was a witch and had the King under her spell. She could find no other reason for his behavior. But how right I was to come to them! They would protect me . . . from the King if need be. She would think up a plan and in the meantime I must behave as though Madame de Noailles had not spoken to me. I must on no account give way to that woman.

The Abbé saw my indignation and asked the cause of it, so I told him; and he went straight to Mercy and told *him*. Mercy immediately saw the dangerous implications and sent an express messenger to Vienna with a full account of what had taken place.

My poor mother! How she suffered from my stupidities! One little word was all that was needed and I would not give it. I was certain that I was right then. My mother was a deeply religious woman who had always deplored light behavior in her own sex and had set up a Committee of Public Morals so that any prostitute found in Vienna was imprisoned in a corrective home; I was sure she would understand and approve my action. I could not see that my refusing to speak to the King's mistress was a political issue—simply because she *was* the King's mistress and I was who I was. I did not see the difficult position in which I was placing my mother. She either had to deny her strict moral code or displease the King of France; and although she might have been a moralist, she was first of all an Empress. I should have realized the gravity of the situation when she did not write to me herself but instructed Kaunitz to do so.

The express messenger returned with a letter from him addressed to me. He wrote:

> "To refrain from showing civility toward persons whom the King has chosen as members of his own circle is derogatory to that circle; and all persons must be regarded as members of it whom the monarch looks upon as his confidants, no one being entitled to ask whether he be right or wrong in doing so. The choice of the reigning sovereign must be unreservedly respected."

I read this through and shrugged my shoulders. There was no express order to speak to Madame du Barry. Mercy was with me when I received the letter and he read it also.

"I trust," he said, "that you realize the seriousness of this letter from Prince von Kaunitz?"

They were all waiting for me to speak to the woman because it was not long before the whole Court knew that the King had instructed Madame de Noailles. They thought this was going to be defeat for me, and I was determined that it should not be. I could be stubborn when I thought I was right and I certainly believed I was right about this. Madame du Barry expected me to speak to her. At every *soirée* or card party she would be waiting . . . expectantly; and every time I would find some excuse to turn away just as she was approaching. Needless to say the Court found this most diverting.

Adelaide and her sisters were delighted with me. They would throw sly looks in my direction whenever we were in public and Madame du Barry was near. They congratulated me on my resistance. What I did not realize was that in flouting the King's mistress I was flouting the King; and this could not be allowed to go on.

The King sent for Mercy and Mercy came to talk to me, as he said, more seriously than he ever had before.

"The King has said, as clearly as it is possible for him to say it, that you must speak to Madame du Barry." He sighed. "When you came to France, your mother wrote to me that she had no wish for you to have a decisive influence in state affairs. She said that she knew your youth and levity, your lack of application, your ignorance—and she knew too of the chaotic state of the French government. She did not want you to be blamed for meddling. Believe me, you are meddling now."

"In state matters! Because I refuse to speak to that woman!"

"This is becoming a state matter. I beg of you to listen carefully. Frederick the Great and Catherine of Russia are seeking to divide Poland. Your mother is against it, although your brother, the Emperor, is inclined to agree with Prussia and the Russians. Morally your mother is right, of course, but she will be forced to give way as not only your brother but Kaunitz is for partition. Your mother is afraid of French reaction to this. If France decided to oppose partition, Europe could be plunged into war."

"And what has this to do with my speaking to that woman?"

"You will learn that the most foolish actions can spark off disasters. Domestic matters have their effect on state affairs. Your mother is particularly desirous at this time of not offending the King of France. He looks to her to settle this silly quarrel between two women which is being discussed throughout the country and perhaps in others. Can you not see the danger?"

I could not. It seemed so absurd.

He gave me a letter from my mother and I read it while he watched me.

"They say you are at the beck and call of the Royal ladies. Be careful. The King will get weary of it. These Princesses have made themselves odious. They have never known how to win their father's love nor the esteem of anyone else. Everything that is said and done in their apartments is known. In the end you will have to bear the blame for it and you alone. It is for you to set the tone toward the King . . . not them."

She does not know, I thought. She is not here.

"I must write to the Empress at once," said Mercy, "and tell her of my interview with the King. Meanwhile I implore you to do this small thing. Just a few words. That is all she asks. And is it much?"

"With a woman of that kind it would not stop at a few words. She would always be at my side."

"I am sure you would know how to prevent that."

"In matters of good behavior I have no need to ask the advice of anyone," I said coldly.

"That is true, I know. But would you feel some remorse if the French-Austro alliance broke down because of your behavior?"

"I would never forgive myself."

A smile cracked his old face and he looked almost human.

"Now I know," he said, "that you will take the advice of your mother and those who wish you well."

But I could not learn my lessons. When I was with the aunts I told them of my conversation with Mercy. Adelaide's eyes flashed fire. It was immoral, she declared.

"I have no choice. My mother wishes it. She is afraid that the King will be displeased not only with me but with Austria."

"The King often needs saving from himself."

"I must do it," I said.

Adelaide was quiet; her sisters sat looking at her expectantly. I thought: Even she accepts the position now.

I should have known better.

It was all over the Court. "Tonight the Dauphine will speak to the du Barry. *La guerre des femmes* is over with victory for the mistress." Well, anyone who wagered against that result was a fool. But it would be amusing to see the humiliation of Little Carrots and the triumph of the du Barry.

In the *salon* the ladies stood waiting for my approach. My custom was to pass among them addressing a word to each in turn—and among them was Madame du Barry. I was aware of her, waiting eagerly, her blue eyes wide with only the faintest trace of triumph. She did not wish to humiliate me, only to ease a situation which was intolerable to her.

I was uneasy, but I knew I had to give in. I could not flout the King of France and the Empress of Austria. Two people only separated her from me. I was steeling myself; I was ready.

Then I felt a light touch on my arm. I turned and saw Adelaide, a sly triumph in her eyes.

"The King is waiting for us in Madame Victoire's apartments," she said. "It is time for us to be going."

I hesitated. Then I turned and with the aunts, left the *salon*. I was aware of the silence in the room. I had snubbed the du Barry as never before.

In their apartments the aunts were twittering with excitement. See how we had outwitted them! It was unthinkable that I—Berry's wife—should speak to that woman.

I waited for the storm and I knew I should not have to wait long.

Mercy came to tell me that the King was really angry. He had sent for him and said coldly that his plans did not seem effective, and he himself would have to take a hand.

"I have sent an express messenger to Vienna," Mercy told me, "with a detailed account of what has happened."

My mother herself wrote to me:

"The dread and embarrassment you are showing about speaking to persons you are advised to speak to is both ridiculous and childish. What a fuss about saying Good Day to someone! What a storm about a quick word . . . perhaps about a dress or a fan! You have allowed yourself to become enslaved and your duty can no longer persuade you. I myself must write to you about this foolish matter. Mercy has told me about the King's wishes and you have had the temerity to fail him! What reason can you give for behaving in such a way? You have none. It is most unbecoming to regard Madame du Barry in any other light than that of a lady whom the King honors with his society. You are the King's first subject and you owe him obedience. You should set a good example; you should show the ladies and gentlemen of Versailles that you are ready to obey your master. If any intimacy were asked of you, anything that were wrong—neither I nor any other would advise you to do it. But all that is asked is that you should say a mere word—should look at her pleasantly and smile—not for her sake, but for the sake of your grandfather, who is not only your master but your benefactor."

When I read this letter I was bewildered. It seemed that everything my mother stood for had been thrust aside for the sake of expediency. I had behaved as she had brought me up to behave and it seemed I was wrong. This letter was as clear a command as she had ever given me.

I wrote to her for she expected an answer:

> "I do not say that I refuse to speak to her, but I cannot agree to speak to her on a fixed hour or a particular day known to her in advance so that she can triumph about that."

I knew that this was quibbling and that I was defeated.

It was New Year's Day when I spoke to her. Everyone knew it would be that day and they were ready. In order of precedence the ladies filed past me and there among them was Madame du Barry.

I knew nothing must prevent my speaking this time. The aunts had tried to advise me against it but I did not listen to them. Mercy had pointed out to me that while they railed against Madame du Barry in private, they were friendly enough to her face. Had I not noticed this? Should I not be a little wary of ladies who could behave so?

Now we were face to face. She looked a little apologetic as though to say: I don't want to make it too bad for you, but you see it had to be done.

Had I been sensible I should have known that was how she sincerely felt; but I could only see black and white. She was a sinful woman, therefore she was wicked all through.

I said the words I had been rehearsing: *"Il y a bien du monde aujourd'hui à Versailles."*

It was enough. The beautiful eyes were full of pleasure, the lovely lips smiled tenderly; but I was passing on.

I had done it. The whole Court was talking of it. When I saw the King he embraced me; Mercy was benign; Madame du Barry was happy. Only the aunts were displeased; but I had noticed that Mercy was right; they *were* always affable to Madame du Barry in person, while they said such wounding things behind her back.

But I was hurt and angry.

"I have spoken to her once," I told Mercy, "but it will never happen again. Never again shall that woman hear the sound of my voice."

I wrote to my mother.

> "I do not doubt that Mercy has told you of what happened on New Year's Day. I trust you will be satisfied. You may be sure that I will always sacrifice my personal prejudices as long as nothing is asked of me which goes against my honor."

I had never written to my mother in that tone before. I was growing up.

Of course the whole Court was laughing at the affair. People passing each other on the great staircase would whisper: "*Il y a bien du monde aujourd'hui à Versailles!*" Servants giggled about it in the bedrooms. It was the catch phrase of the moment.

But at least what they considered my inane remark in the *salon* had stopped them—temporarily—speculating about what went on in the bedchamber.

I was right when I said that the du Barry would not be satisfied. She longed for friendship. I did not understand that she wanted to show me that she had no desire to exploit her victory, and she hoped that I felt no rancor on account of my defeat. She was a woman of the people who by good fortune had become rich; her home was now a palace and she was grateful to fate which had placed her there. She wanted to live on good terms with everyone, and to her I must have seemed like a silly little girl.

What could she do to placate me? Everyone knew that I loved diamonds. Why not a trinket after which I hankered. The Court jeweler had been showing a pair of very fine diamond earrings round the Court —hoping that Madame du Barry would like them. They cost seven hundred thousand livres—a large sum, but they were truly exquisite. I had seen then and exclaimed with wonder at their perfection.

Madame du Barry sent a friend of hers to speak to me about the earrings—casually, of course. I admired them very much, she believed. I said I thought they were the most beautiful earrings I had ever seen. Then came the hint. Madame du Barry was sure she could persuade the King to buy them for me.

I listened in blank silence and made no reply. The woman did not know what to do; then I told her haughtily that she had my permission to go.

My meaning was clear. I wanted no favors from the King's mistress; and at our next meeting I looked through her as though she did not exist.

Madame du Barry shrugged her shoulders. She had had a few words and that was all that was necessary. If La Petite Rousse wanted to be a little fool, let her. Meanwhile everyone continued to remark that there were a great many people at Versailles that day.

5

"Madame, I hope Monsieur le Dauphin will not be offended but down
there are two hundred thousand people who have fallen in love with you."

Maréchal de Brissac, Governor of Paris, to Marie Antoinette

GREETINGS FROM PARIS

One advantage came out of that incident. I learned to be wary of the
aunts. I began to see that that unfortunate affair might never have taken
place but for them. Mercy grimly admitted that it may have taught me a
valuable lesson in which case it must not be completely deplored.

I was no longer the child I had been on my arrival. I had grown much
taller and was no longer *petite*; my hair had darkened, which was an
advantage for there was a brownish tinge in the red so that the nickname
Carrots was no longer so apt. The King quickly forgave me my intransi-
gence over Madame du Barry and my metamorphosis from child into
woman pleased him; I should be falsely modest if I did not admit that I
had ceased to be an attractive child and had become an even more attractive woman. I do not think I was beautiful though. The high forehead
which had caused such concern was still there, so were the uneven slightly
prominent teeth—but I was able to give an impression of beauty without
effort so that when I entered a room all eyes were on me. My complexion
was, I know, very clear and without blemish; my long neck and sloping
shoulders were graceful.

Although I loved to adorn myself with diamonds and fine clothes I
was not exactly vain. I had charmed my way through Schönbrunn and
the Hofburg and I accepted it as natural that I should do so here. I did
not realize that the very qualities which brought me the affection of the
King and the admiring glances of Artois would also stir up a hundred

petty jealousies in the court. I was as careless and heedless as ever. Each little lesson had to be mastered of itself; I could apply my knowledge to nothing, and having discovered the perfidy of the aunts it never occurred to me to look for similar faults in others.

One thing which was pleasing was my new relationship with the Dauphin. He was proud of me. His slow smile would cross his face when he heard compliments about my appearance; I would sometimes catch his eyes on me with a kind of wonder. Then I would be happy and perhaps run to him and take his hand which, while it embarrassed him a little, pleased him.

I was growing fond of him. Our relationship was an unusual one for he seemed constantly to be mutely apologizing to me for being unable to be what was called "a good husband"; and I was trying to convey to him that I knew it was no fault of his. He wanted me to know that he thought me charming, that he was completely satisfied with me; it was simply an affliction which prevented the consummation of our marriage; and as we were growing older we began to understand more of this. He was no longer indifferent to me; he liked to caress me; normal instincts were being awakened in him and there were attempts to which I submitted as hopefully as he did because I believed—as he so desperately wanted to—that one day the miracle would happen.

Mercy wrote to my mother that there was no sign yet of pregnancy but "one may hope every day for that longed for event." But Dr. Ganière, one of the King's doctors who had examined the Dauphin, wrote of my husband:

> "As he grows older his strengthening diet and the presence of this fresh young girl awakens the Dauphin's sluggish senses, but on account of the pain caused at certain moments by his malformation he has to give up his attempts. The doctors agree that only surgery could put an end to the torture resulting from these fruitless and exhausting experiences. But he lacks the courage to submit to it. Nature has allowed him to make some progress, since now he does not immediately fall asleep on reaching the marriage bed. He hopes it will allow him to make more and to be able to avoid the scalpel; he is hoping for a spontaneous cure."

We were growing more tender toward each other. I would scold him for eating too many sweet things which were making him so fat. I would snatch them from him just as he was about to eat them and he would pretend to scowl but he would be laughing and so pleased that I cared.

When he came to our apartments covered in plaster, for he could never see men at work without joining them, I would scold him and tell him that he must mend his ways, which made him chuckle.

Of course Mercy was busily writing of all this to my mother.

> "Nothing the Dauphine can do can turn the Dauphin from his extraordinary taste for everything in the way of building, masonry, and carpentering. He is always having something rearranged in his apartments and works with the workmen, moving material, beams, and paving stones, giving himself up for hours at a time to strenuous exercise from which he returns more tired than a day laborer . . ."

There would be periods when my husband was seized with a frenzy to become normal. During these we would be exhausted physically and mentally; and after a while he would revert to his old habit of going to bed hours before I did so that he was fast asleep when I arrived and he would be up at dawn while I slumbered on.

I became bored. What could I do to amuse myself when Mercy was always at my elbow? What would my mother say to this or that? I was warned that I was eating too many sweets. Did I not know that this could result in *embonpoint*? My dainty figure was one of my greatest assets; my frivolous nature, my *légèreté*, my love of *dissipation* were noticed and frowned on; but at least I had my pretty figure. If I were going to spoil that by this indulgence . . . The lectures went on. I had not cleaned my teeth regularly; my nails were untrimmed and not as clean as they should be. Every time I opened a letter from my mother there was some complaint.

"She cannot love me," I told Mercy. "She treats me like a child. She will go on treating me so until I am . . . thirty!"

He shook his head over me, and murmured that my *légèreté* was alarming. *Légèreté* was a word they seemed to have attached about my neck. I was constantly hearing it. Sometimes I dreamed that I was in bed with my husband and that my bed was surrounded by prying servants who stared at us and shouted *légèreté* . . . *dissipation* . . . *etiquette*.

> "You must furnish your mind," wrote my mother. "You must read pious books. This is essential—for you more than anyone else, for you care for nothing but music, drawing, and dancing."

When I read that letter I was angry. Perhaps it was because my mother was miles away that I could feel so. I am sure I never should if she were beside me.

Mercy watched the indignant color flow into my cheeks and I looked up and caught him.

"She appears to think I am a performing animal." He looked so shocked that immediately a vision of my mother came to me and I felt guilty. "I love the Empress of course," I went on, "but even when I am writing to her I am never at ease with her."

"You have changed," replied Mercy, "when your brother the Emperor reprimanded you as he did so often . . ."

"Oh, so often!" I sighed.

"You did not seem to care enough then. You would smile and forget all about it the moment after he had spoken."

"That was different. He was only my brother. I answered him back . . . and sometimes we had little jokes together. But I could never answer my mother back . . . I could never joke with *her*."

This was immediately reported back to my mother and her next letter said:

> "Do not say that I scold and preach, but say rather: 'Mamma loves me and has constantly my advantage in view; I must believe her and comfort her by following her good advice.' You will benefit from this, and there will then be no further shadow between us. I am sincere and I expect sincerity and candor from you."

But she was disappointed in me for at the same time she wrote to Mercy and he, feeling it would be to my good to see what she wrote, showed me her letter.

> "Notwithstanding all your care and discernment in directing my daughter, I see only too clearly how unwilling are her efforts to follow your advice and mine. In these days only flattery and a playful manner are liked; and when, with the best intentions, we address any serious remonstrance, our young people are wearied, consider they are scolded and, as they always suppose, without reason. I see that this is the case with my daughter. I shall nevertheless continue to warn her when you see that it may be useful to do so, adding some amount of flattery, much as I dislike the style. I fear I have little hope of success in luring my daughter from her indolence."

So the disagreeable pills of advice were to be sugar-coated with a thin layer—a very thin layer of flattery!

When I read the letter I was exasperated, but I loved my mother.

I might toss my head and declare that I was treated like a child but I missed her; I wanted to be with her. There were times when I was quite frightened and then I seemed truly like a child crying for its mother. Once when I went to my bureau I found it open although I knew that I had locked it when I was last there because it was one of the few things I was careful about. Someone must have taken the keys from my pocket while I slept!

I remembered my mother's warning about burning her letters. I had followed this advice faithfully but as I found it difficult to memorize what she had written I had to keep the letters until I had answered them. I slept with them under my pillow; sometimes during the night I would put my hand under to touch the paper.

"Someone has been at my bureau," I told the Abbé.

He smiled. "You forgot to lock it."

"I did not. I did not. I swear I did not."

But he smiled at me, not believing. Such a little featherhead, interested in nothing but pleasure! Was it not the most natural thing in the world that she should forget to lock a desk?

I could confide in no one. I knew that Mercy and Vermond were my friends but everything I told Vermond he reported to Mercy—he dared do nothing else for he held his position through the good graces of Mercy—and Mercy passed it on to my mother.

I sought consolation in lighthearted amusement. There was always Artois ready for a game. He and I made up a little party and went to Marly to see the sunrise. There were several of us though the Dauphin did not accompany us, preferring to stay slumbering in bed. It was beautiful . . . the sun coming up from the horizon to shine on Marly; but it was wrong of course. The Dauphine making excursions in the early hours of morning! For what purpose? No one believed that it was merely to see the sun rise.

I laid myself open to scandal, without realizing, although as yet public opinion was indulgent to me. I was a child, a pretty child, high-spirited and anxious for adventure. But a Dauphine with a husband suspected of impotence should be very careful. The innocent excursion to Marly was noted; and Madame de Noailles pointed out to me that such a reckless adventure should not be repeated.

What to do to relieve the boredom! If I could go to Paris how much more interesting life would be. In Paris there was excitement. It was a busy city; there were balls which were held at the opera house. How I longed to dance, masked, to mingle with the crowds and none know that I was the Dauphine, to escape for a while from that eternal etiquette!

"Your entry into Paris must be official," Madame de Noailles told me.

"When, when?" I demanded.

"That is for His Majesty to decide."

I was frustrated. The great city was so near and yet I was not allowed to visit it. One could reach it in little more than an hour by carriage. How absurd, how ridiculous that I was forbidden to go!

I spoke to the aunts about my desire. They were no longer so affectionate, although Adelaide pretended to be, but Victoire and Sophie could not hide their changed feelings. They watched me furtively when I was in the apartments. I had not obeyed Adelaide over the du Barry affair. I was therefore foolish and unpredictable.

"You could not go to Paris . . . just like that," said Adelaide. "It would have to be arranged."

My husband said that he supposed I should go when the time came. Could he not do something about granting my wish? He wanted to please me whenever he could but this was not a matter for him to decide.

Even Artois was evasive. I came to the conclusion that none of them *wanted* me to go to Paris.

"It would not at this time be etiquette," Artois explained. "You know Grandpapa never goes. He hates Paris because Paris no longer likes him. If you went they would cheer you because you are young and pretty and they would not cheer Grandfather. You can't have the Dauphine cheered and the King insulted. It would not be etiquette."

I decided that I would ask the King myself, for I was sure that if I chose the right moment he would be unable to refuse me for since I had spoken to Madame du Barry and had been less friendly with the aunts he had become very affectionate toward me. He always embraced me warmly when I visited him and complimented me on my appearance. I was growing up charmingly, he said. Sometimes he came to breakfast with me; and when he came he liked to make the coffee himself, and this was more than making a cup of coffee; within the rules of etiquette it meant that he accepted me wholeheartedly as one of the family and one who pleased him very much.

Sometimes I would bring out the waistcoat I was embroidering and show it to him.

"But it is magnificent," he would say. "When, I wonder, shall I have the pleasure of wearing it?"

"Perhaps in five years' time, Papa . . . or ten."

It was a joke between us.

So I chose my moment and said to him: "Papa, I have been your daughter for three years and I have never seen your capital city. I long to go to Paris."

He hesitated and then he said: "Naturally you will go there . . . in time."

"How long, Papa? How long?"

I went to him and, putting my arms about his neck, laughed.

"You are amused?"

"Thinking how fortunate it is that Madame l'Etiquette is not here to see me do this."

He laughed too. He appreciated the name I had given Madame de Noailles for he was a great giver of nicknames himself.

"Fortunate for me," he said, taking my hands and holding them there about his neck.

"Papa, I want to go to Paris. You will give the permission Etiquette demands?"

"Ah, Etiquette and Madame la Dauphine . . . both are irresistible, but Madame more so."

So it was as simple as that. All I had to do was ask prettily and there had been all this unnecessary fuss!

Now I would show them all. The King had given me his permission!

"There will be so much to do," I said. "This is going to delay work on your waistcoat."

"Then I shall not have it within the ten years after all."

I put my head on one side and smiled at him. "I promise you I shall work harder than ever and every flower will be worked with love."

"Which will be far more beautiful than silk I am sure."

Then I embraced him warmly wishing that I could persuade my mother as easily as I did the King of France.

So . . . to Paris. I went triumphantly to my husband and told him that I had persuaded the King. He was mildly surprised but delighted as he always was when my whims were granted.

I told Artois. "To Paris! How I long to dance at the opera ball. Do you know if the King had refused I was going to ask you to make up a party and come with me . . . disguised."

Artois' eyes gleamed. He was adventurous by nature but there was too a love of mischief very similar to that of the aunts. Artois was sympathetic to me and yet he loved trouble for its own sake and he would have enjoyed seeing me involved in it.

"Well," he said, "are you asking me now?"

"But I am going . . . ceremoniously as Etiquette would have it."

He snapped his fingers at Etiquette. "Let's defy the old creature."

"How?"

"By forestalling her. We will dress ourselves in dominoes; we will be masked and drive out from Versailles. Unrecognized we will go to the masked ball."

I looked at him in astonishment but he had seized me and was dancing with me round the apartment. I was caught up in the excitement of the project. What fun! To snap our fingers at Etiquette! Secretly to go to Paris *before* the ceremony she demanded. Why had not Artois thought of this months ago?

He kissed my hands too fervently for a brother-in-law; his bold eyes were caressing. I decided that I would persuade my husband to come with us.

Louis was perplexed. But why go to Paris incognito when in such a short time I could go openly?

"Because it is much more *fun* like this."

He wrinkled his brows to try to understand my sort of fun. Dear Louis! He could no more understand why this adventure appealed to me than I could understand why covering himself with plaster and taking locks to pieces pleased him.

I looked at him appealingly. "I want to go and I know you want me to enjoy myself."

He did. There was a world of understanding between us. He could not apologize for those distasteful sessions in the bedchamber, although he wanted to. His way of doing so was to indulge me all he could. He thought the plan a wild one, but if I was set on doing something so reckless, it would at least be less so if he accompanied me.

So dear kind Louis agreed to come, and late in the evening, our dominoes wrapped around us, our masks disguising our faces we set out along the road to Paris.

It was one of the most thrilling evenings I had so far known. There was an excitement in Paris which caught at me and enveloped me. I had wasted three whole years with this delightful city only an hour or so's ride away and I had never seen it until this night. Artois—I was seated between him and my husband—pointed out the Invalides, the Bastille, the Hôtel de Ville, the Tuileries, and towering Notre Dame. I was aware of the people in the streets for Paris never seemed to sleep. I saw the bridges and the gleaming river, but it was typical of me that what made most impression on me that night was the Opera House.

I shall never forget the excitement—the crowds of people, the music, the dancing. How happy I was! I forgot everything in the joy of dancing; and here the dancers were more abandoned. Several sought to partner me but my husband would not allow that and I was surprised by his quiet dignity which even in his disguise was apparent.

So I danced with him and Artois and some of the members of our little band of adventurers who, on Louis' orders, kept a close guard on me.

The Opera House—it is so clear in my memory now—its great chandeliers, the light from thousands of candles, the smell of pomade and the faint haze of powder in the air. It spells romance to me because of one whom in the not very distant future I was to meet there. I should always feel that the Paris Opera House has a very special place in my most tender memories.

On that night, by great good luck which we did not deserve, nothing unfortunate happened. We had danced well into the night and dawn was breaking when we came back along the road to Versailles.

Next morning we were all at Mass, bright-eyed and innocent, as though we were quite incapable of indulging in such a reckless adventure.

Artois and I congratulated ourselves on having made a gesture of defiance at Etiquette.

The day for the formal entry into Paris arrived and having seen the city by night with all its fascinating contrasts, its magnificent buildings and that air of gaiety which was all its own, I was longing to be there.

Paris! The city that loved me in the beginning and then wearied of me and rejected and hated me. It looked rather like a great ship, with Notre Dame as its stern and its prow the old Pont Neuf raised on the Islet of Cow-Ferryman.

It was a perfect day. There were blue skies and sunshine. All along the road from Versailles to Paris, the people stood waiting for us to pass. When they saw me they shouted a greeting. My husband beside me drew back so that everyone could see me.

"They are shouting for us," I said to him. "They like us."

"No," he answered, "they are shouting for you."

I was delighted for nothing pleased me more than admiration. I responded to it; I sat there smiling and inclining my head and they called out that I was as pretty as a picture.

"Long live our Dauphine," they said.

Provence and Marie Josèphe looked sour, unable to hide their jealousy; and I smiled more dazzlingly and aroused more cheers.

As we approached the city I could scarcely sit still, so excited was I. I saw a mass of faces; flowers were flung at my carriage; flags were waved and there were loyal greetings everywhere.

At the gates of the city the Maréchal de Brissac, who was Governor of the City, was waiting for me with a silver plate on which lay the keys of the city, and amid the roars of approval he handed these to me. Then from the Invalides the guns boomed out, followed by those of the Hôtel de Ville and the Bastille.

Oh, what a wonderful sight! All those people gathered to welcome *me* to their city.

I heard their comments. "Oh, is she not lovely! What a little beauty! As dainty as a fairy!"

Dear people! How I loved them! In a transport of emotion I kissed my hands to them and they responded joyfully.

All the women from the markets wearing their best clothes of black silk had assembled to greet me, and they called out to me that they were pleased to see me in the city. I was struck by the proprietorial air of all these people. This was *their* city not the King's. If the King had no love for Paris—well, Paris could do without him. Paris belonged to the merchants, the market women, the tradesmen, the apprentices. That was the message I received that day. It was theirs and they welcomed me to it because I was young and pretty and had shown that I wanted them to like me. I was in love with Paris, so Paris was in love with me.

What a procession! We were escorted by the King's own bodyguards and behind our coach were three others containing our attendants.

When the keys had been presented to me we drove into the city to Notre Dame where we attended Mass and after that we made our way to the college of Louis le Grand where at Sainte Geneviève the Abbot and his Chapter were waiting for us.

Having listened to his greetings we passed on; under the triumphal arches we went through Paris so that all those who had assembled might have a glimpse of me.

It was one of the most thrilling experiences of my life. I was really happy. I had the glorious feeling that everything was coming right. And at last we came to the Tuileries where we were to dine and the crowd in the garden was bigger than anything I had ever known.

No sooner were we inside than the people began to shout for us.

Monsieur de Brissac said: "They will not be content unless you show yourselves."

"Then," I replied, "we will do so, for I could not disappoint the people of Paris."

So we went onto the balcony and when they saw me there, the people in the gardens began to cheer me and call long life to me; and I stood there smiling and bowing and was very happy.

"But she is adorable," they cried. "She is lovely. May God bless our enchanting little Dauphine."

I was so happy. I had suffered so much criticism from my mother and Mercy that I yearned for approval; and here it was in larger doses than I had ever known before.

"Oh, the dear, dear people!" I cried. "How I love them. *Mon dieu*, what crowds! How many of them there are!"

Monsieur de Brissac, standing beside me, smiled and then bowing he said: "Madame, I hope Monsieur le Dauphin will not be offended but down there are two hundred thousand people who have fallen in love with you."

And that was the most delightful thing, I assured him, that had ever happened to me.

Paris had taken me to its heart and I had taken Paris to mine.

I returned to Versailles as in a dream. I could still hear the applause and the compliments.

The King came to hear how I had fared and I was afraid that if I told him how I had been received he would feel sad because I understood something of the meaning of that almost frenzied greeting. Those people who had shouted for me and for my husband would not shout for the King. They were waiting for him to die because they hated him; Louis the once Well-Beloved was now Louis the Hated. How sad for him, but he did not seem to mind.

He took my hands and kissed them. "I hear you were a triumph," he said.

"Your Majesty is pleased?"

"I should have disowned them if they had not had the good taste to adore you."

Oh, these French! How well they hid their cold cynicism beneath their flowery words!

In a mood of triumph I sat down and wrote to my mother:

"Dearest mother, it is impossible to describe the delight and affection which the people showed us . . . How lucky we are to win the friendship of the people so easily. But I know this friendship is very precious. I am deeply conscious of this and it is something I shall never forget."

I enjoyed writing that letter to my mother. Now she would know that I was not failing as she sometimes seemed to suggest. Mercy might disapprove of much that I did, but the people of Paris had taken one look at me and given no uncertain sign of their approval.

How happy I was as I lay in bed that night! My husband lay beside me, fast asleep. The ceremonies had tired him while they had exhilarated me.

The days of boredom were at an end. Paris had shown me a new way of life and I could hardly wait to begin it.

6

Sa figure et son air convenaient parfaitement à un héros de roman, mais non pas d'un roman français.

Duc de Lévis on Axel de Fersen

"Madame la Dauphine talked to me for a long time without my recognizing her. At last when she made herself known, everyone crowded about her and she withdrew to her box. At three o'clock I left the ball."

From the Journal of Axel de Fersen

THE ATTRACTIVE STRANGER

A few months after my entry into Paris, Artois was married. His bride was the sister of Marie Josèphe. Their father Victor Amédée, the King of Sardinia, had naturally wanted the Dauphin for one of his daughters, so the sisters resented me.

The new bride, Marie Thérèse, was even uglier than her sister. Her only remarkable feature was her nose and that was because of its length; her mouth was enormous, her eyes small and she squinted slightly. She was very small and quite lacking in grace. The King showed clearly that he found her repulsive; as for Artois he did not express disappointment but behaved as though the matter were of little importance. Marie Thérèse seemed to want to hide herself and he was pleased to indulge her in this. He had a mistress already—a very beautiful woman, much older than himself, named Rosalie Duthé, a lady who had served the Duc de Chartres in the same capacity as she now served Artois.

Everyone was amused by Artois' attitude and no one was very sorry for the poor little bride. All their sympathy was for Artois because he was unlucky enough to have such a wife.

The comment in Versailles was characteristic: "Having got indigestion through *gâteau de Savoie* the Prince had gone to take Duthé in Paris."

I was one of the few people who was sorry for Marie Thérèse and I did all I could to be her friend, but she was very disagreeable and curt with me.

However, I was enjoying myself as I had not done since I had come to France, so I did not need the friendship of my sisters-in-law. The Princesse de Lamballe had become my close friend and we chattered together as I used to with Caroline. In fact for the first time I believed I had replaced my sister.

When the snow came I could really imagine I was back in Vienna and one day I found an old sleigh in the stables at Versailles and as the Princesse was with me I told her what fun we used to have in Vienna and how Joseph had had the snow brought down from the mountains when there was none below just because he loved to ride in a sleigh.

"And why should we not?" I cried. "I see no reason why not. Here is the sleigh and there is the snow."

So I ordered the grooms to prepare the sleigh and have the horses harnessed to it and the Princesse and I rode out.

We went to Paris—always Paris; and what fun it was being drawn along the road and finally reaching the Bois de Boulogne. It was bitterly cold but we were wrapped up in furs and it was glorious to feel our faces glowing.

"This is just like Vienna," I cried. "And you remind me of my dearest sister Caroline."

But it was not really like Vienna where there were many sleighs and this was the only way in which one could travel. Ours was the only sleigh in the Bois and we were not traveling; we were playing a game. The people came out to watch us and they seemed very different from those who had welcomed me into their city in the summer. These had pinched blue faces; they stood and shivered and the contrast between them in their inadequate rags and us in our furs was painful. I was aware of this but I tried not to see it because it spoiled the fun.

Mercy came to my apartments looking stern.

"Your new pastime does not please the people of Paris," he told me.

"But why not?"

"It is not a pleasure which is indulged in here."

"Oh," I grumbled. "Etiquette again."

But it was more than Etiquette; and I was not sorry to give it up.

That was an end to our sleigh rides.

The tension in the family circle which had increased since the arrival of Artois' wife was steadily rising. The two sisters were joined in their dislike of me; and my brothers-in-law by their ambition. Of the two brothers Provence was by far the most ambitious. Marie Josèphe had shown no signs of becoming pregnant and it was being said that he suffered the same disability as the Dauphin.

Mercy had warned me of my elder brother-in-law's "little polite trickeries," but as he was continually warning me I paid little heed. Now even I, bent as I was on ignoring unpleasantness and finding new amusements, could not be unaware of the growing tension between the brothers.

"Provence is ambitious and strives in every way to be the dominant member of the household," Mercy said. "I am writing to the Empress to tell her this. I have rarely seen one so young so ambitious."

This ambition was working up to a hatred against my husband. The six of us were often together. Etiquette demanded that we should be. Once, we were in Provence's apartments and my husband was standing by the fireplace and on the mantelpiece was a beautiful china vase, for Provence collected fine china things. My husband had always been fascinated by this particular piece, and I used to watch him and laughingly ask him if he was thinking of giving up bricks and locks for china.

He gravely answered that it might be an interesting study.

As Louis' hands were not made to handle delicate objects Provence was very concerned for the safety of his vase.

I watched him watching Louis and laughingly called attention to his anxiety. Provence was not amused; he stood, his hands behind his back to hide the fact that he was clenching them in fury.

Then . . . it happened. The vase crashed to the floor and was broken into several pieces. Only then did I realize Provence's hatred for the Dauphin. He sprang at him. Louis, taken by surprise, went crashing to the floor. He was heavy and I called out in alarm as he fell, but Provence was on him; he had his hands at my husband's throat. Then Louis had broken free, and they were rolling on the floor, both behaving as though they would kill each other. The sisters stood apart watching; but I could not remain aloof, I ran to them and pulling at my husband's coat shouted to them to stop.

When he saw that I was in danger, my husband cried: "Be careful! Antoinette will be hurt!" My hands were bleeding from a scratch I had received in the scrimmage and the sight of that blood sobered them both.

"You are hurt," said my husband lumbering to his feet.

"It is nothing, but I beg of you do not be so foolish again."

They were both rather sheepish, ashamed to have given way to their tempers over such a matter. My husband apologized for his clumsiness and Provence for his display of temper. But their wives whispered together and they implied that I had been only eager to draw attention to myself by pretending to be so concerned and rushing in and getting scratched.

How difficult it was to be friendly with these girls! But I was friendly by nature and I could not believe that they really disliked me so I tried to think of a way of making them happy. After all, I reasoned with the Princesse de Lamballe, it was small wonder they were so disagreeable. How should we feel if we looked as they did? Poor ugly little creatures.

It did not make life easier because the King so obviously showed his preference for me. When my sisters-in-law knew that he visited me for breakfast and actually made the coffee they were furious! Marie Josèphe did not show it, for she was sly, but her young sister could not disguise her feelings. The aunts were always trying to stir trouble between us but I refused to listen; although I'm sure my sisters-in-law did.

The King knew that I loved the theater and he had said that on every Tuesday and Friday comedies should be performed. I was delighted and I was always there to applaud the actors. But what I longed to do was play on a stage and I conceived the idea that we should do a play among ourselves.

"It would be forbidden if it were discovered," said Provence.

"Then," I retorted, "it must not be discovered."

It was an excellent idea because when we were learning our lines and planning the scenery my sisters-in-law forgot to hate me. And I was so happy to be acting that I forgot everything else.

I discovered some one-act plays; and sometimes we were ambitious enough to try Molière. I shall always remember playing Cathos from Les Précieuses Ridicules. How I would prance across the stage, throwing myself into the part. I loved everyone when I was on a stage. This brought out the best in my brother-in-law Provence who could learn his lines with the utmost ease and had a real gift for playing comedy. I would throw my arms about his neck and cry: "But you are marvelous! You play the part to the life." He would be pleased—so different from the grim young man who bore a grudge against fate which had not made him a Dauphin. Artois of course loved to act, and even my sisters-in-law enjoyed playing. They had such quaint French accents that we were often in fits of laughter in which even they joined.

Sometimes we allowed the young Princesses Clothilde and Elisabeth to play. I pleaded that they should be allowed to because I remembered how I had been kept out because I was too young. They loved it of course; and I grew very fond of little Elisabeth and Clothilde too until her governess turned her against me. She was a goodnatured girl—a trifle lazy, but then she was so fat. The King, with his penchant for nicknames, had already dubbed her Fat Lady. She did not mind. She was wonderfully good tempered and would take the most unrewarding parts with a smile.

This was all the more fun because we had to set out our own stage, which we made with screens; and the approach of anyone not in the secret meant that these had to be bundled into a cupboard hastily and we would all have to try to look as if our costumes were what we would naturally wear and arrange ourselves as though we were merely chatting idly.

My husband was in the secret of course but he would take no part in the play-acting, so he was the audience.

"A very necessary part," I pointed out, "because a play needs an audience."

So he would sit there smiling and applauding and more often than not falling asleep. But I did notice that when I was to the fore he was almost always awake.

So enthusiastic did we become over our amateur theatricals that I called in Monsieur Campan who was my secretary and librarian, and whose services and discretion I valued, and asked him to help us find the exact costumes we would need for our parts. He was very good at this and so was his son who joined us.

The fun continued and everyone noticed how intimate the six of us had become; we even took our meals together.

Amateur theatricals was merely one way of passing the time. I was constantly arranging that we should go into the city and it was usually to the opera ball. I insisted that we all went although my sisters-in-law were not good dancers and were far from eager. The Parisians never cheered them as they did me. They seemed to have forgotten my one lapse into what was considered bad taste—riding through the Bois de Boulogne in my sleigh—and had taken me to their hearts once more. It did not occur to me that the people could love their Dauphine one day and could hate her the next. I knew nothing of the people and although I made many many journeys to the city I knew little of Paris . . . the real city.

I learned a little of it later and wished I had been more perceptive, for the Paris of that day was to change heartbreakingly in little more than a decade and nothing surely could ever be quite the same again.

What a city of contrasts it was—although at that time I was quite blind to this! The elegant Dauphine Square—and those winding streets such as the Rue de la Juiverie, Rue aux Féves, and the Rue des Marmousets in which thieves and prostitutes of the lowest kind lived side by side with the famous Paris dyers whose tubs were set out on the cobbles. Sometimes I would see the red, blue, and green streams running out of these narrow alleys as we passed. I was told they were from the dyers and was content to leave it at that never bothering to learn more of their fascinating trade.

It was a bustling city and a gay one. That was what was most apparent —its gaiety. Sometimes in the early morning rattling back to Versailles after a ball we would see peasants arriving from the other side of the barriers with their produce which they would market in Les Halles. We would see the bakers of Gonesse bringing their bread into Paris. In the dark years ahead these bakers were not allowed to take back any which was unsold for so precious was bread that the authorities kept a tight hold on every loaf that was brought into the capital. Bread! It was a word which was to ring in my ears like the knell of a funeral bell. But at this time they were merely the bakers of Gonesse who came into Paris twice a week and who stopped to stare open-mouthed at our carriages as they carried us back to Versailles.

I knew nothing then of this workaday city into which six thousand country men and women came each morning with their wares. To me Paris was the Opera House, the home of those people who loved me so dearly, the capital city of the country of which I should one day be Queen.

If only I had been taught to know Paris! Madame Campan often deplored this. She said that Vermond had kept me criminally in the dark. I could have learned so much if I had seen Paris at work, Paris as it really was for the Parisians. I should have seen the clerks walking to their work, the traders in Les Halles, the barbers covered in the flour with which they powdered their wigs, the gowned and bewigged lawyers on the way to the Châtelet. I should have been aware of the great contrasts. I should have compared the difference between ourselves in our fine clothes and the poor beggars, the *marcheuses*, those sad creatures who were scarcely human with the scars of debauchery and hardship on their faces, still alive but only just, too worn out to continue their old profession, and who were so called because they were fit only to run errands for the poorest prostitutes. So much poverty on one side, so much splendor on the other! The Paris through which I drove so blithely on my way to and fro was the fertile breeding ground of revolution.

And at the heart was the Palais Royale. Like a small rich town in its own right, the square was as a cloister and after dark all sorts of men and women gathered here. Here was discussed art, the scandals of the court —my marriage must have been a favorite topic—and, as time progressed, the inequalities, the desire for liberty, equality, and the brotherhood of men.

I would feel the excitement envelop me as we left Versailles and drove along the road to Paris. There would be the carriages, the people on horseback, often with an elaborately dressed footman to run ahead of them to show how rich and important they were. And for those who were not so rich there was the *carrabas*, the rather cumbersome vehicle drawn by eight horses which plowed its way back and forth between Paris and Versailles, or the smaller vehicles which had been given the names of *pots de chambre* and which offered more comfort but left the occupants exposed to all weathers.

I was always thrilled to enter the city. It seemed particularly exciting after dark when the street lamps which swung out from the wall on great brackets were alight. As our carriage dashed along showers of mud would be sent up, for Paris was noted for its mud. It was different from any other mud in France, I was told. It had a definite sulphurous smell and if it was allowed to stay on a garment it would burn a hole in it. It was no doubt produced by the refuse which flowed through the streets. Paris was sometimes called Lutetia—the Town of Mud.

Carnival time came with the new year. This was the time of masked balls and comedies, operas and ballets. I could have spent each night at one of these. Because my love of dancing was known there were more masked balls than ever. We always went incognito. That was the greatest fun. Sometimes I would wear a domino and at others a simple taffeta gown or even gauze or muslin. My great delight was to disguise my identity, but I never went to these balls without either my husband or brothers-in-law in attendance. That would not only have been forbidden but highly dangerous; even I realized this.

The day was the 30th of January—a day I shall never forget; I set out with Provence and Artois, my sisters-in-law and several ladies and gentlemen. My husband did not wish to come. I did not try to persuade him because I knew he disliked coming.

I wore a black silk domino as so many dancers did and a black velvet mask hiding my features and as soon as I was in the ballroom I was dancing. Artois partnered me; I preferred that; he was an exquisite dancer and I believed enjoyed dancing with me as much as I did with him. It was exciting, but I had danced many times with Artois. I was aware of being watched as I danced though there was nothing unusual about that. I danced in my own way and several members of my entourage told me that however disguised I was they would know me by the way I moved.

The brilliantly lighted ballroom, the music, the rustle of the silk, the smell of pomade and powder were thrilling—and most of all the anonymity.

I noticed a young man watching me as I danced and although I averted my gaze I went on thinking of him. He was unmasked and handsome in a foreign way. Perhaps that was why I noticed him, because he looked so different. He was tall and slender with very fair hair and what made him so unusual were his dark eyes. His complexion was fair; and he was pale. His was a face of contrasts; at one moment it seemed beautiful as a woman's is, and then one caught sight of dark heavy brows which gave great strength to his face.

Then an impulse came to me, I wanted to speak to him, to hear his voice. Well, why not? This was a masked ball. Why should he know who I was? It was carnival time when manners were free. Why should not a masked domino exchange a few words with another dancer at carnival ball!

We stopped dancing and joined our party. I saw then that the strange man was only a few paces away and instinct told me that he was as curious about me as I was about him for he had taken his stand close to us.

I said: "I wish to amuse myself . . . for a moment." And I went up to the stranger and stood before him smiling.

I said: "It is an amusing ball . . . this."

As I spoke I put up my hand to make sure my mask was secure and I immediately half-wished I hadn't. I was wearing costly diamonds. Would he know how costly? Then I was glad for my hands were beautiful and I was very proud of them.

"I find it very amusing," he answered, and I noticed immediately the foreign accent. Had he noticed mine?

"You are not French."

"Swedish, Madame," he answered. "Or should I say, Mademoiselle."

I laughed. If he knew whom he was addressing what would his reaction be?

"You may say Madame," I answered.

Provence had come closer. I could see that the stranger was aware of

him. I tried to see Provence through a stranger's eyes. He had an air of
the great nobleman. Even when he came to a masked ball he could not
forget that he was almost a Dauphin.

I wanted to know more of the stranger but I was very conscious of
Provence standing there.

"May I say," he said, "that Madame is charming?"

"You may say it if you mean it."

"Then I repeat: Madame is charming."

"What do you do here?"

"I am acquiring culture, Madame."

"At the Opera Ball?"

"One can never be sure where it will be found."

I laughed. I did not know why except that I was happy.

"So you are doing the grand tour?"

"I am doing the grand tour, Madame."

"Tell me where you have been before coming to France."

"To Switzerland, Italy."

"And then you will return to Sweden. I wonder which country you
will like best. Shall you visit Austria? I wonder how you will like Vienna.
I once lived in Vienna." A recklessness seemed to come over me. I went
on breathlessly: "What is your name?"

He said: "It is Axel de Fersen."

"Monsieur . . . Prince . . . Comte . . . ?"

"Comte," he answered.

"Comte Axel de Fersen," I repeated.

"My mother's people came from France."

"That is why there is a look of the French about you," I said. "You
took your fairness from your father, your darkness from your mother. I
saw it at once."

"Madame is observant." He took a step closer and I thought he would
ask me to dance. I wondered what I should do if he did because I dared
not dance with a stranger. Provence was ready to intervene at any moment. Artois was watchful. If the stranger made any move which might
be considered *lèse-majesté*, and which he might easily do after the
encouragement I had given him, Provence would intervene. I saw trouble
ahead, and strangely enough instead of exhilarating me, it alarmed me.

"Madame asks many questions," said the Comte de Fersen, "and I have
answered them. Should I not be permitted to ask a few in fair return?"

Provence was frowning. I acted with my usual lack of thought. I
lifted a hand and removed my mask.

There were gasps of astonishment all about.

"Madame la Dauphine!"

I laughed aloud to hide my elation while I kept my eyes on the Comte de Fersen. How did it feel, I wondered, to indulge in a flirtation with an unknown woman and discover that you had been speaking to the future Queen of France?

He did not hesitate. He behaved with an admirable calm and the utmost dignity. He bowed low and I saw his blond hair touched his embroidered collar. It was the color of sunshine . . . beautiful hair. He must think mine was beautiful too.

The people were closing in on me. They were staring at me. Many may have guessed that I was there but in the masks which covered our faces from forehead to chin no one could be sure. But I had betrayed myself on an impulse and I was creating a scene in that crowded ballroom.

Provence was beside me; with regal dignity he held out his arm. I slipped mine through it. Artois and my party were already signing for the crowd to part and make way for us.

We went straight to our carriages.

Neither Provence, Artois, nor their wives mentioned my action, but I knew when I intercepted their speculative glances that they were considering its significance.

I should have considered it too. It did not occur to me then that these worldly young men had construed my conduct as meaning that I was tired of a marriage which was no marriage. I was a young and healthy woman; I was sexually unfulfilled. A dangerous position for a Dauphine whose offspring would be the Enfants de France. Provence was making up his mind to be watchful. What if I took a lover? What if I produced a child and passed it off as my husband's? It was possible that a bastard could rob him of a crown. Artois' speculations ran along different lines. Was I thinking of taking a lover? If so, he had always found me very attractive.

And their wives, who were beginning to know their husbands well, would be following their thoughts.

And I . . . I was going over every one of those minutes when I had talked to the stranger. I was hearing his voice echoing in my ears. I was thinking of his blond hair against the dark of his coat.

I did not think I should ever see the stranger again but I thought: I shall remember him for a long time. And he will never forget me as long as he lives.

That seemed enough.

7

"A dreadful noise, like thunder was heard in the outer apartment; it was the crowd of courtiers who were deserting the dead Sovereign's ante-chamber to come and bow to the new power of Louis XVI. This extraordinary tumult informed Marie Antoinette and her husband that they were to reign; and by a spontaneous movement which deeply affected those near them, they fell to their knees and in tears exclaimed "Oh God, guide us, protect us for we are too young to rule."

Madame Campan's Memoirs

QUEEN OF FRANCE

Louis was becoming more and more fond of me and I of him. I had written to my mother that if I could have chosen my husband from the three royal brothers I would have chosen Louis. I valued his good qualities more every day, while I became more and more critical of my brothers-in-law. He was as intelligent as Provence although the latter, because he was easily able to express himself, gave the impression of being more so—but it was false. Artois was completely lacking in seriousness; he was not only frivolous which I, more than most, could forgive, but mischievous which I could not.

Mercy had repeatedly warned me against both my brothers-in-law and I was beginning to see that he was right.

But life was too amusing nowadays for seriousness. Mercy was writing to my mother that my only real fault was my extreme love of pleasure. I certainly loved it and sought it everywhere.

But I could be thoughtful; and providing I was made aware of the sufferings of poor people I could be very sympathetic, more so than most people around me.

I often embarrassed Madame de Noailles by this tendency and on one occasion when I was with the hunt in Fontainebleau Forest I committed a breach of etiquette for which she found it difficult to reprove me.

They were hunting the stag and because I was not allowed to ride a horse I had to follow in my calash. A peasant had apparently come out of his cottage at the moment when the terrified stag was passing. He was in its way and the poor creature gored him badly. The man lay by the roadside while the hunt swept by; but when I saw him I insisted on stopping to see how badly hurt he was.

His wife had come out of the cottage and was standing over him wringing her hands; on either side of her were two crying children.

"We will carry him into the cottage and see how badly hurt he is," I said, "and I will send a doctor to tend to him." I commanded my male attendants to carry the man into his home and there I was shocked by the sight of that humble home. Remembering the splendor of my gilded apartments at Versailles, I experienced a sense of guilt and wanted to show these people that I really cared what became of them. I saw that the wound was not deep, so I bandaged it myself and leaving money I assured the wife that I would send a doctor to make sure that her husband recovered.

The wife had realized who I was and she was looking at me with something like adoration. When I left she knelt at my feet and kissed the hem of my gown. I was deeply moved.

I was more thoughtful than usual. "The dear, dear people," I kept saying to myself; and when I was next with my husband I told him of the incident and described the poverty of that cottage. He listened intently. "I am glad," he said with a rare emotion, "that you think as I do. When I am King of this country I want to do all I can for the people. I want to follow in the footsteps of my ancestor Henri Quatre."

"I wish to help you," I told him earnestly.

"Balls, pageants . . . they are an unworthy extravagance . . ."

I was silent. Why, I wondered, could one not be both good and gay?

My pity for the poor was like everything else about me—superficial. But when hardship was thrust under my nose I can say that I cared deeply.

It was the same when I asked one of my servants to move a piece of furniture and the poor old man in doing so fell and hurt himself. He fainted and I called to my attendants to come and help me.

"We will send for some of his fellow servants, Madame," I was told.

But I said no. I myself would see that he was adequately tended because it was in my service that he had hurt himself. So I insisted that they put him on a couch, I sent for water and I myself bathed his wounds.

When he opened his eyes and saw me on my knees beside him, his eyes filled with tears.

"Madame la Dauphine . . ." he whispered in an incredulous wonder and he looked at me as though I were some divine being.

Madame de Noailles might tell me that it was not etiquette for a Dauphine to tend a servant but I snapped my fingers at her; I knew that if I encountered similar incidents like those of the injured servant and peasant I should behave exactly as I had before. My actions were natural and because I invariably acted without thinking at least I had that virtue.

These incidents were talked of and doubtless magnified; and when I appeared in public the people cheered me more wildly than ever. They built up an image which I could never live up to. I was young and beautiful and in spite of the reports of my frivolity, I was good and kind; I cared for the people as no one had cared since the days of Henri Quatre who had said: "Every peasant should have a chicken in his pot every Sunday." I was of the same opinion. And my husband was a good man too. Together we would bring back the good days to France. All they had to do was wait for the old scoundrel to die and a new era would begin.

They began to speak of my husband as Louis le Désiré.

We could not help feeling inspired by this. We wanted to be a good King and Queen when our time came. We remembered though that we were failing in our first duty—to provide heirs. Louis, I knew, was thinking of the scalpel which might free him from his affliction. But would it? Was it absolutely sure? And if it failed . . .

There was another of those shameful periods of experiments of which I prefer not to think. Poor Louis, he was weighed down by his sense of responsibility; he was depressed by his inadequacy and deeply aware of his obligations. Sometimes I saw him at the anvil working in what seemed like a frenzy to tire himself out so that when he went to bed he would immediately fall into a heavy sleep.

We wanted to be good; but so much was against us . . . not only circumstances. We were surrounded by enemies.

I never failed to be astonished when I discovered that someone hated me.

My most careless conversation was commented on and misconstrued. The aunts watched me maliciously, although Victoire did so a little sadly. She really believed that they could help and that in flouting Adelaide over the du Barry incident I had made a great mistake. Madame du Barry might have been helpful but my attitude to her made her shrug her shoulders and ignore me.

She had her own troubles and I believe during those first months of 1774 was a most uneasy woman.

There had been a paragraph in the *Almanach de Liège*—an annual production specializing in foretelling the future—which said: "In April a great Lady who is fortune's favorite will play her last role."

Everyone was talking about this and saying that it referred to Madame du Barry. There was only one way in which she could lose her position and that would be through the death of the King.

Those early months of that year were uneasy ones of mingling apprehension and the most abandoned gaiety. I attended all the opera balls possible and I thought now and then of the handsome Swede who had made such an impression and wondered if I should see him again and what our encounter would be like if I did. But I did not see him.

I discovered a new enemy in the Comtesse de Marsan, governess to Clothilde and Elisabeth, who was a friend of my older antagonist, Louis' tutor, the Duc de Vauguyon. He had disliked me more than ever since I had caught him listening at doors; and when Vermond criticized Madame de Marsan's guardianship of the Princesses I was blamed for this.

Some of my women repeated Madame de Marsan's comments to me, thinking I should be warned.

"Someone said yesterday, Madame, that you carried yourself more gracefully than anyone at Court, and Madame de Marsan retorted that you had the walk of a courtesan."

"Poor Madame de Marsan!" I cried. "She waddles like a duck!"

Everyone laughed heartily but there would be someone who would carry that to Madame de Marsan just as there was someone to carry her disparagements of myself to me.

My animation was praised. "She likes to give the appearance of knowing everything," was Madame de Marsan's comment.

When I favored a new style of hairdressing wearing my hair in curls about my shoulders, which I know was most becoming, it reminded Madame de Marsan of a "bacchanal." My spontaneous laughter was "affected," the manner in which I looked at men "coquettish."

I could see that whatever I did would arouse the criticism of people such as the Comtesse, so what was the use of trying to please them? There was only one course open to me—to be myself.

Change was in the air.

We were staging scenes from Molière and when we were thus engaged my brothers- and sisters-in-law were the characters they were trying to portray which was often a great deal more comfortable than being themselves. My husband loved these theatricals; it suited him absolutely to be the audience and whenever we did catch him sleeping he would retort that audiences often slept through plays and when this was the case actors should blame themselves not the audience. But often he laughed and applauded; and there was no doubt that we were really all happier together when we were playing.

We felt the need to be even more careful. Knowing that Madame de Marsan was so critical, having learned that the aunts were aware of every false step I made, conscious all the time of the ever watchful eyes of Madame l'Etiquette, I was sure that if it were discovered that we were aping players there would be an outcry of indignation and worst of all our pleasure would be forbidden. Knowing this we seemed to enjoy it all the more.

Monsieur Campan and his son were great acquisitions to our little company. Campan Père could play a part, procure our costumes and act as prompter all at once, because he could learn parts so easily that he invariably knew them all.

We had set up the stage and were preparing ourselves. The elder Monsieur Campan was dressed as Crispin and very fine he looked in his costume. The meticulous man had made sure that it was exact in detail and he looked the part to perfection with his brilliantly rouged cheeks and his rakish wig.

The room which served us as a theater was rarely used—which was why we had chosen it—but there was a private staircase leading from it down to my apartments; and when I remembered that I had left a cloak I should need in my apartments I asked Monsieur Campan to go down by the private staircase and get it for me.

I had not thought that there would be anyone in my apartments at this hour but a man servant had come on some errand and hearing a movement on the stairs he came to see who was there.

In the semidarkness the strange figure from another age loomed before him on the dim staircase and naturally he thought he was confronted by a ghost. He screamed and fell backward tumbling down the rest of the stairs.

Monsieur Campan rushed to him and by this time hearing the commotion we all hurried down the staircase to see what was happening. The servant lay on the floor, fortunately unhurt, but white and trembling. He stared at us all—and I am sure we must have presented a strange sight.

However, Monsieur Campan, with his usual goodness, said that there was nothing to be done but explain the situation to the man.

"We are playing at theatricals," he told him. "We are not ghosts. Look at me. You will recognize me . . . and Madame la Dauphine . . ."

"You know me," I said. "See . . . we are only play-acting . . ."

"Yes, Madame," he stammered.

"Madame," said the wise Campan, "we must insist on his silence."

I nodded and Monsieur Campan told the man that he must say nothing of what he had seen.

We were assured that secrecy would be kept, but the man went away looking dazed and we went back to our "stage" but somehow the heart had gone out of our performance. We talked of the incident instead of continuing with the performance and Monsieur Campan was very grave. It was possible that the man would not be able to refrain from mentioning to one or two people what he had seen. We should be watched. All sorts of constructions would be put on our innocent game; we should be accused of orgies; and how easy it would be to attach to our theatrical ventures all sorts of sinister implications. Wise Monsieur Campan—thinking of me and no doubt knowing far more of the evil things which were said of me than I ever could—was of the opinion that we should stop our plays. My husband agreed with him and that was the end of our theatricals.

Without this to amuse me I turned to other pleasures. My old clavichord teacher, Gluck, had arrived in Paris some time before and my mother had written to me urging me to help him make a success in Paris. I was delighted to do this, because I secretly believed that our German musicians excelled the French, yet in Paris I always had to listen to French opera. I naturally had a warm feeling for Mozart; and I was determined to do all I could for Gluck. In fact the Paris Academy had rejected his opera *Iphigénie* but Mercy had prevailed upon them to rescind their decision.

On the night when the opera was performed I made a state occasion of it by begging my husband to accompany me. With us came Provence and his wife and a few friends among whom was my dear Princesse de Lamballe. It was a triumph. The people cheered me and I showed them how pleased I was to be among them. And at the end of the opera the curtain calls for Gluck went on for ten minutes.

Mercy was very pleased about this. He showed me what he was writing to my mother.

"I see approaching the time when the great destiny of the Archduchess will be fulfilled."

I was inclined to preen myself but Mercy would not have that.

He said: "The King is growing old. Have you noticed how his health has deteriorated during these last weeks?"

I replied that I thought he seemed a little tired.

He then put on his most confidential manner which I was always intended to understand meant that what took place between us was of the utmost secrecy and should not be mentioned to anyone.

"If it should so happen . . . soon . . . that the Dauphin were called upon to rule he would not be strong enough to do so by himself. If *you* did not govern him he would be governed by others. You should understand this. You should realize the influence you could wield."

"I! But I know nothing of affairs of state!"

"Alas, that is too true. You are afraid of them. You allow yourself to be passive and dependent."

"I am sure I could never understand what was expected of me."

"There would be those to guide you. You should learn to know and appreciate your strength."

During Lent the Abbé de Beauvais preached a sermon which was soon to be discussed throughout Versailles and I doubted not in every tavern in Paris. There seemed to be a feeling that the King's days were coming to an end and it was almost as though the country were willing him to die. Surely the Abbé would not have dared preach such a sermon as he did if the King had been well. I had discovered that for all his cynicism and sensuality my grandfather was an extremely pious man, by which I mean that he believed wholeheartedly in hell for the sinful unrepentant. He had led a life of such debauchery as few monarchs before him—even French monarchs—and he believed that if he did not obtain absolution of his sins he would surely go to hell. Therefore he was uneasy. He wanted to repent—but not too soon, for Madame du Barry was the one comfort in his old age.

The Abbé therefore dared preach against the ways of the Court and of the King in particular. He likened him to the aged King Solomon, satiated by his excesses and searching for new sensations in the arms of harlots.

Louis tried to pretend that the sermon was really preached against certain members of his Court such as the Duc de Richelieu, notorious as one of the biggest rakes of his day—or anyone else's.

"Ha," said Louis, "the preacher has thrown some stones into your garden, my friend."

"Alas, Sire," was sly Richelieu's retort, "that on the way so many should have tumbled into Your Majesty's park."

Louis could only smile grimly at such a retort; but he was seriously disturbed. He sought a way to silence the outspoken Abbé in the only way he could—presenting him with a Bishopric. This the Abbé accepted with pleasure but went on thundering out his warnings. He even went so far as to compare the luxury of Versailles with the lives of the peasants and the poor of Paris.

"Yet forty days and Nineveh shall be destroyed."

Death seemed to be in the air. My charming grandfather changed visibly. He had become much fatter since my arrival yet he was more wrinkled; but the charm remained. I remember how shaken he was once at a whist party. One of his oldest friends, the Marquis de Chauvelin, was playing at one of the tables and the game having ended he rose and went to chat with a lady at one of the other tables. Quite suddenly his face was distorted; he gripped his chest and then . . . he was lying on the floor.

My grandfather rose; I could see that he was trying to speak but no words came.

Someone said: "He is dead, Sire."

"My old friend," murmured the King; and he left the apartment and went straight to his bedchamber. Madame du Barry went with him; she was the only one who could comfort him; and yet I knew that he was afraid to have her with him for fear he should die suddenly as his friend the Marquis had—with all his sins upon him.

Poor Grandfather! I longed to comfort him. But what could I do? I represented youth—and by its very nature that could only remind him of his own age.

It was almost as though fate were laughing at him. The Abbé de la Ville whom he had recently promoted came to thank him for his advancement. He was admitted to the King's presence but no sooner had he begun his speech of gratitude than he had a stroke and fell dead right at the King's feet.

It was more than the King could bear. He shut himself in his apartments, sent for his confessor; and Madame du Barry was very worried.

Adelaide was delighted. When my husband and I visited her, she talked of the evil life the King had led and said that if he were to make sure of his place in Heaven he had better send that *putain* packing without delay. She was as militant as a general and her sisters were her obedient captains.

"I have told him again and again," she declared. "The time is running out. I have sent a messenger to Louise to ask her to redouble her prayers. It would break my heart if when I reached Heaven it was to find my beloved father—the King of France—locked out."

One day soon after the death of the Abbé de la Ville, when the King was riding, he met a funeral procession and stopped it. Who was dead? he wanted to know. It was not an old person this time, but a young girl of sixteen—which seemed equally ominous.

Death could strike at any time and he was in his middle sixties.

As soon as Easter was over Madame du Barry suggested that he and she should go and live quietly at the Trianon for a few weeks. The gardens were beautiful for spring had come and it was a time to banish gloomy thought and think of life not death.

She could always make him laugh; so he went with her. He went out hunting but felt extremely unwell. Madame du Barry however had prepared remedies for him and she kept declaring that all he needed was rest and her company.

The day after he had left I was in my apartment having my lessons on the harp when the Dauphin came in, looking very grave.

He sat down heavily and I signed to my music master and the attendants to leave us.

"The King is ill," he said.

"Very ill?"

"They do not tell us."

"He is at the Trianon," I said. "I shall go and see him at once. I will nurse him. He will soon be well again."

My husband looked at me, smiling sadly. "No," he said, "we cannot go unless he sends for us. We must wait for his orders to attend him."

"Etiquette!" I murmured. "Our dearest Grandfather is ill and we must wait on etiquette."

"La Martinère is going over," my husband told me.

I nodded. La Martinière was the chief of the King's doctors.

"There is nothing we can do but wait," said my husband.

"You are very worried, Louis."

"I feel as though the universe were falling on me," he said.

When La Martinière saw the King he was grave and in spite of Madame du Barry's protestations insisted that he be brought back to Versailles. This in itself was significant and we all knew it. For if the King's malady had been slight he would have been allowed to stay at the Trianon to recover. But no, he must be brought back to Versailles because Etiquette demanded that the Kings of France should die in their state bedrooms at Versailles.

They brought him the short distance to the palace and I saw him emerge from his carriage for I was watching from a window. He was wrapped in a heavy cloak and he looked like a different person; he was shivering yet there was an unhealthy flush on his face.

Madame Adelaide came hurrying out to the carriage and walked beside him giving orders. He was to wait in her apartments while his bedchamber was made ready—for so urgent had La Martinière declared was the need to return to Versailles that this was not yet done.

When he was in his room we were all summoned there, and I had to fight hard to stop myself bursting into tears. It was so tragic to see him with the strange look in his eyes and when I kissed his hand he did not smile or seem to care. It was as though a stranger lay there. I knew he was not sincere, yet in my way I had loved him and I could not bear to see him thus.

He wanted none of us; only when Madame du Barry came to the bedside did he look a little more like himself.

She said: "You'd like me to stay, France!" which was very disrespectful but he smiled and nodded; so we left her with him.

That day was like a dream. I could settle to nothing. Louis stayed with me. He said it was better we should be together.

I was apprehensive; and he continued to look as though the universe was about to fall upon him.

Five surgeons, six physicians, and three apothecaries were in attendance on the King. They argued together as to the nature of his complaint, whether two—or three—veins should be tapped. The news was all over Paris. The King is ill. He has been taken from the Trianon to Versailles. Considering the life he had led, his body must indeed be worn out.

Louis and I were together all the time, waiting for a summons. He seemed as though he were afraid to leave me. I was praying silently that dear Grandfather would soon be well; I know Louis was too.

In the *oeil-de-boeuf*, that huge anteroom which separated the King's bedchamber from the hall and which was so called because of its bull's-eye window, the crowds were assembling. I hoped the King did not know for if he did he would know too that they believed he was dying.

There was a subtle difference in the attitude of those around us toward myself and my husband. We were approached more cautiously, more respectfully. I wanted to cry out: "Do not treat us differently. Papa is not dead yet."

News came from the sick room. The King had been cupped but this had brought no relief from his pain.

The terrible suspense continued throughout the next day. Madame du Barry was still in attendance on the King but my husband and I had not been sent for. The aunts however had decided that they would save their father; and they were certainly not going to allow him to remain in the care of the *putain*. Adelaide led them into the sick room although the doctors tried to keep them out.

What actually happened when they entered the sick room was so dramatic that soon the whole Court was talking of it.

Adelaide had marched to the bed, her sisters a few paces behind her, just as one of the doctors was holding a glass of water to the King's lips.

The doctor gasped and cried. "Hold the candles nearer. The King cannot see the glass."

Then those about the bed saw what had startled the doctor. The King's face was covered in red spots.

The King was suffering from smallpox. There was a feeling of relief because at least everyone knew now what ailed him and the right cures could be applied; but when Bordeu, the doctor whom Madame du Barry had brought in and in whom she had great faith, heard how pleased everyone was, he remarked cynically that it must be because they hoped to inherit something from him. "Smallpox," he added, "for a man of sixty-four and with the King's constitution is indeed a terrifying disease."

The aunts were told that they should leave the sick room immediately but Adelaide drew herself up to her full height and looking her most regal demanded of the doctors: "Do you presume to order *me* from my father's bedchamber? Take care that I shall not dismiss *you*. We remain here. My father needs nurses and who should look after him but his own daughters."

There was no dislodging them and they remained—actually sharing with Madame du Barry the task of looking after him, although they contrived not to be in the apartment when she was there. I could not but admire them all. They worked to save his life, facing terrible danger; and they were as devoted as any nurses could be. I have never forgotten the bravery of my aunt Adelaide at that time—Victoire and Sophie too, of course; but they automatically obeyed their sister. My husband and I were not allowed to go near the sick room. We had become too important.

The days seemed endless, like a vague dream. Each morning we arose wondering what change in our lives the day would bring. The fact that the King was suffering from smallpox could not be kept from him. He demanded a mirror to be brought to him and when he looked into it he groaned with horror. Then he was immediately calm.

"At my age," he said, "one does not recover from that disease. I must set my affairs in order." Madame du Barry was at his bedside but he shook his head sadly at her. It grieved him more than anything to part with her, but she must leave him . . . for her own sake and for his.

She left reluctantly. Poor Madame du Barry! The man who had stood between her and her enemies was fast losing his strength. The King kept asking for her after she had left and was very desolate without her. I felt differently toward her from that time. I wished I had been kinder to her and spoken to her now and then. How sad she must be feeling now, and her sorrow would be mingled with fear, for what would become of her when her protector was gone.

He must have loved her dearly for while his priests were urging him to confess he kept putting it off, for once he had confessed he would have to say a last goodbye to her, for only thus could he receive remission of his sins; and all the time he must have been hoping that he would recover and be able to send for her to come back to him.

But in the early morning of the 7th of May the King's condition worsened so much that he decided to send for a priest.

From my windows I could see that the people of Paris had come to Versailles in their thousands. They wanted to be on the spot at that moment when the King died. I turned shuddering from the window; to me it seemed such a horrible sight, for sellers of food and wine and ballads were camping in the gardens and it was more like a holiday than a sacred occasion. The Parisians were too realistic to pretend that they were mourning; they were rejoicing because the old reign was passing and they hoped for so much from the new.

In the King's apartments the Abbé Maudoux waited upon him; I heard the remark passed that it was the first time for over thirty years—when he had been installed as the King's confessor—that he had been called to duty. In all that time the King had had no time for confession. How, it was asked, will Louis XV ever be able to recount all his sins in time?

I wished that I could have been with my grandfather then. I should have liked to tell him how much his kindness had meant to me. I would have told him that I should never forget our first meeting in Fontainebleau when he had behaved so charmingly to a frightened little girl. Surely such kindness would be in his favor; and although he had lived scandalously none of those who had shared his debauchery had been forced to do so, and many had been fond of him. Madame du Barry had shown by her conduct that he was not merely her protector but that she loved him. She had left him now, not because she feared his disease but in order to save his soul.

News was brought to our apartment of what was happening in the chamber of death. I heard that when the Cardinal de la Roche Aymon entered in full canonicals bringing with him the Host, my grandfather took his nightcap from his head and tried in vain to kneel in the bed for he said: "If my God deigns to honor such a sinner as I am with a visit, I must receive him with respect."

Poor Grandfather, who had been supreme all his life—a King from five years old—now would be denuded of all his worldly glory and forced to face one who was a greater King than he could ever have been.

But the high dignitaries of the Church would not allow absolution merely in return for a few muttered words. This was no ordinary sinner; this was a King who had openly defied the laws of the Church and he must make public avowal of his sins; only thus could they be forgiven.

There was a ceremony in which we must all take part that his soul might be saved. We formed a procession, led by the Dauphin and myself with Provence, Artois, and their wives following us. We all carried lighted candles and followed the Archbishop from the chapel to the death chamber, lighted tapers in our hands, solemn expressions on our faces and in my heart, and that of the Dauphin at least, a sorrow and a great dread.

We stood outside the door but the aunts went inside; we could hear the tones of the priests and the King's responses; and we could see through the open door that Holy Viaticum was being given to him.

The Cardinal de la Roche Aymon then came to the door and said to all who were assembled outside:

"Gentlemen, the King instructs me to tell you that he asks God's pardon for his offenses and the scandalous example he has set his people, and that if his health is restored to him he will devote himself to repentance, to religion, and the welfare of his people."

As I listened I knew that the King had given up all hope of life for while he lived he would cling to Madame du Barry, and what he had said meant that he had dismissed her for the time that was left to him.

I heard him say in a slurred voice so different from the clear and musical tones which had enchanted me on my arrival:

"I wish I had been strong enough to say that myself."

That was not the end. It would have been better if it had been. But there were a few days of horror left. My fastidious grandfather! I hope he did not know what happened to the handsome body which had once charmed so many. Putrefaction set in before death and I heard that the stench from the bedchamber was horrible. Servants who must wait on him retched and fainted in that room of horror. His body was blackened and swollen, but he could not die.

Adelaide and her sisters refused to leave him. They performed the most menial tasks; they were with him throughout the days and nights, and they were on the verge of exhaustion, but still they would not allow anyone to take their places.

My husband and I were not permitted to go near the sick room but we must remain at Versailles until the King was dead. As soon as he expired we should leave Versailles with all speed for the place was a hotbed of infection. Already some of the people who had crowded in the *oeil-de-boeuf* when the King had been brought over from the Trianon had taken sick and died. In the stables everything was ready for us. We were to leave for Choisy the moment the King died; but Etiquette insisted that we be at Versailles until that moment.

In one of the windows a candle was burning; and this was meant to be a signal.

When the flame was snuffed out that would be a sign to all that the King's life was over.

My husband had taken me to a small room and there we sat in silence.

Neither of us spoke. He had imbued me with his sense of foreboding. He had always been serious but never quite so much as at this time.

And then suddenly as we sat there we heard a great tumult. We half-rose, looking at each other. We had no idea what it could be. There were voices . . . raised, shouting it seemed; and this overwhelming clamor.

The door was flung open suddenly. People were running in, surrounding us.

Madame de Noailles was the first to reach me. She knelt and taking my hand kissed it.

She was calling me: "Your Majesty."

Now I understood; I felt the tears rushing to my eyes. The King was dead; my poor Louis was King of France and I was the Queen.

They pressed in on us as though it were a *joyful* occasion. Louis turned to me and I to him.

He took my hand and spontaneously we knelt together.

"We are too young," he whispered; and we seemed to be praying together:

"Oh God, guide us, protect us. We are too young to govern."

8

"I marvel at the design of Fate which has chosen me, the youngest of
your daughters, to be Queen of the finest Kingdom in Europe."

Marie Antoinette to Maria Theresa

"You are both so young and the burden which has been placed on your
shoulders is very heavy. I am distressed that this should be so."

Maria Theresa to Marie Antoinette

"Petite Reine, de vingt ans,
Vous, qui traitez si mal les gens,
Vous repasserez la barrière . . ."

Song being sung in Paris a month after Marie Antoinette's accession
to the throne

FLATTERY AND REPRIMANDS

As soon as the King was dead there was no reason why anyone should
remain any longer at Versailles. Our carriage had been waiting for days so
there was nothing to delay us. We were to leave at once for Choisy.

The aunts, in view of the fact that they had been in close contact with
the late King and were therefore undoubtedly infectious, were to live in a
house by themselves as it was considered of the greatest importance that
my husband should remain in good health.

We were all very solemn as we rode away from Versailles. In our carriage
were Provence and Artois with their wives and we said very little. I kept
reminding myself that I should never see my grandfather again and that
now I was a Queen. We were all truly griefstricken, and it would have
needed very little to set us all sobbing. Louis was the most unhappy of us

all and I remembered that remark of his about feeling that the universe was about to fall upon him. Poor Louis! He looked as though it were already falling.

But in truth how superficial our grief was! We were all so young. Nineteen is very young to be a Queen—and a frivolous one at that. Perhaps I make excuses; but I could never sustain an emotion for long—particularly grief. Marie Thérèse made some comment and her odd pronunciation set my lips twitching. I looked at Artois, he was smiling too. We couldn't help it. It seemed so funny. And then suddenly we were laughing. It may have been hysterical laughter, but it was laughter nonetheless; and after that the solemnity of death seemed to have receded.

They were busy days at Choisy, particularly for Louis. He had put on new stature, was more dignified and, although modest, he had the air of a King. He was so earnestly eager to do what he believed to be right, so deeply conscious of his great responsibility.

I wished that I had been cleverer so that I could have been of some use to him; but I did immediately think of the Duc de Choiseul who should be recalled. He had been a friend of mine and a friend of Austria and I was certain that my mother would wish me to use my influence with my husband to have him brought back.

It was indeed a new man I discovered at Choisy for when I mentioned the Duc de Choiseul a stubborn expression crossed his face.

"I never cared for the fellow," he said.

"He was responsible for making our marriage."

He smiled at me tenderly. "That would have come about without him."

"He is very clever, I have heard."

"My father did not like him. There was a rumor that he was involved in his death."

"Involved in your father's death, Louis? But how?"

"He poisoned him."

"You can't believe that! Not of Monsieur de Choiseul!"

"At least he failed in his duty to my father." He smiled at me. "You should not concern yourself with these matters."

"I want to help you, Louis."

But he just smiled. I heard that he had once said: "Women taught me nothing when I was young. All that I learned was from men. I have read little history but I have learned this: mistresses and even lawful wives have often ruined states."

He was too kind to say this directly to me but he held firmly to this belief.

The aunts however had some influence with him. Although they occupied a separate establishment they were allowed to visit us which they did. They could tell the King so much of the past, they said; and he seemed to believe them, for he listened.

There was much coming and going between Choisy and Paris. Everyone was wondering how much influence the aunts would have with the new King, how much influence I should have, and whom the King would choose for his mistress. That made me want to laugh. Had they forgotten that a wife was too much of a burden for the King, let alone a mistress? That reminded me of course that our distressing and perplexing problem would now be more pressing than ever.

Louis at the moment was concerned with choosing a man who could advise him in the conduct of affairs and he believed that he needed someone of great experience to make up for his own lack. His first thought was for Jean Baptiste d'Arouville Machault who had been Comptroller General of Finances until the antagonism of Madame de Pompadour had brought him down. He was certainly experienced, and it was due to the schemes of the King's mistress that he had fallen—all of which endeared him to Louis who wrote summoning him to Choisy for he was very eager to begin working for his country.

While he was writing the letter the aunts arrived, and I was with my husband when they were announced. Adelaide declared that she had come at once to her dear nephew's aid for she was sure she could give the information he must be in need of.

"You see, dear Berry . . . Ha, I must not say Berry now, Your Majesty . . . I have lived so long and so close to your grandfather . . . and I know so much that can be of use to you." She included me in her smile and I was so full of admiration for the manner in which she nursed her father that I felt a rush of affection for her.

"You are sending for Machault. Oh no . . . no . . . no . . ." She put her ear close to the King's and whispered "Maurepas. Maurepas is the man."

"Is he somewhat old?"

"Ah, Your Majesty is somewhat young." She laughed shrilly. "That is what makes it such an excellent arrangement. You have the vigor and vitality of youth. He has the experience of age. Maurepas," she whispered. "A most able man. Why when he was twenty-four he controlled the King's household as well as the Admiralty."

"But he lost his posts."

"Why? . . . why? Because he was no friend of Pompadour. That was our father's mistake. However able a man, if one of his women did not care for him . . . it was the end."

She went on enumerating the merits of Maurepas and eventually my husband decided to destroy the letter he had written to Machault and instead wrote to Maurepas. I was there when he wrote the letter which seems to convey so much of his feeling at that time.

> "Amidst the natural grief which overwhelms me and which I share with the entire kingdom, I have great duties to fulfill. I am the King; the word speaks of many responsibilities. Alas, I am only twenty [my husband was not even that. He had three months to wait for his twentieth birthday] and I have not the necessary experience. I have been unable to work with the ministers as they were with the late King during his illness. My certainty of your honesty and knowledge impels me to ask you to help me. You will please me if you come here as soon as possible."

No King of France ever ascended the throne with a greater desire for self-abnegation than my husband.

Having secured the appointment of Maurepas the aunts were triumphant, believing they were going to be the power behind the throne. They watched me suspiciously and I knew that when I was not present they warned the King against allowing his frivolous little wife to meddle.

He was so good; he immediately had two hundred thousand francs distributed to the poor; he was greatly concerned about the licentiousness of the Court and determined to abolish it. He asked Monsieur de Maurepas how he could set about bringing a state of morality to a Court where morals had been lax for so long.

"There is but one way, Sire," was Maurepas' answer. "It is one Your Majesty must take to set a good example. In most countries—and in particular in France—where the Sovereign leads, the people will follow."

My husband looked at me and smiled, very serenely, very confidently. He would never take a mistress. He loved me; and if he could only become a normal man, we would have children and ours would be the perfect union.

But there was so much to think of at that time that that uneasy subject was forgotten.

Louis was kind. He could not even be cruel to Madame du Barry. "Let her be dismissed from the Court," he said. "That should suffice. She shall go to a convent for a while until it is decided to what place she may be banished."

It was lenient, but Louis had no wish to punish. Nor had I. I thought of that time when I had been forced to say those silly words to her. How angry I had been at the time, but now it was all forgotten; and I could only remember how she had stayed with the King when he was so ill and she was in danger of catching the dreaded disease. Let her be banished. That was enough.

Louis quickly grasped that the country's finances were in disorder and determined on household economies. I was beside him and declared that I too would economize. I gave up my *droit de ceinture* a sum of money which was given by the state for my private purse which hung on my girdles. "I have no need of this," I said. "Girdles are no longer worn."

This remark was repeated in the Court and in the streets of Paris.

Paris and the whole country were pleased with us. I was their enchanting little Queen; my husband was Louis le Désiré, and one morning when the traders started their early morning trek to Les Halles it was noticed that during the night someone had written Resurrexit on the statue of Henri Quatre which had been erected on the Pont Neuf.

When my husband heard of this his eyes shone with pleasure and determination. In every Frenchman's opinion Henri Quatre was the greatest King France had ever had, the King who had cared for the people as no other monarch had before or since.

Now they were saying that in Louis le Désiré this great monarch was born again.

At Choisy it was easy to forget those last nightmare days at Versailles. I was Queen of France; in his way my husband loved me; everyone was eager to pay me homage. Why had I been apprehensive?

I knew that my mother would be anxiously watching events. No doubt it had already been reported to her how I had conducted myself during the King's illness and death; but I myself would write to her.

With the new flush of triumph on me I wrote: rather arrogantly (I excuse myself for I was freshly savoring the flattery which is paid to a Queen):

> "Although God chose that I should be born to high rank, I marvel at the design of Fate which has chosen me, the youngest of your daughters, to be Queen of the finest Kingdom in Europe."

My husband came in while I was writing this letter and I called to him to see what I had written. He looked over my shoulder smiling. He knew of my difficult penmanship and said that was very good.

"You should add something to the letter," I told him. "It would please her."

"I should not know what to say to her."

"Then I will tell you." I thrust the pen into his hand, and jumping up pushed him into my chair. He chuckled under his breath, half embarrassed, half delighted by my spontaneous gestures as he so often was.

"Say this: 'I am very pleased, my dear mother, to have the opportunity to offer you proof of my affection and regard. It would give me great satisfaction to have the benefit of your counsel at such a time which is so full of difficulties for us both . . .'"

He wrote rapidly and looked at me expectantly.

"You are so much cleverer than I with a pen," I retorted. "Surely you can finish it."

He continued to laugh at me. Then as though determined to impress me with his cleverness he began to write rapidly:

". . . but I shall do my best to satisfy you and by so doing show you the affection and gratitude I feel toward you for giving me your daughter with whom I could not be more satisfied."

"So," I said, "you are pleased with me. Thank you, Sire." I dropped a deep curtsey. Then I was on my feet, snatching the pen from him.

I wrote below his message.

"The King wished to add his few words before allowing this letter to go to you. Dear Mother, you will see by the compliment he pays me that he is certainly fond of me, but that he does not spoil me with high-flown phrases."

He looked puzzled and half ashamed.

"What would you wish me to say?" I laughed snatching the letter from him and sealing it myself.

"Nothing that you have not already said," I replied. "Indeed, Sire, Fate has given me the King of France, with whom I could not be more satisfied."

This was typical of our relationship at this time. He *was* satisfied with me, although he did not wish me to meddle in politics. He was the most faithful husband at Court; but I was not sure at this time whether this was due to his devotion to me or to his affliction.

One of the most anxious women in Europe was my mother. She was so wise. She deplored the fact that the King was dead. If he had lived another ten or even five years we should have had time to prepare ourselves. As it was we were two children. My husband had never been taught how to rule; I would never learn. That was the position as she saw it. And how right she was! I often marvel that while all those people close at hand were dreaming of the ideal state which they fancied two inexperienced young people could miraculously turn the country into, my mother from so far away could see the picture so clearly.

Her answer to my thoughtless letter—the one to which I had made my husband add his comments was:

"I do not compliment you on your new dignity. A high price has been paid for this, and you will pay still higher unless you go on living quietly and innocently in the manner in which you have lived since your arrival in France. You have had the guidance of one who was as a father to you and it is due to his kindness that you have been able to win the approval of the people which is now yours. This is good, but you must learn how to keep that approval and use it for the good of the King, your husband, and the country of which you are Queen. You are both so young, and the burden which has been placed on your shoulders is very heavy. I am distressed that this should be so."

She was pleased that my husband had joined with me in writing to her and hoped that we should both do all we could to maintain friendly relations between France and Austria.

She was extremely worried about me—my frivolity, my *dissipation*, (by which she and Mercy meant my preoccupation with matters which were of small importance) my love of dancing, and gossip, my disrespect for etiquette, my impulsiveness. All qualities my mother pointed out, to be deplored in a Dauphine but not even to be tolerated in a Queen. She wrote:

"You must learn to be interested in *serious matters*. This will be useful if the King should wish to discuss state business with you. You should be very careful not to be extravagant; nor to lead the King to this. At the moment the people love you. You must preserve this state of affairs. You have both been fortunate beyond my hopes; you must continue in the love of your people. This will make you and them happy."

I replied dutifully that I realized the importance of my position. I confessed my frivolity. I swore that I would be a credit to my mother. I wrote and told her of all the homage, all the ceremonies, how eager everyone was to please me. She wrote back, sometimes tender, often scolding; but her comment was: "I fancy her good days are over."

Four days after we arrived at Choisy a messenger came from the aunts' house nearby to tell us that Madame Adelaide was suffering from fever and pains in the back. It would seem too much to ask that they should all three escape the infection, and indeed it was proved that Adelaide had the smallpox; and as Victoire and Sophie always followed her in what she did, very soon they too were suffering from the dreaded disease.

There was consternation at Choisy. I had already had a mild attack so that I was not vulnerable, but what of the new King? I persuaded him to be inoculated which I knew resulted in a very mild attack and made one immune; and as a result he was treated together with Provence, Artois, and Artois' wife. Louis was always thoughtful of others and immediately gave orders that no one who had not had the smallpox was to come near him.

The inoculation was considered a dangerous procedure, but I was absolutely certain that it was the right thing. Mercy however warned me that if all went well I should be judged wise but if things went the other way I should be blamed. He watched me severely hoping I should see the lesson in this. But I merely laughed at him and said I *knew* my husband and the others would be grateful to me for having persuaded them to this measure.

As it happened I was right—but I could so easily have been wrong.

I wrote exultantly to my mother to tell how many spots my husband had. I told her too about the aunts.

"I am forbidden to go to them. It is dreadful for them to pay so quickly for the great sacrifice they made."

I should have liked to have visited them to tell them how much I admired what they had done, but I had to obey the order to keep away from them.

During those days our popularity grew. The people had so hated Louis XV that they would have loved my husband merely for the fact that he was different. They loved his youth, his friendly manners toward them and his simplicity. He had ordered eight suits of frieze cloth and this was discussed through Paris. Not silk, brocade, and velvets but frieze cloth! Being a King to him meant serving his people not having them admire him; and he was more at ease with them, so it was said, than he was with noblemen. Once at Choisy he went for a walk by himself and when he returned I, with my sisters-in-law, met him in the park and we sat on a bench eating strawberries. The people came to look at us and we smiled at them. They were delighted; I heard later that we made a charming picture.

Sometimes we walked arm in arm in the alleys at Choisy and the people said that it was pleasant to see such domestic felicity. How different was a King who could take pleasure in simple pastimes than one who had neglected his wife and cared for nothing but his mistresses.

It was decided that in view of the fact that the aunts were suffering from smallpox we should leave Choisy and go to La Muette and I was certainly glad to be nearer Paris. The people came out in thousands to see us arrive and we had to go out on the balconies and smile and bow to them. During Grandfather's reign the gates of the Bois de Boulogne had been closed, but my husband ordered them to be opened so that the people could walk about wherever they liked. This delighted them and they would come out as early as six in the morning hoping for a glimpse of us. As there was nothing Louis liked better than to please the people and nothing I liked better than to be admired, everyone was happy.

Louis would walk among the people unguarded, unceremoniously, and on foot. One day he had been out walking and I was riding; I was leaving the château and he was returning and when I saw him, I dismounted and gave my horse to one of the guards and ran on foot to greet my husband.

The people stood in silence watching and Louis embraced and kissed me on either cheek.

The cheers were deafening. Some of the women wiped their eyes. Their emotions were very easily aroused; Louis took my arm and we walked back, the people following us and when we reached the château we had to appear on the balcony and they kept shouting for us and would not let us go.

"Long live the King and Queen. Long live Louis le Désiré and our beautiful Queen."

It was wonderful. Louis and I held hands, kissed each other, and I threw kisses to the people.

It was a very happy day and of course every incident was reported to my mother.

She seemed pleased at last. She wrote:

"I cannot describe my joy and consolation at what I hear . . .
A King of twenty, a Queen of nineteen; and they act with hu-
manity, generosity and prudence. Remember that religion and
morals are necessary to win God's blessing and thus keep your
people's affections. I pray God that he will keep you in His care
for the good of your people, for the good of your family and for
that of your mother to whom you give new hope. How I love
the French! What vitality there is in a nation which feels so
strongly." Characteristically she added: "One only wishes they
will acquire more constancy and less frivolity. By correcting
their morals these happy changes might be brought about."

She was right as usual. These were surely the most inconstant people
in the world.

Naturally the first thing I had done on becoming Queen of France was
to rid myself of the tiresome Madame l'Etiquette, and freedom, I think,
went to my head. I was determined to do all in my power to flout their
stupid etiquette. Surely as Queen I could set the tone of the Court. The
people adored me; I knew that all the young members of the Court were
looking forward to a wonderful time. The laughter I could so easily provoke was as music in my ears. I was tired of all the old ladies. I was going
to have friends . . . young and gay like myself.

I said a great many foolish things.

I thought people over thirty were ancient. "I cannot understand," I
said lightly, "how people of *that* age can come to Court."

I was encouraged by all the ladies of my acquaintance who laughed
heartily at everything I said. How I hated it when I had to receive the old
ladies who had come to pay their mourning respects. How hideous they
looked! I remarked behind my fan to the Princesse de Lamballe that the
centenarians had come to see me. She giggled and we had to keep our
faces hidden by our fans for they looked like crows in their plain dresses
of *raz de Saint Maur*; they all wore black stockings and black gloves, coifs
like nuns, and even their fans were made of black crepe.

And there was I with my ladies of honor waiting to receive them. I
could hear the young Marquise de Clermont-Tonnerre tittering behind
me. She was a gay little creature and I was fond of her because she
laughed so readily.

I heard the giddy creature say that she was tired of looking at centenarians and would sit on the floor. No one would know because Her Majesty's
dress and that of the ladies in the front row would hide her.

But she did not content herself with that. I caught her just as the black-

est of the black crows was bowing before me, peeping round the panniers of my gown and I could not, much as I tried, restrain my features. I
put my fan up to my lips but the gesture was seen and I was aware of
the glances of the old Princesses and Duchesses.

When I spoke I heard the laughter in my voice and I could not stop.

As soon as the ceremony was over I retired to my apartments and I
and my ladies were almost hysterical with laughter.

"Do you think they saw us, Your Majesty?" asked little Clermont-
Tonnerre.

"What do I care if they did. Should the Queen of France care for the
opinion of . . . of *bundles* . . . like that."

Everyone thought that was very funny; but oddly enough very soon the
whole Court was talking of my frivolous behavior at the mourning ceremony; and the old ladies declared that they would never come to pay their
respects to that *petite moqueuse* again.

When I heard this I laughed aloud. I was the Queen of France, did I
care for the old ladies; they were *collets montés*, and if they did not come
again to my court that suited *me* very well.

My conduct at the mourning ceremony was discussed everywhere. So
was my silly remark about people of thirty being too ancient to come to
Court. I had forgotten how many people over thirty there were at Court.

My enemies had produced a song which was meant to be a warning to
me:

> "*Petite Reine, de vingt ans,*
> *Vous, qui traitez si mal les gens,*
> *Vous repasserez la Barrière*
> *Laire, laire, laire, lanlaire, laire, lanla.*"

So if I were to misbehave they would send me packing. It should have
been a warning as to the fickleness of the people.

Frivolous as I was, it was generally supposed that I should have great
influence with the King. He was clearly very indulgent toward me and he
always tried to please me in every way. I knew that it was the wish of my
mother and Mercy that I should guide him through them and I fancied
myself in the part of King's adviser.

That unpleasant little rhyme I discovered could have been set in motion by the Duc d'Aiguillon's friends—no doubt he himself had had a part
in it. He had been a great supporter of Madame du Barry who was now
safely housed in the Convent of the Pont aux Dames, but he was still at

Court to plague me. I pointed this out to Louis and I prevailed upon him to see that the Duc was my enemy. My husband promised to send him into exile. I did not want that because I knew what it meant to men such as he was to be sent away from Paris, so I asked the King merely to dismiss him from his post and leave it at that.

How blind I was! He knew he had me to blame for his dismissal, and he did not thank me for softening the blow; in Paris he and his friends set about libeling me as they so well knew how to do; and that was the beginning of hundreds of damaging pamphlets and songs which in the next few years were to be circulated about me.

But at the time I was flushed with triumph. I had had Aiguillon dismissed; now I would bring back my dear friend Monsieur de Choiseul.

"Poor Monsieur de Choiseul," I said one day to my husband when we were alone in our apartment, "he is sad at Chanteloup. He longs to be back at Court."

"I never liked him," my husband replied.

"Your grandfather liked him . . ."

"And in time dismissed him."

"That was due to du Barry. She brought that about. Your Majesty would not be influenced by a woman like that!"

"I shall always remember what he said to me one day. 'Monseigneur,' he said, 'I may one day have the misfortune to be your subject, but I shall never be your servant.'"

"We all say things at times which we do not mean. I am sure I do."

He smiled at me tenderly. "I am sure you do too," he said.

I put my arms about his neck. He flushed slightly. He liked these attentions but they made him uncomfortable. I believe they brought back memories of those embarrassing embraces in the bedchamber.

"Louis," I said, "I want you to allow me to invite Monsieur de Choiseul to return to Court. Can you deny me such a *little* thing?"

"You know that I find it difficult to deny you anything but . . ."

"I knew you would not disappoint me." I released him, thinking: I've won.

I lost no time in making it clear to Monsieur de Choiseul that the King had given him permission to return to Court and Monsieur de Choiseul lost no time in coming.

He was full of hope and when I saw him, although he had grown much older since our last meeting, I still thought him a fascinating man, for with his odd pug face he had never been handsome.

I was to learn something about my husband. He was not to be led. He was fond of me; he was proud of me; but he really believed that women must be kept out of politics and he was not going to allow even me to interfere.

He looked coolly at Choiseul and said: "You have put on weight since we last met, Monsieur le Duc; and you have grown balder."

Then he turned away leaving the Duc disconsolate. But there was nothing he could do; the King had turned away and dismissed him.

It was significant. I was not going to influence my husband. That would be a matter for his ministers.

I was sorry—but for Monsieur de Choiseul not for myself. I was ready to give up my dreams of power; nothing as serious as politics could hold my attention for long and Mercy would have to tell my mother that the King was a man who would go his own way and that they must not expect me to meddle.

Mercy told me that my mother was not sorry Monsieur de Choiseul had not been taken back. I had asked the King to receive an ex-minister and the King had shown his respect for me by doing so. That pleased her. As for Monsieur de Choiseul, she did not think his character was such as would allow him to be of much help to the French nation at this stage of its history. At the same time I had done well to bring about the dismissal of the Duc d'Aiguillon.

It was always pleasant to have praise from my mother; but I could not enjoy her approval for long.

9

"If the price of bread does not go down and the Ministry is not changed we will set fire to the four corners of the Château of Versailles.

"If the price does not go down we will exterminate the King and the entire race of Bourbons."

Placards attached to the walls of the Château of Versailles during La Guerre des Farines, *1775*

THE GRIM REHEARSAL

Soon after we became King and Queen, Louis gave me the gift which brought more pleasure to me than anything else I ever possessed.

He came into our bedchamber one day and said rather sheepishly that it was the custom of each King of France to present his Queen on her accession to the throne with a residence which should be all her own to do with as she will. He had decided to present me with Le Petit Trianon.

Le Petit Trianon! That enchanting little house! Oh, it was delightful. I loved it. Nothing, I declared, could have made me happier.

He stood smiling at me while I threw my arms about his neck and hugged him.

"It is very small."

"It's a doll's house," I cried.

"Hardly grand enough for the Queen of France perhaps."

"It's beautiful!" I cried. "I wouldn't exchange it for any château in the world."

He began to chuckle quietly as he often did at my wild enthusiasm.

"So it is all mine!" I cried. "I may do as I like there? There I can live like a simple peasant. I'll tell you one thing, Louis, there is one guest who will not be invited there. It is Etiquette. That may remain behind in Versailles."

I summoned the Princesse de Lamballe and with some of my youngest ladies went to look at Le Petit Trianon without delay. It looked different from when I had glanced casually at it *en passant*. I suppose because it was entirely mine. I loved it because it was small . . . a refuge, situated just far enough from the palace to be a retreat and not far enough for one to have to make a journey to reach it.

It was delightful—a villa. This was how humbler people lived; and how often during the life of a Queen, with so many tiresome ceremonies to be performed did one long to be *humble*. Little Clermont-Tonnerre cried that it had been the *maison de plaisir* of Louis XV—the little love nest where he and Madame du Barry had taken refuge from Versailles.

"That is all over," I said firmly. "Now it will be known as the refuge of Marie Antoinette. We will change it. We will make it entirely *my* house so that nothing remains of that woman."

"Poor creature. Doubtless she would like to change Pont aux Dames for the Trianon now."

I frowned. I did not want to gloat over my enemies' misfortunes. I never did. I merely wanted to forget them.

There were eight rooms only, and we were all very amused by the odd contraption which was a kind of table and which could be made to rise from the basement to the dining room. This had been constructed for the use of Louis XV, so that when he brought a mistress to the Petit Trianon who did not wish to be seen by servants, a meal could be prepared in the basement and sent up to the dining room without any servants appearing. We shrieked with laughter as the old thing creaked up and down.

The house was tastefully furnished. My grandfather would doubtless have seen to that. I did not think the furniture with its delicately embroidered upholstery was the choice of du Barry.

"Oh, it is perfect . . . perfect!" I cried running from room to room. "What fun I shall have here!"

I ran to the windows and looked out on beautiful lawns and gardens. I could do so much here. I could refurnish it if I wished, although I liked the present furniture. There must be nothing overpoweringly splendid to remind me of Versailles. Here I would entertain my dearest friends and we should cease to be Queen and subjects.

I could not see Versailles from the windows which was an added charm. Here I could come when I wanted to forget the château and court life.

I was delighted that my husband had given me this *little* house. How much more charming than Le Grand Trianon which Louis XIV had built for Madame de Maintenon. I could never have felt so pleased with that.

I could scarcely wait to get back to Versailles to tell my husband how enchanted I was with his gift.

In February my brother Maximilian visited me. My mother had sent him on a tour of Europe in order to complete his education, so naturally he came to see me. He was eighteen and as soon as I saw him I realized how my years in France had changed me. This was young Max who had sat with Caroline and me in the gardens of Schönbrunn and watched our elder brothers and sisters perform. He had always been chubby, now he had grown fat; and he seemed awkward and decidedly inelegant.

I was rather ashamed of him, particularly now, knowing the French so well, I could imagine what they were saying about him, although they received him so graciously. But graciousness was lost on Max; he didn't recognize it; he didn't see what mistakes he made, because he thought everyone who didn't agree with him must be wrong. He was like Joseph but without my eldest brother's good sense.

Louis asked him to sup with us privately and behaved as though he were a brother, and I was pleased to ask questions about home and my mother. Yet the more I listened, the more I realized how far from the old life I had grown. It was five years since I had shivered naked in the *salon de remise* on that sandbank in the Rhine. I felt I had become French and when I looked at Max—heavy, awkward, humorless—I was not sorry.

It was inevitable that there should be gossip about my brother; all his little gaucheries were recorded and exaggerated. Through the Court they spoke of him as the Arch-Fool instead of the Archduke and stories about him were circulated through the streets of Paris by my enemies.

Max was not only ignorant of French etiquette but determined not to bow to it; and because of this a contretemps arose. As a visiting royalty it was his duty to call on the Princes of the Blood Royal and they awaited a call from him; but Max stubbornly said that as *he* was a visitor to Paris it was their duty to call on him first. Both were adamant and a difficult situation was created for none of them would give way, and consequently Max did not meet the Princes. Orléans, Condé, and Conti declared this was a deliberate insult to the Royal House of France.

When my brother-in-law Provence gave a banquet and a ball in honor of my brother, the three Princes of the Blood Royal made their excuses and left the city. It was a clear insult to my brother.

That in itself was bad enough but when the Princes returned, very ostentatiously, to Paris, the people crowded into the streets to cheer them and murmur against Austrians.

When Orléans came to Court I reproached him.

"The King invited my brother to supper," I said, "which you never did."

"Madame," replied Orléans haughtily, "until the Archduke called on me I could not invite him."

"This eternal etiquette! It wearies me."

How impulsively I spoke! That would be interpreted as: "She pokes fun at French customs; she would substitute those of Austria." I must guard my tongue. I must think before I spoke.

"My brother is only in Paris for a short time," I explained. "There is so much for him to do."

Orléans coldly inclined his head; and my husband, seeing him, expressed his annoyance by banishing Orléans, with Condé and Conti, from the Court for a week.

That was small consolation for the Princes were constantly appearing in public and being cheered by the people as though they had done something very brave and commendable in refusing to be kind to my brother.

I was not sorry to see Max go. My sister Maria Amalia was causing a certain amount of scandal through her behavior in Parma. This was discussed in Paris, and it was considered that I had somewhat disreputable relations.

"But what can you expect of Austrians?" people were asking one another.

After Max's visit I don't think the people of France were ever quite so fond of me as they had been before.

While I was occupied with the Trianon—and in fact I gave little serious thought to anything else at this time—a very grave situation had arisen in France.

I did not clearly understand it but I knew that the King was very worried. He did not wish to speak to me of these anxieties for my attempts to get him to reinstate Choiseul had strengthened him in his desire to keep me out of politics. He liked to see me happy with the Trianon; and that kept me busy.

As I saw it, what happened was this.

In August Louis had appointed Anne Robert Jacques Turgot as Comptroller General of Finances. He was a very handsome man, about forty-seven, with abundant brown hair which hung to his shoulders; he had well-cut features and clear brown eyes. My husband was fond of him because there was a similarity between them. They were both awkward in company. I once heard that when he was a child Turgot used to hide himself behind a screen when there were visitors at his home and only emerge after they had gone. He was always awkward and blushed easily; and this *gaucherie* rather naturally endeared him to my husband.

Louis was very pleased at the appointment and talked to me a little about Turgot, but I was too much immersed in my own affairs to listen for long; but I did gather that the finances of the country were, in my husband's opinion, such as to cause grave concern and that Turgot had what he called a three-point programme which was:

> No bankruptcy.
> No increase in taxation.
> No loans.

"You see," said my husband, "there is only one way to make possible Turgot's programme. Complete economy to reduce expenses. We must save twenty millions a year and we must pay off our old debts."

"Yes, of course," I agreed, and I was thinking: Pale blue and pale cherry for the bedroom. My bedroom! A single bed where there will not be room for my husband . . .

Louis was looking apologetic. "Turgot has told me that I must look to my own expenses and that my first duty is to the people. He said: 'Your Majesty must not enrich those he loves at the expense of the people.' And I agreed with him wholeheartedly. I am fortunate to have found such an able minister."

"So fortunate," I agreed. No stiff satin, I thought. No heavy brocade. That is suitable for Versailles. But for my darling Trianon . . . soft silks in delicate shades.

"Are you listening?" he asked.

"Oh yes, Louis. I agree with you that Monsieur Turgot is a very good man and we must economize. We must think of the poor people."

He smiled and said that he knew I would be beside him in all the reforms he intended to make because he knew that I cared about the people as much as he did.

I nodded. It was true. I did want them all to be happy and pleased with us.

I wrote to my mother that day:

> "Monsieur Turgot is a very honest man, which is most essential
> for the finances."

I realize now that it was one thing to have good intentions and another
to carry them out. Monsieur Turgot was an honest man but idealists are
not always practical and luck was against him because the harvest that
year was a bad one. He established internal free trade but that could not
keep the price of corn down because of the shortage. Moreover, roads were
bad and the grain could not be brought to Paris. Turgot met this situation
by throwing on the market grain from the Royal Granaries which had
the effect of bringing down the price but as soon as it was used up the
price rose again and the people were more discontented than ever.

Then there was a distressing rumor that in various parts of the country
people were starving and there was murmuring against Turgot.

The news got worse. Riots broke out at Beauvais, Meaux, Saint-Denis,
Poissy, Saint-Germain; and at Villers Cotterets a crowd collected and
started to raid the markets. Boats on the Oise which were carrying grain
to Paris were boarded and sacks of corn were split open. When the King
heard that the raiders had not stolen the precious grain but thrown it into
the river he was very disturbed.

He said gravely: "It does not sound like hungry people, but those determined to make trouble."

Turgot, who was suffering acutely from the gout and had to be carried
to my husband's apartments, was constantly there.

I had been at Le Trianon reveling in the paintings of Watteau which
adorned the walls and deciding that I should not attempt to alter the
carved and gilded paneling, and I returned to find my husband preparing
to leave for the hunt. He had spent many hours in close consultation with
Turgot and he told me that he wanted to get away for a while to think
about the depressing situation. Then Turgot and Maurepas had left for
Paris, for word had come to them that organized agitators were planning
to lead raids on the markets there. My husband decided to take a short
respite; in any case he could always think more easily in the saddle.

I was in my apartments when the King came bursting in on me.

"I had just left the Palace when I saw a mob," he said. "They are coming
from Saint-Germain and are on their way to the Versailles market."

I felt the blood rushing to my face. The mob . . . marching on Versailles. Old Maurepas and Turgot away in Paris and no one to send them
away. No one . . . that was . . . but the King.

He looked pale but resolute. "I find it hard to bear when the people are against us," he said.

Then I thought of that moment when we had known we were King and Queen of France and how we had both cried out that we were too young, and I forgot the Trianon; I forgot everything but the need to stand beside him, to support him, to will him to be strong. I took his hand and he pressed my fingers.

"There is no time to be lost," he said. "Action, prompt action is necessary." Then the old look of self-doubt was in his face. "The right action," he added.

The Princes of Beauvau and de Poix were in the château and he sent for them . . . poor substitutes for Maurepas and Turgot. He briefly explained the situation. He said: "I will send a message to Turgot and then we shall have to act."

I knew he was praying silently that the action he took would be the right one. And I prayed with him.

He sat down and wrote to Turgot:

> "Versailles is attacked . . . You can count on my firmness. I have ordered the guards to the market place. I am pleased with the precautions you have taken in Paris, but it is what could happen there that alarms me most. You are right to arrest the people of whom you speak, but when you have them remember I wish there to be no haste and many questions. I have just given orders what shall be done here, and for the markets and mills of the neighborhood."

I stayed with him, and I was gratified that that seemed to please him.

"What alarms me is," he said, "that this should appear to be an organized riot. It is not the people. The situation is not as bad as that. There is nothing that we could not set to rights . . . given time. But this is organized . . . planned . . . the people are being incited against us . . . why?"

I thought of how the people had cheered me when I first went to Paris and Monsieur de Brissac had said two hundred thousand people had fallen in love with me; I thought of the people cheering us in the Bois de Boulogne.

"The people love us, Louis," I said. "We may have our enemies but they are not the people."

He nodded and again I realized by the way he looked at me that he was glad I was there.

That was a terrible day. I could eat nothing; I felt faint and slightly sick. The waiting was terrible and when I heard the sounds of shouting approaching the château I was almost relieved.

That was my first glimpse of an angry mob. There they were in the grounds—unkempt, in rags, brandishing sticks and howling abuse. I stood a little way back from the window watching. Someone threw something; I could see it on the balcony. It looked like moldy bread.

Louis said he would speak to them and bravely he stepped on to the balcony. There was a moment's silence and he cried: "My good people . . ."

But his voice was drowned in their shouting. He turned to me and I saw the tears in his eyes.

"You tried. You did your best," I assured him, but I could not comfort him. He was sad and depressed, but he was like a different man from the Louis I had known before. There was a resolution about him. I knew that he would not be afraid whatever happened and that he had one purpose: to bring cheap bread to his people.

I saw the guards come into the courtyard led by the Prince de Beauvau. No sooner had he appeared than the mob turned on him; they threw flour at him . . . the precious flour needed for bread . . . and he was covered in it from head to foot.

"We shall march on the château," cried a voice in the crowd.

The Prince cried: "What do you want the price of bread to be?"

"Two sous," was the answer.

"Then two sous shall it be," said the Prince.

There was a wild shout of triumph and the people turned to rush to the bakers demanding bread at two sous. Thus ended the riots at Versailles; but several of those who had been arrested turned out to be not starving peasants at all but men of substance—one of them was Artois' chief cellarer; and some of the sour bread of which the people had complained was picked up and turned out to be bread mixed with ashes.

This was very disturbing indeed.

Louis wrote at once to Turgot:

"We are peaceful now. The riot was beginning to be violent but the troops calmed them. The Prince de Beauvau asked them why they had come to Versailles and they replied that they had no bread . . . I have decided not to go out today, not through fear but so that all may be calm and settle down. Monsieur de Beauvau tells me that a foolish compromise was made which was to let them have bread at two sous. There was no other thing to do, he says, but let them have it at this or its present price. The bargain is made now but precautions should be made to prevent their believing they can make laws. Give me your advice on this."

Turgot returned at once to Versailles. "Our consciences are clear," he told the King; "but the current price of bread must be restored or there will be disaster."

In spite of Turgot's precautions there were riots in Paris; the Chief of Police Lenoir was dilatory; it may have been that he did not wish to show himself against the rioters.

This was all very alarming; Lenoir refusing to do his duty, and more bread being found which had been turned moldy by a special process. Turgot acted promptly and dismissed Lenoir, replacing him by a man named Albert who was a supporter of his and immediately went into action. Arrests were made and order was restored; the entire Parlement was summoned to Versailles where the King received them.

"I must stop this dangerous brigandage," he said. "It could quickly become rebellion. I am determined that neither my good town of Paris nor my kingdom shall suffer. I rely on your fidelity and submission when I am determined to take measures which ensure that during my reign I shall not have to take them again."

He was determined, as he had told me, before receiving the Parlement, that order should be brought back to his kingdom, and that the real culprits of this rising should be discovered and dealt with.

But the riots in Paris continued; and once again those who were arrested proved to be not poor people in need of bread but men and women with money in their pockets.

Louis was very distressed.

"This is a plot," he told me, "a plot against us. That is what disturbs me so."

"But you are behaving like a true King, Louis. I have heard it said again and again. They tell me that the manner in which you spoke to the Parlement has won everyone's admiration."

"I always find it easier to talk to fifty men than to one," he said with his shy smile.

I cried: "You will discover who made this plot, and then all will be well. I think the French are happy to understand that they have a strong King whom they can trust."

He was delighted and murmured: "You jump to conclusions. It is not all over yet."

Nor was it. As he and I passed out of his room we saw a notice pinned on the door. I read it and gasped. It said:

> "If the price of bread does not go down and the Ministry is not changed, we will set fire to the four corners of the Château of Versailles."

I stared at it in horror. I looked at my husband who had turned pale. "Louis," I whispered, "it is as though they hate us."

"It is not the people," he cried. "I will not believe it is the people."

But he was shaken. And so was I. It was like a cold wind blowing through the palace.

Albert reported that he had made many arrests. A wigmaker and a gauze maker had been caught stealing and it was decided to make an example of them. They were hanged on two gallows eighteen feet high so that they could be an example to the rioters.

Louis was distressed.

"I wish they could find the ringleaders," he said again and again. "I do not wish the people who have only been led away to be punished." If he could he would have pardoned those two men but Turgot insisted that there must be an example; and certainly the hanging of these two men sobered the people. The rioting died down; the insurrection "La Guerre des Farines" was over.

It was clear that some organization, some secret band of men, was using the grain shortage to build a revolution. Fortunately the resolution of the King and the prompt action of Turgot, the replacement of Lenoir by Albert and the solidarity of the Parlement had avoided that.

Everyone was speculating as to who could have been behind it. Some said it was the Prince de Conti whom Max had so offended when he had visited us. It was whispered that he hated me and my family so much that he wished to bring down the Monarchy.

It seemed ridiculous but it was true that the riots had started in Pontoise and he had a house there.

There were all sorts of whispers; I listened for a while. I even heard that Conti was a member of a secret organization suspected of all kinds of subversive activities.

We ought to have been thankful for a grim warning; we should not have rested until we found out the truth of these rumors. Surely it could not have been difficult had we really tried.

But we were all too thankful that "La Guerre des Farines" was over to wish to resurrect causes. We wanted to forget it.

10

"It is very surprising and so comforting to be so well received after the revolt and in spite of the price of bread which is still dear. But it is characteristic of the French to be carried away by evil suggestions and then return immediately to good sense. When we hear the people's acclamations and see these proofs of their affection, we are all the more committed to work for their good."

Marie Antoinette to Maria Theresa

"I am sorry you could not share the satisfaction I have felt here. It is my duty to work for a people who give me so much happiness. I shall give myself up to this absolutely."

Louis XVI to Maurepas

CORONATION

A month had elapsed since the last of the bread riots and everyone was talking about the Coronation. Coronations were rare events with such long-lived Kings as Louis XIV and Louis XV, both of whom had reigned for so many years. Louis XVI was dreading it, of course, for it was the sort of occasion he preferred to avoid. He would be extremely clumsy at the most significant moments; and he hated dressing up. Moreover the ceremony would be archaic, the same that had been carried out since the earliest days of the French Monarchy. Louis would have given a great deal to escape it.

Mercy and my mother were hoping that I would be crowned too and to tell the truth I did not share my husband's horror of the ceremony. I should have been in my element, a glittering figure, receiving the homage of my subjects, and was secretly disappointed when it was decided that there was to be no coronation for me.

"It would mean even more expense," said Louis, "at a time when there is urgent need for economy everywhere. There will be Clothilde's wedding and the lying-in of Artois' wife . . ."

He looked sheepish; the delicate subject was being raised again. I felt unhappy too. Artois was the first of the brothers to be a father. How I envied my sister-in-law! I had thrown myself wildly into making changes at Le Trianon hoping to forget my envy. Lucky, lucky woman! What did it matter if she were small and ugly and squinted and had a long thin nose? She was to be a mother!

"So," said Louis, "you will not be crowned with me. I know you do not wish it. And how I wish that I could avoid the fuss."

But it was decided that there must be a coronation so on the 5th of June I with my brothers- and sisters-in-law left for Rheims. It was midnight when we saw the city in moonlight. The people leaned out of their windows—those who were not lining the streets—and they cheered us wildly; they were almost as enthusiastic as the people of Paris had been when I first had officially entered their city.

As we had arrived the day before the King, I was thrilled to see his entry. His carriage was eighteen feet high and we saw him receive the keys of the city from the Duc de Bourbon who was the Governor of Champagne.

Long before the King was due to arrive at the Cathedral I had taken my place in a gallery near the high altar so that I could have a good view of the proceedings, and never before in my life had I been so moved.

I knew that at seven o'clock the quaint ceremony of bringing the King had begun and that the Bishops of Beauvais and Laon had headed the procession which had arrived at his apartments. The Grand Chorister then knocked on the door and was asked by the Grand Chamberlain: "What is your wish?"

"We wish for the King," was the answer.

"The King sleeps."

This little exchange was repeated twice and then the Bishop said: "We ask for Louis XVI, whom God has given us to be King."

Then the door of the apartment would be opened and Louis would be seen lying on the state bed in all his gorgeous coronation robes.

Then after the blessing and sprinkling of holy water the journey to the Cathedral would begin.

I shall never forget seeing my husband as he came to the high altar. He was in gold and crimson, his mantle was of silver cloth and his velvet cap decorated with diamonds and plumes. There were times when he, being so deeply conscious of his state, was indeed a king, dedicated, noble. I had glimpsed this during the Guerre des Farines when he had faced a murderous mob without fear. He might be shy of great gatherings, awkward in company, embarrassed by our situation in the bedchamber, but he was a brave man.

I watched the sprinkling from *la sainte ampoule* which had been handed down from the days of Clovis, the first King of the Franks; and after that there followed the coronation oath. The sword was presented to the King and he knelt at the altar. Then he was prepared for the annointing and afterward dressed in his robes of purple velvet decorated with fleurs-de-lis. He sat on his throne while the crown of Charlemagne was placed on his head. I had never before seen such splendor. I kept thinking that that crown had been worn by all the Kings of France and I thought of my grandfather who had been very young when it had been placed on his head—young and so handsome, far more so than this present Louis; and I remembered him as I had last seen him, lying on his death bed . . . his lips cracked, his eyes wild, and the horrible smell of death in the apartment.

Louis glanced up at me. For several seconds he kept his eyes on my face as though he had forgotten the solemn ceremony, everything but ourselves; and I felt that too. It was a wonderful moment. A turning point in our lives, I thought afterward. We were together—as one person. And although I felt no great and surging passion for my husband I knew that I loved him and that he loved me. It was a quiet devotion, a bond that was nonetheless strong because it was passionless.

I realized suddenly that the tears were running down my cheeks.

The doors were flung open and people surged into the Cathedral. I could smell the incense; I heard the exclamation as birds were let loose as a symbol of peace. The guns began their salute and the sounds of trumpets and drums mingled.

I joined the royal procession from the Cathedral; and as we came out the shouts of "*Vive le Roi*" filled the air.

Everyone was happy on that day.

I wrote to my mother:

> "The coronation was a great success in all ways. Everyone was delighted with the King and he with them . . . I could not keep my tears from flowing . . . It is very surprising and so comforting to be so well received after the revolt and in spite of the price of bread which is still dear. But it is characteristic of the

French to be carried away by evil suggestions and then to return immediately to good sense. When we hear the people's acclamations and see these proofs of their affection, we are all the more committed to work for their good."

My husband came to me while I was writing this and I showed it to him. He still seemed a little shy in my presence and we were both deeply conscious of that scene in the Cathedral.

"It was a wonderful experience," he said. "I felt as though God had spoken to me."

I nodded.

"I have written to Maurepas and this is what I have said."

I read the letter which had the same theme as mine.

"I am sorry that you could not share the satisfaction I have felt here. It is my duty to work for a people who give me so much happiness. I shall give myself up to this absolutely . . ."

"We think alike," I said.

He took my hands and kissed them; then he said: "It was a splendid occasion, was it not? A deeply moving occasion. Yet nothing touched me so much as when I looked up at the gallery and saw your tears."

I threw myself into his arms.

"Oh Louis . . . Louis . . . I have never felt so moved."

At Rheims Louis performed the ritual of touching for the King's Evil—another of those old customs which dated back to Clovis. Victims of scrofula from all over France had come to Rheims for this ceremony; and two thousand four hundred sufferers lined the avenue kneeling while Louis passed along. It was a horrible sight, so many people so far gone in this terrible disease; the weather was warm and the stench revolting. Yet Louis did not flinch. His eyes shining with purpose his bearing kingly as it could be at times like this, touched each one—from forehead to chin and then on either cheek, while he said: "May God heal you; the King touches you."

Two thousand four hundred times he said those words and as though he meant them; no King of France ever performed this sacred duty with more sincerity, and those poor sick people looked up at him with something like adoration.

I was proud—not only to be Queen of France but the wife of such a man.

He gave no sign of weariness when the long duty was over and Provence and Artois played their part—which was to bring first the vinegar which was to disinfect his hands and then the orange flower water with which to wash them.

When I was alone with him I told him he was magnificent and he was very contented.

We would work together, he implied; and I wondered whether had I asked him at this stage to give Monsieur de Choiseul a place in his government he would have agreed. I believe he would for he could have denied me nothing. But Monsieur de Choiseul was of the past; besides my mother did not wish him to be restored.

I wanted only one thing of Louis: children. The only thing he could not give me—but I know he longed for them as much as I did.

11

"On the most unhappy point which troubles my dear mother I am most unhappy to be unable to tell her anything new. This is certainly no fault of mine. I can only rely on patience and sweetness."

Marie Antoinette to Maria Theresa

"Here we have a spate of lampoons. No one at court is spared, including myself. They have been generous in my case. They give me many illicit lovers, both male and female."

Marie Antoinette to Maria Theresa

"I hear that you have bought bracelets which have cost two hundred and fifty thousand livres with the result that your finances are in disorder . . . I know how extravagant you can be, and I cannot keep quiet about this because I love you too well to flatter you."

Maria Theresa to Marie Antoinette

"She called him [Jacques Armand] my child, and lavished tenderest caresses upon him, still maintaining a deep silence respecting the affliction which constantly occupied her heart."

Madame Campan's Memoirs

EXTRAVAGANCES

My longing for children was growing more and more intense. I had increased my little family of dogs but although I loved them dearly they could not compensate me for my overwhelming desire to be a mother.

When my sister-in-law gave birth to a son I longed to be in her place. When she called out in agony I wished that agony were mine. She lay exhausted yet somehow exalted—quite unlike the unattractive little creature I had known before this. The miracle had happened to her.

I heard her voice raised half hopefully half fearfully; and I could imagine her feelings when she received the answer.

"A little Prince, Madame . . ." The words every Princess and Queen must wish to hear.

She answered: "My God! How happy I am!"

And how well I understood!

The child was well and healthy; the sound of his crying filled the apartment; it seemed the most magical sound in the world.

We left the apartment, I with my attendants, the chief of whom was the Princesse de Lamballe, my dear friend whom I had set up in place of Madame de Noailles. I grew fonder and fonder of my dear Lamballe every day and I did not know what I would do without her. I had now secured the services of Jeanne Louise Henriette Genet, the little lectrice. She was now Madame Campan having married Monsieur Campan's son. She was devoted and good and I did not know what I would do without her either, but of course she was not of the same rank as the Princesse and had her role as one of my trusted attendants, rather than a close friend who could accompany me to *fêtes* and balls.

As we came out of the lying-in chamber and through the château we were met by a crowd of women from the Halles of Paris. It was the custom of the public to be present at the time of royal births although it was only the Queen who must give birth publicly; at the births of lesser members of the royal family only the family need be present. But the fact that a royal child was being born was the nation's concern and although the people were not allowed to enter the Comtesse's bedchamber they were in the château.

Thus as I walked through to my apartments, the Princesse de Lamballe beside me and Madame Campan a few paces behind, I found that the women from Les Halles were all about me. They looked at me with that frank curiosity to which I had grown accustomed. I tried hard not to wrinkle my nose against the smell of fish—for these were the *poissardes* who above all the Paris traders were noted for their frankness of expression —as they crowded about me, touching my clothes, my hands. My hands fascinated them particularly; my fingers were so long and slender, the skin so soft and white and of course they were aglitter with my beloved diamonds.

One woman thrust her face close to mine and, jerking her head toward the lying-in chamber, said: "You ought to be in there, Madame. You ought to be breeding heirs for France not fondling your lady friends."

I saw the Princesse flinch; and I believe my color heightened a little, but I merely held my head high and tried to walk through the crowd.

"You should sleep with the King instead of dancing through the night and early morning."

These women may have seen me riding home from the Opera at dawn when they were making their way to the markets.

Someone laughed. "They say he can't . . . Is it true?" The coarse laughter. "You should see that he can, Madame . . ."

This was becoming unbearable. The stench of these bodies, the insulting words which were growing more and more crude every moment! Was it not enough that I had had to see my sister-in-law with her newly born son in her arms? Must I now have to listen to coarse insults which I did not deserve?

Madame Campan was beside me! I saw her with calm dignity making a path, forcing a way through the crowd. My dearest Lamballe was not much use on such an occasion.

"The Queen is exhausted . . ." said Madame Campan.

The crude jest which followed that made me shudder; but I would have no more of it. After all I was Queen of France. In my most regal manner I walked through that crowd of shouting women as though I could not see them, could not hear them, as though they did not exist. When I was in my apartment I heard their shouting behind me; I saw the tearful face of the Princesse, the calm one of Madame Campan.

I said: "Leave me . . . with Madame Campan."

And when the door shut on us I could restrain myself no longer. I threw myself onto my bed and wept.

When I told my husband of the incident, he was saddened.

"It is so unfair . . . so unfair . . ." I stopped. "Is it my fault?" And seeing the stricken look on his face: "Is it *our* fault?"

He tried to comfort me and I whispered to him. "There is only one answer. The *petit operation*."

"Yes," he replied. "Yes."

I gripped his shoulders, my face alight with hope.

"You will . . . ?"

"I will consider."

I sighed. For so long he had been considering. It was nearly six years. What was he afraid of? The scalpel? Surely not. He was no coward. It was the indignity. The people would know; they would speculate; they would watch. Even now every time he came to my bedchamber they knew; they doubtless calculated the number of hours he spent there. It was this continual watchfulness which was ruining our lives. If only they would have left us alone!

"You will . . . you will see the doctors?"

He nodded. He wanted to give me all I asked; and I had made it clear that I wanted children above all things.

When he had left me I sat down and wrote to my mother:

"I have high hopes that I shall persuade the King to undergo that little operation which is all that is necessary."

My mother wrote back that I must keep her informed, and I obeyed her. I told her everything, but I do not think she could understand the effect this continuing situation was having on me. I was twenty; I was young, extremely healthy. It was not as though I lived the life of a normal virgin. There were these constant frustrating attempts which failed. I was restless and unhappy; I turned away from my husband and then toward him. He had seen the doctors; he had asked for all details of the necessary operation; he had examined the instruments which would have to be used and had come back to me.

"I believe," he said, "that in time this will right itself of its own accord."

My heart sank. He could not face the operation. We were to go on in the old unsatisfactory way.

Every time he came to my apartments by way of the *oeil de boeuf* the crowds would be there watching him. The lampoons and chansons were increasing. We were no longer the young King and Queen who were going to create a Miracle and make France a land flowing with milk and honey; we had had the Guerre des Farines; we were an impotent young man and frivolous young woman. The knowledge that while we were together those people were speculating on our actions disturbed us. We both began to dread these encounters. Yet we must do our duty. It was my idea that we should have a secret staircase built between the King's bedchamber and mine so that he could visit me without anyone's knowing when.

We did this and it comforted us but the position was unchanged and I knew it would be until he submitted to the *petit operation*.

I wrote to my mother:

"On the most unhappy point which troubles my dear mother, I am most unhappy to be unable to tell her anything new. This is certainly no fault of mine. I can only rely on patience and sweetness."

But I was anxious for her to know that although my husband failed me in this one thing, in all other matters I had nothing of which to complain. Oh yes, I was fond of Louis, but he was failing me.

There is really no excuse for the manner in which I behaved during the next phase of my life. I am sure it caused great consternation to my mother who was watching so anxiously from afar. I can only plead the excuse of youth, my aroused senses which were never satisfied, the unhealthy atmosphere in which I lived.

I needed children. No woman was meant to be a mother more than I. Every time I rode through the country and saw the little ones playing I would envy those humble cottage women with little ones clinging to their skirts. My entire being yearned for children. If any of my women had children I would ask that they be brought to me. I would romp with them and my dogs in a manner which Mercy felt was most unbecoming.

In the circumstances what had I but the pursuit of perpetual amusement? I did not want time on my hands to meditate on my unsatisfactory life.

I began to suffer from violent headaches and became feverish and giddy. Mercy called them "nervous affectation." He did not believe that I could be ill. In fact I looked extremely healthy; I had great vitality. But I would sometimes find myself crying for little reason. It was most disturbing.

I longed for affection—demonstrative affection—which I could not get from Louis and I was beginning to realize the danger of my mood. I was surrounded by handsome virile young men, who delighted to pay me compliments and who showed me in a hundred ways that they desired me. Their courteous manners, their lingering glances excited me and all the time I was aware of a warning voice—that sounded like my mother's —continually ringing in my ears. This is danger. The children you bear will be Les Enfants de France. It would be criminal if they should have any father but the King.

I could not resist a little light flirtation. Perhaps Madame de Marsan was right and I was a coquette by nature; but I never allowed myself to be alone with any young man. I knew I was watched; that I was surrounded by people who hoped to see me rush to disaster; I knew that shocking things were written of me and that there were many people who believed perhaps that I did lead a scandalous life.

Mercy reproached me for my restlessness. I was never in bed before the dawn; I seemed to have an endless craving for excitement. I surrounded myself with the young and giddy members of the Court and had no time for those who could help and advise me.

I tried to explain to him. I felt I could be frank with Mercy. He at least would not supply the *chansonneurs* with material for their libels.

"I am perplexed by my strange position," I cried in desperation. "You have seen the way in which the King leaves me alone. I am afraid of being bored. I am afraid of *myself*. To prevent myself brooding I must have continual action. I must have novelty."

He looked at me severely and of course went straight to his apartment and reported what I had said to my mother.

I had to have someone on whom to lavish my affections. I loved little Elisabeth and kept her with me whenever possible. Clothilde had now married and left us. My dearest friend was Marie Thérèse Louise, the Princesse de Lamballe. I found her enchanting, for she was so gentle and sweet, although many thought her stupid. She had a habit of swooning which Vermond said was affectation; she would swoon with pleasure at a gift of flowers or with horror at the sight of shell fish. She confided in me that she had suffered so much through her marriage that it had made her afraid of her own shadow. Poor dearest Lamballe! During those days of uncertainty she was my closest companion. She was so devoted to me; she said she would be happy to be one of my dogs so that she could sit at my feet every day. We used to walk through the gardens arm in arm like two schoolgirls, which naturally shocked everyone who saw us for it was no way for a Queen to be seen in public. But the more frustrated I became, the more determined I was to show contempt for their etiquette.

And then I met the Comtesse Jules. She was the loveliest creature I had ever seen. She had large soulful blue eyes and thick brown curling hair which she wore hanging about her shoulders. She wore no jewels; I discovered that she had none; but on the first day I saw her there was a red rose in her corsage.

Her sister-in-law was the Comtesse Diane de Polignac, lady-in-waiting to the Comtesse d'Artois and it was Diane who had brought her to Court.

As soon as I saw her I wanted to know who she was and commanded that she be presented to me. She was twenty-six at our first meeting but she looked as young as I. Her name was Gabrielle Yolande de Polastron and at seventeen she had been married to the Comte Jules de Polignac.

I asked why I had not seen her at Court before, for I was certain that had she been there I should have noticed her. She answered frankly that she was too poor to live at Court; nor did she seem to care about this. My dearest Gabrielle (she was always known to others as the Comtesse Jules) was completely without ambition. Was that why I was so taken with her? She did not care for jewels; she did not care for honors; and she was a little lazy, I was to discover, and I found all this enchanting. As she talked to me she made me feel that I was not a Queen but a person and that she was drawn to me as I was to her.

She was leaving Court shortly, she told me, but I said she must not do so. I would arrange that she stayed at Court. I felt we were going to be friends.

She did not express surprise; in fact it was not easy to persuade her to accept. She did not really believe that she would care for Court life.

But I was determined, and as the Polignacs was perhaps the most ambitious family at Court they soon prevailed on Gabrielle to accept the honor which I was thrusting upon her.

This was a most important encounter, for it set up a change in my affairs.

I was no longer bored. I wanted Gabrielle to be with me constantly. She enchanted me; she had a lover, the Comte de Vaudreuil; she told me about him, explaining that all ladies had lovers and their husbands had mistresses. It was the accepted state of affairs.

For ladies of the Court perhaps, but not for the Queen.

Vaudreuil, I found to be a rather terrifying character. He was a Creole and, Gabrielle told me, entirely fascinating, although she was afraid of him. I would see how charming were his manners; but his jealous rages were violent. I was to discover that he was extremely ambitious, too.

The Princesse de Lamballe was naturally jealous of my new favorite; and was constantly criticizing her which I fear made me lose patience with her. But I was still fond of her and kept her about me, although I was completely fascinated by my adorable Gabrielle.

The Polignacs had formed themselves into a coterie and their object was of course to make a nucleus about me; they would use me doubtless for their own ends but I was too foolish to see this.

Everything I was doing was unwise, of course. My friendships for women were noticed and commented on. I guessed that reports of these would be carried to my mother and I was anxious to mention this to her before she did to me.

"Here we have a spate of lampoons," I told her. "No one at Court is spared, including myself. They have been generous in my case. They give me many illicit lovers, both male and female."

My shrewd mother must have been wondering how she could bring pressure on my husband to end this trying situation.

By bestowing the post of equerry on the Comte Jules de Polignac I insured that Gabrielle could be at Court and near me. I was now caught up in the gaiety of life. There was no more boredom. The Polignac set saw to that. I was mixing with gay young people and I was the gayest of them all. Gabrielle's apartment was at the head of the marble staircase next to my own and I could see her without ceremony. Without ceremony! That was what I was always seeking.

I found these people so interesting and unusual. There was the Princesse de Guéménée, who had become governess after Madame de Marsan to the young Princesses. I had been very fond of her for some time; she was quite fascinating; she loved dogs as I did and I always enjoyed visiting her to see them—there must have been twenty adorable little creatures whom she swore had special powers which helped her to get into touch with the other world. She had left her husband the Prince de Guéménée and her lover was the Duc de Coigny.

Coigny was charming, seeming old to me being about thirty-eight years old; but his manners were exquisite and I was no longer so stupid as to believe that no one over thirty should come to Court. Then there was the Prince de Ligne, a poet, and the Comte d'Esterhazy, a Hungarian whom I felt justified in seeing because my mother had recommended him. There were also the Baron de Besenval and the Comte d'Adhémar, the Duc de Lauzan, and Marquis de La Fayette who was very young, tall, and redheaded and whom I christened Blondinet.

All these people congregated in Gabrielle's apartments and there I went to them to escape the stifling strain of etiquette in the *petits appartements*.

It was the Princesse de Lamballe who brought Rose Bertin to my notice. The Duchesse de Chartres also recommended her. She was a *grande couturière* with a shop in Rue Saint-Honoré and was considered extremely clever.

As soon as she was brought to me she went into ecstasies about my figure, my coloring, my daintiness and natural elegance. All she needed to make her happy was to dress me. She brought with her some of the most exquisite materials I had ever seen in my life and draped them around me scarcely asking permission to do so. In fact she was completely lacking in that respect which I was accustomed to receive and she behaved as though dressmaking was of more importance than the Monarchy. I was not so much a Queen as a perfect model for her creations. She made me a gown which I thought the most elegant I had ever had. I told her so and the next day she had "discovered" another material which was created for me; no one else should have it; if I did not she would throw it aside. She would make up this material for no one but the Queen of France.

I was amused by her. She never waited in the anterooms but came straight in to my apartments. When one of my attendants referred to her as a dressmaker she was shocked.

"I am an artist!" she retorted.

And she was. She fascinated me with her talk of silks and brocades and colors; she came to me regularly with designs and sometimes I would make a suggestion.

"If Madame had not been the Queen of France she would have been an artist! Now she must be content to *show* these masterpieces to the world."

My clothes were becoming more and more elegant. There was no doubt about that. My sisters-in-law tried to copy me. Rose Bertin would laugh secretly in my apartments. "Have they the figures of Aphrodite? Do they walk as though on a cloud? Have they the grace and the charm of an angel?"

They had not, but they were rich enough to be allowed to make use of Rose Bertin's talents.

Between us she and I set the fashion of the Court. Whenever I entered a room everyone waited breathlessly to see what I was wearing. Then they would go to Rose Bertin and beg her to copy it.

She chose her clients with care, she told me. This one was too thin, that one too fat; another completely ungainly.

"What do you think, Madame, a merchant's wife had the impertinence to call at my establishment yesterday. Would I work for her? The arrogance. Although she was a very *rich* merchant's wife, I said, 'I have not time to spare to talk to you, Madame. I have an appointment with Her Majesty.'"

It added a new interest to life; and when the bills came in I scarcely looked at the large figures at the bottom of the paper.

I just scrawled "*payez*" on the bottom.

Rose Bertin was very contented with me—and I with her.

Oh, the folly of those days! I refused to see what was going on in the world about me. I did not listen when people talked of France's uneasy relationship with England which might break into war at any moment. I had completely forgotten the Guerre des Farines. I danced until three or four in the morning, or played cards and I was beginning to gamble heavily now.

I had done a great deal to abolish etiquette but I had naturally not been completely successful. When I awakened one of my attendants would bring to my bed an album in which patterns of my dresses had been fixed. As soon as a new dress arrived this would be fixed into the album. My first task on awaking was to decide what I would wear for the whole of the day and because of that I must have an account of all my engagements—perhaps a reception in the morning, *négligé* for afternoon and a sumptuous Bertin gown for evening. Another attendant would stand by the bed holding a tray of pins and when I had made my choice I would stick one of these into the elect. When I had made my choice the album would be taken away, the dresses brought out in readiness for when they would be needed.

The ceremony of getting up was tiresome. I thought longingly of the Trianon and determined to spend as much time there as possible. To awake in my own little room. What joy that was! To leap out of bed and look at my gardens which I was having made to my designs. Perhaps to run out with a robe thrown over my night attire. What fun, what joy to feel the dew on the cool grass with my bare feet. That was one of the joys at the Trianon.

How different from Versailles where etiquette seemed to suffocate me and rob me of my natural vitality.

One winter's morning my *lever* was carried to excess. To dress me I must have a lady of honor on one side and a tirewoman on the other; and as if this was not enough my first *femme de chambre* must be in attendance besides two of the lower servants.

It was a lengthy business and on that cold morning I did not relish this. It was the tirewoman's duty to put on my petticoat and hand me my gown and the lady of honor to perform the more intimate tasks of putting on my underclothes and pouring out the water in which I should wash. But when a Princess of the Royal Family was there, the lady of honor must allow her to give me my linen; and this had to be most scrupulously observed, because there might be occasions when two or three Princesses were present and if one usurped the duty of the other—thereby implying she was of higher rank—this would be a major breach of etiquette.

On this particular day I was undressed waiting for my undergarments to be handed to me and just about to take them from the maid of honor when the door opened and the Duchesse d'Orléans came in. Seeing what was happening, she took off her gloves and, receiving the garment from the maid of honor, handed it to me; but at that moment the Comtesse de Provence appeared.

I sighed deeply, my irritation rising. There was I without my clothes; already delayed by the Duchesse d'Orléans and now here was my sister-in-law who would be deeply affronted if anyone but herself put on my clothes. I handed her the garment, folded my hands across my breasts and with an expression of resignation, waited, grateful for only one thing: there could not be a lady of higher rank than my sister-in-law to come and repeat this stupid performance.

Marie Josèphe, seeing my impatience and that I was cold, did not stop to remove her gloves but put the shift over my head and knocked my cap off while doing so.

I could not contain myself. "Disgraceful!" I muttered. "How tiresome!"

Then I laughed to hide my irritation; but I was more determined than ever to put my foot through their silly etiquette. I understood that it was probably necessary on certain state occasions but to carry it to these lengths was quite ridiculous.

Thus I reveled in bringing Rose Bertin into my private apartments where no tradesman had been admitted before. And I spent more and more time at the Trianon.

The really great ceremony of the day was that of dressing my hair. Naturally I employed the best hairdresser in Paris, which probably meant in the world. Monsieur Léonard was as important a personage in his way as Rose Bertin was in hers. Every morning he drove to Versailles from his establishment in Paris to dress my hair, and people used to come out to watch him in his splendid carriage drawn by six horses. No wonder there was growing discontent about my extravagance. As Rose Bertin invented new fashions for me alone, he invented new hair styles. My high forehead had been a cause of complaint years before but now styles were worn high to suit high foreheads, and hair styles gradually became more and more fantastic. The hair was stiffened with pomades and made to stand straight up from the head, then padded with hair of the same color; as far up as eighteen inches from the forehead Monsieur Léonard would then begin his original creation. He would create fruit, birds, even ships and landscape scenes with artificial flowers and ribbons.

My appearance was a constant topic of conversation throughout Versailles and Paris; it was written and joked about, while my extravagances were deplored.

Mercy, of course, was reporting; but my mother did not need him to learn about this.

She wrote reprovingly:

"I cannot refrain from commenting on a subject which many newspapers have brought to my notice. I mean your manner of hairdressing. I gather that from the roots on the forehead it rises as much as three feet and on top of that are feathers and ribbons."

I replied that the lofty headdresses were fashionable and that no one in the world thought them in the least strange.

She wrote back:

"I have always held that it is well to be in the fashion but one should never be outré in one's dress. Surely a good-looking Queen, blessed with charm, has no need of such foolishness. Simplicity of attire enhances these gifts, and is much more suitable to exalted rank. Since, as Queen, you set the fashion, all the world will follow you when you do these foolish things. But I, who love my little Queen and watch her every footstep, must not hesitate to warn her of her frivolity."

There was a different tone in my mother's letters these days. She warned; she did not command; and constantly she was telling me that she advised me through her great love for me.

I should have paid more attention to her; but it was so long since I had seen her; and even her influence was beginning to wane. I no longer trembled at the sight of her handwriting; after all, if she were an Empress, I was the Queen—and the Queen of France. I was a woman now and could act as I pleased. I continued to consult with Rose Bertin; my dress bills were of enormous proportions and my hair styles grew more preposterous each day.

Moreover Artois and his cousin Chartres were encouraging me to gamble. We played faro at which it was possible to lose a great deal of money. The money which the King gave me to pay my debts each week all seemed to go at the gambling table.

I had no sense of money; all I had to do was scribble "*payez*" on the bills which were presented to me and let my servants deal with the matter.

My husband was too indulgent. I think he understood that driving passion not to be bored, not to stop and think, and blamed himself for it. Always he must have been conscious of the shadow of the scalpel which he could not bring himself to face. He paid my debts and never lectured me; but he did try to curtail the gambling; not for me, only, but for the whole Court.

But what excited me more than anything—more than clothes, gambling, dancing, and hair styles—were diamonds. How I loved those gorgeous sparkling stones; and they became me as no others did. They were cold yet full of fire; and I was too. I never once allowed a young man to be alone with me; I was frigid, it was said; but beneath the frigidity there was a brilliant fire which like a diamond could flash in certain circumstances.

I had many jewels. Some I had brought from Austria and then there was the casket my grandfather had given me for a wedding present; but a new jewel could always fascinate me. If the people grumbled at my extravagance at least the tradespeople were delighted. The court jewelers, Boehmer and Bassange, who had come to France from Germany, were as delighted with me as Rose Bertin and Léonard were. They would present their beautifully set stones to me, looking so delicious in their satin and velvet cases that I found them altogether irresistible. When they showed me a pair of diamond bracelets I was fascinated by them and I did not think of the price until I had decided I must have them.

This brought protests from my mother.

> "I hear that you have bought bracelets which have cost two hundred and fifty thousand livres, with the result that you have thrown your finances into disorder and are in debt . . . This deeply disturbs me, particularly when I contemplate the future. A Queen degrades herself by decking herself out in this ostentatious manner, and still more so by lack of thrift. I know how extravagant you can be, and I cannot keep quiet about this matter because I love you too well to flatter you. Do not lose through your frivolous behavior the good name you acquired when you arrived in France. It is well known that the King is not extravagant, so blame will rest on you. I hope I shall not live to see the disaster that will ensue unless you change your ways."

The warning continued for news of my gambling debts had reached her.

> "Gambling is without doubt one of the worst pleasures. It attracts bad company and provokes gossip . . . Let me beg of you, my dear daughter, do not give way to this passion. Let me beg of you to stop this habit. If I do not hear that you accept this advice I

shall be forced to ask the King's help in this matter so that I may save you from greater misfortune. I know too well what consequences will ensue and you will lose caste not only with the people of France, but abroad also—which will distress me deeply, for I love you so tenderly."

I wanted to please her and tried to for a while, but soon I was slipping back into the old ways. When Mercy reproached me I answered: "I do not think my mother can understand the difficulties of life here."

I think he, who was closer at hand, did, as did the Abbé Vermond. Perhaps this made them a little less severe in condemning my follies.

The Trianon was a delight. I was laying out the gardens afresh with the help of the Prince de Ligne who had made for himself one of the loveliest gardens in France at Bel Oeil. There was a fashion for everything English at this time. Frenchmen tried to dress like Englishmen in long coats cut close and thick stockings, with stock hats—not at Court of course, where they were most elaborately attired, but we noticed this in the streets of Paris. Signs were hung outside shops: ENGLISH SPOKEN HERE; lemonade sellers now sold punch and everyone was drinking *le thé*. Artois had introduced horse racing to France and I often went with him to the races. It was another excuse for gambling. So of course I must have an English garden at the Trianon. I was planning a little temple in the gardens which was to surround an exquisite statue of Eros by Bouchardon. I decided on Corinthian pillars about the statue and I would call it the Temple of Love. It became clear to me that the Prince de Ligne was in love with me; and I was sad about this because I enjoyed his company so much and I dared not allow that friendship to develop.

My feeling for him must have been noticed for my mother wrote and said that she thought it wrong that he should spend so much time in Versailles so I told him to join his regiment for a while and then come back. I was surprised how sorry I was that he must go away.

But it was clear to me that I had to be careful.

Mercy came to me and spoke to me severely. I had made many new friends; I was constantly in their company. They seemed to him to be people of questionable morals. Was I being wise?

I looked at him slyly because I knew that he had a mistress, an opera singer, Mademoiselle Rosalie Levasseur; he had lived with her for years, and although theirs was a very respectable relationship, as far as it could be in the circumstances, it was one without benefit of clergy.

I did not mention this. I contented myself with a lighthearted rejoinder that one must enjoy oneself while one was young. "When I grow older I shall be more serious; then my frivolity will disappear."

I was surprised that old Kaunitz understood my position far better than my mother or my brother. He wrote to Mercy: "We are young yet, and I fear we shall be so for a very long time."

This time was difficult for my husband too.

The kingly bearing he displayed at the time of the Guerre des Farines seemed to have disappeared; he asserted himself in odd ways. He liked to fight with his attendants and often I would go to his apartments and see him wrestling on the floor. He always got the better of his opponents for he was much stronger than they were; this must have given him the feeling of superiority he needed to feel.

He was the absolute antithesis of everything that I was. He did not complain of my extravagance but he was so thrifty that he was almost mean; there was no subtlety about him. Sometimes he would fix one of his friends by his expression and walk toward him so that the poor man had to retreat until he was standing against a wall. Then Louis would find he had nothing to say and would laugh loudly and walk away.

His appetite was voracious. I have seen him eat for breakfast a chicken and four cutlets, several slices of ham and six eggs all washed down with half a bottle of champagne. He worked at the forge which he had had installed on the top story and there he would hammer away and make boxes of iron, and keys. Locks were his passion. He had a workman up there named Gamain who treated him as though he were a fellow worker and even jeered at his efforts, all of which Louis took in the utmost good humor declaring that in the forge Gamain was a better man than he was.

At his *coucher* he was as impatient of etiquette as I was and would take his *cordon bleu* and throw it at the nearest man. Stripped to the waist he would scratch himself before the courtiers and when the noblest present tried to help him into his nightgown he would run round the room leaping over the furniture, forcing them to chase him which they did until they were out of breath. Then he would take pity on them and allow them to put on his nightgown. The nightgown on, and his breeches loosed, he would engage them in conversation, walking about the room with his breeches about his ankles so that he was obliged to shuffle.

It was the Duc de Lauzan who made me realize how dangerously Louis and I had drifted apart. At a party at the house of the Princesse de Guéménée, Lauzan appeared in a very splendid uniform and on his helmet was the most magnificent heron's plume. I thought it very beautiful and impulsively said so. The very next day a messenger came from the Princesse de Guéménée with the feather and a note from the Princesse which said that the Duc de Lauzan had begged her to implore me to accept it.

I was embarrassed but I knew that to return the feather would be to wound him deeply and impulsively decided that I would wear the feather once and then lay it aside.

Monsieur Léonard used it for my headdress and when Lauzan saw it his eyes gleamed with pleasure.

The next day he presented himself at my apartment and begged an interview. Madame Campan was in attendance and I granted the interview as I should have done to anyone. He wished, he said, to speak to me privately if I would so honor him.

I glanced at Madame Campan; she knew the signal. She would go into the anteroom and leave the door open, because she knew that I was never alone with men.

When she had disappeared he threw himself onto his knees and began kissing my hands.

"I was overcome with joy," he cried, "when I saw you wearing the aigrette. It was your answer . . . the answer I longed for. You have made me the happiest man in the world . . ."

"Stop," I said. "Are you mad, Monsieur de Lauzan?"

He stumbled to his feet, the color draining from his face. He said: "Your Majesty was gracious enough to show me by our token . . ."

"You are dismissed," I told him.

"But you . . ."

"Will you go, Monsieur de Lauzan? Immediately . . . Madame Campan . . . come here please."

She was there as I knew she would be.

There was only one thing Lauzan could do. He bowed and retired.

I said to Madame Campan: "That man shall never again come within my doors."

I was shaking with apprehension. I was both angry and alarmed. I knew that I was to blame in a way. I had behaved coquettishly; and I had been so foolish as to wear the plume. Why could not these people understand that I merely wanted to be amused!

Lauzan never forgave me. His feelings for me were indeed strong and if he could not be my lover he could at least become my enemy. He was that—in the years when I so needed friends.

There were times when I longed to escape from the Court; and there was the Petit Trianon waiting to welcome; but sometimes I felt as though I wanted to get far away; I wanted to ride out in my calash and be alone —which was strange for me. Not that I was alone. There was ceremony even when I went riding informally in this way; I must have my coachman and postilions.

We rode through villages and I looked out at the children at play—beautiful creatures whom I should have been so happy to call mine; as we rode along suddenly one of these little ones ran out of a cottage and almost under the horses' hoofs. I cried out, the coachman pulled up sharply; the little boy lay sprawling in the road.

"Is he hurt?" I cried, leaning out.

The child began to scream wildly as one of the postilions picked him up.

He kicked furiously, and the postilion grinned. "I cannot think much ails him, Your Majesty. But he's frightened."

"Bring him to me."

He was brought. His clothes were ragged but not unclean; he stopped crying as I took him and looked up at me wonderingly. He had large blue eyes and light-colored waving hair. He was like a little cherub.

"You are not hurt, darling?" I said. "And there is nothing to fear."

A woman had come out of the cottage; two children, older than the little boy, ran after her and I caught a glimpse of others.

"The boy . . ." began the woman; and she looked at me in astonishment. I was not sure if she knew who I was.

"Jacques, what are you doing?"

The little boy on my lap turned his head from her and nestled closer to me. That decided me. He was mine. Providence had given him to me.

I beckoned to the woman and she came closer to the calash.

"You are his mother?" I asked.

"No, Madame. His grandmother. His mother—my daughter—died last winter. She has left five children on my hands."

I was exultant. "On my hands!" It was significant.

"I will take little Jacques. I will adopt him. I will bring him up as my child."

"He is the naughtiest of them all. One of the others . . ."

"He is mine," I said, for I loved him already. "Give him to me and you will never regret it."

"Madame . . . you are . . ."

"I am the Queen," I said. She dropped a clumsy curtsey and I added: "You shall be rewarded." And my eyes filled with tears at her gratitude for like my husband I loved to help the poor when I was made aware of the difficult lives they led. "And this little one shall be as my own child."

The little one sat up suddenly and began to cry: "I don't want the Queen. I want Marianne . . ."

"His sister, Madame," said his grandmother. "He is very wayward. He will run away."

I kissed him. "Not from me," I said, but he tried to wriggle away from me. I signed to Campan to take the name of the woman and to remind me that something should be done; and then I gave orders to return to the palace.

Little Jacques kicked all the way and kept screaming that he wanted Marianne and his brother Louis. He was a bright little fellow.

"You do not know, darling, what a happy day this is for you," I told him, "and for me."

I told him of the toys he should have . . . a little pony of his own. What did he think of that? He listened and said: "I want Marianne."

"He is a faithful little fellow," I said. "Not to be bribed."

And I hugged him which made him wriggle more than ever. His little woolen cap fell off and I was enchanted for he was much prettier without it. I thought how delightful he would look in the clothes I should plan for him. We should soon discard that red frock and the little sabots.

When we reached the palace there was some astonishment to see me hand in hand with a little peasant boy, who was now too bewildered by all he saw to continue with his tears.

The Queen's latest folly, was what they called it. But I did not care. At last I had a child even though he was not of my flesh and blood. I found a nurse for him immediately—the wife of one of my menservants who had children of her own and whom I knew to be a good mother. I gave orders that he was to be suitably dressed as became his new station in life. And then with Madame Campan's help I set about making arrangements to send my little darling's brothers and sisters to school.

Those were the happiest days I had known for a long time and when I saw my little one in a white lace-trimmed frock with a rose-colored sash trimmed with silver fringe, and a little hat decorated with a feather, I thought he was the most beautiful creature I had ever seen.

I embraced him; I wept over him; and this time he did not object; he lifted those wondering and most beautiful blue eyes to my face and called me "Maman."

I called him Armand. That was his family name and it seemed more suitable at Court than Jacques. Every morning he was brought to me; he would sit on my bed before my *lever;* and we would breakfast together; sometimes we would dine together too. The King would join us and he grew quite fond of little Armand.

I was the only one who could tame his waywardness. He liked to sit on the bed and play with the feathers and ornaments of my headdresses. When I was most elaborately dressed for some ball or banquet I would go and show myself to him.

If I loved him, he loved me too. It did not occur to me that a child could be capable of deep emotions—perhaps deeper than my own.

No one could doubt that the state of affairs between my husband and myself was unsatisfactory. Although he never showed anything but kindness for me it was clear that he preferred the company of others to mine. He spent more time with Gamain than with me. I was completely outside political affairs; he showed clearly that, indulgent as he was toward me— permitting my extravagances, often paying my debts, practising, as it seemed, parsimony to counterbalance my extravagance, even allowing me to bring a peasant child into the family circle—he was not going to allow me to interfere in political affairs.

The uneasiness of my mother, Mercy, Vermond, and Kaunitz was apparent. And my mother had her enemies in Europe, the chief of whom was Frederick of Prussia—known as the Great to so many and to my mother as the Monster.

Frederick had his spies everywhere so he was well-informed of the King's inability to consummate our marriage, and an idea occurred to him that an experienced woman might achieve what a frivolous young girl had failed to do. Such a woman was the well-known actress of the Comédie Française, Louise Contat. She was more than beautiful; a woman of sensitivity, understanding, and great charm, she was sought after by many a nobleman.

Such a mistress, Frederick the Great was certain, could greatly help the King. In any case it was worthy of a try. And it should be ascertained before the liaison was encouraged that the delectable Contat would be the friend of Prussia.

But for the vigilance of Vermond and Mercy I have no notion what would have grown out of this; but of one thing I am sure my husband would never have been unfaithful.

Mercy was, however, soon writing to my mother. What a flutter there must have been in the Hofburg! I imagined the conferences between Joseph and my mother. Joseph had grown more pompous than ever and as head of the family believed it was his duty to castigate his family and keep it in order.

He had visited Naples to see Caroline and her conduct did not please him. Poor Caroline! What had the years done to her? She was creating scandal in Naples with the husband to whom she had gone so reluctantly. Joseph had plenty to lecture her about. Caroline's excuse was that she never entertained a lover until she was pregnant by her husband. As though as long as she secured the rightful succession nothing else mattered. Maria Amalia had been creating scandal in Parma ever since she had been there. And here was I in France, with the eyes of the world on me, frivolous and extravagant, but at least faithful to my husband—although rumor accused me of a hundred obscenities.

And now there was a possibility of my place in my husband's affections being taken by a brilliant and attractive actress who would be eternally grateful to my mother's greatest enemy for putting her into this exalted position.

Action must be taken without fail. It should have been long before.

My brother Joseph was coming to Versailles to discover the true state of affairs for himself and to see what could be done about them.

12

"Do you look for opportunities? Do you sincerely respond to the affection the King shows you? Are you cold and distrait when he caresses you? Do you appear bored or disgusted? If so can it be expected that a man of cold temperament could make advances and love you with passion?"

"In truth I tremble for your happiness because I believe in the long run things cannot continue as they are now . . . The revolution will be a cruel one and perhaps of your own making."

From the Emperor Joseph's Instructions to Marie Antoinette

"I have attained the happiness which is of the greatest importance to my whole life . . . My marriage was thoroughly consummated. Yesterday the attempt was repeated and was even more successful than the first time . . . I don't think I am with child yet but I have hopes of becoming so at any moment."

Marie Antoinette to Maria Theresa

"I hope that next year will not go by without my giving you a nephew or niece . . . It is to you we owe this happiness."

Louis XVI to the Emperor Joseph

IMPERIAL VISITOR

News was brought to me that my brother had arrived in Paris and was staying at the Austrian Embassy, being entertained by Mercy. What, I wondered, was Mercy telling my brother about me at this moment? It could scarcely be anything flattering. I thought of the all reproachful letters I had received from Vienna. Nothing would have been kept from my brother the Emperor of Austria and co-ruler with my mother.

The last time I had seen him was when I had said goodbye to my home and he had traveled the first stage of the journey with me. I remembered yawning while I listened to his recounting my good fortune and how many horses were being used to carry me on my journey. I had not then been sorry to say goodbye to Joseph; but now I was both delighted and apprehensive at the prospect of seeing a member of my very own family.

Joseph had given instructions that there was to be no fuss, no ceremony. He was not even traveling as the Emperor of Austria but as Count Falkenstein, and had arrived at the Embassy in an open carriage in the heavy rain. This need not have happened, of course. He could have come in state.

I guessed that he would lecture me on my extravagance; it was something he particularly deplored for he enjoyed living a Spartan life; he had always wanted to be a ruler whose first thought was the betterment of his people, and he liked to travel among them incognito, doing good by stealth; but malicious people said that although he remained incognito for a while he always liked his identity to be revealed at the climax of his adventures, when he would arrange for someone to betray him. Then he could dramatically declare: "Yes, I am the Emperor."

I refused to believe this. It was more malicious gossip; but at the end of Joseph's visit, I was not so sure. In fact it was rather tiresome of him to come incognito. Why should he stay at the Embassy? He had said that while he was at Versailles he had no intention of lodging at the château or the Trianon. Two furnished rooms must be found for him in the town for he did not wish to be treated as the Emperor of Austria, but as an ordinary citizen.

Today, I thought, will be the day.

I was at my toilette. My hair was hanging about my shoulders for Monsieur Léonard's six in hand had not yet rattled along the road between Paris and Versailles when I heard the clatter of horses' hoofs in the courtyard. It was half-past nine, and I paid little attention, therefore I was most surprised when I was told that the Abbé Vermond was without and he had a visitor to see me. The visitor did not wait to be announced but burst in on me unceremoniously.

"It is . . ." I cried. "It really is . . . my brother Joseph."

Then I forgot everything but that this was my brother; and I felt like a child again, as though I were in the Schönbrunn about to be reproached for something and I ran to him and threw my arms about him. Joseph was moved too and as he embraced me there were tears in his eyes.

"My little sister . . . my beautiful little sister!"

"But, Joseph, it is wonderful to see you . . . It is so long . . . and I have thought of you so much and our dearest mother and home . . ."

I was chattering incoherently in German, for I had slipped back to my native tongue unconsciously. "Oh, Joseph, it is wonderful. It is like being a little girl again."

Joseph said it did him good to look at me and at that moment he was not a bit like the stern brother who had been so critical of my frivolity back in Vienna. But we Germans are a sentimental people. Living so long with the French I had forgotten how much so.

We went on chattering. And how is dear Mamma? And what of the Schönbrunn gardens? Do the fountains still play as they did? What of our little theater in the Hofburg where we used to perform our plays? What of the servants? What of my dogs . . . those I had to leave behind? Is Mamma well and happy? I'm afraid she has been anxious. How I should love to see her. You must tell her, Joseph . . . tell her that I long to see her again.

We were laughing and crying and Joseph said I had grown beautiful. I had been a pretty little creature when I left; now I had become a beautiful woman. If he could find a woman as beautiful as I was he would marry again.

This was just the excitement of our reunion. We reveled in it for that first hour or so, before he embarked on the unpleasant task which had brought him to France, which was of course to lecture me, to criticize me, and to teach me how to rectify my follies.

When my almost hysterical joy in reunion was over I was able to look at him clearly and, I have to admit, critically. He was scarcely handsome; he was purposely very plainly dressed for his suit was meant to be of service rather than to flatter. It was of a color known in the Court as puce since Rose Bertin had made me a dress in a silk of the same shade and the King seeing it had cried out that it was the color of a flea. From then on "puce" had become fashionable. But it scarcely suited my brother. I disliked his short boots which gave him a look of the people; and the way in which his hair was dressed was certainly not becoming to an Emperor; he wore it in a single curl. He stooped a little and had aged a great deal since I had last seen him.

"You are thinking that I do not look like the Emperor of Austria. Confess it."

"You look like my brother Joseph and that is all I ask."

"Ah, they have taught you to pay fancy compliments here but I am a plain man and I like plain speaking. Now let us be completely alone together for I wish to talk to you."

"You will wish me to conduct you to the King who will be anxious to meet you."

"All in good time," said Joseph. "First I want to hear from your own lips if these rumors are true. You must be frank with me, because it is on account of this that I am at Versailles . . . on account of this and other matters. And I must know the truth with nothing held back."

I conducted him into a small antechamber and shut the door.

"The whole of Europe," he said, "talks of your marriage. It is true, is it not, that the King is unable to consummate that marriage?"

"It's true."

"Although he has made many attempts."

"He has made many attempts."

"And the doctors have examined him and find that the knife is necessary to make him a normal man."

I nodded.

"He shrinks from this operation?"

I nodded again.

"I see. He must be made to see his duty."

Joseph walked up and down the apartment as though communing with himself. In spite of his plain garments he adopted what I thought of as a very Imperial attitude. I began to wonder then whether Joseph was as modest as he wanted us to believe.

He asked many intimate questions and I answered him frankly.

He said: "It was time I came."

I sent a messenger to tell the King that my brother was in the château and I proposed bringing him to him without delay; then I slipped my arm through that of Joseph and led him to the King's apartments.

Louis hurried to my brother and embraced him.

I noticed that Louis was taller and although he was by no means the most elegant man at Court he looked distinguished beside Joseph. But Joseph had the manner of the elder brother. He might like to travel incognito but he immediately made it clear that he considered the King of France inferior to the Emperor of Austria. Louis was at the moment in purple velvet because he was in mourning for the King of Portugal who had died a short while before.

They exchanged pleasantries and Louis assured my brother that the whole of the château was at his disposal, to which Joseph laughed shaking his head.

"No, brother," he said, "I prefer to live as a simple man. My lodgings in Versailles will suit me very well. I have two rooms which are good enough for me in the house of one of your bath attendants."

"You will surely not find the comfort to which you are accustomed there."

"I do not give much thought to comfort, brother, and I am not so accustomed to it as you are. A camp bed and a bearskin is all I ask."

He looked round the gilded apartment as he spoke and his gaze was a little scornful as though there was something sinful in our splendor.

He must meet the members of the royal family, said the King; and some of his ministers, most certainly Monsieur de Maurepas. Nothing would delight him more, replied Joseph; and the morning was spent in receiving people and presenting them to him. I felt a little uncomfortable because my hair was not dressed and there was no time to have this lengthy ceremony performed. Poor Monsieur Léonard, I guessed was in despair but naturally I could not leave my brother. If he had given us a time when he would arrive, how much more comfortable it would have been for us all! But Joseph's simple habits were to make life considerably more complicated for us during his stay.

We took dinner in my bedchamber. No ceremony, demanded Joseph, so a table was brought and we sat on stools which was somewhat uncomfortable. So there we were perched on our stools—eating in the bedchamber, the three of us most informally; we were none of us quite at ease and I was sure both Louis and I would have been less strained if we had eaten in the normal way.

We talked a great deal together during the next few days. Joseph had come to France with a threefold purpose: to warn me to repent of my frivolous ways; to cement the alliance between France and Austria; and, perhaps most important of all, to discover the truth behind my unsatisfactory marriage and set it to rights. It was characteristic of Joseph that he believed himself capable of achieving all three.

During the first days the sentimental feelings aroused by our reunion continued. I could see though that he thought the French Court a very extravagant place and he was very critical of it.

On the second day Joseph took an intimate supper with the family in Elisabeth's apartments. I wanted my brother to be fond of Elisabeth because I was, and she was growing into an enchanting creature. The idea crossed my mind that Joseph needed a wife; he had suffered two unhappy marriages, first with the beautiful and strange Isabella whom he had loved and then with the wife whom he had hated; his only child was dead. He was Emperor of Austria and he needed an heir . . . although of course he had brothers to follow him. Yet if Elisabeth married Joseph she would go away from France and that did not seem to me such a good idea.

I fancied that Artois was laughing at my brother behind his back. He and Provence would consider Joseph inelegant and uncultured.

So that was an uneasy meal. Oh dear, how I wished Joseph would behave like normal visiting royalty!

Something seemed to have happened to all three brothers that night. I daresay it was provoked by Joseph's stilted conversation; but when we rose Provence stuck out a leg and Louis tripped over it; then Louis fell on Provence and they wrestled together; Artois joined in. It was only a game but it seemed extraordinary to Joseph. I had seen my husband and his brothers romp in this way before, sometimes it was half in fun, at others half in anger, for Provence I believe was so jealous of Louis that this kind of fighting relieved his feelings. As for Louis himself he always enjoyed this sort of game, perhaps because he usually emerged the victor. Artois of course was mischievous enough to delight in something which would shock the visitor.

Elisabeth and I exchanged glances of horror, but Joseph ignored the romping young men and talked to us, showing not the slightest surprise.

Later I said to him: "Madame Elisabeth is already quite the woman!" and he replied sternly: "It would be more satisfactory if the King were quite the man."

I was eager to show Joseph the Petit Trianon and the next day I took him there, with only two ladies in attendance, because I told Joseph: "The Trianon is my retreat and there I can live simply."

With pride I took him to see the English garden which was almost finished.

He was not interested. He began to lecture me.

Did I not realize that I was heading for disaster? I surrounded myself with men and women of questionable morals. It was small wonder that my own morals were questioned. "You are a featherhead," he cried. "You think of nothing but pleasure."

"I must occupy my time."

"Then occupy it worthily."

"If I had children . . ."

"Ah. That's at the core of the matter. But your behavior toward the King displeases me."

"Displeases you."

"A wife should be subservient to her husband. You do not seek to please him enough. You should court him. You should go out of your way to please him."

"His tastes are very different from mine."

"You should make his tastes yours."

"Can you see *me* at the forge." I held out my hand. "Can you see me making locks . . . wrestling on the floor with my sisters-in-law perhaps? It is quite impossible for me to follow the King's tastes."

"You should not do these things, of course. But you should be more submissive. You should show that you find pleasure in his company. You could do a great deal to make him normal."

I was silent. And Joseph went on to lecture me on my dancing throughout the night, on my gambling, on my choice of friends and my extravagances.

I said meekly: "I shall try to mend my ways, Joseph." And indeed since I had adopted little Armand I had improved a little. But somehow, though I loved the little boy he only made me long the more for children of my own.

Joseph refused to leave his furnished rooms and declared that he wished to see Paris as a tourist, not as an Emperor. He would ride out of Versailles in his little open carriage, somberly dressed in his plain puce-colored coat, taking with him two servants in quiet gray. When he reached the capital he left his carriage and walked about the streets hoping to be taken for a man of the people, but somehow doing it so ostentatiously that most people guessed he was a personage, and as it was known that my brother was visiting us and was a simple man who liked to remain unrecognized, his identity was quickly revealed.

He would go into shops and make purchases, having the article wrapped and taking it away himself while the lackeys waited outside. If he heard whispers of "It is the Emperor" he pretended not to hear and become more bourgeois than ever.

He would return from these trips a little bespattered by the Paris mud but pleased with his journeys. I could see that Paris was beginning to enchant him. He talked of the sunset from the Bourbon Quay and the imposing silhouette of Notre Dame. To stand apart and look at Paris was an enchanting sight he told me. Had I ever looked back at the spire of the Sainte-Chapelle and the turrets of the Conciergerie? No, he answered for me. There was only one spot in Paris that I showed any interest in: the Opera House where I danced.

He lectured Louis, too. What did he know of his people? It was a ruler's duty to mingle with his people . . . incognito, of course. Louis should be up one morning to see the peasants from the country arriving at Les Halles with their produce; he should mingle with the bakers of Gonesse. He should see the gardeners wheeling their barrows into the city full of fruit and vegetables; he should see the clerks on their way to work and the waiters at the lemonade shops serving early customers with their coffee and rolls; he should buy coffee from one of the coffee women who carried their urns on their backs and he should stand there in the street and drink it from an earthenware cup. He should ride on the *carrabas* and take a trip in a *pot de chambre*. It was the way for a King to know what his people were thinking of its government and its King. And he must do all this incognito.

In fact it seemed that Joseph was far more interested in the people of France than any members of the royal family. He included in his tour museums, printing houses, and factories; he wanted to see how the dyes were made and wandered about the Rue de la Juiverie, the Rue de Marmousets, and such like unsavory places to chat with the workers. His accent, his clothes, his determination not to be recognized, all gave him away. In a very short time the people of Paris were aware that the Emperor of Austria was among them and they looked out for him. They recognized him at once in his plain puce garments, his unpowdered hair, its simple style, and his earnest endeavor to show them that he was one of them and dispense with all etiquette. They delighted in him and he was extremely popular; on the rare occasions when he was seen with us all the cheers were for him.

I noticed his secret satisfaction and I knew then that his favorite role was the Emperor who was discovered to be an Emperor.

From the soap works he went to the tapestry makers, the botanical gardens, and the hospitals. These interested *him* far more than the theaters and the opera balls, although he did deign to visit the Comédie Française. He called on Madame du Barry who was at this time at Louveciennes, which her old friend Maurepas had arranged should be hers after the two and half years she had spent at the Pont aux Dames.

This gesture I did not understand in my brother unless he was curious to see a very beautiful woman; or perhaps to show that he was a tolerant freethinker who was not shocked by the life she had led. It was surprising that he had no time for the Duc de Choiseul who had been a good friend to Austria until the time of his disgrace and was responsible for arranging my marriage.

It seemed ironical too that the people who had criticized me for flouting their etiquette should so admire Joseph for doing the same.

But my brother did not confine himself to visiting Paris; he sought to set our household in order. Not only was I subjected to lectures, which I have no doubt I deserved, but my brothers-in-law were also.

He told Artois that he was a fop. He should not think because he was the third brother he could devote himself to a life of frivolity. He should be more serious. During his stay he, Joseph, would endeavor to have more private conversations with Artois who should discuss his difficulties with the Emperor; then he could be given the benefit of Imperial advice. I could imagine Artois' reactions to this. He listened demurely enough; but I heard the laughter coming from his apartments and guessed how he was entertaining his friends.

Of Provence he was a little uncertain. He did not offer him advice but he did warn me of him. "There is something cold about him. As for that wife of his she is an intriguer. She's not a Piedmontese for nothing. She's coarse and ugly but don't dismiss her as of no importance on that score."

Naturally the aunts were very eager for his company. They had so much to tell him, Adelaide assured him; and Joseph never missed an opportunity for receiving information. However, he was rather startled when Adelaide invited him into a small room to show him some pictures and then fell upon him and embraced him passionately.

Joseph expressed his astonishment for while she caressed him in a loverlike way she assured him that it was perfectly all right. Such liberties must be allowed an old aunt.

Joseph, on telling me this, warned me to make sure he was never alone with any of the aunts again.

"They have always behaved a little oddly," I told him.

"Indeed it is so, but they count for nothing in this Court. It is the others of whom you must be watchful. Provence, cold as a snake and his intriguer of a wife. The other one is too frivolous and his company is not good for you. He is the only one who can beget children and when I have shown your husband how to overcome his infirmity and you become pregnant it would be as well not to have been too friendly with Artois. You are too much in his company. It could give rise to talk."

I assured my brother that I did not exactly *like* Artois; but he was the gayest member of the family and he and I enjoyed the same kind of pastimes. He could always amuse me and I so badly needed to be amused.

"Tut tut tut," said Joseph. "You will have to learn that there is more in life than amusement."

Joseph's pontifical manner was beginning to tire us all. I wished that he had been a little frivolous, that he would gamble and lose heavily, that he would show some interest in the lighter amusements of the Court. But that was quite foreign to his nature.

As the days passed he took to criticizing me in front of my women which I did not like. He would wander in when I was at my *toilette* and show disapproval of my elaborate gowns. When my rouge was being applied he looked on with cynical amusement. I might have retorted that it was as necessary to wear rouge as Court dress. Even Campan when she had first come to Court as the humble lectrice had been obliged to wear it.

He glanced at one of my attendants who was very highly rouged and said: "A little more. A little more. Put it on *furiously* like Madame here."

I was so annoyed about this that I determined to ask my brother to spare me his criticisms in front of people. When we were alone I did not mind what he said, but it was certainly undignified for the Queen of France to be reprimanded before her subjects as though she were a child. What could be more damaging to her prestige than that?

Smarting with indignity I sat before my mirror while Monsieur Léonard dressed my hair.

"Ah, Madame," he said, "we will have such a confection that the Emperor himself must admire it."

I smiled at Léonard in the mirror and as he proceeded to excel himself, Joseph with his usual lack of ceremony strolled in.

"Brother, do you like this style?" I asked.

"Yes," he answered in a bored tone.

"You do not sound very enthusiastic. You are thinking that it is unbecoming?"

"Do you wish me to speak frankly?"

"When, Joseph, did you not?"

"Very well. I think it is over fragile to carry a crown."

Monsieur Léonard looked as though my brother had been guilty of the greatest *lèse majesté* possible; my attendants and friends were shocked that my brother should speak to me thus in their presence, for on this occasion he was not so much criticizing my headdress as myself as the Queen of France.

When I remonstrated with him, he replied: "I am an outspoken man. I cannot prevaricate. I say what I mean."

I had deplored artifice, the artifice of French conversation, but a few weeks of Joseph's company made me long for it.

Mercy was made a little uneasy by the manner in which Joseph was behaving. I imagined that Kaunitz had tried to advise my brother how to deal with me, and my brother of course would accept advice from no one. Joseph had forgotten that seven years had passed since I left Austria; he saw me still as the silly little girl, his baby sister.

Joseph himself told me that Kaunitz had prepared a written document of the instructions he was to pass on to me. "But I have no need of documents," said my brother. "I am here to see you and talk to you. And I have a firsthand knowledge of the scene."

So he continued to advise us; and he did make some impression; he made me see how I was grieving my mother by my conduct; he impressed on me the folly of my ways. He had been among the people of Paris; he had seen hardship and poverty. What did I think these people would feel when they knew of my extravagances. He moved me to tears of repentance.

"I will be different, Joseph," I said. "Pray tell my mother that she must not worry. I will be more *sérieuse*. I promise."

And I meant it.

It was unfortunate that when he accompanied me to the apartments of the Princesse de Guéménée there should have been a scene. He had been reluctant to go but I had persuaded him. They were playing faro and the free manners between the sexes shocked my brother; their conversation sparkled but it was a little risqué and, most unfortunate of all, Madame de Guéménée was accused of cheating.

Joseph wished to leave.

"It's nothing but a gaming hell," he declared; and there followed a long lecture on the dangers of gambling. I must give up gambling. No good could come of it. I must choose my friends with greater care.

Everything we did seemed to be the excuse for a lecture, but we listened to Joseph and, like so many of his kind, much of what he said was right and true.

He was often closeted with my husband, for the purpose of his visit had been to strengthen Austro-French relations and, of course, that other matter.

I did not know what he said to my husband, but I have no doubt that he pointed out his duty, that he told him of the dangers of a Monarchy that could not produce heirs. Artois had a son; but Provence would come before him. There were jealousies and antagonisms when the succession was not from father to son.

Joseph himself had no son but he would not allow this fact to interfere with his lecture to the King on his duties. And Louis admitted to him that what he longed for more than anything was to have children.

His visit was of the utmost importance for he extracted from Louis the promise that he would not allow this unsatisfactory state of affairs to continue. Something must be done and Louis would see that it was.

He left at the end of May, having been with us since mid-April.

His parting words to me were that I was too frivolous and featherheaded for him to be able to make much headway with me in conversation; I so deplorably lacked the power of concentration. This was true, I was well aware. Therefore he had written his "instructions" and I was to study them carefully after his departure.

Oddly enough much as he had irritated me, now that he was going I was filled with sorrow. He was a part of my home and childhood; he had brought back so many memories. He had talked of our mother and brought her closer to me. I wept bitterly to part with him.

He embraced us warmly—both myself and the King. And when he had gone, Louis turned to me and said with the utmost tenderness: "During his visit we were together more often and for longer periods. Therefore I owe him a debt of gratitude."

It was a charming compliment; and there was a new purpose in my husband's eyes.

When I was alone I read Joseph's instructions. There were pages of them.

"You are grown up now and no longer can be excused on account of being a child. What will happen to you if you hesitate? Has it ever occurred to you to ask yourself? An unhappy woman is an unhappy Queen. Do you look for opportunities? Do you sincerely respond to the affection the King shows to you? Are you cool or *distrait* when he caresses you? Do you appear bored or disgusted? If this is so, can it be expected that a man of cold temperament could make advances and love you with passion?"

I thought about this seriously. Was it true? Joseph for all his pomposity was a shrewd observer. Had I betrayed my feelings? For often I did experience these emotions when the King approached me.

Joseph went on to criticize me in the light of his observations.

"Do you ever give way to his wishes and suppress your own? Do you try to convince him that you love him? Do you make any sacrifices for his sake?"

There were pages about my conduct toward my husband of which he was highly critical. He blamed me for the state of affairs, yet while implying that I was not responsible for my husband's infirmity, he hinted that it might have been overcome by sympathy and understanding on my part.

My relationships with certain people at Court were a scandal. I had a genius for attaching the *wrong* kind of people to myself.

> "Have you ever troubled to think of the effect which your friend-ships and intimacies may have upon the public? . . . Bear in mind that the King never plays games of chance and therefore it is scandalous for you to give such bad customs *your* patronage . . . Then think of the contretemps you have had at the opera balls. I suggest that of all your amusements this is the most dan-gerous and unseemly, especially as your escort on these occasions, as you tell me, is your brother-in-law who counts for nothing. What use then is there in going incognito and pretending you are someone else . . ."

I smiled. What use, brother Joseph, in your disguises? I could hear his voice, a little pained at the frivolity of the question. My disguise is to prevent people knowing who their benefactor is; yours to seek wild and dangerous pleasure.

"Do you honestly believe you are not recognized?"

Not always, dear Brother—no more than you do!

> "Everyone knows who you are and when you are masked people make comments which should not be made in your presence and say things which are not suitable for you to hear . . . Why do you wish to rub shoulders with a crowd of libertines? You do not go there simply to dance. Why this unseemliness . . . The King is left alone at night at Versailles while you mix with the *canaille* of Paris."

Had I forgotten my mother's advice? Had she not, ever since I left Vienna, been imploring me to improve my mind? I should take up read-ing . . . *serious* reading of course. I should read for two hours a day at the very least.

Then he said a strange thing, used a strange word which I was to remember later:

> "In truth, I tremble for your happiness because I believe that in the long run things cannot continue as they are now . . . The *revolution* will be a cruel one and perhaps of your own making."

He did not underline that terrible word. I do it now.

It did occur to me then that that was an odd expression, but now

I can see the paper clearly and the word seems to jump out of the page
. . . written in red, the color of blood.

I did try to improve my ways after Joseph had left. I knew he was right;
I should not gamble; I should try to be more serious. I even tried reading.

I wrote to my mother that I was following my brother's good counsels.
"I bear them written on my heart," I said extravagantly. I did not go to the
theater very often; I went even less to the opera balls; and I tried to like
hunting; in any case I went with my husband on several occasions; I was
always careful to be gracious to the centenarians and the bundles.

I was really trying very hard.

So was Louis.

He kept his promise to Joseph and the little operation was performed.
It was a success.

We were delighted. I wrote to my mother:

> "I have attained the happiness which is of the greatest impor-
> tance in my entire life . . . My marriage was thoroughly consum-
> mated. Yesterday the attempt was repeated and was even more
> successful than the first time. I thought at first of sending a
> special messenger to my beloved mother, but I was afraid this
> might arouse too much gossip . . . I don't think I am with child
> yet, but I have hopes of becoming so at any moment."

The change in my husband was great. He was delighted; he behaved like
a lover; he wished to be with me all the time; nor was I eager to avoid him.
I kept saying to myself: Soon my dream will come true. I have now as
much chance as any other woman of becoming a mother.

Louis said he must write to my brother to whom we owed all this.

> "I hope that next year will not go by, without my giving you a
> nephew or niece . . . It is to you we owe this happiness."

The news was going all round the courts. The aunts insisted that they
hear all about it. Adelaide was in a mood of great excitement and she
explained everything in detail to her sisters.

Louis had mentioned to Aunt Adelaide in a rush of confidence: "I
find the pleasure very great and I regret that so long a time had passed
without my being able to enjoy it."

The King was excessively cheerful; the Court looked on with interest
and made bets as to when there would be proof of the newly acquired
royal virility. Provence and his wife tried to hide their annoyance but I
was aware of it. Artois mischievously tried to provoke Provence while he

made jesting references behind our backs to the King's newly acquired prowess.

Our lives were certainly at the mercy of those about us. There was no privacy. It was noted that I looked tired in the mornings, which provoked titters and furtive observation. Everyone was watchful.

I did not care.

I was longing for the day when I could announce that I was about to become a mother.

13

"Madame, my dear mother, my first impulse, which I regret not having followed some weeks ago was to write to you of my hopes. I stopped myself when I thought of the sadness it would cause you if my hopes proved false . . ."

Marie Antoinette to Maria Theresa

". . . the torrents of inquisitive people who poured into the chamber were so great and tumultuous that the rush was near destroying the Queen. During the night the King had taken the precaution to have the enormous tapestry screens which surrounded her Majesty's bed, secured with cord. Had it not been for this foresight they would most certainly have been thrown upon her."

"The windows were caulked up; the King opened them with a strength which his affection for the Queen gave him at that moment."

Madame Campan's Memoirs

"We must have a Dauphin. We need a Dauphin and an heir to the throne."

Maria Theresa to Marie Antoinette

THE ARRIVAL OF MADAME ROYALE

Each day I thought of my new hopes. I longed for a sign that I was pregnant. I tried hard to follow Joseph's instructions and considered what would please my husband. He was equally attentive. At least we both desired the same thing. I dreamed about my own little Dauphin. When I had him I would ask nothing more of life. My desire for a child was a burning intensity.

That August I gave a *fête* at Trianon, setting up a fair in the gardens with stalls; I allowed the shopkeepers of Paris to bring their stalls in the gardens and I myself took on the role of *limonadière* and was dressed as a waitress in the most delightful muslin and lace specially created for me by my ever-accommodating Rose Bertin. Everyone declared that they had never seen such a *limonadière* and they hurried to be served by me. I and my ladies felt it was the greatest fun in the world to serve lemonade. The King was constantly at my side and everyone noticed how tenderly we behaved toward each other.

All through that year I hoped and dreamed and nothing happened. I began to wander whether it ever would. I would have little Armand brought to me each morning; he delighted me for he had grown very affectionate and his great blue eyes would look so mournful when I had to leave him; but he always made me long more than ever for a child of my own.

Perhaps, I thought gloomily as the year came to its close, even though our marriage has been consummated it may not be fruitful.

I was in despair. I sought the old pleasures to console myself. Artois was always at my side determined to bring me out of my solemn mood, he told me, and make me enjoy life again. Let us disguise ourselves; let us go to the opera ball.

It was carnival time and I longed to go to the ball but when my husband asked me if I were going I said No, because I believed he would prefer I did not. He hastily replied that he would not dream of keeping me from my pleasure and that I should go to the ball as long as I was accompanied by the Comte de Provence. So I started dancing again. I began visiting the Princesse de Guéménée's apartment and playing heavily. Joseph's warnings were forgotten and I was back with the old bad habits.

We played games and tricks together and on each other. Artois was always playing practical jokes and I and the Prince de Ligne decided to play one on him. We often had music in the Orangery and very high up in a niche on the wall, there was a bust of Louis XIV. When the concert was over and we were leaving the Orangery, Artois always bowed low to this statue and cried: "*Bonsoir, Gran'père*." I thought it would give him a shock if the statue answered so I arranged that we should get a ladder and the Prince de Ligne should climb up to the statue; we would then remove the ladder and the Prince would answer Artois in deep serious tones.

We were convulsed with laughter thinking how alarmed Artois would be believing that he had called the shade of his great and formidable ancestor from his grave by his frivolous raillery.

However the Prince refused at the last moment because he had been told by one of his friends that someone had decided to carry the joke a bit further by refusing to bring the ladder back by which he would descend, so that he would not be able to get down.

The Prince had no great desire to spend the night high up in the Orangery with the bust of Louis XIV and the joke fell through. But that was the sort of life we were leading.

And when I was in the depth of my despair believing I should never have a child, to my great joy I guessed I might be pregnant. I was so excited I could scarcely go about my normal affairs. I was terrified that I might be wrong; and I was determined I was not going to say anything until I was sure. Everyone watched me expectantly at first, now they ceased to do so; and I was glad of it.

I did not want to do anything but dream about the child. I pretended to be ill—one of my "nervous affectations"—so that I could be alone to think.

"Monsieur le Dauphin," I said to myself a hundred times a day.

I studied my body but there was no difference as yet. I was very careful getting in and out of my bath lest I should slip. My bath was shaped like a sabot and for the sake of modesty I wore a long flannel gown buttoned to the neck when I sat in it; and when I came out I always made one of the two bathing women in attendance hold a cloth in front of me so that my attendants should not see me. Now I felt this to be doubly necessary. Not that my body had changed one little bit.

The weeks passed and I clung to my secret and at last I felt convinced. I was certain I had felt the child move within me.

My husband should be told first. I was so excited that I did not know how to break the news. I knew he would be overcome with emotion too. Did he not desire this as much as I did?

I went to his apartments. I was half-laughing, half-crying.

He rose when he saw me and came toward me in consternation.

Laughing I cried: "Sire, I have come to lodge a complaint against one of your subjects."

He was startled. "What has happened?"

"He has kicked me."

"Kicked you!" Indignation and horror.

I burst out laughing. "In the womb," I answered. "He is young yet so I hope Your Majesty will not be too severe . . ."

He looked at me, wonder dawning on his face. The child had not kicked; he was too young yet; but perhaps I imagined that I could feel him moving; I wanted him so much.

"Can it be?" whispered my husband.

I nodded; then he embraced me; and we remained clinging to each other for some minutes.

We were so happy; yet we both wept.

I wrote to my mother:

> "Madame, my dear mother, my first impulse, which I regret not having followed some weeks ago was to write to you of my hopes. I stopped myself when I thought of the sadness it would cause you if my hopes proved false . . ."

I no longer wanted to dance. It would be bad for the child. I wanted to sit and dream.

I wrote again to my mother:

> "There are still moments when I think it is only a dream, but this dream goes on and I think I need no longer doubt . . ."

Had I ever been so happy? I did not think so. A child . . . all of my own!

I was a little absentminded when Armand came to sit on my bed. I did not see him. I saw another child. My own . . . my baby Dauphin.

I was writing to my mother frequently of all my hopes, how I was going to care for my Dauphin, what I was preparing for him. I was taking care of myself. I took quiet walks in the gardens of Versailles and Trianon; I liked to sit and talk in the *petits appartements*, listening to gentle music and doing a little needlework. I was planning my baby's clothes. I wanted to do so much for him myself. I could not wait for him to be born.

I wrote to my mother:

> "The manner in which they are brought up now is much less constricting. Babies should not be swaddled. They should be in a light cradle or carried in one's arms. I learn that they should be out of doors as soon as possible so that they can grow accustomed to fresh air by degrees and they end by being in it almost the whole of the day. I believe it to be good and healthy for them. I have arranged for my baby to be lodged downstairs, and there shall be a little railing separating him from the rest of the terrace. This will teach him to walk early . . ."

How I longed to have him with me. I was impatient of the waiting.

The discomforts of pregnancy did not worry me in the least. I welcomed them. I was never tired of talking of babies and I gathered about me those people who had had them so that they could talk of their experiences.

But how long the waiting seemed! I began to grow so weary of it; sometimes I was almost sick with longing for my child.

My baby was due in December and the summer seemed endless; and then a strange event occurred which for a short while made me less aware even of my coming baby.

It was August and I was in the crowded *salon* with my husband and brothers- and sisters-in-law, and I was beginning to feel a little tired. I knew I only had to catch Louis' eye and he would dismiss the assembly. He was always so solicitous of my health and terrified, as I was, that the baby might be jeopardized.

Then it happened. He was some little distance from us and neither my husband nor his brothers knew him. But I did. I took one look at that unusual and most handsome face, at the contrast of fair hair and dark eyes, and I was transported back to an opera ball where as Dauphine I had danced disguised . . . until I had revealed myself.

"Ah," I cried impulsively. "Here is an old acquaintance!"

"Madame." He was standing before me, bowing low over my hand. I felt his lips against my fingers and I was happy.

"Comte de Fersen," I said thoughtlessly.

He was delighted that I should remember him. Others watching me—were they not always watching me?—were surprised and naturally would not let the matter pass.

He had changed a little since we had last met; but then so had I. We had both become more mature. I asked him to tell me what had happened to him after the opera ball.

He had been to England, he said, and after that to Northern France and Holland before returning to the Château of Löfstad which was his home in Sweden.

"And you were happy to be home."

He smiled; he had the most charming smile I had ever seen. "The Court of Sweden seemed a little dull after that of France."

I was pleased, loving compliments.

"But it is your home," I reminded him.

"I had been so long away . . . Brussels . . . Berlin, Rome, London, Paris . . . in particular Paris."

"I am pleased that our capital pleased *you*."

He looked steadily at me and said: "There is something here that . . . enchants me."

I was excited. I knew what he meant.

"You have a family though . . . a large family?"

"A younger brother and three sisters, but they were always away from home. They all held posts at Court."

"Naturally. But I know what it means to live in a large family and leave it . . ."

I dare not talk to him much longer for we were being noticed. He was courtier enough to realize this.

I said conspiratorially: "We will talk together again."

Being thus dismissed he bowed and I turned to my sister-in-law who was standing beside me. Marie Josèphe would be beside me at such a time. I was sure she had listened to every word.

What strange days they were. I don't think I had ever been so happy in the whole of my life. I would wake in the night and put my hands on my body to feel the child; and I would picture my little boy lying in my arms or I would be teaching him to walk and say *Maman*.

Then I would think of Comte Axel de Fersen, with his strangely beautiful face and his ardent eyes. Of course I was happy. I had never carried a child before; I had never before known a man with whom I felt so completely at peace. I had strange thoughts—perhaps women do during pregnancy. I wished that I lived in a little house with a husband like Axel de Fersen and babies . . . lots of them. I believed that if I could do that I should ask for nothing else. What were gambling, dancing, practical jokes, glorious silks and brocades, fantastic headdresses, diamonds . . . a crown . . . what would all these things amount to when compared with that simple life of complete contentment.

I can be honest with myself now and say that if I could have had that I should have been happy. I see myself now as an ordinary woman, not clever, unsubtle, sentimental, a woman who was meant most of all to be a mother.

But I had been miscast in the role of Queen.

It was a pleasure to discover more and more of Axel de Fersen. His love of music delighted me. I sent him invitations to concerts; sometimes I would invite him with a few intimate friends. I would play the harpsichord to them and sometimes sing. I had not a very good voice but it was pleasant enough and everyone applauded me naturally whenever I sang. But the singing was for him though we could never be alone together since we were watched at every turn. I remember my brother Joseph's warning about my sister-in-law, Marie Josèphe. She was not a Piedmontese for nothing, he had said; and she was certainly constantly setting people to spy on me. She was a jealous woman. Provence could not get children; and his one hope and hers had been that I should die childless and leave the way to the throne clear for them. Now I was with child; there might be many more children once we had proved we could have them. And they were naturally disconsolate.

But although Axel and I were not alone together we did enjoy many conversations. He made me see his affectionate mother; his father for whom he had a deep respect and who, he admitted, was a little parsimonious and wondered when his son was going to give up wandering about Europe and settle down to a career. He even told me of Mademoiselle Leyel, a Swedish girl who lived in London and to whom he had been sent to pay court.

"Her vast fortune greatly appealed to my family," he said gravely.

"And to you?" I asked.

"I am not averse to a large fortune."

"And she is beautiful?"

"She is reckoned so."

"I am interested in your adventure in London. Tell me more."

"I was a guest in her parents' luxurious mansion."

"That must have been most pleasant."

"No," he said. "No."

"But why not?"

"Because I was an unenthusiastic wooer."

"You surprise me."

"Surely not. I was pursued by a dream. Something happened to me once . . . years before . . . in Paris. In the Opera House there."

I was afraid to speak to him for I was very much aware of my two sisters-in-law silently watching.

"Ah! And did you not ask for her hand?"

"I asked her. It was my father's wish and mine to please him."

"So you are to marry this rich and handsome woman?"

"By no means. She refused me."

"Refused you?"

"Your Majesty sounds incredulous. She was wise. She sensed my inadequacies."

I laughed lightheartedly. "We should not have cared for you to go to London . . . so soon. You have only just arrived in Paris."

And so the days passed. Great events were happening to us but I paid no heed to that. It was only later that I gave them a thought. Throughout the Court the conflict between England and her colonists in America was being talked of—and with great glee because it delighted all Frenchmen to see their old enemies the English in trouble. Although in Paris English habits were followed slavishly there was an inherent hatred for our neighbors on the other side of the Channel.

Frenchmen could not forget the defeats and humiliations of the Seven Years' War and all they had lost through that to the English; and ever since 1775, at the beginning of our reign, we had been applauding the Americans; in fact there were many Frenchmen who believed that France should declare war on England. Some time before, I remember my husband's telling me that if we declared war on England it was very likely that this might bring a reconciliation between England and her colonies; after all, they were all English and they might well stick together if a foreign power attacked. Louis never wanted war. "If I went to war," he said, "I could not do my people all the good I wished."

Nevertheless when America declared Independence on July 4th, 1776, we were delighted and wished the settlers well. I remember three American deputies coming to France at that time: Benjamin Franklin, Silas Deane, and Arthur Lee. How solemn they were! How somber with their suits of cloth and their unpowdered hair. They stood out oddly among our exquisite dandies, but they were received everywhere and were quite the fashion and when the Marquis de La Fayette left for America to support the colonists many Frenchmen followed him. They were pressing the King to declare war but Louis continued to stand out against it although we sent help secretly to America in the form of arms, ammunition, and even money. At this time however the battle between our *Belle Poule* and the British *Arethusa* occurred and Louis was reluctantly obliged to declare war against England—at least at sea.

I had listened to what Axel had told me about the American fight for independence; he was a fervent supporter of freedom; and I repeated his arguments to my husband. It was one of those rare occasions when I interested myself in state affairs.

Louis was anxious to please me at this time, and I do believe my voice, added to that of others, was to some extent instrumental in bringing him to the decision to declare war at sea.

I was wildly enthusiastic for the Americans against the English; but when someone asked my brother Joseph for his opinion, he answered: "I am a Royalist by profession." Mercy repeated this remark to me. It was a warning, reminding me that I was giving wholehearted support to those who were rebeling against Monarchy. The rights or wrongs of the dispute were neither here nor there. Kings and Queens who believed it was right and proper for subjects to rebel against them in any circumstances—were they taking a risk? It seemed my brother Joseph thought so; and he was more experienced than I.

The weather during that summer was very hot and I began to feel my pregnancy. Unable to take much exercise I liked to sit on the terrace in the cool of evening often by the light of the moon or in starlight. We had had the terrace illuminated with fairy lights and an orchestra played every night in the Orangery. The public were allowed to walk about freely in the gardens and they made full use of this—particularly during the warm summer evenings.

I and my sisters-in-law would sit on the terrace together and for these occasions we always wore simple white gowns perhaps of muslin and cambric and big straw hats with light veils over them to shield our faces. Thus we were often unrecognized; and now and then people would sit beside us and talk to us without knowing who we were.

This of course resulted now and then in unpleasant incidents. A young man came and sat beside me once in the gloom and made advances. I had spoken to him without realizing his intentions and had to get up and walk abruptly away for he had made it clear that he knew he was speaking to the Queen.

Such incidents were extremely unpleasant particularly as my sisters-in-law were nearby and would probably report perhaps to the aunts, who now criticized everything I did and made much of every little happening, or to the Sardinian Ambassador who would be pleased to embellish the story and spread it abroad. It was sure to be said that I encouraged amorous strangers. They were making up the most scandalous stories about me now; in fact it seemed to be a favorite pastime.

I decided as the autumn came that I would retire more and more from the public. I had every reason for doing so. So I kept to my own apartments surrounded only by my most intimate friends like my dearest Madame de Polignac, the Princesse de Lamballe, and the Princesse Elisabeth who as she grew older was becoming more and more close to me.

Axel de Fersen was frequently at my gatherings; we sang, played music, and talked. They were very pleasant days. As for my husband he was in a state of constant anxiety and I would laugh at him, for ten times a day he would come to my apartments to ask anxiously how I was feeling; and when he was not asking me he was summoning the doctors and *accoucheurs* demanding to know that everything was as it should be.

The ordeal of birth! It stays with me now. For any woman giving birth to her first child is a frightening though, I admit, exalting experience. But with a Queen it is all that and a public spectacle at the same time. I might be giving birth to the heir of France and therefore all France had a right to see me do it.

The town of Versailles was full of sightseers. It had been impossible to get a room anywhere since the first week of December. Prices shot up. Well, what could one expect? They were all determined to see me give birth to my child.

It was a cold December day—the 18th, I remember well—when my pains started. Immediately all the bells of the town started to ring to let everyone know that I was in labor. The Princesse de Lamballe and my ladies-in-waiting hurried to my bedchamber; my husband came in some consternation. Our marriage had been such a topic of conversation for so many years that he feared there would be even greater interest than there usually was over a royal birth. He himself fastened the great tapestry screens about my bed with cords. "So," he said, "that they should not be easily overthrown." How right he was to take this action! When he had done this he despatched guardsmen to Paris and Saint-Cloud to summon all the Princes of the Blood Royal who, tradition demanded, should be present at the birth.

No sooner had the Princes arrived than the spectators stormed the château and many of them forced their way into the bedchamber. An effort, I gather, was made to prevent too many entering the room but there were at least fifty people all determined to see a Queen in labor.

My pains were growing more and more frequent. I tried to console myself; this was the moment for which I had longed all my life; this was becoming a mother.

I had arranged with the Princesse de Lamballe that she should let me know, without speaking, the sex of my child, and I was aware of her close to my bed during the agonizing hours that followed. The heat was tremendous for the windows had been caulked up to keep out the cold night air; but we had not bargained for such a crowded lying-in chamber. Packed close together so that there was no room for anyone to pass between them, some standing on benches to get a better view, leaning heavily against the tapestry screens so that, but for my husband's foresight in using those thick cords, they would have collapsed onto the bed, the spectators whispered together. I felt I could not breathe; I was grappling not only with the ordeal of birth but with the fight for breath. The smell of vinegar and essences mingled with that of sweating bodies and the heat was unbearable.

All through the night I fought to give birth to my child . . . and for my life; and at half-past eleven on the morning of December 19th my child was born.

I lay back exhausted; but I must know whether the child was a boy. I looked at the Princesse; she was near the bed; she shook her head, in the arranged signal.

A girl! I felt a sick disappointment . . . and then . . . I was fighting for my breath.

I was aware of faces about me . . . a sea of faces . . . those of the Princesse de Lamballe, the *accoucheur*, the King.

Someone shouted: "My God, give her air. For God's sake move away . . . and give her air."

Then I fell into unconsciousness.

I heard from Madame Campan afterward what happened. None of the women could force their way through the crowds to bring the hot water. Air was absolutely necessary for all the doctors agreed I was on the point of death by suffocation.

"Clear the room," shouted the *accoucheur*. But the people refused to move. They had come to see the show and it was not yet over.

"Open the windows! For God's sake open the windows."

But the windows had been pasted all round with strips of paper and it would take hours to remove it that they might be opened.

There were moments in my husband's life when he was indeed a King among men and this was one of them. He pushed his way through the crowd and with a strength which no one would have thought possible in one man, he wrenched open the windows and the cold fresh air rushed into the room.

The *accoucheur* told the surgeon that I must be bled immediately without hot water since it was unobtainable and an incision was immediately made in my foot. Madame Campan told me afterward that as the blood streamed forth I opened my eyes and they all knew that my life had been saved.

Poor Lamballe fainted—as might have been expected—and had to be carried out; the King ordered that the room be cleared of all spectators but even then some of them refused to go and the *valets de chambres* and the pages had to drag them out by their collars.

But I was alive; I had given birth to a child—albeit a daughter.

When I was conscious of what was going on I was aware of the bandage about my foot, and I asked why it was there.

The King came to my bedside and told me what had happened. Everyone seemed to be weeping and embracing each other.

"They are rejoicing," he told me, "because you have recovered. We feared . . ."

But he could not go on. After a pause he said: "It shall never happen again. I swear it."

"The child . . ." I said.

And the King nodded. The child was brought to me and laid in my arms; and from the moment I saw her, I loved her and I would not have had her different in any way.

My happiness was complete.

"Poor little one," I said, "you may not be what we wished for, but you are not on that account less dear to me. A son would have been rather the property of the State; you shall be mine. You shall have my undivided care, shall share all my happiness and console me in my troubles."

I named her after my mother. She was called Marie Thérèse Charlotte; but she was known from the beginning throughout the Court as Madame Royale.

Couriers were despatched. My husband himself wrote at once to Vienna; and throughout Paris there was general rejoicing, with processions and bonfires; the sky was so bright that all through the night it was like day; and the sounds of fireworks and gun salutes filled the palace.

Everything was going as it should after that first ordeal when I had been unable to breathe in that overpopulated room. The people crowded round the palace to demand how I was and bulletins were issued daily. I was tremendously happy. I had my baby and the people were so interested in my welfare that they demanded constant news of my health. The King was in ecstasies. He was so delighted to be a father; he kept coming into the nursery to see his daughter and marvel at her. "What a darling she is!" he kept murmuring under his breath. "Look at these fingers . . . She even has nails, ten of them, and they are perfect . . . *perfect.*"

I laughed at him but I felt exactly the same. I too wanted to look at her all the time, to marvel at her; my own daughter, my very own!

We were young. We would have many children yet. The next would be a Dauphin. I was certain of it.

Meanwhile the birth of Madame Royale must be celebrated.

A strange incident occurred a few days after the birth of my baby.

The Curé of the Madeleine de la Cité called at the palace and asked to see Monsieur Campan. When alone with Monsieur Campan the Curé produced a box which he said had been given to him in the confessional, so he could not reveal the name of the person who had given it to him. Inside the box was a ring, which, so the confession ran, had been stolen from me that it might be used in sorcery to prevent my having children.

Monsieur Campan brought the ring to me which I recognized as one I had lost seven years ago.

"We should try to discover who has done this," said Monsieur Campan.

"Oh, let it be. I have the ring and the sorceries were not successful. I do not fear them."

"Madame, would you not wish to know one who was such an enemy?"

I shook my head. "I would prefer not to know those who hate me so much."

I could see that Monsieur Campan did not agree with this and thought we should have made some endeavor to discover our enemies but my dislike of trouble prevailed and I gave orders that the matter should be forgotten.

Perhaps once again I was wrong. Perhaps had I pursued the inquiries Monsieur Campan thought I should make, I might have discovered some enemies who were living very close to me.

I quickly forgot all about the ring; there were so many other more amusing things to occupy me. The King and I were to go to Paris for my churching. On this day one hundred poor girls were married and I gave them all a dowry. When I arrived at the church they were all assembled there with their hair most unnaturally curled and they were married in Notre Dame. We arrived in the King's carriage with the trumpeters going on ahead to announce us and twenty-four footmen resplendent in the royal livery and six pages on horseback. The Prévôt came to the door of the carriage and made a speech to which the King replied.

The procession passed through Paris. On a balcony in the Rue St. Honoré, Rose Bertin had lined up her assistants and stood at the head of them. They all dropped fine curtseys as we passed. From Notre Dame we went to Sainte Geneviève's and on to La Place Louis XV; and although many people came out to watch us there were hardly any cheers.

I was bewildered. What did they want! They had had their fireworks, buffets of cold meat and wine; certain prisoners had been liberated; the brides had had their dowries. I had given the first of the Enfants de France. What was wrong with them? Why this cold reception? Why these sullen looks?

When we returned to the château I summoned Mercy and told him of our reception.

He nodded gravely. Of course he had heard of it already.

"It is incredible," I said. "What do they want?"

He answered: "They have heard much of your extravagances. There have been many scandalous stories. Hardly a day passes when a new song and a rhyme about you is not being circulated. Your *légèreté*, your *dissipation*, are the cause of this. This is a time of war, but you think only of amusing yourself. That is why the people are against you."

I was hurt and a little frightened. It had been alarming to ride through those crowded silent streets.

"I will be different," I said firmly. "I will give up these too conspicuous amusements. I am a mother now . . ."

I meant it. I wanted to.

My mother wrote from Vienna, she was delighted that I had come safely through childbirth and that my daughter was healthy.

"But we must have a Dauphin," she wrote. "We need a Dauphin and heir to the throne."

14

"I must confess to Your Majesty that the Comte de Fersen has been so well received by the Queen that it has given umbrage to several persons. I must admit that I cannot help believing that she has an inclination for him; I have seen indications too obvious to leave me in doubt in the matter. The conduct of the young Comte de Fersen has, on this occasion, been admirable in its modesty and reserve and above all in the decision he has taken of going to America."

From a letter written by the Swedish Ambassador at Versailles to King Gustavus III of Sweden

"My dear mother can feel reassured with regard to my conduct. I feel too much the necessity of having children to neglect anything on that score . . . Besides, I owe it to the King for his tenderness to me and his confidence on which I congratulate myself."

Marie Antoinette to Maria Theresa

"Up to now I have been discreet but I shall grow importunate. It would be a crime if there were no more royal children. I am growing impatient and at my age I have not much time left to me."

Maria Theresa to Marie Antoinette

TRAGIC NEWS FROM VIENNA

I was indeed, as my brother Joseph had said, a featherhead. The incident of the ring should have warned me that I had enemies close to me who felt it important that I should remain unfertile. I should have been warned by the sullen looks of the people. There was a war in progress and wars mean increased taxation and hard living for the people; and when they hear stories of a Queen's extravagance, and actually see evidence of it with their own eyes, they become resentful. No, that is too mild a word. They become murderous with hate. I was blamed for their poverty, I, the silly little Queen, who thought of nothing but dancing and buying fine clothes and jewels. The King had given hundreds of examples of his care for the poor; he even dressed more soberly than most of the Court gallants. But he was under my spell; he gave way to me as a doting husband will to a pretty wife. My absorption with amusements and indifference to their needs were responsible for the high price of bread; and I was a foreigner.

They began to call me the Austrian Woman. What right had I—a foreigner and an Austrian at that—to come to France and presume to rule the French!

A spate of lampoons showered over Paris. Every careless little act of mine was turned into an example of extravagance, indifference to the people and, chiefly, obscenity. I only had to address a word to a man and he was my lover; I only had to smile at a woman and my relations with her were unnatural.

I knew all this. I could not help knowing it. But I shrugged it aside, as I had been shrugging aside warnings all my life.

I seemed to have a genius for making enemies and selecting friends who could only add to my troubles. I made excuses for myself by saying that I was just an ordinary woman thrust into an extraordinary role which I had not the ability to play; but perhaps I should say I lacked the concentration to play because had I been serious, had I listened to the warnings of my true friends—the King, my mother, Mercy and Vermond, and in her small way my dear Campan—I might have turned my course even at this time. Yes, I am sure there was time then. I was on the downhill path; I had started to trip blithely down but I had not yet begun that headlong rush from which it was impossible to stop myself.

Perhaps if my husband had been different . . . But I should not blame him. His education had been neglected; he had never been taught anything of the intricacies of statecraft. I remember often how when he first knew he was King he had cried: "They have taught me nothing!" And his grandfather, Louis XV, seeing that his own end could not be far off had remarked, "I can see the working of this state machine, but I do not see what will become of it when I am gone and how Berry will extricate himself." My poor husband, so kind and yet so ineffectual except in those rare moments when he threw aside his doubts of himself as he could do.

But at this time I saw none of this. Scurrilous verses. Lies. Scandals.

There had always been plenty of them. It did not occur to me to wonder who it was who was circulating them. It did not occur to me that it might be my own brothers-in-law, my sisters-in-law, Condé, Conti, Orléans, those Princes whom I had offended.

The wild dance toward destruction had begun but I was unaware of it. There was so much to make me happy. There was my darling little daughter. There was Axel de Fersen, haunting me like a shadow, always at my side, or even if he were not close to me I was aware of his glances across the room; there was the King, forever grateful because I had given proof of his virility, always kind and tender but never so much as now; there was the adored Trianon which was gradually changing its character and losing all sign of the house in which Louis XV had entertained his mistresses. It was *my* house. I was changing the gardens. I was having the library painted white and had had great fun choosing my apple-green taffeta curtains. The bookshelves were lined with plays for I intended to give plays at Trianon. I had such plans. I was building a theater there and I was already planning whom I should invite to join my little troupe of players. I never thought of the cost of this. I never thought of money at all. I would demand that the work be finished in record time. "No cost should be spared, Madame?" "No. Finish it, that's all." In a year my embellishments to the Petit Trianon had cost over three hundred and fifty thousand livres. And the country was at war; and the people of Paris were complaining of the price of bread! Perhaps I had indeed started that mad downhill rush.

But I was happy. Two months after the birth of my baby I felt a great urge to go to the opera ball. It was Shrove Sunday and I told Louis that I longed to dance there. In his uxorious mood he said he would come with me.

"And you will go masked?" I asked.

He said he would and we went together; no one recognized us and we mingled freely among the dancers, though always together. But I could see that he was bored.

"Please, Louis," I said, "let us go to the next ball which is on Shrove Tuesday. It has been such fun tonight."

Weakly, as he so often did, he agreed; but on the Monday he pleaded an excess of state business. I was so disappointed that he immediately said I should go with one of my ladies but I should take care not to be recognized. I chose the Princesse d'Hénin, an inoffensive woman, and arranged that we should drive to the house of the Duc de Coigny in Paris where we should change into an ordinary carriage which he would have waiting for us. Everything had been arranged at such short notice that the carriage, which must necessarily have no distinguishing marks on it, was old and unfit for service. It was, the Duc told us, the only one he could acquire at short notice without disclosing for whom it was intended. Consequently the thing broke down before we reached the opera. Our footman said that he would call a fiacre and the Princesse and I had to go into a shop while he did so. This was amusing to me because I had never before ridden in a public vehicle and I could not resist boasting of it to my friends. How foolish I was! It was the ideal basis on which to build a scandalous story. The Queen traveled about Paris in a fiacre. She called at the house of the Duc de Coigny! For what purpose? Could there be any doubt? This was known as L'aventure du fiacre, and there were various versions of it.

And all the time I was growing more and more dependent for my happiness on the presence of Axel de Fersen. People were beginning to notice how happy I was in his company. I loved to hear about his sisters Fabian, Sophie, and Hedda; I loved to hear about his home in Sweden and his travels in various countries. I was less reticent than he was; he understood how we were watched. He was careful of my reputation; he knew that I was surrounded by spies and enemies; he did not tell me this for we preserved the fable that there was nothing unusual in our relationship. He was merely a visiting foreigner at my Court and I was therefore naturally a little more hospitable to him than I would be to a Frenchman.

It was an idealistic relationship. We both knew that it could be no more; but as such it was very precious to us. He could not become my lover. My duty was to bear the Enfants de France and they could have no father but the King. But we allowed ourselves to dream wild dreams, beautiful dreams; it was like the love of a troubador for a lady whom he can only adore from afar.

It suited my mood, and I did not look beyond the present. I invited him to my card parties and when I learned that he had come to one on one of the evenings when I had decided not to attend I wrote to him and told him how sorry I was. I had heard that he was a Captain of his King's Light Dragoons and I expressed the desire to see him in his uniform.

The very next time he appeared before me he was wearing it. I shall never forget the sight of him in that romantic costume . . . blue doublet over a white tunic, with tightly fitting chamois breeches, his cylindrical military cap decorated with two feathers, one blue and one yellow.

Several people noticed how overcome I was by emotion at the sight he presented; and I could not take my eyes from him. With his pale skin, his fair hair and those glowing dark eyes he seemed godlike.

I thought: I have never experienced this emotion before for any other person.

After that my friendship for him was discussed freely and he was named as one of my lovers.

The spell was broken, and shortly afterward he said: "I can bring you only harm by remaining."

A cold fear struck me and I replied quickly that I was accustomed to calumnies. A few more could do me no harm.

"I would challenge to a duel any who spoke one word against you in my presence."

The hero of romance! He was perfect in every way. He meant it. He would willingly die for my sake and I knew it. He would even go away for my sake.

Gabrielle de Polignac sought to comfort me.

"How unlucky I am to be treated so," I said. I laughed. "But if it is malicious of people to suppose I have lovers, it is certainly odd of me to have so many attributed to me and to do without them all."

Gabrielle certainly thought it was odd of me. It was something hardly any woman in our set did without. Of course I was foolish to surround myself with these people. No wonder I was suspected of behaving as they did. Even Gabrielle was Vaudreuil's mistress. And all these women's lovers were said to be mine as well because I met them frequently in the apartments of my friends. I should have been content with the companionship of the Princesse de Lamballe and my dear little sister-in-law Elisabeth.

Then Axel who had always felt very strongly about the cause of American Independence made up his mind that he would go to America and help to further it.

I was heartbroken, but must keep up a pretense of mere regret at saying goodbye to someone I respected and liked to chat to. Not that I deceived anyone.

"What!" cried one Duchesse when she heard he was going. "Are you deserting your conquest?"

I pretended not to hear this and I went on smiling blankly at Artois who was watching me maliciously.

"If I had made one," Axel answered, "I should not abandon it. I go without leaving anyone behind to regret my going."

He would lie for me, because he knew of my feelings. It was the only thing to do. He dared not stay.

So he left. Well, I would devote myself to my child.

Rumors of my behavior had of course reached my mother, though not of Axel specifically.

I wrote to her:

> "My dear mother can feel reassured with regard to my conduct. I feel too much the necessity of having children to neglect anything on that score. If in the past I was in the wrong it was due to my youth and irresponsibility, but now you can be sure I realize my duty. Besides I owe it to the King for his tenderness to me and his confidence on which I congratulate myself . . ."

I meant that. I was deeply grateful to my husband for his goodness to me. It was not only fear of having another man's child which had made me agree that Axel should go away, it was the desire to be a faithful wife and worthy of my husband. I knew that he had never been unfaithful to me; he had never had a mistress. Was he the first King of France to aspire to this virtue? How many women at this Court could say they possessed a faithful husband? His kindness to me, his desire to please me, that ever-abiding *tendresse*, surely it demanded some reward?

Besides there was our child.

My little Madame Royale! How I adored her! I saw less of little Armand now. He was bewildered and sad and I would suddenly realize this and send for him and let him lie on my bed with me while I fed him with sweetmeats. But the position was changed. He was no longer my little boy. He was merely Armand, to be cared for by servants. What time I had was given to my own little daughter. He was well fed, he had all the material comforts that he had enjoyed before. It did not occur to me that I had acted in my usual thoughtless manner when I had taken him from his home, pampered and petted him and then cast him aside. I forgot this but he never did. He was to remember it in the years to come; he became one of those bitterest enemies who did his share to destroy me.

So even when I had meant to be kind I was helping to build that great force which was to come against me and envelop me and sweep me on to destruction.

My mother was writing as often as ever and the theme of her letters was: There must be a Dauphin.

I was keeping late hours, she had heard from Mercy. Was that the way to get a Dauphin? The King went early to bed and rose early. I went late and rose late. She had heard that at the Trianon where I often was I slept alone. She disapproved of the *lit à part*. Each month she wanted to hear that I was pregnant and there was no news of this happy situation.

> "Up to now I have been discreet, but I shall grow importunate. It would be a crime if there were no more royal children. I am growing impatient and at my age I have not much time left to me."

I too longed for a Dauphin.

I did try to live more quietly. I read as my mother would have wished though perhaps not the books she would have chosen; I liked novels of romance; I did a little needlework and I gambled now and then although not so heavily as before; but my greatest happiness was with Madame Royale.

The first word she said was "Papa" which pleased me as much as it did the King. I wrote to my mother:

> "The poor little thing is beginning to walk. She has now said 'Papa'; her teeth are not through yet but I can feel them. I am glad she began by naming her father."

Each day there was some progress. How thrilled I was when she took her first tottering steps toward me.

I wrote and told my mother of course.

> "I must confide to my dear mother a happiness I had a few days ago. There were several people in my daughter's room and I asked one of them to ask her where her mother was. The poor little thing, without a word being said to her, smiled and came to me her arms outstretched. She knew me, the little darling. I was overjoyed and I love her even more than I did before."

Mercy was grumbling to my mother that I could be talked to of nothing for I would interrupt and tell him that my daughter had her first tooth, had said "*Maman*," had walked farther than ever before; that I spent almost the whole day with her; that I listened to his conversation even less than I had before.

It seemed I could never give satisfaction.

Meanwhile my mother continued to write:

"There must be a Dauphin."

To my great joy I believed I was pregnant again. I was determined to say nothing of this to anyone but the King and a few of my friends. I could not resist whispering it to Gabrielle and I told the Princesse de Lamballe and my dear Elisabeth and Madame Campan, but I did make them all swear to secrecy until I was absolutely sure.

Then a dreadful thing happened. While I was traveling in my carriage I was suddenly aware of a cold wind and without thinking I jumped up to shut the window. More effort was needed than I had believed and I strained myself with the result that a few days after the event I had a miscarriage.

I was heartbroken. I wept bitterly and the King wept with me.

But we must not despair, he said. We should have our Dauphin in a very short time, he was sure. And in the meantime we had our adorable Madame Royale.

He comforted me and I declared how glad I was that I had not mentioned my condition to anyone except those whom I could trust. I imagined what the aunts or my sisters-in-law would have made of it. They would have blamed me, my love of pleasure, my indifference to duty . . . anything to discredit me.

I told my husband how glad I was and he said that we should keep the secret and I must tell all those who knew of the affair to say nothing of it. I was quite ill for a few days but my health was so good generally that I quickly recovered.

Then I caught measles and as the King had not had this complaint I went to the Trianon that I might be alone. I was followed there by those who had had it or decided to risk infection; Artois and his wife, the Comtesse de Provence, the Princesse de Lamballe and Elisabeth. It was not to be expected that we should stay there without male company and the Ducs de Guines and de Coigny came with the Comte d'Esterhazy and the Baron de Besenval. These four men were constantly in my bedroom and did their best to amuse me. This caused a great deal of comment and scandal, naturally. The men were called my sick nurses; and it was whispered that the measles were nonexistent; they provided the excuse. They were asking which ladies the King would choose to nurse him if he were ill?

Mercy for once had said that he could see no harm in my having friends at the Trianon to amuse me and help me recover from my illness. The King saw nothing wrong either. Kings and Queens had received visitors in their bedrooms for as long as anyone could remember. It was a tradition to do so.

When I was better I stayed on at the Trianon. I wanted to be there all the time. There were protests from Vienna, and Mercy told me that he had my mother's permission to remind me that a great court must be accessible to many people. If it were not, hatreds and jealousies would arise; and there would be trouble.

I listened, yawning, thinking of the play I would be putting on in my theater very soon. I should play the principal part myself. Surely everyone would agree that that was fitting.

The result of this interview was that I wrote to my mother and assured her that I would spend more time at Versailles.

She answered me:

> "I am very glad that you intend to resume your State at Versailles. I know how tedious and empty it is, but if there is not State the disadvantages which result from not holding it are greater than those of doing so. This applies particularly to your country where the people are known to be impetuous."

I did try to do what she suggested and held State at Versailles but so many people whom I had offended stayed away. I rarely saw the Duc de Chartres, for one. He had retired to the Palais Royale and entertained his friends there. I did not know what they discussed there; nor did it occur to me to wonder.

There seemed no point then in holding court at Versailles; why should I not spend more and more time at the Petit Trianon where life was so much more fun, surrounded as I was by the friends I had chosen.

The blow struck me suddenly. I had not even known that she was ill.

The Abbé Vermond came to my apartments and said he must speak to me alone. His eyes were wild, his lips twitching.

I said: "What is wrong?"

He replied: "Your Majesty must prepare yourself for a great disaster."

I rose staring at him. I saw the letter in his hand and I knew.

"The Empress . . ."

He nodded.

"She is dead," I said blankly, for I knew it was true. I was conscious of a terrible loneliness such as I had never known before.

He nodded.

I could not speak. I was numbed. I felt like a child who is lost and knows it will never feel entirely safe again.

"It cannot be," I whispered.

But he assured me that it was.

I said unsteadily, "I want first to be alone . . ."

He nodded and left me and I sat on the bed and thought of her as I had known her in Vienna. I saw her at her mirror while her women dressed her hair; I could feel the cold Viennese wind, sharper than anything I had known since I left Austria; I could picture her bending over my bed when I was pretending I was asleep. I could hear her voice. "You must do this. You must do that. Such *légèreté* . . . such *dissipation* . . . You are rushing on to destruction. I tremble for you."

Oh tremble for me, Mamma, I whispered, for without you I am so alone.

The King came and wept with me. He had waited a quarter of an hour before coming. I heard him in the anteroom where the Abbé had waited, respecting my wishes to be alone.

My husband said: "I thank you, Monsieur l'Abbé, for the service you have just done me." And I knew then that he had sent the Abbé to break the news to me.

He came in then and embraced me.

"My dear," he said, "this is so sad for us all but mostly for you."

"I cannot believe it," I said. "I had letters from her so recently."

"Ah, you will miss her letters . . ."

I nodded. "Nothing will be quite the same again."

And as he sat beside me on the bed, his hand in mine, I seemed to hear her voice admonishing me as it had all my life; I must not grieve. I had my husband; I had my daughter; and I must not forget that France needed a Dauphin.

I ordered Court mourning to be made and meanwhile I put on temporary mourning. I shut myself in my apartments and saw no one but members of the royal family, the Duchesse de Polignac, and the Princesse de Lamballe. I remained thus, aloof from the Court for several days; and I thought of her continually.

When I received Mercy he told me what he had heard of her end. She had been very ill since the middle of November and the doctors had said that she was suffering from hardening of the lungs.

On the 29th of the month she said to her women who came to her bedside, "This is my last day on earth, and my thoughts are of my children whom I leave behind." She mentioned us all by name, raising her hands to heaven as she did so.

And when she came to me she kept murmuring, "Marie Antoinette, Queen of France"; and she burst into tears and wept long and bitterly.

All the day she lived and it was eight in the evening when she started to fight for her breath.

Joseph, who was with her, whispered: "You are very ill."

And she answered: "Ill enough to die, Joseph."

She signed to the doctors.

"I am going now," she said. "I pray you light the mortuary candle and close my eyes."

She looked at Joseph who took her into his arms and there she died.

15

"Monsieur le Dauphin begs leave to present himself."

Louis XVI to Marie Antoinette

"I saw our little Dauphin this morning. He is very well and as lovely as an angel. The people's enthusiasm continues the same. In the streets one meets nothing but fiddles, singing and dancing. I call that touching and in fact I know no more amiable nation than ours."

Madame de Bombelles to Madame Elisabeth

"Catherine de Medicis, Cleopatra, Agrippina, Messalina, my crimes surpass yours, and if the memory of your infamous deeds still causes people to shudder, what emotions could be aroused by an account of the cruel and lascivious Marie Antoinette of Austria."

Quotation from a pamphlet in circulation before and after the Revolution called Essai Historique sur la Vie de Marie Antoinette

"France, with the face of Austria, reduced to covering herself with a rag."

Written under a portrait of Marie Antoinette dressed in a simple Creole blouse

THE AUSTRIAN WOMAN

Once again I was brought to bed of a child. Almost a year had passed since the death of my mother, for it was October. How I missed those letters which had arrived for ten years with such regularity. I remembered often how I used to tremble as I opened them and sometimes feel irritated by the continual complaints, but how often during the last year I had longed to receive them. How I should have enjoyed telling her that once more I was pregnant. But what was the use? She had gone forever; yet I knew that forever her memory would keep her with me.

I longed for a son, but I dared not pin my hopes on this. I could not love a child more than I loved my little daughter. I prayed: "A son . . . please God, but if You see fit to send me a daughter, she will seem all that I desire."

This *accouchement* was different from the last. The King had said that the public were not to be admitted for I was not again going to be exposed to the sort of risk I had run before, and only members of the family and six of my ladies—including the Princesse de Lamballe who was a member of the family—together with the *accoucheur* and the doctors were present.

My pains started when I woke on that morning—it was the 22nd of October—and they were so slight that I was able to take a bath; but by midday they had increased.

It was an easier labor than that of my little Madame Royale but when the child was born I was half-conscious and too weak to be entirely sure of what was happening.

I was aware of the people about my bed; there seemed to be a deep silence and I was afraid to ask for news of the child. The King had made a sign that no one was to speak to me; he had been very anxious during the latter weeks of my pregnancy and had commanded that when the child was born no one was to say what its sex was, for if it were a daughter I should be disappointed and if a Dauphin so overjoyed that either emotion might be bad for me in the state of exhaustion I should surely experience after the delivery.

I was aware of the silence about my bed. I thought: It is a girl. Or worse still: It is still-born. No! I heard the cry of a child. I had a baby; I wanted to cry out: Give me my child. What matters if . . .

Then I saw the King; there were tears in his eyes and he seemed overcome by his emotion.

I said to him: "You see how calm I am. I have asked no questions."

His voice was broken and he said: "Monsieur le Dauphin begs to present himself."

A son! My dream was fulfilled. I held out my arms and they laid him in them. A boy . . . a perfect boy!

There was excitement in the bedchamber and the adjoining rooms where the ministers and members of our household waited.

I heard afterward that everyone there started kissing and embracing. I heard voices: "A Dauphin. I tell you it is true. We have a Dauphin." Even my enemies were caught up in the excitement. Madame de Guéménée, who was to take charge of him, sat in a chair with wheels and he was handed to her; she was then wheeled to her apartments close by and everyone crowded round her to see the child. They wanted to touch him, or his shawl or even the chair in which the Princesse sat.

"He must become a Christian without delay," said the King.

Our little Dauphin was baptized at three o'clock.

One hundred and one guns were fired immediately so that Paris should be aware of the sex of the child. That was the signal for the city to go wild with joy. Bells were ringing; processions were formed; at night bonfires were lighted and there were the usual firework displays. I could scarcely believe that these were the people who took such joy in those disgusting lampoons which were circulated about me; now they were asking God to protect me, the mother of their Dauphin. Now they were dancing, drinking my health, crying: "Long live the King and Queen. Long live the Dauphin."

As my mother said they were an *impetuous* people.

I was delighted with my new baby. I sent for Madame Royale that she might see her little brother and we stood hand in hand admiring him as he lay in his cradle. She was three years old and growing lovelier every day, besides being very intelligent.

I caught sight of Armand standing at the door scowling at us and I smiled at him but he dropped his eyes. And as I passed him I ruffled his hair. He was no longer as pretty as he had once been; but perhaps I was comparing him with my own little ones.

The tocsins rang for three days and nights. When I awoke I heard them and the realization of my great joy would come flooding over me. A two-day holiday was declared throughout Paris. Wine flowed freely in the streets; buffets of meat were set up; and people wore garlands of artificial flowers about their necks and called to each other "Long live the Dauphin!" as a kind of greeting.

Festival followed festival. Each of the guilds sent representatives to Versailles; and for nine days the ceremonies continued. The whole Court assembled to receive them and there was great hilarity when the sedan-chairman's guild sent a chair with a model of a wet nurse and a Dauphin seated in it. The nurse was a copy of the one we had engaged who had been speedily nicknamed Madame Poitrine. The chimney sweeps brought a model of a chimney on which small chimney sweeps sat and sang praises of the new born heir to the throne; the tailors brought a miniature uniform; the blacksmiths an anvil on which they played a tune. The market women put on their black silk dresses which they kept for years and brought out only on the most auspicious occasions and sang praises of me and my little son. But the most unusual of all were the locksmiths who felt they had a special affinity with the King because of his interest in their profession. They brought a huge lock which they presented to the King and their leader asked if His Majesty would care to try to unlock it. To do so was the task of a true locksmith and if the King would prefer one of their band to demonstrate he had but to command, but knowing His Majesty's skill . . . and so on. The King, thus challenged, determined to have a try and amid great applause he very quickly succeeded. And as he turned the lock, from it sprang a steel figure which was seen to be a marvelously wrought tiny Dauphin.

The celebrations continued. When I rode out into the streets of Paris the people cheered me.

I believed my indiscretions and follies of the past were forgotten because I had given this country what it wanted; an heir, a little Dauphin.

Looking back I think I reached the peak of my contentment then. The King shared my emotions. Almost every sentence he uttered contained the words, "My son" . . . or "the Dauphin." All the servants adored him; people would wait for hours for a glimpse of him. He was a wonderful baby, a beautiful contented child—the center of our lives. Louis went about giving his hand to everyone, listening avidly to their conversation—about the Dauphin of course; tears came into his eyes every time the child was referred to, so, as can be imagined, he was constantly in tears. Elisabeth told me that at the baptism—she was his godmother—the King had been unable to take his eyes from the child.

Madame Poitrine was an important person in our lives. The name fitted her; she was enormous and the doctors agreed that her milk was excellent. She was the wife of one of the gardeners and she regarded the Dauphin as her own and as he was the most important person in the palace she took second place. She shouted like a grenadier; she swore often; but her placidity was remarkable; neither my presence nor that of the King ruffled her in the least. She would say: "You can't touch him now. I've just got him off. I won't have him disturbed." Which amused us and made us laugh and be very content for we knew how she cared for our baby. She accepted the clothes we gave her, the laces and fine linen, with a shrug, but absolutely refused to use rouge or powder on her hair. She just did not hold with all that, she said, and she couldn't see what good it would do her baby.

Long after Elisabeth showed me a letter which at the time she had received from a friend, Madame de Bombelles. It brought those days back so clearly and we both wept over the paper.

"I saw our little Dauphin this morning. He is very well, and lovely as an angel. The people's enthusiasm continues the same. In the streets one meets nothing but fiddles, singing, and dancing. I call that touching and in fact I know no more amiable nation than ours."

Oh yes, they were happy then, and pleased with us. Why did it not remain so?

I look back over the last years and I try to see where all the tragedies could have been prevented. There must have been a way of stopping them.

Ever since I had been Queen I had had periodic visits from the two very clever court jewelers Boehmer and Bassenge. Madame du Barry had admired their work. Perhaps it was because of this that they had made a fantastic necklace which they had hoped to sell to her. They had collected the finest stones in Europe, sinking their capital in this project. Unfortunately for them Louis XV died before it could be offered and then there was, of course, no hope of Madame du Barry's having it.

They were in despair and their first thought was of me. When they showed it to me I was dazzled at the sight of all those magnificent stones but secretly I thought the necklace, which was rather like a slave collar, a little vulgar. It was not the great temptation the jewelers had thought it would be and perhaps the knowledge that it had been made with Madame du Barry in mind did not attract me either.

The jewelers were astounded and horrified. They had thought I should be enchanted and find some means to get it, knowing my passion for diamonds.

They showed the necklace to the King who called me to look at it. "You like it?" asked my husband.

I was in one of my penitent moods at the time, having been severely reprimanded by my mother for extravagance, and I said that I thought we had more need of a ship than a diamond necklace.

The King agreed with me but like the jewelers he was surprised. They pleaded. They must sell the necklace and they had hoped that I would have it. But I was firm; I was not going to incur the expense and my mother's anger—for she would surely hear of the purchase—for something I did not very much like.

The King told me that if I wanted the necklace he would empty his privy purse of everything he possessed to please me.

I laughed and thanked him. He was so good, I told him, but I had enough diamonds, and 1,600,000 francs for an ornament that would only be worn four or five times a year was ridiculous.

I forgot all about the necklace and then several years later when I was with my little daughter Boehmer called and asked if he might see me.

Thinking he had some small trinket to show me which my daughter might like to see I said he should be admitted. As soon as he came in I saw how distressed he was; for he flung himself on his knees and burst into tears.

"Madame," he cried, "I shall be ruined if you do not buy my necklace."

"That necklace!" I cried. "I thought we had heard the last of it."

"I am on the verge of ruin, Madame. If you do not buy my necklace I shall throw myself into the river."

My daughter moved closer to me, gripping my skirts; she was staring in horror at the hysterical man.

"Get up, Boehmer," I said. "I do not like such behavior. Honest people do not have to beg on their knees. I shall be sorry if you kill yourself but I shall in no way be responsible for your death. I did not order the necklace and I have always told you that I do not want it. Please do not speak to me of it again. Try to break it up and sell the stones instead of talking of drowning yourself. I am displeased that you should make such a scene in my presence and that of my daughter. Please do not let this happen again and now go."

He went and after that I avoided him. I heard though that he was still desperately trying to sell the necklace and I asked Madame Campan to find out how he was succeeding for I was sorry for the man.

Madame Campan one day told me that the necklace had been sold to the Sultan of Constantinople for his favorite wife.

I sighed with relief.

"How glad I am that now we shall have heard the last of that vulgar necklace."

I was spending more and more time at the Petit Trianon. My theater was now completed and I was longing to put on some plays. I had formed my troupe which consisted of Elisabeth, Artois and some of his friends, the Polignacs and theirs.

My sister-in-law Marie Josèphe refused to join us, saying it was beneath her dignity to act on a stage.

"But if the Queen of France can act, surely you can too."

"I may not be the Queen," she replied, "but I am the stuff of which they are made."

That made me laugh, but she refused to join us; so she was always a member of the audience instead. Monsieur Campan was of great help as prompter and part-producer, the role he had occupied in those days when we had played secretly in the room at Versailles. This was different. This was a real theater. I threw myself into acting with a wild enthusiasm; we did several plays and comic operas. I remember the names of some of them: *L'Anglais à Bordeaux, Le Sorcier, Rose et Colas.* In *Le Sabot Perdu,* I had the part of Babet who is kissed on the stage by her lover; Artois played the lover and this was talked of and written of as something like an orgy.

The people seemed to have forgotten the devotion they had shown me at the time of the Dauphin's birth. Pamphlets were coming out at an alarming rate and I was always the central figure portrayed. I could not understand why they should have chosen me. I believed it was because I was not French. The French had hated Catherine de Medicis, not because of her evil reputation but because she was not French. They had called her the Italian Woman; now I was the Austrian Woman.

Les Amours de Charlot et 'Toinette, was a popular little book which was supposed to be an account of my relationship with the Comte d'Artois, with whom, ever since I had come to France, my name had been coupled.

One day the King found a booklet called *Vie Privée d'Antoinette* in his private apartments which showed that I had enemies inside the palace for one of them must have placed it there.

I refused to read them. They were so absurd, I said. Anyone who knew me would simply laugh at them. I did not realize that my enemies were building up a public image of me and that was the woman so many people believed me to be.

There was one pamphlet which was supposed to have been written by me for it was in the first person. This seemed sillier than any, for it was ridiculous to imagine that if I were guilty of all the crimes they attributed to me I should have made a confession and allowed it to be printed and circulated.

"Catherine de Medicis, Cleopatra, Agrippina, Messalina, my crimes surpass yours, and if the memory of your infamous deeds still causes people to shudder, what emotions could be aroused by an account of the cruel and lascivious Marie Antoinette of Austria . . . A barbarous Queen, an adulterous spouse, soiled with crimes and debaucheries . . ."

When I saw this I laughed and tore it up. No one would take it seriously. But this infamous document called *Essai Historique sur la Vie de Marie Antoinette* was sold, reprinted again and again and is in circulation at the time I am writing.

Why did I not understand that there were people who were determined to believe these things of me? The only way I could have shown them up as the ridiculous lies they were was by living a quiet and thrifty life.

And what did I do? I retired in disgust to the Petit Trianon. It was my little world. Even the King could only come there at my invitation. He respected this and gravely waited to be invited. He enjoyed those visits for to him, grappling with state affairs, it was indeed a boon to escape from ceremonies and tiring interviews with statesmen.

When we were not acting plays we played childish games. The favorite game was called *Descampativos*, which had derived from blind man's buff. One of the players was sent out of the room and when he or she had left, the rest of us would cover ourselves completely with sheets. Then the one who was outside would be called in; in turn we would touch him and he would have to guess who we were. The great point about this game was the forfeits which had to be paid and these became wilder and wilder. Everything we did was exaggerated; the simplest pleasure was described as a Roman bacchanalia. Another game was *tire en jambe* in which we all mounted sticks and fought each other. This gave rise to a lot of horse play and although the King liked to wrestle and play rough games he had little liking for this.

My garden occupied a great deal of my time. I was constantly planning and replanning. I said I wanted it to look as little like Versailles as possible. I wanted a natural garden. Oddly enough it seemed more costly to create that than the symmetrical lawns and fountains which Louis XIV had made so popular. I had plants brought from all over the world; hundreds of gardeners were employed to produce a natural landscape. I wanted a brook running through a meadow, but there was no spring from which the water could be obtained. "You cannot obtain water!" I cried. "But that is ridiculous." And water had to be piped and brought from Marley. Some comments were that it was gold not water that filled the charming little stream at the Trianon. Rustic bridges were built over the stream; there was a pond and an island; and all these had to be created as though nature had put them there.

The price of all this was staggering, only I never considered it. I would yawn as I looked at the amounts; I was never quite sure of the number of noughts; but I was constantly thinking of how I could improve my little world and it occurred to me that I should create a village, for no rustic scene was complete without people. There should be cottages, I decided, eight of them; little farms with real people and real animals. I summoned Monsieur Mique, one of the most famous of our architects, and told him what I planned. He was enchanted with the idea. Then I asked the artist Monsieur Hubert Robert to work with Mique. They must build for me eight little farmhouses, with thatched roofs and even dung heaps. They must be charming but natural.

The two artists threw themselves into the project with enthusiasm, sparing no expense. They were constantly suggesting improvements and I enjoyed my conferences with them. The farmhouses must be made to look like real farmhouses. The plaster would have to be chipped in places; the chimneys must look as if smoke had poured through them.

Natural was the order of the day and no artifice or expense should be spared to achieve it.

When the farmhouses were ready I peopled them with families, selecting them myself. Naturally I had no difficulty in finding peasants who were happy to make their home there. So I had real cows, pigs and sheep. Real butter was made; my peasants washed their linen and spread it out on the hedges to dry. Everything, I said, must be *real*.

Thus was created my Hameau. My theater had cost 141,000 livres; I did not stop to calculate the cost of the Hameau at the time; and later I dared not.

But I was happy there. I even dressed simply there, although Rose Bertin assured me that simplicity was a great deal more difficult to achieve than vulgarity—and naturally more costly.

In a simple muslin gown I wandered along by the brook or sat on a grassy bank so cleverly built up that none would have guessed it had not always been there. Sometimes I caught fish and these were cooked; for I had had my stream well stocked with fish as it naturally would be in the country. Sometimes I milked cows, but the floor of the cowhouse was always cleaned before I came and the cows brushed and cleaned. The milk would fall into a porcelain vase marked with my monogram. It was all very delightful and charming. The cows had little bells attached to them and my ladies and I would lead them by blue and silver ribbons.

It was enchanting. Sometimes I would pick flowers and take them into the house and arrange them myself. Then I would take a walk past the farmhouses to see how my dear peasants were getting on and making sure that they were behaving naturally.

"At least," I said with satisfaction, "the people in my Hameau are content."

And that seemed a very good thing and made worth while the great sums of money which continued to go into making the place, for I was constantly adding to its beauties and discovering new ways of improving.

Letters were arriving from Joseph but they did not have the same effect as those of my mother. Moreover that intense devotion which she had felt for me was lacking. Joseph thought me foolish—and he was certainly right in this—and lectured me, but then he lectured everyone.

He was writing to Mercy of course and Mercy remained my watchdog as he had during my mother's lifetime.

Mercy, who was no respecter of persons and never minced his words, showed me what he had written to Joseph. I suppose in the hope that I would profit from it.

"Madame Royale is never apart from her mother and serious business is constantly interrupted by the child's games, and this inconvenience so fits in with the Queen's natural disposition to be inattentive that she scarcely listens to what is said and makes no attempt to understand. I find myself more out of touch with her than ever."

He sighed as I read, for my attention was straying even as he put the paper into my hands and I was wondering whether a pale pink sash would be more becoming for my darling child rather than the blue one she was wearing.

Poor Mercy! The heart had gone out of him since my mother's death. Or was he realizing at last that the task of rescuing me from my follies was hopeless.

Money! It seemed the constant topic of conversation—and such a boring one! There was apparently a deficit in the country's finances which it was imperative to rectify, so said Monsieur Necker who had been appointed as Comptroller General of Finances. Turgot's policy had failed and he had been followed by Clugny de Nuis who had not given satisfaction. This man had not been successful although he had the support of the

Parlement (largely because he had tried to undo all the work Turgot had done). He had established a state lottery which had not worked out as he had planned it should and his methods were leading to financial disaster. When he died there was a sigh of relief and my husband turned to Jacques Necker.

Necker was a Swiss, a self-made man who owned the London and Paris bank of Thellusson and Necker. He had proved his ability to juggle successfully with finances and was at the same time beloved of the philosophers, having won a prize for a literary work from the Académie Française; he had written several attacks on property owners and deplored the contrast between rich and poor. He was a man of great contrasts—perhaps more so than most. He was an idealist yet he yearned for power. He refused to accept payment for his work; but then he was an extremely rich man and did not need money. He wanted to improve the conditions of the poor; he wanted to bring the country to prosperity, but he wanted all to know that he, Necker, and he alone was responsible for the good which was being done.

He was a Protestant and since the reign of Henri IV no Protestant had been allowed to hold office. It indicates the impression Necker made on the King for this rule to be waived. Louis who, since he had been King had made a great effort to understand public affairs, was certain that the country needed Necker at this time.

Necker was a big man with thick eyebrows below a high forehead above which was a high tuft of hair. His complexion was yellow and his lips tight as though he were calculating the cost of everything. He looked incongruous in fine velvets; I said to Rose Bertin that he would look better in a Swiss bourgeois costume and that she had better make him one.

"Madame," she replied, "I choose my clients with the utmost care. Since I serve the Queen of France, it is my duty to do so."

Necker, looking round for a means of cutting expenses, examined the royal household. We had too many servants. Madame Royale herself had eighty people in her household. None of us ever moved without being accompanied by a retinue of servants. Four hundred and six people lost their posts on the first day the resolution had been put into action; others followed.

But there seemed no perfect solution, for although we economized in our household, those who were dismissed were without employment.

Necker and his wife felt strongly about the state of our hospitals and the King always ready to further such good causes was entirely in accord with them. The conditions at the Hôtel-Dieu in Paris were truly shocking. My husband went, incognito, and wandered through the wards and when he came back he was in tears and very melancholy. But France did not want tears; it needed action. He knew this and planned to pull down the old building and replace it by four new hospitals. But where was the money to be found? He had to abandon that grand scheme and satisfy himself with enlarging the old building and adding three hundred beds.

And while this was happening my bills at the Hameau were steadily mounting.

Why was my folly not brought home to me? Why did everyone wish to indulge me? And was it indulging me? Was it not giving me a helping hand toward my doom. Before our daughter had been born my husband had indulged me because he was so apologetic for the embarrassing situation in which he had placed me; afterward he could not thank me enough for proving to the world that he could be a father.

But why should I blame others? I was told of these things; but I did not listen. I would weep when I heard of conditions at the hospital. After the birth of Madame Royale I had asked if I could found a lying-in hospital. This I had done. It salved my conscience. I could stop thinking about unpleasant things like dying people lying on the floor of the Hôtel-Dieu tormented by vermin while the rats leapt over them and there was no one to attend them or feed them.

Necker was constantly trying to bring in reforms—hospitals, prisons, the state of the poor. He instituted a new rule of loans not taxes, which made the people cheer him but did nothing to alleviate the situation.

Necker wanted popularity; he never criticized me. I know now that it was because the King doted on me and wished me to have my diversions; although Necker wanted to do good to France he wanted most of all to bring power to Necker. Without the King's support he could not do this and therefore he must continue to please the Queen.

The lack of money seemed to affect everyone. There was a great scandal when the Prince de Guéménée became bankrupt. This ruined several traders who had been supplying him for years. His enormous retinue of servants were in despair. The affair reverberated throughout Versailles and Paris; and naturally his wife could not hold her post as governess to the Enfants de France.

In her place I chose my dearest Gabrielle. She was not eager. Perhaps what I loved most about the dear creature was her indifference to power. I think Gabrielle would have been happiest if she could have lived quietly in the country away from courts. She had no desire for jewels, not even fine clothes. Perhaps she knew she was beautiful enough to do without them. She was lazy and liked nothing better than to lie on the lawns at the Trianon—just with myself and perhaps a few of our very intimate friends—and idly chatter. She declared that she was not suited to the post. The Dauphin needed a nurse who was constantly watching over him.

"But I shall watch over him," I declared, "and so will his father and many others. We shall be together more than ever. You must accept, Gabrielle."

Still she hesitated. But when her lover Vaudreuil heard he insisted that she took the post. I often wondered what happened between them. She declared she was terrified of him . . . terrified but fascinated. So Gabrielle became the children's governess. I now know that this friendship between myself and Gabrielle was one of the main causes of complaint against me. How strange! It was so beautiful really—a loving friendship; the desire of two people who had much in common to be together. Where was the harm in it? Yet it was misconstrued. I do not refer to the evil construction which was put on that friendship. There must always be libels about me and my friends. I ignored them; they were so ridiculous. But her family was ambitious. I persuaded Louis to make Gabrielle's husband a Duke which meant that she had the *droit au tabouret*; then her family were constantly producing some member who needed a post at Court. Large sums were constantly being paid to that family from the ever diminishing treasury.

Money!

One lovely June day I was seated in my gilded apartment playing the harpsichord and my thoughts were wandering from the music. I was contemplating that I was growing old. I was nearly twenty-eight! My little daughter would be five years old in December and my little Dauphin two in October.

Ah, I sighed inwardly, I am no longer young; and a sadness took possession of me. I could not imagine myself old. What should I do when I could no longer dance, play, and act? Arrange marriages for my children! Lose my sweet daughter to some monarch of a far-off country. I shuddered. Never let me be old, I prayed.

There was a scratching at the door.

I looked up from the harpsichord and signed to the Princesse de Lamballe to see who wished to enter.

It was an usher to announce a visitor.

I started as I saw him in the doorway. He had aged a good deal, but he was none the less attractive for that.

He is more distinguished than ever, I thought.

Count Axel de Fersen was approaching. I rose. I held out my hand; he took it and kissed it.

I felt suddenly alive, glad of these moments. All my gloomy thoughts of encroaching age had disappeared.

He had come back.

What glorious days followed. He came constantly to my drawing room, and although we were never alone we could talk together and we did not need words to convey our feelings for each other.

When he talked to me of America he glowed with enthusiasm. He had been awarded the Cross of Cincinnatus for bravery but he did not wear it. It was forbidden by His Majesty Gustave of Sweden, but the latter had been impressed by its bestowal for he had made Axel a Colonel in his army.

"Now," I said, "you will stay in France for a while."

"I shall have to have a pretext for doing so."

"And you have none?"

"My heart has a reason; but I cannot declare that to the world. There must be two reasons . . ."

I understood. His family was pressing him to return to Sweden and settle down. He should marry . . . a fortune. He should consider his future. How could that be furthered in France.

He told me of these matters and we smiled at each other in a kind of enchanted hopelessness. Never from the beginning did we believe we could be lovers in truth. How could we? I was a very different woman from the woman portrayed in the pamphlets. I was fastidious; I was essentially romantic. A sordid bedchamber interlude had no charms for me. I believed in love—love that is service, devotion, unselfishness . . . idealized love. It seemed to me that Axel gave me that. In his Swedish Army uniform he looked magnificent—apart from all other men. I saw him like that and that was how he would always be to me. I was not looking for transient sensations, the gratification of a momentary desire. I dreamed that I was a simple noblewoman, that we were married, that we lived our idealistic lives in a little house somewhere like the Hameau where the cows were all clean and the butter was made in Sèvres bowls and the sheep were decorated with silver bells and ribbons. I wanted nothing sordid to enter my paradise.

Moreover I had my babies. To me they were perfect. And they were Louis' children. I would not have them different in any way, and my little Madame Royale already had a look of her father.

There was no logic in my dreams; there was no practical reasoning. I wanted romance . . . and romance is not built on the realities of life.

Nevertheless I wished to keep Axel in France.

I was delighted when Louis showed me a letter he had received from Gustave of Sweden. It ran:

> "Monsieur my brother and cousin, the Comte de Fersen having served with approbation in Your Majesty's armies in America and having thereby made himself worthy of your benevolence, I do not believe I am being indiscreet in asking for a proprietary regiment for him. His birth, his fortune, the position he occupies about my person . . . led me to believe he can be agreeable to Your Majesty, and as he will remain equally attached to my own, his time will be divided between his duties in France and in Sweden . . ."

It did not take me long to persuade Louis that this was an excellent idea.

Axel now had the opportunity to be more often at Versailles without arousing comment. He could come in the uniform of a French soldier.

"My father is not pleased," he told me. "He feels I fritter away my time."

"Alas," I replied. "I fear it too."

"I never frittered more happily."

"There is a concert tonight. I shall look for you."

And so it went on.

Fersen père was an energetic man. If his son determined to waste his time in France he must marry. There was a very eligible young woman who would suit him admirably. She had a fortune; her father was a power in France, but what she needed was a husband with birth and title. Germaine Necker, daughter of the Comptroller, was the chosen bride.

When Axel told me this I was dismayed. If he married our romance would be shattered. It was true that I was married, that there could never be a chance of my marrying Axel, but who ever heard of a married troubador! How could he be in constant attendance on *me* if he had a wife and such a wife as Germaine Necker, a democrat and reformer, a woman of strong ideals learned from her parents.

"It must not be," I said.

Fersen agreed but he was gloomy. The Neckers had already been informed of the proposition and they thought it an excellent one. Mademoiselle Necker would be mortally offended if he failed to propose marriage to her.

"We must find another suitor for her," I declared. "One whom she will like better."

I was horror-stricken. How could any woman like anyone better than Axel!

Germaine Necker was a very determined woman. She would marry whom she pleased, she announced; and oddly, it seemed to me, she did not propose to marry Axel. For some time she had been in love with the Baron de Staël; she made up her mind to marry him and being the forceful young woman she was in a very short time Germaine Necker had become Madame de Staël.

Axel showed me a letter he had written to his sister Sophie of whom he was very fond and with whom he was always outspoken. She would understand his true feelings, he assured me.

"I will never assume the bond of matrimony. It is against my nature . . . Unable to give myself to the person to whom I wish to belong and who really loves me, I will give myself to nobody."

Romance had been preserved.

Even so he could not stay indefinitely in France. Family affairs called him back to Sweden. But I knew that he was mine forever. He would never marry; he had said so.

A few months later he was back in Paris whither he had come with his master, Gustave. I remember well the day the news was brought. Louis was on a hunting expedition and staying at Rambouillet, and when the news was brought that Gustave had arrived, my husband dressed so hastily to receive him that the King of France greeted his guest wearing one gold buckled shoe with a red heel and one with a black heel and a silver buckle. Not that Gustave, who was clearly indifferent to his own appearance, cared about that. But the important fact was that Axel was back in France.

I betrayed my emotions in a hundred ways. I immediately declared that we must give a fête at the Trianon in honor of the King of Sweden and I was determined that never should there have been such a fête.

Those about me raised eyebrows; they tittered and whispered behind their hands. In whose honor was this fête being given?

I had never before liked Gustave because the last time he had come to France—I was Dauphine then—he had given a diamond necklace to Madame du Barry's favorite dog. This I had said was silly and vulgar too, for he had done more honor to the King's mistress than to the future King of France.

But now he was Axel's King and I longed to entertain him because then I should be entertaining Axel too.

We gave a performance in the Trianon theater of Marmontel's *Le Dormeur Eveillé*; and after that we went into the English gardens. Lights had been hidden in trees and bushes; and I had ordered that trenches be dug behind the Temple of Love and these trenches were filled with faggots which when lighted made the Temple look as though it were supported by the flames.

Gustave commented that he could believe he was in the Elysian Fields. That was the intention I had meant to convey; that was why I had commanded that everyone be dressed in white, so that they could wander about like inhabitants of paradise.

In this setting Axel and I could be closer than we ever had before. We could touch hands; we could even kiss. In a white garment, and in the dusk of that enchanted night we could believe that we were in another world, a world of our own where duty and reality had no place.

When supper was served we could no longer be together and I walked from table to table seeing that my guests were served with venison which the King had killed in the chase, sturgeon, pheasants, and all the delicacies known to us. This was how I wished it to be for in spite of all the splendor—and never had there been such a splendid *fête* even at this Court—I liked to preserve my illusion of living simply at the Trianon.

There were not many more opportunities for talking to Axel and I knew that when Gustave departed he would have to go with him. A few days later after our Elysian entertainment Axel and I, with Gustave and other members of our Court and the Swedish entourage, watched two men, Palâtre de Rozier and a man named Proust, rise high above our heads in an air-inflated balloon. This had been embellished with the arms of France and Sweden and the name of the balloon was the Marie Antoinette. I could scarcely believe my eyes and everyone else was greatly impressed expecting imminent disaster, but the balloon traveled from Versailles to Chantilly and everyone was talking about the wonders of science.

But I was thinking of Axel and that soon there must be another of those partings—each one harder to bear than the last.

I wanted to give him a memento, something by which he could remember me. So I gave him a little almanac on which I had embroidered the words:

> "Foi, Amour, Espérance,
> Trois, unis à jamais.

Then he went back to Sweden with his King.

Madame Vigée-Le Brun was painting my portrait. She was a charming dainty creature and I was attracted to her. I liked to chat with her while she worked. I watched the picture grow on her canvas and one day I said: "If I were not a Queen, one would say that I looked insolent, do you not think so?"

She turned the remark aside as one not expecting an answer. She might have replied that even though I was a Queen there were many who thought I looked insolent and haughty. The petulant lower lip which had been noticed when my appearance was being so freely discussed by the French envoys at my mother's Court had become more pronounced. It was an inheritance from my Hapsburg ancestors. I told Madame Le Brun this and she smilingly replied that she despaired of ever reproducing my complexion.

"It is so fresh, so flawless that I have no colors to match it."

Flattery for a Queen! But I certainly did possess this brilliant complexion and it would be false modesty to deny it.

My clothes were discussed at this time very freely throughout Paris as well as Versailles. It was discovered that I had paid 6000 livres for one dress. Madame Bertin was expensive, I knew, but then she was an artist, the finest couturière in Paris. It was not that she was my sole dressmaker; she was the designer of my gowns and hats; but I had my sewing women; there were special work people for riding habits and dressing gowns; there were makers of hoops and collarettes, flounces and petticoats.

My extravagances were a popular theme so I decided that Madame Vigée-Le Brun should paint me in a gaulle which was a blouse worn by the Creoles. This was as simple as a chemise and made of inexpensive lawn.

The picture was charming and was exhibited. The people flocked to see it and it soon became apparent that nothing I could do was right.

The Queen was playing at being a chambermaid, was one comment. What she wishes to do is to ruin trade for the silk merchants and weavers of Lyons so that she can help the drapers of Flanders. Are they not her brother's subjects?

That was bad enough. But the most damaging and most significant comment was scribbled under the picture as it hung in the Salon:

"France, with the face of Austria, reduced to covering herself with a rag."

16

"Provided I don't speak in my writings of authority, religion, of politics, of morality, of the officials of influential bodies, of other spectacles, of anyone who has any claim to anything, I can print anything freely, under the inspection of two or three censors."

"Calumny! You don't know what you are disdaining when you disdain that. I have seen people of the utmost probity laid low by it. Believe me, there is no false report however crude, no abomination, no ridiculous falsehood which the idlers in a great city cannot, if they take the trouble, make universally believed—and here we have tittle-tattlers who are pastmasters of the art."

Beaumarchais

"The Cardinal has made use of my name like a vile and clumsy forger. It is probable that he did so under pressure and an urgent need for money and believed he would be able to pay the jeweler without anything being discovered."

Marie Antoinette to the Emperor Joseph

THE DIAMOND NECKLACE

In May of the year 1785 a great joy came to me when I gave birth to my second son. My confinement was attended with the same ceremony as that which there had been at the birth of my little Dauphin. My husband declared that never again should I be submitted to the danger I had faced at the time of my daughter's birth.

Louis himself came to my bedside and emotionally declared: "We have another little boy!" And there was my dear Gabrielle holding the child in her arms coming to my bed.

I insisted on holding him. A little boy . . . a perfect little boy! I wept; the King wept; in fact everyone was weeping with joy.

My husband commanded that messages be sent to Paris with the news. My little son was baptized in Notre Dame by Cardinal de Rohan—as his brother had been—and he was christened Louis-Charles. Te Deums were sung; the tocsins were sounding; the salute of guns was fired.

There was rejoicing in Versailles for four days and nights.

I was so happy. My dreams were coming true. I had two sons and a daughter. I would often bend over the little newcomer as he lay in his beautiful cradle.

"You will be happy, my darling," I told him.

Oh, if I could have foreseen the misery into which I had brought this unfortunate child! How much better if he had never been born!

There was one man whose name was on every lip. It was the author Beaumarchais who had written a play called *Le Mariage de Figaro* in which there was tremendous interest throughout the Court and I believe the country. The author had had difficulty in getting the play performed because the Lieutenant of the Police, the magistrates, the Keeper of the Seals, and strangely enough the King did not think it would be good for the country to see it.

I had thought what fun it would be to put it on at my Trianon theater and Artois agreed with me, seeing himself in the part of the Barber.

He flitted about my apartments, doing the rogue of a barber to the life. It was small wonder that people had suggested that Artois and I were closer friends than propriety permitted. We were completely in tune on matters such as this. He could not see why we should not do the play any more than I could.

I see it now, of course; I see how that dialogue is full of innuendo. I can see that Figaro is meant to represent the People; and that the Comte Almaviva is the old régime, the tottering structure of aristocracy. Almost every line of the dialogue is charged with meaning. This was not a play about a Comte who commits adultery as naturally as eating and breathing; it is not an account of the shrewdness of a wily barber. It was a picture of France—the uselessness of the aristocracy and the growing awareness of the shrewd people of the state of their country; it was meant to set them wondering as to how it could be remedied.

I think of little snatches of dialogue.

"*I was born to be a courtier.*"

"*I understand it is a difficult profession.*"

"*Receive, take, ask. There's the secret of it in three words.*"

"*With character and intelligence you may one day rise in your office.*"

"*Intelligence to help advancement? Your lordship is laughing at mine. Be commonplace and cringing and one can get anywhere.*"

"*Are you a prince to be flattered? Hear the truth, you wretch, since you have not the money to recompense a liar.*"

"*Nobility, wealth, rank, office—that makes you very proud! What have you done for these blessings? You have taken the trouble to be born, and nothing else.*"

I was too immersed in my own affairs to be fully aware of the crumbling society in which I was living. I saw nothing explosive in these remarks. To me they were merely excessively amusing. But my husband saw the dangers immediately.

"This man turns everything to ridicule—everything which should be respected in a government."

"Then won't it be played?" I asked, showing my disappointment.

"No, it will not," replied my husband, quite sharply for him. "You may be sure of that."

I often think of him now, poor Louis. He saw so much that I could not understand. He was clever; he could have been a good King. He had the best will in the world; he was the kindest, the most amiable of men; he sought nothing for himself. He had his ministers—Maurepas, Turgot who was replaced by Necker in his turn replaced by Calonne—but none of these ministers was great enough to carry us safely over the yawning abyss which was widening rapidly beneath our very feet. Dear Louis, who wanted to please. But it was so difficult to please everyone. And what did I do? I was the tool of ambitious factions and did nothing to help my husband, who wanted to please me and wanted to please his ministers, and vacillated between the two. That was his crime; not cruelty, not indifference to the suffering of others, not lechery—not all those crimes which had undermined the Monarchy and set the pillars on which it was erected moldering to dust; it was vacillation in which he was helped by a giddy thoughtless wife.

This affair of the play was characteristic of Louis' weakness and my frivolity.

When *Figaro* was banned everyone became greatly interested in it. When Beaumarchais declared that only little men were afraid of little writings, how clever that was! And how well he understood human nature! There was no one who wished to be thought a "little man," and his supporters were springing up everywhere. Gabrielle told me that her family believed the play should be performed. What sort of a society was this where artists were not allowed to speak their minds! The play could not be performed, but what was to prevent people's reading it?

"Have you read *Figaro*?" It was the constant question asked everywhere. If you had not, if you did not burst into immediate praise, you were a "little man or woman." Clever Beaumarchais had said so.

There was one section of society which placed itself firmly behind Beaumarchais. Catherine the Great and her son the Grand Duke Paul expressed their approval of the play and declared they would introduce it into Russia. But the most important supporter was Artois. I think he longed for us to play it and therefore he was determined to see it performed. He was as lightminded as I and even went so far as to order a rehearsal in the King's own theater—Menues Plaisirs. Here my husband showed himself firm for once. As the audience was beginning to arrive he sent the Duke de Villequier to forbid the performance.

Shortly afterward the Comte de Vaudreuil, that most forceful lover of Gabrielle's, declared that he could see no reason why the play should not be performed privately and gathered together actors and actresses from the Comédie Française, and the play was put on in his château at Gennevilliers. Artois was there to see it performed. Everyone present declared it a masterpiece and demanded to know what was going to happen to French literature if its most important artists were muzzled.

Beaumarchais made fun of the censorship in the play itself:

> "Provided I don't speak in my writings of authority, religion, of politics, of morality, of the officials of influential bodies, of other spectacles, of anyone who has any claim to anything, I can print anything freely, under the inspection of two or three censors."

This was, many people were declaring, not to be tolerated. France was the center of culture. Any country which failed to appreciate its artists was committing cultural suicide.

Louis was beginning to waver, and I repeated all the arguments I had heard. If certain offensive passages were removed . . .

"Perhaps," said the King. They would see.

It was a half victory. I knew that he could soon be persuaded.

I was right. In April 1784 in the theater of the Comédie Française, *Le Mariage de Figaro* was performed and there was a stampede to get tickets. Members of the nobility stayed all day in the theater to make sure of their places and all through the day the crowd collected and when the doors were open they rushed in; they were standing in the aisles; but they listened spellbound to the performance.

Paris went wild with joy over *Figaro;* he was being quoted all over the country.

A victory for culture! What the nobility did not realize was that it was a step further in the direction of the guillotine.

I believe that I had been right to add my voice to those who persuaded the King. I wished to show my appreciation of Beaumarchais and to honor him, so I suggested that my little company of friends should perform his play *Le Barbier de Séville* at the Trianon, in which I myself would play Rosine.

At the beginning of August in that year 1785 five months after the birth of my adorable little Louis-Charles I was at the Trianon; and I intended to stay there until the festival of Saint Louis, and while I was there to play in *Le Barbier de Séville.*

As always, I was happier there than anywhere else. I remember walking round the gardens to look at the flowers and to see what progress my workmen had made—there were always changes being made at the Trianon—and pausing close to the summerhouse to look at my theater with its Ionic columns, supporting a pediment on which a carved cupid held a lyre and a wreath of laurels. I remember the thrill I always experienced when I entered the theater and the joy I took in its white and gold decorations. Above the curtain concealing the stage were two lovely nymphs holding my coat of arms and the ceiling had been exquisitely painted by Lagrenée. It looked very small with the curtain hiding the stage—that stage which was my pride and delight—and which was enormous, large enough for the performance of any play; and if the space provided for the audience was small, well, it was a family affair, so we did not need the space of an ordinary theater.

What I enjoyed most at the Trianon—apart from acting—was what were called the Sunday balls. Anyone could attend if suitably dressed. I had said that mothers with children and nurses with their charges were to be presented to me and I enjoyed talking to these guardians of the little ones about their charming ways and their ailments. I talked to the children and told them about my own. I was happiest then. Sometimes I would take part in a square dance, passing from partner to partner, to let the people know that the Trianon was conducted without the formality of Versailles.

I was particularly happy at that time having no idea that a storm was about to break. Why should I have had? It all began so simply.

The King was giving a present of a diamond epaulet and buckles to his nephew, the Duc d'Angoulême, son of Artois, and had ordered these through Boehmer and Bassange, the Court jewelers; he asked them to deliver them to me.

After the manner in which Boehmer had behaved about his diamond necklace before my little daughter I had ordered that he was not to come into my presence but should deal with my *valet de chambre*.

I was with Madame Campan rehearsing my part in *The Barber* when the epaulet and buckles were delivered to me. The *valet de chambre* who brought them told me that Monsieur Boehmer had delivered a letter for me at the same time as he had brought the jewels.

I sighed as I took it. I was really thinking of my part.

"That tiresome man," I said. "I do believe he is a little mad."

One of the women was sealing letters by a lighted wax taper and I went on talking to Madame Campan: "Do you think that I put enough emphasis into that last sentence? Do you think she would have said it in that way? Try it . . . show me how you would do it, dear Campan."

Campan did it excellently. What a way she had with words! Not that she looked in the least like Rosine . . . my dear serious Campan!

"Excellent!" I said and opened the letter. I ran my eye over it yawning slightly. Boehmer always made me want to yawn.

> "Madame,
>   We are filled with happiness and venture to think that the last arrangements proposed to us, which we have carried out with zeal and respect, are a further proof of our submission and devotion to Your Majesty's orders and we have real satisfaction in the thinking that the most beautiful diamonds in existence will belong to the greatest and best of Queens . . ."

I looked up and gave the letter to Madame Campan. "Read it and tell me what that man means."

She read it and was as mystified as I was.

"Oh dear!" I sighed taking the letter from her. "That man was born to torment me. Diamonds! He thinks of nothing else. If he had not sold that wretched necklace of his to the Sultan of Turkey he would be pestering me about that, I am sure. Now apparently he has some more diamonds which he would like me to buy. Really, Campan, when you next see him, tell him that I do not like diamonds now and that I will never buy any more as long as I live. If I had the money to spare I would rather add to my property at St. Cloud by buying the land around it. Now do be careful to impress this on him. Tell him what I have told you and make him understand."

"Would Your Majesty wish me to make a point of seeing him?"

"Oh no, there is no need for that. Just speak to him when the opportunity arises. To talk to him specially might set some other notion going in his crazy head. He will get an obsession with emeralds doubtless if he thinks I no longer care for diamonds. But do make it clear to him . . . without making it seem as though I have specially commanded you to do so."

"He visits my father-in-law frequently, Madame. It may well be that I shall meet him some time at his house."

"That's an excellent idea." I smiled at her. "You are so discreet . . . so reliable. I am thankful for that, dear Madame Campan."

I was still holding Boehmer's letter and looked down at it with distaste. Then I held it in the flame of the taper and watched it burn.

"Now," I said, "no more of Monsieur Boehmer and his diamonds."

How mistaken I was!

Madame Campan left Versailles for a few days to stay at her father-in-law's country estate at Crespy. I missed her because no one else—not even Gabrielle and Elisabeth—were as good as Madame Campan at rehearsing with me and I made up my mind that I should call her back very soon. I was obsessed by the play. It was going to be the best we had ever done. Rosine was a perfect part for me. I liked to read Beaumarchais' description of her:

> "Imagine the prettiest little woman in the world, gentle, tender, lively, fresh, appetizing, nimble of foot, slender-waisted with rounded arms, dewy mouth; and such hands, such feet, such teeth, such eyes . . ."

The aunts said: Was that a fitting description of the Queen of France? It sounded to them more like a coquette. It was undignified of the Queen of France to ape *commoners* on the stage.

I laughed at them. Louis was a little uneasy but I could always bring him to my way of thinking. He knew how much I wanted *The Barber* to be played; and that I should have been heartbroken if I had not taken part in it. So he refused to listen to the aunts' criticism and was only delighted to see me so happy over my part. After all had I not only just given him another son!

Madame Campan had not been gone more than a few days when Monsieur Boehmer presented himself at Trianon and begged for an audience with me, saying that Madame Campan had advised him to see me without delay.

One of my women came to me to tell me this adding that he seemed very agitated.

I could not understand why he should come if Madame Campan had delivered my message correctly. But of course she had and he, construing it that I was no longer interested in diamonds, had come with emeralds or sapphires or some such stones. He had worried me with his diamonds; I was not going to allow him to repeat the performance with other jewels.

"I will not see Monsieur Boehmer," I said. "I have nothing to say to him. He is mad. Tell him I will not see him."

A few days after that I decided that I must have Campan to help me with my part, so I sent for her. If I had not been so immersed in the production—for I liked to do more than play the most attractive parts and I would supervise the costumes and scenery and plan the décor—I should have noticed that Madame Campan was very uneasy.

When I had run through my part however I did say to her: "That idiot Boehmer has been here asking to see me and saying that you advised him to come. I refused to see him, but what does it mean? What could he want? Have you any idea?"

She burst out: "Madame, a very strange thing happened at my father-in-law's house. I wanted to speak to you of it as soon as I was admitted to your presence. Have I your permission to tell you all?"

"Please do so."

"When Monsieur Boehmer came to dine with my father-in-law, I thought this would be an excellent opportunity to pass on your message to him. Madame, I cannot describe his astonishment. Then he stammered out that he had written a letter to you and had had no reply. I understood it was the one which had come with the King's gift to Monsieur d'Angoulême. I told him I had seen it and it had not seemed very comprehensible. He replied that he supposed it would not be to me but that the Queen would understand. Other guests were arriving and it was my duty to help receive them so I tried to excuse myself but Monsieur Boehmer asked me if I would allow him to talk to me later. His manner was so extraordinary that I said we would take a walk in the gardens at a suitable moment and then he could tell me what he wished to."

"The man is quite mad, I am sure of it."

"Madame, it is such an extraordinary story but he swears it is true."

"Pray go on."

"He said: 'The Queen owes me a large sum of money.' "

"I'm sure that is not true. His account has been settled."

"Madame, he went on: 'The Queen has bought my diamond necklace.' "

"Oh, no! Not that thing again. The Sultan of Turkey has it."

"He says that is not so, Madame. That was merely a tale he was asked to put about. I told him that he must be dreaming. I said: 'The Queen refused to buy the necklace long ago and as a matter of fact I knew that His Majesty had offered to buy it for her and still she refused it.' He said: 'She changed her mind.' "

"Oh, Campan, what does all this nonsense mean?"

"I do not know, Madame, but Boehmer tells a very strange story. He assured me that you had bought the necklace. I replied that it was impossible. I had never seen it among your jewels. Boehmer said that he had been told you were to wear it on Whitsunday and was very surprised that you did not."

"My dear Campan, this is the most utter nonsense. I told you Boehmer was mad."

"Yes, Madame, but he talked so earnestly. He seemed so sensible . . . so sure. I asked when you had told him that you had made up your mind to buy the necklace for I knew you would not see him and had not done so for a very long time. He then said a strange thing, Madame. He said that the Cardinal de Rohan acted for you."

"The Cardinal de Rohan! Then he is quite quite mad. I loathe Rohan. I haven't spoken to him for eight years."

"I told Boehmer this, Madame, and he said Your Majesty *pretended* to be on bad terms with Rohan, but in fact you were very great friends."

"Oh, this grows madder and madder."

"As it seemed to me, Madame. I pointed this out to Boehmer but he was so insistent that he spoke the truth and indeed, Madame, if he is mad he makes a very good show of being sane. He had an answer to everything. He said that Your Majesty's commands were transmitted to him by letters which bore Your Majesty's signature and that he had to use them to satisfy his creditors. The necklace was to be paid for in installments, and that he had already received 30,000 francs which Your

Majesty had given the Cardinal to give to him, Boehmer, when the necklace was handed over."

"I don't understand this," I cried; but it no longer seemed a joke. There
was something very mysterious going on.

"I believe," I said, "that a great fraud may well have been played on
Boehmer. We must get to the bottom of this. I will send for him at once."

I sent a messenger to Paris and commanded the jeweler to come to
the Trianon without delay.

"Monsieur Boehmer," I said, "I wish to know why I am expected to
listen to mad assertions that you have sold me a necklace which I have
often refused to buy."

"Madame," he answered, "I am forced to this unpleasant business because I must satisfy my creditors."

"I fail to see where your creditors concern me."

"Madame," he replied, in great distress, "it is too late to pretend. Unless Your Majesty will be so good as to admit you have the necklace and
give me some money, I shall be declared bankrupt and the reason will be
known to all."

"You talk in riddles, Monsieur. I know nothing of this necklace."

The man was almost in tears. "Madame," he said, "forgive me, but I
must have my money."

"I tell you I owe you nothing. I did not buy your necklace. You know
that I have not seen it . . . nor you, for a long time."

"Madame, the Cardinal de Rohan paid me the first installment when
I handed the necklace to him. I must have the money owing to me . . ."

I could not bear to look at the man.

I said: "There has been some fraud here. It must be examined. Go now,
Monsieur Boehmer, but I promise you that I will look into this matter
without delay."

He left me and I went into my bedchamber where I remained. I was
trembling with apprehension. Something very strange was happening
about me and at the center of it was that sinister man, the Cardinal de
Rohan.

It was a fraud, of course. The man was a scoundrel. He had acquired
the diamond necklace and pretended that I had bought it.

I had heard a great deal about him since that day he officiated at Strasbourg when I had first come to France. My mother was constantly writing
to me about him when he was Ambassador to Austria and she had urged
Mercy to do all he could to get him recalled. "All our young and plain

women are bewitched by him," she had written. "His language is extremely improper and this ill becomes his position as priest and minister. He insolently uses these expressions no matter what company he is in. His suite follow his example—they are without merit or morals." Neither I nor Mercy had been in a position to have him removed from Vienna, but when my husband became King it was a different matter. My mother wrote that she was pleased to see an end to "his horrible and shameful embassy." She had written warning letters, I must be wary of this man; he would bring me no good, I must not be charmed by him for he was a flatterer and could be very amusing. I saw him as a kind of ogre and had refused to receive him. My feelings toward him were not softened when I heard that he had written a letter to the Duc d'Aiguillon about my mother and that Madame du Barry had read this aloud at one of her *salons.*

In this he wrote:

> "Marie Thérèsa wept over the misery of oppressed Poland, but she is an adept at concealing her thoughts and seems to produce tears at will. In one hand she holds a handkerchief to dry her tears and in the other a sword, so as to be the third sharer."

This letter had arrived at the time when I was making matters worse by refusing to speak to Madame du Barry and my mother, while making stern rules against the prostitutes of Vienna, was urging me not to irritate the situation between France and Austria by persisting in this refusal.

I loathed the man. I ignored him; and I believe that the desire to find a way into my good graces obsessed him. The more I ignored him, the more he tried to gain my favor, and I was determined not to give it.

He had scored over me in one way. It was not my wish that he should hold the post of Grand Almoner of France. I had been annoyed when I had heard that he had baptized my babies; but what could be done about it when he held that high post?

Madame de Marsan, Rohan's cousin, had asked my husband, without my knowledge, that the post should be Rohan's, and Louis, who liked to please people, had given his word that it should be. When I discovered this, I determined to prevent it, particularly as Mercy and my mother were urging me to do this. I told Louis that he could not allow a man who had insulted my mother to hold the post of Grand Almoner of France. It was unfortunate, said my husband, but he had promised Madame de Marsan, and he did not see how he could go back on his word.

"I can see!" I cried. "It is impossible. This man has insulted *me* . . .

through my mother. Could you grant such a favor to a man who had
insulted your wife?"

"I could not, of course . . ."

"Then you must tell him he cannot have the post. You are the King."

"My dear, I have given my word . . ."

It seemed imperative that I have my way. If I did not my mother would
say that I had no influence with my husband. I began to cry. I was
of no importance, I wept. My husband preferred to grant favors to other
women rather than to me.

Tears always distressed Louis. It was not so. He would do anything to
please me. What about those chandelier earrings I had admired. They
contained some of Boehmer's best diamonds.

I continued to weep. I did not want diamonds. I wanted him to forget
his promise to Madame de Marsan. Was it much to ask?

He would do it, he said. He would tell Madame de Marsan that she
would have to forget his promise.

I threw my arms about his neck. He was the best husband in the world.

I had counted without Madame de Marsan.

She complained bitterly. The King had given his word. Was she not
to rely on the King's word?

"Madame, I cannot grant your wish," Louis told her. "I have given the
Queen my word."

Because Louis was kind he was also weak. Had his grandfather or Louis
Quatorze declared that they wished to break their word, it would have
been accepted as law. But with my husband it was different. People
were ready to reason with him, even to criticize him . . . and in this case
threaten him.

"I respect the Queen's wishes, Sire," said the impertinent Marsan, who
had always hated me, "but Your Majesty cannot have two words. The
Queen would not wish that the King, in order to please her, should do
what the threat of death would not force from the meanest gentleman.
I therefore must respectfully take the liberty of assuring Your Majesty
that having published the promise he gave me, I should find myself reluctantly compelled to make it known that the King had broken it to please
the Queen."

As Louis explained to me afterward, there was nothing he could do but
give way for it was true that he had given his word to her first.

I was angry but I knew that neither tears nor pleading could help, so I
accepted the situation and forgot about it—until now.

But Cardinal de Rohan was a man I would never accept. I had disliked him even more than ever. Then I had in fact ceased to think of him. Now I was forced to.

As my anger subsided I began to tell myself that the only reason I had become so agitated was because the Cardinal de Rohan appeared to be so deeply implicated. All the same I must tell my husband about it without delay.

Louis listened gravely and said that Boehmer should be immediately commanded to give his account of what had happened. Knowing that Mercy would most certainly have communicated something of the affair to my brother Joseph—for he still wrote to Vienna, although not as frequently as he had when my mother was alive—I myself wrote to my brother . . . giving him what at the time seemed the most logical explanation.

"The Cardinal has made use of my name like a vile and clumsy forger. It is probable that he did so under pressure and an urgent need for money and believed he would be able to pay the jeweler without anything having been discovered."

I was very angry. I hated that man. Not only had he slandered my mother but he had slandered me. I wanted revenge and I was determined to have it.

When Boehmer sent in his account of how he had been approached by the Cardinal with orders to buy the necklace for me, my fury increased. He had sworn on oath that he had received the commission from me.

I said: "He shall be disgraced. He shall be robbed of all his posts. Louis, you must promise to arrest him."

"Arrest the Cardinal de Rohan! But my dear . . ."

"He has used my name. He has lied and cheated. He shall be arrested. Louis, you must swear it."

Louis was uneasy. "We must look into this matter. We are a little in the dark at the moment."

"In the dark! We have Boehmer's word that he went to them with this story . . . this lie. If you do not arrest that man it will be as though *you* believe this story against me."

"That I would never do but . . ."

"Then arrest him." I put my arms about his neck. "Louis, you must arrest him. If you do not it will seem that even *you* are against me. Promise me . . . promise me now that you will arrest the Cardinal."

My poor Louis! Was there ever a more clear example of a man who had the intelligence to know what was the wise thing to do and lacked the will power to do it? Louis wanted peace. He wanted to hurt no one; he could not stand up against my blandishments even though he knew that I was acting against my own interests. He could not reason against tears and the fury of featherbrained women.

"The Cardinal shall be arrested," he promised; and I was satisfied.

It was the 15th of August, the Feast of the Assumption. The King summoned the Baron de Breteuil, Minister of his Household, and Monsieur de Miromesnil, Keeper of the Seals, to his cabinet. I was there.

The King quickly explained the reason for our presence there and added that he intended that the Cardinal de Rohan should be arrested without delay.

Monsieur de Miromesnil immediately protested: "Sire, Rohan's rank and family entitle him to be heard before he is arrested."

Louis wavered, in fact agreeing with Miromesnil, but I put in hastily: "He has forged my name. He has behaved like a common swindler. I insist that he be arrested."

I saw Breteuil's eyes gleam. He hated the Cardinal as much as I did because he had followed the Cardinal as Ambassador to Vienna and since then the Cardinal had made him a butt of his malicious wit.

Breteuil said: "It is clear what has happened. Rohan is the most extravagant man in France. Not only has he rebuilt the episcopal palace in Strasbourg—think how much that must have cost him—but he has a retinue of women on whom he lavishes a fortune. He has taken up with that sorcerer Cagliostro who lives at his palace in luxury and who, although he is reputed to make gold and jewels for his patron, costs the Cardinal a great deal to maintain. He has been embarrassed for money for years—in spite of his great revenues. He is undoubtedly in debt and this is his means of satisfying his creditors."

"He has disgraced his cloth and his name," I said hastily. "He does not deserve any considerations because of them."

I could see my husband wavering between what he considered right and what would please me and I threw him my most appealing glance; Monsieur de Breteuil, unable to hide his satisfaction in an enemy's imminent downfall, came in decisively on my side.

The King decided that Rohan should be arrested.

The Feast of the Assumption happened to be my name day and there was to be a special levée at Versailles that I might receive congratulations. Thus the galleries and the *oeil de boeuf* were crowded. As Grand Almoner of France it was the Cardinal's duty to celebrate Mass in the royal chapel. Unaware of what lay before him he came in his lace rochet and scarlet soutane. He was told that the King wished to see him in his cabinet at midday. He must have been surprised that neither the King nor I had appeared in state as was expected on such an occasion; but he came in blithely enough, completely unaware of what was about to break over his head.

He bowed low to the King and me; I deliberately turned my head and behaved as though I did not see him. I was aware of the effect my conduct had on him.

Louis came straight to the point.

"My dear cousin," he said, "did you buy diamonds from Boehmer?"

The Cardinal turned pale but he answered: "Yes, Sire."

"Where are they?"

"I believe they have been given to the Queen."

I gave an exclamation of anger but the King went on as though he had not noticed: "Who gave you the commission to buy these diamonds?"

"A lady called the Comtesse de la Motte-Valois. She gave me a letter from Her Majesty the Queen. I thought that I should please Her Majesty by carrying out this commission."

I could no longer contain myself. "Do you think, Monsieur, that I should entrust such a commission to you to whom I have not spoken for eight years! And could you really believe that I would choose to carry through the negotiations by means of this woman?"

The Cardinal was trembling. "I can see that I have been cruelly deceived. I will pay for the necklace." He turned to me and his expression was one of humility as though he were begging me for a little sympathy. He would certainly not get it. "My desire to please Your Majesty blinded me. I did not suspect fraud . . . until now. I am deeply sorry. May I show Your Majesties how I became involved in this matter?"

The King gave his permission and with shaking hands the Cardinal took a paper from his pocket which he handed to the King. I went swiftly to my husband's side. There was an undoubted order to buy the necklace; it appeared to have been written by me and addressed to a Comtesse de la Motte-Valois.

"That is not my writing," I cried triumphantly.

"And see," said the King, "it is signed 'Marie Antoinette de France.'" He turned sternly to Rohan who looked as though he would faint. "How could a Prince of the House of Rohan and the King's chaplain believe that this is how a Queen of France would sign herself? Surely you know that Queens only sign their Christian names, and that even Kings' daughters have no other signature, and that if the royal family added any other name it would not be 'de France.' I have a letter here. It is signed by you and addressed to Boehmer. Pray look at me and tell me if this is a forgery."

The Cardinal swayed slightly. Louis thrust the letter into his hand. "I . . . I have no recollection of writing this," he said.

"It bears your signature. Is that your signature?"

"Yes, Sire. It must be authentic if it bears my signature."

"I must have an immediate explanation of these matters," said the King. I could see that he was feeling sorry for Rohan. Such a proud arrogant man, accustomed to making fun of others; now he was about to be brought low. That would seem pathetic to Louis, no matter how villainous the fellow was.

He said gently: "My cousin, I do not want to find you guilty. I should like you to justify your behavior. Now explain to me the meaning of all this."

"Sire," stammered the Cardinal, "I am too distressed to reply to Your Majesty at present . . . I am not in the condition . . ."

The King said kindly: "Try to calm yourself, Monsieur le Cardinal, and go into my study. There you will find paper, pens, and ink. Write what you have to tell me."

He left us.

"He is a very guilty man," said Breteuil; but the King was silent. An affair like this distressed him greatly.

We waited for a quarter of an hour. Outside in the *oeil de boeuf* the crowds must be becoming restive. They would know there was something wrong. The King sat at his table frowning, now and then glancing at the clock. Miromesnil looked very uneasy.

It was fifteen minutes later when the Cardinal appeared with the paper on which he appeared to have written very little.

I stood beside the King and read it with him. It was only about fifteen lines and seemed very confused. All I could gather was that a woman calling herself the Comtesse de la Motte-Valois had persuaded him that the necklace was to be bought for me, and that he knew now that this woman had deceived him.

The King sighed and laid down the paper. I would not look in Rohan's direction but I was aware how his eyes kept turning toward me. I had never hated him so much.

"Where is this woman?" asked the King.

"I do not know, Sire."

"Where is the necklace?"

"In the hands of this woman, Sire."

"Where are the documents purported to be signed by the Queen?"

"I have them, Sire. They are forged."

"We well know they are forged!"

"I will bring them to Your Majesty."

"I want to warn you, cousin," said the King, "that you are about to be arrested."

He looked stricken. "Your Majesty knows I shall always obey your orders, but I beg you spare me the pain of being arrested in these pontifical robes."

I saw my husband waver. He wanted to spare the man this disgrace. I clenched my hands. Louis glanced at me almost apologetically and my lips tightened. He was going to allow his pity for my enemy to overcome his desire to please me.

I showed him by my expression how I should regard such an action and he said: "I fear it must be so."

"Your Majesty will remember the close ties of our families," went on Rohan.

I could see that my husband was visibly moved and the tears of rage filled my eyes. He saw these tears and he said: "Monsieur, I shall console your family as best I can. I should be extremely pleased if you can prove yourself innocent. But I must do my duty as a King and a husband."

Monsieur de Breteuil was on my side. He signed to the Cardinal to make his way to the door which opened onto the Salon de la Pendule. On such an occasion this was naturally crowded; all members of the Court were present, some in the *oeil de boeuf*, others in the long gallery, in the council and state rooms.

Breteuil shouted to the Captain of the bodyguard the extraordinary command. It echoed through the Galerie des Glaces:

"Arrest the Cardinal de Rohan."

I was triumphant—triumphantly blind. "There," I said, "that matter is settled. This wicked man will be proved to be a cheat and be punished for all his sins."

I sat down to write to my brother Joseph:

"As far as I am concerned I am delighted at the thought of not having to hear this miserable business talked of again."

I do not understand now how I could have deceived myself and whether

I actually believed that or deep in my heart, realizing the enormity of this affair, refused to see it. I have come to believe I was adept at deceiving myself.

I expected congratulations from my friends. I expected them to say how pleased they were to see that wicked man brought to an account of his sins at last. But there was an odd brooding silence in my apartments. Gabrielle did not visit me; it did not occur to me that her family might be advising her to keep away. Madame de Campan was quiet and restrained as though she were involved in the affair. I should have been warned. She really cared for me and when I was in danger her love for me would make her anxious while her intelligence would not allow her to deceive herself. The Princesse de Lamballe agreed with me that it was a good thing, but then as Vermond had once pointed out she had a reputation for stupidity; and Elisabeth was sad, but then she was so pious that she always deplored trouble of any sort even for those whom she knew deserved it. My sisters-in-law seemed smugly pleased. But there was so much to think of. What of *The Barber of Seville?* Nothing must interfere with that production.

I decided to leave Versailles at once for the Petit Trianon.

"We must continue with the rehearsals this ridiculous affair of the necklace has interrupted," I declared.

So I went to the Trianon and thought of nothing else but my part.

When Campan told me that Rohan's family were furious because he had been arrested and sent to the Bastille I merely laughed. "It is where he should have been long ago," I retorted. "Now hear me in the first act."

How strange that the dialogue in this very play was like a grim warning. I remember now Basile's speech on calumny but strangely enough I took no heed of it then.

Now it comes back to me:

> *"Calumny! You don't know what you are disdaining when you disdain that. I have seen people of the utmost probity laid low by it. Believe me there is no false report however crude, no abomination, no ridiculous falsehood which the idlers in a great city cannot, if they take the trouble, make universally believed—and here we have tittle-tattlers who are past masters of the art . . ."*

How true that was to prove and how foolish I was to believe that I had heard the last of the affair of the diamond necklace.

But I thought of nothing then but my performance.

At the end I stood triumphantly on the stage to receive the applause; I had played as rarely before.

Such a play in my own theater, myself playing the principal role! I was happy and excited with my success, and I had no notion then that this was the last time I should play there.

17

"Madame de Boulainvilliers once saw from her terrace two pretty little peasant girls, each labouring under a heavy bundle of sticks; the priest of the village who was walking with her, told her that the children possessed some curious papers, and that he had no doubt they were descendants of a Valois, an illegitimate son of one of the Princes of that Name."

Madame Campan's Memoirs

"The face of this woman (Baronne d'Oliva) had from the first thrown me into that sort of restlessness which one experiences in the presence of a face one feels certain of having seen before without being able to say where . . . What had puzzled me so much in her face was her perfect resemblance to the Queen."

Beugnot

"After this fatal moment (the meeting in the Grove of Venus) the Cardinal is no longer merely confiding and credulous, he is blind and makes of his blindness an absolute duty. His submission to the orders received through Madame de la Motte is enchained to the feelings of profound respect which are to affect his whole life. He will await with resignation the moment when her reassuring kindness will fully manifest itself, and meanwhile will be absolutely obedient. Such is the state of his soul."

Monsieur de Target advocate for the Cardinal de Rohan at the time of the trial

EVENTS LEADING TO THE TRIAL

Looking back, I see the affair of the necklace as the beginning, as the first rumble of thunder in the mighty storm which was to break about my head. I was determined that Rohan should be judged and found guilty; he must be exposed as the swindler I believed him to be. Should he be excused because he was a prince of a noble family? I owed it to my mother as well as my own dignity as Queen of France to have him proved guilty of all the sins which I was certain he had committed.

I laughed when I considered what I was sure his family expected. They would imagine that the King would exercise his right to inflict a mild punishment on the Cardinal, perhaps send him a *lettre de cachet* which would mean a brief exile; then he could return to Court and the incident be forgotten.

I was determined that this should not be.

Louis, as usual, wavered. His good sense told him that he should listen to wise counselors and obey his own instincts in the matter which were that the less universally known about the matter the better for us all; but his sentiments toward me—and he loved me truly—insisted that he listen to my outbursts of fury against a man who had dared presume that I would enter into an underhand negotiation with him. Whenever Rohan's name was mentioned, I would burst into an angry tirade which often ended in tears.

"The Cardinal must be punished."

Louis pointed out that the Cardinal belonged to one of the oldest families in France; he was related to the Condés, the Soubises, and the Marsans; they believed that they had been personally insulted since a member of their family had been arrested publicly like a common felon.

"Which he is!" I declared. "And the whole world should know it."

"Yes, yes," replied my husband, "you are right of course. Yet not only his family but Rome itself is displeased that a Cardinal of Holy Church should have been submitted to this insult."

"And why not," I demanded, "when he deserves his fate more than some man who steals bread because he is hungry."

"You are right," said my husband.

I embraced him warmly. "You will never allow a man who has insulted *me* to go free, I know."

"He shall have his just rewards."

All the same Louis allowed the Cardinal to decide whether he would be judged by the King or the Parlement.

He quickly made his choice and wrote to the King, and it struck me at the time that the man who had written that letter to my husband had changed a great deal from the frightened creature who had been summoned to the King's cabinet on the day he was arrested.

He had written:

"Sire, I had hoped through confrontation to obtain proofs that would have convinced Your Majesty beyond doubt of the fraud of which I have been the plaything and I should then have desired no judges except your justice and your kindness. Refused confrontation and deprived of this hope, I accept with most respectful gratitude the permission which Your Majesty gives me to prove my innocence through judicial forms; and consequently I beg Your Majesty to give the necessary orders for my affair to be sent and assigned to the Parlement of Paris, to the assembled chambers.

Nevertheless if I could hope that the inquiries which have been made, and which are unknown to me, could have led Your Majesty to decide that I am only guilty of having been deceived, I should then beg you, Sire, to decide according to your justice and your kindness. My relations, penetrated with the same sentiments as myself, have signed.

I am, with the deepest respect,

> Cardinal de Rohan,
> De Rohan, Prince de Montbazon.
> Prince de Rohan, Archbishop of Cambrai.
> L.M. Prince de Soubise."

When my husband read this letter he was disturbed. He too was struck by the change in Rohan. His imprisonment in the Bastille had changed him from a very frightened man to an arrogant one.

I could see the speculation in his eyes. He said to me: "If I admitted that the Cardinal is merely a man who has been deceived into taking part in this fraud, he would not wish to be tried by the Parlement."

I laughed aloud. "I daresay not. He would rather have your leniency than a judicial sentence when he is proved guilty."

"What if he is not proved guilty?"

"You are joking. Of course he will be proved guilty. He *is* guilty."

My husband looked at the letter; he was staring at those names at the foot of it—some of the most influential in the country.

I knew that he was hoping that the matter might be hushed up in some way, which I told myself was just what Rohan's noble family wanted. But I was determined to bring this affair into the open.

My folly makes me shudder even now.

The most important affair in France was the trial. Information was leaking out daily. The Comtesse de la Motte-Valois had been arrested; so had Cagliostro, the notorious magician, and his wife; and so had another creature, a girl of light morals who was known as the Baroness d'Oliva and who was said to have impersonated me. The story was growing more and more fantastic every day. There had been nothing compared with this since the ascent of the balloon which had amazed everyone. But this was even more exciting; this was a trial of a great Cardinal; it was the story of great fraud, a fabulous diamond necklace which had disappeared completely from the scene; it was a story of scandal and intrigue and at the very heart of it was the Queen of France.

I was unaware then of all the twists and turns of this incredible story; but I have since heard many versions of it. In fact I have never ceased to hear of it. It was not really so much the Cardinal de Rohan who stood on trial; it was the Queen of France.

How could I have prevented what was to happen? By being a different woman. By never having entered on a life of selfish pleasure. I was not guilty of all of which I was accused in this nightmare story of a diamond necklace. My tragedy was that my reputation was such that I could have been.

I must set down the story of the Diamond Necklace, which gradually came to my knowledge while the tension was growing over that trial— and during it.

As I learned it I lost my carelessness. I believe this was the first time I really began to understand the mood of France, that I first became aware of that crumbling pedestal which supported the Monarchy.

The Prince de Rohan was at the very center of the drama; he was the dupe, it seemed; but how a man of his education and culture could have been so easily duped it is difficult to understand; perhaps it had something to do with the strange Cagliostro who was arrested with Rohan and who remains a vague and shadowy figure, the mystery man—magician or charlatan? That is something I shall never know. Perhaps the most important figure in the whole unsavory affair was the Comtesse de la Motte-Valois, that woman who, from afar, since this unfortunate affair occurred has been writing her sensational lying and pornographic stories of my life—my enemy whom I have never met, to whom I have done no harm except to have ascended the throne of France. Hers was an unusual story. She claims descent from the royal Valois, that branch of the family of France which ruled before the Bourbons. She was the daughter of a certain Jacques Saint-Rémy who claimed descent from King Henri II. This appeared to be the truth for Henri II had had an illegitimate son by a certain Nicole de Savigny and this child, christened Henri after him, was legitimized by him and created Baron de Luz and de Valois.

Jeanne suffered great poverty in her childhood but she had heard that she was descended from the Valois and never forgot it. In the days when she was living on the proceeds of her great fraud she bore the arms of her family—*d'argent a une fasce d'azur, chargée de trois fleurs de lis d'or*—on her carriage, in her house, anywhere she could put it.

The child Jeanne was brought up in a state of abject poverty and this, added to the knowledge that she was of royal blood, may well have been at the root of her hatred for me and her desire to gain, at any cost, the status which she believed belonged to her.

No doubt when Henri de Saint-Rémy, son of Henri II lived in the château it had been a beautiful place but during the years which followed, the Saint-Rémys found it impossible to keep up their standard of living; the ditches about the château became filled with stagnant water; the roof had fallen in and the upper part was exposed to the weather. By the time Jeanne's father was born, it was a ruin. He was a man of great physical strength but had no desire to regain his family's fortunes if it meant work. He was only interested in drink and debauchery and gradually sold, little by little, all that remained of the château.

He seduced one of the village girls named Jossel and when their child was born married her. She was a woman of loose morals and as Jeanne's father cared only for drink she soon began to dominate the household.

Jeanne was one of three children; neither parent cared for them, and they were kept in a miserable hut, naked, for they had no clothes and they would have starved to death but for the efforts of the Curé and some of the peasants who took pity on them.

When I think of all this now, I can forgive her, because I know misery even greater than she must have endured as a child; but at that time it was difficult to understand. Now I see that she felt a need to take revenge on society; and I can even feel it in my heart to be sorry for this woman.

How wretched the child must have been, but while she was naked and shivering with cold and hunger, she never lost sight of the fact that she was descended from the royal Valois.

There came a time when the family decided to take to the road. There were four children, Jacques, Jeanne, Marguerite-Anne, and Marie-Anne. Poor little Marie-Anne was a year and a half and could only totter so they decided they could not take her with them; they wrapped her in swaddling clothes and hung her on the door of a farmhouse. Leaving her there they set out and now began the real nightmare for the children. Their mother was a strong handsome peasant and she decided to make use of her attractions; their father was ailing so she turned him out and took up with a soldier as depraved and cruel as herself. The children were sent out to beg and if they did not return with money were severely beaten. Then came Jeanne's stroke of luck. Her cry when she stood by the roadside begging was: "Give alms to a poor orphan sprung from the blood of the Valois." This naturally provoked jeers now and then but it did attract some attention and one day the Marchioness de Boulainvilliers passing in her carriage heard what the child said, was curious, and stopped to question her. She was immediately struck by the child's beauty and proud bearing; she believed the story of royal descent and decided to help. She took Jeanne and her little sister Marguerite-Anne and sent them to school, where very soon Marguerite-Anne caught smallpox and died. Meanwhile Jeanne's father had died in great poverty in the Hôtel Dieu in Paris; her mother's paramour left her and she returned with Jacques to Bar-sur-Aube her native town where she took up a life of prostitution. Jacques ran away to sea and joined a ship at Toulon where with the help of Madame de Boulainvilliers he made a good career in the Navy and actually died at the time the affair of the necklace came to light.

Jeanne had left her nightmare childhood behind her; and it is not surprising that she made up her mind that never would she fall into such dire misery again.

Madame de Boulainvilliers was good to her and when she was old enough to leave school placed her with a dressmaker in the Faubourg Saint-Germain; but Jeanne was too proud to remain there. In her autobiography, which she produced after the trial and which of course everyone was eager to read, she said she became a "Washerwoman, a water carrier, a cook, an ironer, a needlewoman, everything except a happy and respected girl."

That was what Jeanne craved for above everything—to win the respect which she considered due to her rank.

Madame de Boulainvilliers was a kindly woman; she realized that Jeanne could never settle down and understood the reason, so she took her into her home and there Jeanne lived for a while as a member of the household. Madame de Boulainvilliers did not forget little Marie-Anne who had had the good fortune to be taken in by the good-hearted farmer when he had discovered her hanging on his door; the good lady sent for her and since she had grown into a well-mannered girl decided that she should go with her sister Jeanne to a finishing school for young ladies. Now Jeanne was not only a beautiful young woman of twenty-one, she was an educated one, but remembering she had sprung from the Valois, she wanted to be treated as a royal personage.

When Jeanne was twenty-four she was still restless and dissatisfied and she then met a soldier some two years older than herself. This was Mark-Antoine-Nicolas de la Motte, an officer in the *gendarmerie*. They became lovers and it was necessary for them to marry hastily. Twins were born a month after the wedding but in a few days they were dead. Jeanne was the leading spirit in this union, it appeared, and de la Motte soon learned that he must do as he was told. One of the first things he was obliged to do was to assume the title of Comte. He obeyed his wife, and her haughty manners, her habit of reminding everyone that she was descended from the Valois soon made everyone accept the title as a natural one. They became known as the Comte and Comtesse de la Motte-Valois.

Jeanne and her husband, in need of money, for how could a descendant of the Royal House of Valois be expected to live on the pay of an officer of the *gendarmerie*, immediately began to make plans. An opportunity arose when Madame de Boulainvilliers visited Strasbourg as a guest in the château of Saverne, the magnificent home of the Cardinal de Rohan. Jeanne remembered that the Cardinal was notoriously fond of women and she was undoubtedly attractive. With her air of haughty refinement, her lovely chestnut hair and blue eyes under black eyebrows, her coloring was startling.

She decided to use the Cardinal, but at this stage she was not sure how. That wildest of plans would occur to her later when a series of strange events fell into their places setting the stage and making possible this plot which would otherwise have seemed too incredible for reality.

I have already written much of the Cardinal de Rohan. I shall never be able to get that man out of my mind and even now when I have become resigned to my fate and my understanding of others has grown—I still feel a great revulsion every time I hear his name or allow his image to cloud my thoughts.

I suppose he was handsome in his way for he was known as La Belle Eminence. Sometimes I think he was an extremely foolish man—indeed he must have been, for who but a simpleton would have allowed himself to be used as he was?

I can recall his face clearly; there is something childlike about it—round and like a doll's, unwrinkled and highly colored; the only aging feature was his white hair which grew far back from his forehead and even this merely accentuated the ruddy roundness of his face. He was very tall and carried himself with grace and great dignity; and in his Cardinal's robes he was a figure of magnificence. He held the Bishopric of Strasbourg which was the richest in France; he was a Prince of the Empire, Landgrave of Alsace, Abbé of the Grand Abbey of Saint-Vaast and Chaise-Dieu, Provisor of Sorbonne, Grand Almoner of France, Superior-General of the Royal Hospital of the Quinze-Vingts, and Commander of the Order of the Holy Ghost. And this was the man who had been arrested at Versailles like a common felon—as his family said.

At the time he made the acquaintance of Jeanne de la Motte-Valois the Cardinal was under the spell of Cagliostro.

I do not know the truth about Cagliostro. Who does? Some laugh at him. Others say that he was in possession of some of the great secrets of the universe. The fact remains that while he was close to the Cardinal, the Cardinal accepted ridiculous falsehoods as truth.

There were so many stories about the magician. I have heard descriptions of him from my servants who waited in the streets to catch a glimpse of him. His coat was of blue silk, his shoes were fastened by buckles made of diamonds; even his stockings were studded with gold; he glittered as he walked for diamonds and rubies covered his hands; his flowered waistcoat was set with gems which sparkled so fiercely that they dazzled the eyes of all who beheld them.

When he was arrested, shortly after the Cardinal, I heard many stories of his strangeness. The one which most impressed me was that of how he stopped in the square of Strasbourg before a crucifix and declared in a loud voice which could be heard by all those around—and there was always a crowd following him: "How could an artist who had never seen him have made such a perfect likeness?"

"Your lordship knew Christ?" asked a hushed voice close by.

"We were on terms of friendship," was the answer. "How many times we strolled together on the shady shore of Lake Tiberias. His voice was of great sweetness, but he would not listen to me. He loved to walk on the shore where he picked up a band of fishermen. This and his preaching brought him to a bad end." Then to his servant he added: "Do you remember that day when they crucified Christ in Jerusalem?"

Then came the astonishing climax to the story: "No, my lord," replied the servant in the hushed tones of reverence with which the great man was addressed. "Your lordship forgets I have only been in your service for the last fifteen hundred years."

He was a small fat man with the appearance of being in his forties; he had large bright animated eyes, and a strong voice. He was undoubtedly fascinating for often those who went to him to jeer at him and expose him as a fraud became his most earnest admirers.

Of course there were those who said he talked gibberish which people thought was brilliant wit and wisdom because they could not understand it. He had a formula for certain questions and when he was asked who he was would reply: "I am he who is!" and would add: "I am he who is not!" which was so baffling that most people who heard became very deferential and pretended they were the wise ones who could understand the meaning of his imagery.

There were countless sinister murmurs about him. He was a Freemason and wished to set up Egyptian Freemasonry in France; he was in the pay of secret societies and his motives were more devious than the duping of a foolish Cardinal. He had discovered the philosopher's stone and could transmute base metals into gold and make precious stones. Stories of the cures he had affected on his journeys were told everywhere. He could look at a man who was crippled and make him walk. He would not give his attention to all sufferers, however, and he reserved the right to treat those whom he favored.

There was a Comtesse de Cagliostro—a young woman of charm and beauty who was said to be "not of this world." No one knew where she came from any more than they knew her husband's origins. She was "an angel in human form who had been sent to soften the days of the Man of Marvels." Cagliostro was a faithful husband who never gave one amorous glance in any other woman's direction. All he was interested in was his own doctrine.

In spite of the wild life he had led, there was about the Cardinal a touch of innocence; he was a lecher, but a romantic one; superstitious in the extreme he was very much attracted by the occult. Moreover he delighted in splendor; he admired fine clothes and above all magnificent jewelery; and Cagliostro was a magician who, by his great wisdom, could bring sparkling jewels from his crucible. Such an achievement could not fail to impress the Cardinal and in a very short time he had invited Cagliostro to Saverne, where the two became great friends.

The Cardinal wore an enormous jewel, the size of an egg which he declared he had seen Cagliostro pluck from the crucible. How the Cardinal was duped, whether the Cardinal was duped, remains a secret, but it was a fact that Cagliostro lived in great splendor with his Comtesse in the palace of Saverne and that the Cardinal could scarcely bear him out of his sight.

And then in the private apartments of the Cardinal's palace these two men began to talk of me. I had become an obsession with the Cardinal. I had stubbornly refused to receive him at Court; I had remembered my mother's warnings about him; I had tried to prevent his being Grand Almoner; he knew that I disliked him, and he wanted my favor with the desperation of a man who has only had to take what he desires all his life and suddenly finds something denied him.

There was something even more sinister which had crept into the Cardinal's mind. He wanted to be my lover. The thought of this took possession of his mind. He began to think of little else. Did he talk of me to Cagliostro? Did he ask what chances he had of success with me? If he had talked with *me* instead of the magician I could have told him that never . . . never *never* should I have looked at him with favor even if I had been the kind of woman who forgets her marriage vows.

Why did Cagliostro lend himself to this mad scheme? Did he know what was going on? Could it be true that he had gifts like Mesmer's and could make people act as he wished at certain times? And did he wish me to be caught up in this gigantic scandal because his masters of some of the secret lodges of the world were eager to see the end of the Monarchy in France?

At the time it seemed that this was merely the story of a gullible man, a scheming woman and a man of mystery. I was involved—the central figure in the plot, the character who never makes an actual appearance during the whole of the play, but without whom there would be no play.

Jeanne de la Motte-Valois speedily became the Cardinal's mistress; that was an inevitable sequel. She also became Cagliostro's friend. Did she suspect he was a charlatan? Did he know that she was a scheming woman? Which ever way one turns in this incredible story there is mystery.

Jeanne would soon have discovered the Cardinal's obsession with me. Then the Comtesse saw a way of improving her status with the Cardinal; it may have been then that it all began.

She had become friendly with a comrade of her husband's, Rétaux de Villette, a handsome young man of about thirty, with blue eyes and a fresh complexion although his hair was already beginning to turn gray. He was an adept at writing verses, imitating well-known actors and actresses and he could write in various styles, even delicately as a woman. This young man became the lover of the Comtesse—perhaps she was genuinely fond of him, or perhaps because the plot was already beginning to form in her mind and she wished to bind him to her.

Jeanne hinted to the Cardinal that I had shown some favor to her. This did not seem impossible for my friendships were the source of a great

deal of gossip and it was known that it was women with charming looks
such as the Princesse de Lamballe and Gabrielle de Polignac who attracted me. Jeanne was extremely attractive; she was also a member of the
House of Valois; it was not therefore an impossibility that I should have
noticed her and favored her. So far the story progressed reasonably enough.

Jeanne must have been overwhelmed with joy by her success, for the
Cardinal showed clearly that he believed her and confided in her his
great desire to be received by me.

It might be, she told him, that she could put in a word for him with
the Queen. But Jeanne knew that vague promises would not satisfy him;
this was where Rétaux de Villette could be useful; he could write in a light
feminine hand and if he signed his letters with *my* name, why should not
the Cardinal believe that they had been written by me? They were addressed to my dear friend Madame la Comtesse de la Motte-Valois and
in them were many expressions of friendship.

How could he have believed that I had written such letters to this
woman! Yet it seemed that he did. It has been suggested that Cagliostro
was in the plot with the de la Mottes to delude the Cardinal and that
the sorcerer mesmerized him into accepting the letters as written by me.
I should have said this was ridiculous but for the fact that they had that
absurd signature "Marie Antoinette de France." Surely if he had his wits
about him the Cardinal must have realized they were false by that alone.

I have seen some of these letters which were said to have been written
by me. I shudder to look at them; and even now with most of the facts in
mind I am still mystified.

Jeanne had led the Cardinal to believe that if he could write a justifica-
tion of his misdeeds over the past years I would be willing to consider it
and perhaps forgive him.

Delightedly he immediately prepared a long apologia on which he spent
days—rewriting and correcting and when it was finished the Comtesse
took it promising that she would deliver it to me at the earliest possible
moment.

A few days later Rétaux de Villette wrote a letter on gilt edged paper
with a little fleur-de-lis in the corner.

> "I am delighted that I need no longer regard you as blameworthy.
> It is not yet possible to grant you the audience for which you
> ask, but I will let you know as soon as it is possible. In the mean-
> time please be discreet."

This letter signed Marie Antoinette de France produced the desired effect on the Cardinal. He was overcome with emotion; he was ready to lavish handsome gifts on the woman who could help him to such progress in his relationship with me. The fact that he did not question the veracity of this shows that he must have been the biggest fool in France. Yet he was not in truth that. Cagliostro had looked into the future for him and *advised* him to carry on with the project nearest his heart. How often have I asked myself what the magician's role was in the mystery!

Jeanne knew that she could keep the Cardinal believing I was writing to him but whenever I was at a gathering in which he was present I refused to look his way. For a while this situation might be explained but it could not go on.

But Jeanne was never at a loss and she devised a grandiose scheme with her husband—the self-styled Comte de la Motte-Valois—and her lover Rétaux de Villette. They were short of money, but Jeanne saw a means of becoming very rich. The Cardinal was a man of tremendous resources; he might suffer temporary embarrassments but his assets were great. He would be the milch cow who should be milked with the gentlest, cleverest hands. They must plan carefully though. The Cardinal must be brought face to face with the Queen; the Queen must show her favor toward him. I can imagine those two men, whose wits were so much duller than hers, demanding: "How?" And her cool reply: "We must find someone to play the part of the Queen."

How they must have gaped at her; but she was the brains behind the plot. Had it not worked out so far as she had told them it would? They should leave it to her. Now, what they needed was a young woman who looked sufficiently like me to be passed off as me. Everyone knew what I looked like. There were portraits of me in the galleries. They must find someone who had my coloring. They could teach her the rest.

She was a forceful woman; and both men were her slaves. It was the so-called Comte de la Motte who found Marie-Nicole Lequay, later known as the Baroness d'Oliva. The girl was young, about six years younger than I; her hair was similar in color to mine; she had blue eyes and an ample bosom. In fact she was known among her friends as the "Little Queen"; so her resemblance to myself had often been noticed. She was a milliner but followed another occupation—though more amateur than professional —besides that of making hats and at this time had a protector, Jean-Baptiste Toussaint. She was apparently a gentle creature, an orphan who had been placed with a guardian whose means of earning a living was to take in children to board—and from whom she had run away after being badly treated. She had had many lovers—not necessarily lovers who paid her; she was an easygoing gentle girl who was generous with her favors.

The Comte de la Motte met her in the Palais Royale where gay young people sauntered or sat in order to make each other's acquaintance. He was immediately struck by her likeness to me and brought her to the house in Rue Neuve-Saint-Gilles which was where the da la Mottes lived when in Paris.

Jeanne immediately saw the possibilities and it was she who changed the girl's name to Baroness d'Oliva—a near anagram of Valois. Soon she was telling the girl that the Queen would be grateful to her forever if she would do one little thing for her.

The poor simple girl was so overwhelmed that she was easily persuaded. Jeanne must have summed her up as too stupid and innocent to do much more than make an appearance and perhaps, with careful coaching, say one sentence; but that would be enough, as long as Jeanne was present to conduct the operation and step in quickly if things should go wrong.

Jeanne de la Motte must be the most audacious woman in the world. Who else would have conceived such a plan? Others might have been as villainous, but who would have been so wildly adventurous? Perhaps it was because she was certain of her powers to succeed that she did it. She had everything ready for the girl. Her hair was carefully powdered and dressed high though not elaborately. She had copied that simple dress of mine in which Vigée-Le Brun had painted me . . . the long white *gaulle* which had been called a chemise, and which had caused such a stir when the picture had been exhibited in the *salon* a short while before. This was made in muslin. Over the dress was put a mantle of fine white wool and on her head a very wide-brimmed hat to shade her face. With more than a slight resemblance to me the girl might well, in the dusk, be mistaken for me.

Rosalie, Jeanne's maid, a girl of about eighteen, black-eyed and saucy, who found living in the household of the Comtesse de la Motte an exciting adventure helped her to dress and during this process Jeanne taught her her words which were: "You may hope that the past will be forgotten." The poor girl had no idea what this meant. She had to concentrate on suppressing the accent of the Paris streets, on acquiring a faint foreign accent, on making a graceful gesture with her hands.

I can imagine the poor child, dominated by these people—particularly Jeanne—excited at playing the role of a Queen whom she had often been told she resembled, and at the same time being paid for it. Jeanne had hinted that not only would she be recompensed by herself and the Comte but that the Queen herself would no doubt wish to show her gratitude. Why should she ask what it was all about? She would not have been given an explanation and if she had, she would not have been able to grasp it. No! Her part was to do as she was told and she doubtless only hoped that she could play it to satisfaction. In the pocket of her muslin gown was a letter which she must take out and give to the man whom she would meet; she must also hand him a rose and not forget her words.

It was a dark night—no moon no stars—ideal for the scene. Everything was quiet in the park—the only sound that would be heard would be that of the water playing in the fountains. The Comtesse and her husband led the young girl in her muslin dress across the terrace and through the pines and firs, the elms, willows, and cedars to the Grove of Venus.

A man arrived dressed in something which the girl would readily accept was the livery of one of the gentlemen of my household.

"So you have come," said the Comte; the man bowed low. This part was played by Rétaux de Villette.

Oliva was told where to stand and wait while the Comte and Comtesse and Rétaux disappeared among the trees. Poor girl! She must have found it rather eerie standing there alone in the grove at night. I wonder what her thoughts were at that moment.

But a man had appeared—tall, slim, in a long cloak and a wide-brimmed hat turned down to hide his face. It was the Cardinal de Rohan.

Oliva held out the rose. She must have been astonished by the fervor with which he accepted it. I imagine him, kneeling, kissing the hem of her muslin gown.

Then he lifted his eyes and she said what she had been told: "You may hope that the past is forgotten."

He rose, approached, and a torrent of words burst from him. He was in ecstasy. He wanted to prove his devotion and so on. Poor little Oliva. What could she understand of this. She was unaccustomed to such fluency. How relieved she must have been to find the Comtesse at her side, taking her arm, pulling her into the shadows! "Come quickly, Madame. Here comes Madame and the Comtesse d'Artois."

The Cardinal bowed low and hurried away. The Comtesse, still gripping Oliva, was full of triumph. Oliva had forgotten to hand over the letter but the plan had succeeded even beyond her hopes.

And after that they had the foolish Cardinal in their web. He really believed that the Comtesse had arranged that meeting with me. How could he have been so foolish? Did he really think that I would come out into the park at night to meet a man! But then he had heard those scurrilous lampoons which had assigned to me a hundred lovers and like so many people in France he believed them. Perhaps that was why he had this impossible dream of becoming one of them.

A friend of Jeanne's, a young lawyer, happened to have called at the house at Rue Neuve-Saint-Gilles and was there when the carriage arrived bringing the adventurers back from the Grove of Venus; he wrote an account of what he saw and which I have since seen:

> "Between midnight and one in the morning we heard the sound of a carriage from which emerged Monsieur and Madame de la Motte, Rétaux de Villette and a young woman from twenty-five to thirty years of age with a remarkably good figure. The two women were dressed with elegance and simplicity . . . They talked nonsense, laughed, sang, so that one scarcely knew whether they were on their head or their heels. The lady I did not know shared in the general hilarity, but was timid and kept within bounds. The face of this woman had from the first thrown me into a kind of restlessness which one experiences in the presence of a face one feels certain of having seen before without being able to say where . . . What had puzzled me so much in her face was its perfect resemblance to that of the Queen."

Maitre Target of the French Academy who was one of the counsels for the Cardinal's defense wrote:

> "It is not surprising to me that in the darkness the Cardinal should have mistaken the girl d'Oliva for the Queen—the same figure, same complexion, same hair, a resemblance in physiognomy of the most striking kind."

So the first little plot had succeeded and now it was time to begin the greater one.

Target puts the case clearly when he stated on behalf of his client:

> "After this fatal moment (the meeting in the Grove of Venus) the Cardinal is no longer merely confiding and credulous, he is blind and makes of his blindness a duty. His submission to the orders received through Madame de la Motte is linked to the feeling of profound respect and gratitude which are to affect his whole life. He will await with resignation the moment when her reassuring kindness will manifest itself, and meanwhile will be absolutely obedient. Such is the state of his soul."

Madame de la Motte realized this. She must have been anxious as she felt her way, for even her optimistic mind must have realized that one false step could bring the entire edifice of fraud and deceit tumbling to the ground.

Jeanne sought an interview with the Cardinal very shortly after the meeting and told him that the Queen most clearly favored him for she, who was the most generous of women, wished to bestow fifty thousand livres on a noble but impoverished family. She was a little short of money at the moment but if the Cardinal could lend her this amount . . . and give it to Madame de la Motte to bring to her . . . she would know he was truly her friend.

How could the man be such a fool! The old question which I and countless others have asked themselves since this wretched business came to light.

He believed what they said because he wanted to believe; but all the time he was in close touch with Cagliostro who assured him that he could see into the future and there he saw the Cardinal reaping great benefits from his association with a person of very high rank. That satisfied the superstitious and gullible Cardinal.

Being short of money he borrowed from a Jewish moneylender assuring him he would be honored if he knew to what purpose the money was to be put.

In this manner Jeanne began to extract more money from the Cardinal, enough for her to be able to buy a mansion in Bar-sur-Aube, where she had once lived in such wretchedness and where she could continue with the fiction that she was now respectfully received at Court on account of her relationship with the royal family.

Had she been content with what she had managed to purloin she might have lived for the rest of her life in comfort. But she was an insatiably ambitious woman and she conceived the plan for the necklace.

It was at one of her parties that she had heard of the jewelers' trouble. Boehmer and Bassange talked of nothing but the diamond necklace which they could not sell. They had built their hopes on the Queen and the Queen did not want their necklace. Madame de la Motte had been boasting about her influence with the Queen; she and her husband had already extracted money from various people on the pretext that they could help them to rich posts at Court. So it was natural that the anxious jewelers should speak to her about the necklace and ask her if she could use her influence to interest me in it.

Madame de la Motte replied that this might be possible—and from that moment the scheme was conceived.

She would do her best to advise the Queen to reconsider buying the necklace. Could she herself see it? Nothing easier. The jewelers would bring it to the Rue Neuve-Saint-Gilles.

I can well imagine how the de la Mottes were dazzled by it. I remembered when I had first seen it how startled I was. It was in truth composed of some of the finest gems in Europe. I would never have wished to wear it. Secretly I thought it vulgar; but it was certainly a magnificent piece—in fact the most splendid I have ever seen.

I can remember it perfectly now. I have seen it so often in the drawing of me which circulated through Paris, for there were many ready to believe that I had stolen the necklace and when they wished to be particularly insulting they drew it about my neck.

In a necklace fitting closely to the neck were seventeen diamonds almost as large as filberts, and this in itself would have been dazzlingly beautiful; but the jewelers had added to this loops with pear-shaped pendants, clusters and a second rope of diamonds; there was even a third row decorated with knots and tassels of the precious stones and one of the four tassels in itself would have been worth a fortune. There were two thousand eight hundred carats in the necklace, and there had never been one like it. There never would be again—neither such a valuable necklace nor such a fateful necklace.

Once having seen it Madame de la Motte could not get it out of her mind. She did not want it as a necklace but through those brilliant loops and tassels she saw herself living like a Queen for ever more. If she possessed the necklace and broke it up and sold the stones she would be a rich woman for the rest of her life.

Her energetic mind was working fast.

"We would give a thousand louis to anyone who could find us a buyer for the necklace," tempted Boehmer and Bassenge.

How she must have laughed. A thousand louis. And the necklace worth sixteen hundred thousand livres! She would speak to the Queen, she replied haughtily, but she would not wish her friends the jewelers to reimburse her if she were able to arouse the Queen's interest.

I can readily imagine their joy. Meanwhile Madame de la Motte was planning her most ambitious scheme of all. The purchaser must naturally be the Cardinal de Rohan. A few letters purporting to come from me and the foolish man was like a fish on the hook. Of course he would enter into negotiations for the necklace if it were my wish.

Madame de la Motte told the jewelers that the purchase would go through. A very great nobleman would make it on behalf of the Queen. She, Madame de la Motte did not wish her name to be mentioned in the affair—it would be between the Cardinal de Rohan, the Queen, and the jewelers.

Overcome with joy, seeing a way out of all the anxieties of the past, the jewelers offered Madame de la Motte a precious stone in payment for her services. This she refused. She was only too happy to help, she said.

To the Cardinal she explained that I wished to buy the necklace without the King's knowledge; and that I should need to do so on credit since I was short of money at the time.

"Her Majesty will pay by installments," she explained, "and this will fall due at intervals of three months. Naturally, for such an arrangement the Queen must have an intermediary. She at once thought of you."

The Cardinal during the trial explained what had happened:

> "Madame de la Motte brought me a supposed letter from the Queen in which Her Majesty showed herself anxious to buy the necklace, and pointed out that, being without the necessary funds for the moment, and not wishing to occupy herself with the necessary arrangements in detail, she wished that I would treat the affair and take all the steps for the purchase and fix suitable periods for payments."

On receipt of this letter the Cardinal was delighted. He would be happy to do anything for Her Majesty. He would feel honored to make any arrangement she desired. The price was fixed at sixteen hundred thousand livres, payable within two years in four six-monthly installments. The necklace would be handed to the Cardinal on February 1st and the first installment would be due on August 1, 1785. He drew up this agreement in his own hand and gave it to Madame de la Motte to show to her dear friend the Queen. Back came the note on gilt-edged paper with the fleur-de-lis in the corner signed "Marie Antoinette de France" to say that the Queen was satisfied with the arrangements made and deeply grateful to the Cardinal.

It is strange that when the Cardinal saw the necklace he had his first doubts. This man who believed that I would meet him by night in the Grove of Venus, who believed that he had a chance of becoming my lover, was astonished that I could wish to wear such a vulgar ornament as the diamond necklace.

He wavered. He would wish, he told Madame de la Motte, to have a document signed by the Queen authorizing him to buy the necklace for her.

Madame de la Motte was not disturbed. Why not? Rétaux de Villette had provided other documents. Why not this one? In due course it was produced signed in the usual way "Marie Antoinette de France" and the word "Approved" was written beside each clause in what purported to be my handwriting.

How could the Cardinal have looked at that signature and not known it false? How could he have believed I would sign myself thus?

I remember these questions being asked continually during the trial and afterward; and one pamphleteer gave a possible answer:

> "People are so easily persuaded as to the truth of what they desire . . . It was such a mistake as might easily have been made by a man with a lively agitated mind like that of the Cardinal who was pleased, delighted even with an arrangement which fed some sentiment, some new view in the endless labyrinth of his imagination."

The deal was made. On February 1st Boehmer and Bassenge brought the necklace to the Cardinal, who, that same day, took it to the Rue Neuve-Saint-Gilles where Madame de la Motte was waiting to receive it. He was invited to wait in a room with a glass door through which he could watch the transfer of the necklace. He saw a young man in the Queen's livery present himself to the Comte and Comtesse de la Motte with the words "By order of the Queen." He took the casket and disappeared.

The Cardinal took his leave and as soon as he had gone, Rétaux de Villette, who had played the part of Queen's messenger returned with the casket; and the conspirators sat down at a table to gloat over the finest diamonds in Europe.

But they had not made this plan merely to look at diamonds. They must be broken up and sold.

They got to work without delay.

The whole story might have been discovered much earlier, for a few days after the Cardinal had handed over the necklace a jeweler called at the headquarters of the Paris police to give the information that a man had brought him some extraordinarily fine diamonds which had obviously been taken from their settings by an unskilled person. As a result Rétaux, returning to the shop, was arrested.

With great plausibility Rétaux explained that the diamonds had been placed in his possession by one of the King's relatives, the Comtesse de la Motte-Valois. He was able to prove this and at the name of Valois the police retracted and Rétaux was released.

But it had been a warning that it was a mistake to try to dispose of the best diamonds in Paris and the Comte set out for London to sell the stones. When he returned he was a rich man—although the London jewelers had benefited greatly by the sale for naturally he did not get the full value of the diamonds. Now Madame de la Motte was in her element. She was a woman who could live in the present and did not much concern herself with the future—an attitude of mind which I understood perfectly.

She made a royal departure to Bar-sur-Aube with servants in splendid uniform; a carriage drawn by four English horses—carpets, tapestries, furniture, and clothes; she needed twenty-four carts to carry all her possessions with which she intended to furnish her mansion. On her English berlin of a delicate pearl gray color she had the arms of the House of Valois engraved with the motto: *Rege ab avo sanguinem, nomen, et lilia.* From the King my ancestor I derive my blood my name and the lilies.

There she lived royally as she must always have longed to live since she had heard that she had Valois blood in her veins. But surely she must have known that it could not last. There must be a reckoning.

Perhaps like myself she had to learn that what one sows one must reap. The Cardinal had been arrested and had told his story implicating Jeanne. Two days later guards arrived at Bar-sur-Aube. Jeanne knew resistance was useless; she was taken prisoner and lodged in the Bastille.

18

> "The Queen was innocent and to give greater publicity to her innocence she desired the Parliament to judge the case. The result was that the Queen was thought guilty and that discredit was thrown on the Court."
>
> *Napoleon at St. Helena*

> "I saw that he [de Rohan] would be unable to appear any more at Court. But the action which will last several months may have other results. It began by the issue of a warrant of arrest which suspends him from all rights, functions and faculty of performing an civil act until judgment is pronounced. Cagliostro, charlatan, La Motte and his wife together with a girl named Oliva, a mudlark of the gutters, are in the same boat. What associates for a Grand Almoner, a Rohan and a Cardinal!"
>
> *Marie Antoinette to Joseph II*

> "The Queen's grief was extreme . . . 'Come,' said Her Majesty to me, 'come, and lament for Your Queen, insulted and sacrificed by cabal and injustice . . .' The King came in and said to me: 'You find the Queen much afflicted; she has great reason to be so.'"
>
> *Madame Campan's* Memoirs

THE TRIAL

All the actors in the Diamond Necklace affair were in the Bastille with the exception of the Comte de la Motte, who had escaped to London with what was left of the necklace, and the whole of the Court and the country was working itself up into a fever of excitement and expectation.

Each day Paris was filled with excited crowds. No one talked of anything but the coming trial. The Cardinal had changed completely. He was lodged in a fine apartment at the Bastille, very different from that used by ordinary prisoners, and there he took three of his servants to look after him. He paid one hundred and twenty livres a day for his lodging; and he was allowed to receive visits from his family, his secretaries, and of course his counsel with whom he was preparing his defense. The drawbridge of the Bastille had to be kept lowered all through the day, so many visitors were there; he even gave a banquet in his rooms where champagne was served. He continued to administer the business his position demanded as though the Bastille were another of his palaces which for the sake of convenience he was temporarily obliged to occupy. He took daily exercise in the Governor's garden or walked on the platform of the towers.

Supported by his powerful family he was gaining confidence. When he heard that Louis had appointed Breteuil as one of his interrogators he immediately protested on the grounds that Breteuil was an enemy. Louis, eager to be fair, at once agreed to make a change and substituted Vergennes, the Minister of Foreign Affairs, for Breteuil, and instead of Breteuil's assistant he ordered that Marshal de Castries, Minister of Marine, should assist Vergennes.

In less comfortable quarters in the Bastille Madame de la Motte was preparing her defense. Her fertile imagination was to invent many a fantastic story during the trial; but when Rétaux and the Baroness d'Oliva were arrested she must have been very uneasy. She had warned Oliva that she might be arrested for it was very much to Madame de la Motte's interest that the girl was not able to tell of that scene in the Grove of Venus. Oliva had tried to escape with her lover, Toussaint de Beaussire, but they had been arrested at Brussels. Rétaux de Villette was caught in Geneva; and these two with the Comte and Comtesse de Cagliostro were in the Bastille. So important was the affair considered that great efforts had been made to bring the Comte de la Motte back to France. England did not recognize extradition and would do nothing to help, so the Comte was wiser than his co-adventurers in escaping to that country. His whereabouts were discovered to be on the border between England and Scotland; an elaborate plot was made and a ship was sent to Newcastle-on-Tyne where his landlord and landlady were asked to slip a drug into his wine so that he might be bundled into a sack carried on board and brought to France; but he discovered the plot in time and escaped.

When the prisoners were arrested wild rumors filled the streets. The Cardinal was named as the biggest scoundrel France had ever known.

Stories of the orgies which took place at Saverne were circulated; every woman whose name was temporarily in the news was said to have been his mistress.

Paris was against the Cardinal; but the Court was against me. I suddenly became aware of this in the looks which came my way and in the sorrow of friends like my dear Campan and Elisabeth. Gabrielle was uncertain; she was surrounded by her family and the Cardinal belonged to one of the greatest houses in France. That was the crux of the matter. The Cardinal had been publicly arrested and that was an insult to the nobility.

It gradually began to dawn on me how much I was hated, and to doubt the depth of these people who had always shown me such respect and, as I thought, affection.

Then suddenly public opinion changed—as it will without reason it seems—but I suppose nothing happens without reason. The people of Paris, so quick to sense a turn in affairs were now giving their allegiance to the Cardinal. He had ceased to become the villain of the piece; he was the maligned hero. There had to be a villain, of course—or a villainess. The Comtesse de la Motte? Well, she was deeply involved but the story would be more intriguing if there was a sinister and shadowy figure in the background—and that figure was a Queen.

But for the Queen, it was whispered, none of this could have happened.

Every day accounts of the affair were published. One printer produced a day-to-day account of events, and people could scarcely wait for his sheets to come from the press. The Cardinal was again the Belle Eminence—so dignified, so handsome; and the fashionable color for ribbon was half red half yellow called *Cardinal sur la paille*. Stories were told about him. His lechery had now become gallantry. When he had been arrested he had managed while pretending to latch his shoe to scribble a note to his confidant the Abbé Georgel asking him to destroy certain papers concerning the necklace affair which were in his Paris mansion. The Abbé had obeyed, removing a great deal of valuable evidence. This was talked of now and instead of accepting the fact that the Cardinal had made a bid to avoid incriminating himself, this was construed as his desire to prevent a Certain Person's being involved.

I was pregnant again; I was worried about the health of my eldest son. I was becoming more *sérieuse*, more aware, and this must necessarily depress me. I was spending more and more time with my family but the affair of the diamond necklace could not be kept out of my private life. I was deeply involved—even though I had taken no part in it.

The Cardinal's counsels were the finest in Paris. Men such as Target, de Bonnières, and Larget-Bardelin; Target was recognized as one of the shining lights of the French Bar. Sixty-year-old Maitre Doillot acted for Madame de la Motte and she so fascinated him that he became merely her mouthpiece and in fact she defended herself through this medium. As this turned out it was not an advantage for the prisoner, but it did mean that the most fantastic explanations of what had taken place were given. Oliva was given a young advocate fresh from school who was immediately attracted by her.

The excitement was becoming more and more intense. There was no conversation except that which concerned the affair of the necklace. Madame Cagliostro had been released as she was proved to have had nothing to do with the affair. She went to her hotel in the Rue Saint-Claude, there to await the verdict; and when the highest people in the land called to imply that they believed she had been wronged, she received them with signs of weeping on her face. Indeed, it was considered fashionable to call on the lady.

This was an indication of how popular feeling was going. The people were already beginning to whisper that it was one who was not standing trial who was really guilty.

According to custom the consultations between prisoners and their advocates were published; these were sold in large numbers; the speeches for the defense were published before they were spoken and therefore the people could follow the way the trial was going.

So much has been written of this affair; so many theories have been brought forward; and how can I say which is the true one?

I believed then that the Cardinal was guilty; I could not understand how he could have been deceived as so many people believed he had been. But everyone else believed him innocent.

Madame de la Motte made the most extraordinary allegations about everyone, but she did not mention my name. When one of her stories was proved wrong she would immediately produce another. In the court, where one accused was allowed to question another, she confounded the Cardinal when he asked her how she came by such sudden wealth. He should know, was her answer. He was a generous lover and she had been his mistress; she reproached Oliva for her loose conduct; Cagliostro so incensed her that she picked up one of the candlesticks and threw it at him.

Cagliostro responded with his own invective . . . words, which most could not understand; they concerned his mysticism and his aloofness from ordinary men.

But when she was confronted with Oliva's and Rétaux de Villette's account of the scene in the Grove of Venus she raged and stormed, and since she could not deny this took place, fainted. When the turnkey tried to help her she revived suddenly and bit him in the neck.

With Madame de la Motte's wild behavior and Cagliostro's weird pronouncements the Cardinal stood out as a man of great breeding and even honor. Each day his popularity rose and as the stories emerged and the judges and the people tried to make sense of them, they became more and more certain that the Cardinal had been the dupe of scoundrels.

Oliva, who in the Bastille had given birth to a child which her lover immediately accepted as his, made an instant appeal to the spectators' chivalry. She had done no wrong. She had impersonated me it was true but she had had no idea for what purpose and when she was called to give her evidence she was feeding her newly born baby and begged the Lords of Parlement to be kind enough to wait until her little son had finished his meal. Everyone was deeply moved and the lords patiently waited and it was reported in the news sheets that "The Law was silenced in the presence of Nature." What an impression she made with her bodice loosened and her long hair, so much like my own, escaping round her shoulders. When she showed signs of faintness the severest of the lawyers was ready to catch her in his arms. Everyone was convinced that such a charming creature had been the tool of scheming people and was herself entirely innocent—which I am sure was the case.

And then Cagliostro in green silk embroidered with gold:

"Who are you and whence do you come?" he was asked.

"I am an illustrious traveler," he cried in loud tones which provoked laughter but he soon silenced that with his colorful invective; and I believe that there were many who though they laughed in the courtroom by day were in truth afraid of what such a notorious sorcerer might do to them.

And so they stood before the judges—the handsome Cardinal, the wild, beautiful and scheming Comtesse, the charming young courtesan with her baby at her breast, the adventurer Villette and the fantastic magician, sorcerer, or wise man. Everyone was awaiting the verdict of the judges which was of the utmost importance to all these people on trial—and perhaps equally so to me.

The judgment was given on Wednesday, 31st May, and the court opened at six o'clock in the morning. From five o'clock the streets had been filling and crowds had gathered in front of the Palais de Justice. Guards, mounted and on foot, kept the crowds in order from the Pont Neuf to the Rue de la Barillerie.

In the entrance of the Grande Chambre members of de Rohan's family had assembled; they were all dressed in mourning and had doubtless placed themselves there as a warning to the judges who must pass them by. They wished to imply that to do anything but acquit the Cardinal would be an outrage against the nobility.

It became quite clear that the de Rohans were determined to bring their relative out of that court acquitted of all guilt. For this reason, as Madame de la Motte was judged first and judged guilty—for how could it be otherwise in view of the evidence—two of the judges declared their intention to press for the death penalty. This was a ruse on the part of these men because if a case was being judged which might incur the death penalty no cleric must sit in judgment. Of the thirteen clerics among the judges only two were favorable to Rohan, therefore, by removing them from the seat of judgment, although the Rohans lost two votes in their favor they rid themselves of eleven against. Such was the power of the Rohans.

Madame de la Motte was not sentenced to death but she was condemned to be whipped naked by the executioner, marked with the letter V for *voleuse* on her shoulder, and imprisoned in the Salpêtrière for the rest of her life. Her husband though not present to pay the penalty of his crimes was sentenced to the galleys for life; Rétaux de Villette was exiled and Oliva was acquitted but not without blame for she had actually taken part in the scheme to impersonate me.

Cagliostro was dismissed from every charge.

There remained the chief figure in the drama—the one whose presence in it was responsible for the great interest throughout the country.

An absolute acquittal was demanded. The Cardinal had been the dupe of scoundrels—but his good faith was undeniable. He was absolutely innocent.

"It is innocence, gentlemen," declared his counsel, "that I am defending, as a man and as a judge; and I am so thoroughly penetrated with my belief that I would allow myself to be hacked to pieces in maintaining it."

The battle was over. After sixteen hours of deliberation the Cardinal was acquitted without a stain on his character.

In the streets they were shouting. The women of the fishmarket had assembled outside the Bastille with roses and jasmine. The Parisian crowds—the most easily excited in the world—were roaring their approval. "Long live the Parlement. Long live the Cardinal."

When I heard the verdict I suddenly realized its implication.

This was the biggest defeat I had ever suffered. In giving their verdict the Parlement had implied that it was not unnatural for the Cardinal de Rohan to expect that I would make arrangements to meet him in the park at Versailles; it was not unnatural to think that I could be bought by a diamond necklace!

I was overcome with horror. I threw myself onto my bed and wept. When Madame Campan found me there she was alarmed by my wild grief and sent for Gabrielle to come and comfort me.

When I saw them there in my bedchamber, those two dear women whom I trusted and knew to be my friends I cried: "Come and lament for your Queen, insulted and sacrificed by cabals and injustice." Then I was angry suddenly. The French hated me. In that moment I hated them. "But rather let me pity you as Frenchwomen," I went on. "If *I* have not met with equitable judges in a matter which affected my reputation what could you hope for in a suit in which your fortune and your character were at stake?"

The King came in and shook his head sadly.

He said: "You find the Queen much afflicted. She has great reason to be so. They were determined throughout the affair to see only an ecclesiastical Prince—a Prince de Rohan; while he is in fact a needy fellow. And all this was but a scheme to put money in his pockets, in endeavoring to do which he found himself the party cheated instead of the cheat. Nothing is easier to see through; and it is not necessary to be an Alexander to cut this Gordian knot."

I looked at him, this kind but most ineffectual man; and I thought then of that day when they had brought us news that we were King and Queen of France and how we had cried: "We are too young to rule."

How right we were! We were more than too young; we were unequal to this great task—he through his inability to make a decision even when he knew the right one and I . . . I was the foolish featherhead my brother Joseph had said I was—the silly child my mother had known me to be and feared so much because of it.

But at least now I knew this; and it was something I had not fully realized before.

The sentence was carried out on Madame de la Motte on the steps of the Palais de Justice. As was expected she did not submit lightly. She struggled and bit her jailers and when the V was about to be branded on her shoulder she writhed so violently that she received it on her bare breast instead. Afterward she was carried off fainting to the Salpêtrière clad in sackcloth with only sabots for her feet, to live on black bread and lentils for the rest of her life. No sooner had her punishment been carried out than the people of Paris declared her to be a heroine. The Duc and Duchesse d'Orléans collected on her behalf; good things were sent to the Salpêtrière. My foolish Lamballe was caught up in the general enthusiasm and took some delicacies to the prison which immediately gave rise to the rumor that I had sent her because my conscience troubled me. Then came the rumor that the story told by Madame de la Motte was true; that she had indeed acted on my behalf. It seemed, although I did not know it then, that the diamond necklace would never be forgotten.

A few weeks after her incarceration in her prison Madame de la Motte was allowed to escape and it was whispered that I had arranged it.

But when the libels began to pour in from England, for Madame de la Motte took to her pen when she reached that country, people still repeated this ridiculous story. The self-styled Comtesse was received in various English houses where she told lurid stories of life at the French Court and I was always a prominent feature in them.

Having wronged me once it seemed she was impelled to go on doing so.

This was a turning point in our lives and we knew it, both Louis and I. He was so good to me. He believed in my virtue, and I was grateful to him. He was tender and kind; but he did not understand how the earth was opening before us.

Now I know that had he stood firm then he might have saved us. Had he shown himself resolute in the face of the Parlement he might have kept some of that long standing respect for the Monarchy which was fast crumbling away.

He should have been strong with me in the first place. He should never have allowed the affair of the necklace to be publicly known. It should have been investigated in private and settled in private.

"No one is more pleased than I am that the innocence of the Cardinal has been established," he declared.

But because I was so unhappy, so upset sensing the great disaster of this affair he sent a *lettre de cachet* to the Cardinal exiling him to his Abbey of Chaise-Dieu.

He exiled Cagliostro and his wife. This was his weakness.

If he disagreed with the Parlement he should have shown that disagreement. Instead of which he accepted it and then agreed to the exile.

I could not rid myself of the terrible depression which had come to me. Mercy wrote to my brother:

> "The Queen's distress is greater than seems reasonably justified by the cause."

It was true. But some intuition warned me that what had happened to me was the greatest disaster I had ever faced. I did not understand fully. I merely knew that it was so.

I had lost my lightheartedness. I felt I would never be gay and carefree again.

19

"When waste and unthrift deplete the royal treasury there arises a cry of
despair and terror. Thereupon the finance minister has recourse to disastrous measures, such as, in the last resort, that of debasing the gold cur-
rency or the imposition of new taxes . . . It is certain that the present
government is worse than that of the late King in respect of disorderliness
and extortion. Such a condition cannot possibly continue much longer
without catastrophe resulting."

Comte de Mercy-Argenteau

"I am worried about the health of my eldest boy. His growth is somewhat awry for he has one leg shorter than the other and his spine is a
little twisted and unduly prominent. For some time now he has been inclined to attacks of fever and he is thin and frail."

Marie Antoinette to Joseph II

"Four wax tapers were placed on her toilette; the first went out and I
relighted it; shortly afterward the second and the third went out also,
upon which the Queen squeezing my hand in an emotion of terror said
to me: 'Misfortune has power to make us superstitious. If the fourth
taper goes out like the rest, nothing can prevent my looking on it as a
fatal omen.' The fourth taper went out."

Madame Campan's Memoirs

MADAME DÉFICIT

Nothing could ever be quite the same again. For one thing I myself had
stepped across the threshold of awareness. I was no longer the frivolous
child. I had become conscious of my growing unpopularity and what had
once seemed the height of pleasure now seemed a waste of time.

The leader of fashion, the frivolous seeker of pleasure who threw herself so wholeheartedly into games such as *descampativos* and *guerre panpan*, seemed like a silly child. I had grown up. Moreover at the time of the verdict which had so distressed me I was heavily pregnant and about a month afterward I gave birth to another daughter. My little Sophie Béatrix was delicate from birth. Perhaps the grief and anger I suffered at the time of the verdict undermined my health and that of the child; but the baby took my mind completely from that affair; and I would sit nursing the whimpering child and tell myself that I did not mind what happened to me as long as she grew up strong and healthy.

I had now four children. It was what I had always wanted. To be a mother; to live with my children and for my children.

The libels about me grew wilder and they were everywhere. Pictures of me were stuck on the walls of Paris buildings and in all of them I was depicted wearing the Diamond Necklace. The story was that it was in my jewel box; that I had made a scapegoat of poor Madame de la Motte. If ever I rode out I was given sullen looks and silence. I thought often of my first visit to Paris when Monsieur de Brissac had told me that two hundred thousand Frenchmen were in love with me. How different it was now! Where had I gone wrong? I had been extravagant, careless, I knew, but I had never been vicious. Before my friends the Polignacs had urged me to interfere in the giving of appointments I had kept aloof from state affairs. But I had to admit that my desire to please them had caused me to interfere. Strangely enough, my husband, who was a shrewd man in many ways, seemed to trust my judgment. I think he was bemused because of the admiration my appearance excited in others, and yet I was not a promiscuous woman. I had been a faithful wife, which was something which could be said for few women at the Court of France. I was a romantic; the sensations I craved were for continual excitement, the daring escapade, the preliminaries of love-making, flirtations—I was a coquette by nature—but I had no deep sexual desires which must be gratified at all costs. Perhaps that early initiation which had been so frustratingly humiliating had had its effect upon me. Although I had always been surrounded by an admiring group of men and women who professed passionate friendships for me these relationships had never been physical. I did not desire that. The very idea would have been repulsive to me. My life must be rather like a Watteau painting—charming, delicately romantic. But how could the people understand this? And my conduct was such as to give credence to the terrible stories of sexual orgies which were attached to my name. The King however preserved a reverence for me. I had been patient with his inadequacies, I had shared those humiliating attempts over a number of years and never complained to him nor blamed him, now I shared his triumphs. His manhood had been vindicated and I had played a very large part in the vindication. Therefore he wished to please me. And when I asked favors for my friends he was very loathe to refuse them, even though his common sense might have told him it would have been wise to do so.

I often think of him now with great tenderness. I remember his love for our children. How people would smile when he spoke of "my son" and "the Dauphin," seeking opportunities to bring the children into the conversation. And our children loved us. We were never King and Queen to them, but dearest Papa and darling darling Maman. I knew they had this special feeling for me. I was happy in my nursery; and I knew now more than ever that Louis and I should have been born in a humbler station of life. We could have been good simple parents. This was our tragedy.

How did the fearful disasters come upon us? Even now, I cannot entirely say. Even now I ask myself when that moment had come, the turning point in affairs of men which can lead to greatness . . . or disaster. If my dear Gabrielle had not possessed such rapacious relations perhaps things might have been different. No, that was too small a matter.

I was accused of working against France for Austria. Every little incident was turned to my disadvantage, as people will do when they appear to be consumed by an all absorbing hate. I was Austrian and because of this was resented in France.

My brother Joseph was at war with Turkey and Prussia and the French alliance with Austria had laid down that in such circumstances money or men should be sent to aid their ally. I knew of course that what Joseph needed was men, not 15,000,000 livres which Monsieur de Vergennes and his Council had decided to send. I asked Vergennes to see me that I might ask that men should be sent and give my reasons why. Monsieur de Vergennes informed me that it was not politic to send Frenchmen to fight in the service of the Emperor Joseph; therefore the money would go. I explained that there was no lack of money at Vienna and that it was men who were needed, to which Vergennes asked me to remember that I was the mother of the Dauphin and cease thinking of myself as the sister of the Emperor. It was as though he believed I wished to sacrifice France for the sake of Austria, which was quite untrue. The money was sent. I was deeply distressed. I talked of it to my dear Campan who, during these days of uneasiness, seemed to grow closer to me.

"How can they be so wicked!" I cried. "They have sent all that money from the general post office making it known publicly that the carriages which are being loaded with French money are going to my brother in Austria. I, they say, am sending money from France, where it is so badly needed, to my brother. And in truth I had not wished the money to be sent—and it would have been sent if I had belonged to any other house. Oh, my dear Campan, what can I do? What can I say? But does it matter —for whatever I do or say they will be against me."

I try to understand now what was happening in France during those days when we were coming nearer and nearer to the precipice. In the days of Louis XIV the Monarchy had been supreme. His power had been absolute; and he kept it intact because under his rule France had become great. In war, art, and science he led France to become premier among nations. He was an autocrat but he was a King of whom France could be proud. The pomp and etiquette of his Court did not appear to be ridiculous because he was in fact as grand as his setting. He was not named the Roi Soleil for nothing.

And there was his great grandson, our dear grandfather who had been so charming to me on my arrival. It was during his long reign that the pedestal on which the Monarchy was placed had begun to crumble. Madame Campan's father was right. It had begun long before we came to the throne. The people's heritage had been squandered in careless and extravagant debauchery. It was later said that not since the days of ancient Rome was there such profligacy as was practiced at the Court of Louis XV. But when my husband became King there should have been a change. There could never have been a King of France less given to extravagance and he had never in his life practiced debauchery. He wanted to be good; he cared passionately for his people; he asked nothing for himself, only their confidence in the belief that he was their little father who would make France great again. Maurepas was there to advise him; he listened to Maurepas; but when I made my requests he would listen to me; and he was never sure to which of us he should give his support. He wavered. Was that what destroyed us? He was unable to think quickly, unable ever to make up his mind. This was not stupidity—quite the reverse. He was too ready to see both sides of a dispute, which was often the true aspect of the case, but it prevented his making a decision. Hence he would go a little way in one direction, hesitate, turn . . . give way and then sway again. My poor Louis, whose intentions were always so unselfish, who desperately sought to find the right course and seldom succeeded.

He had trained himself to be calm in all situations and in this he was helped by his own nature. Yet all his good qualities worked against him; for this very calmness prevented his seeing disaster when it loomed right ahead of him. He would say: "Oh, it will pass. It is only a bagatelle."

Had it not been for the state of the finances, we might have avoided tragedy. Was it our fault that the country's finances were tottering on the edge of bankruptcy? To some extent perhaps I was to blame. My dear Trianon was like a greedy monster who put his head into the treasury and drank deep. My white and gold theater, my exquisite gardens, my Hameau . . . they were all very expensive. But I did not think of the cost because they were so beautiful, and they made not only me but thousands of others happy.

Turgot, and Necker, had tried to right these finances and their methods had failed. Then we called in Calonne. His policy was to borrow from the people and decrease taxation. The yearly deficit was over 100,000,000 livres.

Everyone was talking of the Deficit. They had given me a new name. My picture, with the necklace was seen everywhere and underneath it were the words Madame Déficit.

When Calonne had first taken over we had all felt optimistic. We did not realize then that he was thinking only of the immediate present and that the fact that things did seem to improve was due solely to the confidence he inspired. But confidence was not enough. Whenever I asked if something might be done he would bow courteously and say: "If what Your Majesty asks is possible, the thing is done; if it is impossible it shall be done."

This seemed a most encouraging and clever answer; but it was not the way to solve our difficulties.

Then I forgot all these tiresome financial matters because the health of two of my children began to worry me and occupy my thoughts exclusively. I had accepted the certainty that little Sophie Béatrix would be a difficult child to rear; but now my eldest son, my little Louis-Joseph, the Dauphin, was showing signs of weakness. The trouble began with rickets and in spite of all the careful attention which I and the doctors bestowed on him his condition worsened.

It soon became apparent that his spine was affected and my darling was going to be deformed. I was desperately unhappy; and my great consolation was in the good healthy looks of my dearest Madame Royale and her younger brother, the Duke of Normandy, who was healthy and lovely with his blue eyes and fair hair.

He was a strange child, my little Dauphin; perhaps it was because he was not as strong as other boys—he was introspective, and clever—a little old man, he seemed at times. I loved him fiercely as one does a child whose health gives continual cause for anxiety; I was constantly in the nursery so that I might keep an eye on the baby Sophie Béatrix. Gabrielle was my close companion for she was governess to the children and it was very disturbing when the Dauphin took a dislike to her. I could not understand how anyone could dislike Gabrielle—she was so lovely in appearance, so gentle in manner, and she adored children. But there had always been intrigues against the Polignac family and although Gabrielle was unlike the others she was a Polignac and no one forgot it. The Dauphin's governor was the Duc d'Harcourt, and I believe he bred this hatred in the Dauphin for his governess. I tried to stop it and this was noticed. I soon realized that I, too, was not to be allowed complete freedom in the management of my own nurseries.

I remember one day taking marshmallows and jujube lozenges to Louis-Joseph for he was very fond of sweetmeats. The Duc d'Harcourt respectfully pointed out that the Dauphin was only allowed to eat such sweets as the faculty prescribed for him. I was momentarily angry that I should not be allowed to give him sweets and then when I looked at his poor little body I thought perhaps it was the doctors who should decide.

It was only a few days later when Gabrielle told me that the Dauphin had sent her from the room.

"You are too fond of using perfumes, Duchesse," he said, "and they make me feel ill."

"But," protested Gabrielle with tears in her eyes, "I was not using perfume."

In some ways I found greater pleasure in my younger son; who was nearly two years old. He adored me and liked to climb all over me, examining Monsieur Léonard's elaborate headdress with the greatest interest and glee. He was gay and a little self-willed and very interested in everything about him; and because he was not such an important little person as his elder brother I thought of him as entirely my own.

Little Sophie Béatrix was growing weaker. I could not leave her; it was heartbreaking to see the wan little creature fighting for her breath. I shall never forget the day she died in my arms. I looked down at the still little face and until that time I had never known such unhappiness.

I laid her gently in her cradle and tried to comfort myself with thoughts of the other children; but looking back it seemed that perhaps that was the beginning of all my sorrows.

The financial affairs of the country were getting worse and whenever people talked of the Deficit they mentioned my name. My extravagances were responsible for it all; I was the Austrian woman who worked against France for the sake of Austria; I had crippled the finances of France by buying the Diamond Necklace, by the expenses of the Trianon. I was indifferent to these slanders. I thought only of the deterioration in the health of my elder son.

He was an extremely clever boy and would talk so wisely that it seemed incredible in one so young; but as I watched his deformity become more pronounced with the weeks I wept for him. He could not play as his little brother did, but would sit with his dog Moufflet always beside him, for all the children had inherited from me a love of dogs.

My husband mourned with me for the loss of our little daughter and the poor state of our Dauphin's health. I'm sure he was more disturbed on that score than by Calonne's suggestions to call together certain members of the nobility and clergy—the Notables—that they might give their advice as to how the country could be extricated from the alarming position into which it was falling.

Calonne's idea was to abolish privilege and levy taxes equally. It was an idea which needed the most solemn examination. "Only an Assembly of Notables could fulfill it."

My husband was alarmed. He knew that the calling together of this assembly was a direct blow at the power of the Monarchy; but Calonne pointed out that the great Henri Quatre had made use of it. Vergennes was against the idea and for a time Louis wavered between his ministers, and then the alarming state of the exchequer decided him to come down in favor of Calonne's suggestion. This assembly would consist of seven Princes of the Blood, fourteen Archbishops and Bishops, thirty-six Dukes and Peers, twelve Councilors of State, thirty-eight Magistrates, twelve Deputies of State and twenty-five Municipal Officers of large towns, and was meant to be a cross section of the people who could be most use in advising the King and Parlement.

Once he had made the decision to call the Assembly of Notables Louis was pleased.

He told me on the morning of the 30th of December: "I have not slept a wink—but my wakefulness was due to joy."

Poor Louis! What little grasp he had of the true state of affairs. How he believed that everyone was of the same disinterested outlook as himself!

He went on: "The maxim of our kings has been: 'As willeth the King so willeth the law.' Mine shall be: 'As willeth the happiness of the people, so willeth the King.'"

He was happier than he had been since the death of Sophie Béatrix, believing that this measure would solve our problems. La Fayette, recently returned from America was firmly in favor of the summoning of the Notables and the abolition of privilege. He had come back with ideas of a new liberty, and he was not the only one. The philosophers were writing of liberty, preaching liberty. And in the Palais Royale the domain of our old enemy the Duc d'Orléans, meetings were held in the gardens at which further abolitions were talked of. Liberty, Equality, and Fraternity were discussed. Frenchmen had helped to fight for these across the sea, so why not in France?

It was hardly likely that the Notables should succeed. Were the nobility of France going to agree to pay taxes? Were they going to take on a greater share of the country's finances? The Notables were impotent. It was said that they were not in a position to impose taxes. The only assembly which could do that was a States General.

That was the first whisper of those words.

The Notables were a failure. In the streets they were using the Anglo-French title of Not-Ables. This assembly could only resign and was a sign for the downfall of Calonne who had been responsible for calling them.

The people were demanding the recall of Necker.

Who to replace Calonne? The Abbé Vermond was at my elbow. His friend Loménie de Brienne, Archbishop of Toulouse, was the man for the task. He was certain of it. I always wanted to please my friends and Vermond had been close to me since my arrival in France—and even before—therefore I longed to make this appointment. The King did not wish for it; everyone was against it; he wavered; but I persisted and eventually he gave way.

Now I was caught up in state affairs. Loménie de Brienne was not the man for the job; in fact the Parlement was against him and everything he suggested was opposed. The very fact that I had helped to make his appointment set them against him; and when in a futile effort to please me he brought forward the proposal that I should have a place at the meetings of the council and so have a say in the actual government of the country the result was naturally to make me more unpopular than ever.

In the streets the people were shouting: "Shall we be governed by Madame Déficit? Never." They paraded with placards on which were crude drawings of me—always wearing the necklace, always inscribed Madame Déficit.

In the Palais Royale opinion against me was steadily whipped up; at Bellevue, which Louis had given to the aunts, my wickedness and depravity were talked of and fresh stories—the more fantastic the better—were concocted.

"It is the Queen," was the cry. "The Queen who is responsible for the woes of our country. Who else but the chief character in the case of the Diamond Necklace, who but the Austrian Woman, Madame Déficit.

Brienne had no new ideas. I was fast realizing that I had been wrong to ask for his appointment. He could only think of borrowing, and wanted to float new loans. The Parlement disagreed with his propositions and the King, in a rare moment of decision, decided to support the minister.

"I command you to carry out the orders of Monsieur de Brienne," cried Louis.

Orléans was on his feet reminding the King that what he had said was illegal.

Knowing that Orléans was a danger, having some notion of the nightly gatherings in the Palais Royale, Louis for once was stern, and banished Orléans to his estates at Villers-Cotteret.

Now there was a division between the King and the Parlement; and all the Parlements of the country stood firmly behind the Parlement of Paris.

"Brienne must go," was the cry not only in the capital but throughout the country. There was rioting in several towns; people were demanding the recall of Necker and he could only come back if Brienne was dismissed.

The cry went up: "The country needs the States General!"

Madame Louise, the youngest of the aunts, died at that time. I think of her now as one of the lucky ones who did not live too long as most of us did.

She had died in her convent sure of her place in Heaven for as she passed away she cried in her delirium as though to her coachman: "To Paradise, quick. Full speed ahead."

I think she must have been the happiest of the aunts, removed from the stresses which had become so much a part of our lives.

I was spending more and more time at the Trianon, walking in the gardens, talking to my peasants at the Hameau. I felt so strongly the need to escape. I kept the children with me—my two healthy ones and my Dauphin, who was growing visibly thinner every day.

Rose Bertin came with new patterns. She had an exquisite silk—and also the most delightful satin I had ever seen.

"Everything is changed now," I told her. "I have many dresses in my wardrobe. They must suffice."

She looked at me incredulously and then smiled her roguish familiar smile. "Wait until Your Majesty sees the new blue velvet."

"I have no wish to see it," I replied. "I shall not be sending for you so often now."

She laughed and called to one of her women to unroll the velvet, but I turned away and walked to the window.

She was angry; I saw that as she left the apartment; her cheeks were pink and her eyes were half-closed. I wondered why I had ever liked the woman; and I was to wonder still more when I understood that she, growing more and more angry when she realized I really meant that I should not send for her, discussed my follies and extravagances with her customers and even went into the market places to do so.

I really had no desire for new dresses. I had changed. I must set a good example. I must cut down my expenses. I told the Duc de Polignac that I should have to relieve him of his post of Master of my Horse. It was in any case almost a sinecure and one which cost me fifty thousand livres a year. I had created it for the sake of Gabrielle. I also relieved her lover, the Comte de Vaudreuil, of his post of Grand Falconer.

"This will make us bankrupt!" cried the infuriated Comte.

"Better you than France," I replied with some sharpness. I was beginning to see how foolish I had been in bestowing such gifts on these people; I was realizing how they had battened on my careless generosity, which was in fact no generosity at all for I was giving away something which did not belong to me.

I felt these people were already turning from me—not Gabrielle, who had never asked for anything for herself, only favors for her family because they pressed her to; not the Princesse de Lamballe who was a disinterested friend; and my dear sister-in-law Elisabeth who cared deeply for my children and so had made an even deeper bond between us. These were my true friends. But perhaps even at this stage the others had already begun to desert.

But there was one friend who had returned to France and of whom I was very much aware. This was Comte Axel de Fersen. He appeared at gatherings and I never had more than a discreet word or so with him. But I was conscious of a great serenity because he was there. I felt that he was awaiting that moment when I should give the sign and then he would be at my side.

The Dauphin was growing weaker. I was constantly in his apartments, watching over him. My anxiety for him could make me forget for a time these state affairs. Here was tragedy and one which was more real to me, more heartrending than the difficulties of France.

I was writing to Joseph about him:

"I am worried about the health of my eldest boy. His growth is somewhat awry for he has one leg shorter than the other and his spine is a little twisted and unduly prominent. For sometime now he has been inclined to attacks of fever and he is thin and frail."

I wanted to be with him the whole of the time, nursing him myself. But that was not possible. The Opera House had requested that the King and I attend a gala performance and Louis said that he thought it would be expected that we should show ourselves.

I dreaded it. I told him so. They wished to see him; they loved him, but they hated me. They were fed on the cruelest lies about me. I hated the thought of going to the Opera House, which in itself would be a reminder of those days when I had danced so madly at the opera balls.

"It is our duty to go," said Louis somberly.

I went as I often did to the nurseries to show the children my gown; little Louis-Charles shrieked with delight and stroked the soft silk of my skirt.

"Beautiful beautiful Maman," he said. And he insisted on showing me Moufflet's latest tricks. Moufflet was the cleverest dog in the world and he wished he were his. My poor little Dauphin was lying in his bed, his misshapen body hidden; I wanted to weep as I bent over and kissed him. He put his arms about my neck and clung to me; he loved me when there was no one there to poison him against me.

I left for the opera with the memory of my nurseries staying with me. It was a brilliant occasion and I was delighted that the King was so loudly cheered. There were no cheers for me though, and I heard the shout of "Madame Déficit!" and "Where is the Diamond Necklace?"

As I stepped into the royal box I saw the paper which had been pinned there. It was hastily removed but not before I had caught sight of the words, "Tremble, Tyrants."

I did tremble, throughout the opera, uncontrollably. But Louis sat beside me smiling with that calm smile which, it seemed, nothing could shake.

What joy it was when my son seemed to be recovering his health a little. I forgot all my anxieties in letting myself believe that he was really growing stronger. He was such a clever child and he was always amusing me with his sayings.

"He will be a very wise King," I told his father; and Louis agreed with me.

They had put him into a corselet to try to straighten his spine and he never complained. He was like a little man.

I was anxious that he should learn how to manage his finances. Finances were very much in my mind at that time and I had ordered his governor and governess not to give him more than his allowance. He was very taken with a mechanical doll he had seen and greatly desired it. I planned to give it to him, for he told me he had asked God to see that he received it.

He told me that one of his attendants had reminded him that it was better to ask God for wisdom than riches.

"To which, Maman," he told me with a smile, "I replied that while I was about it I saw no reason not to ask for both at once."

What could one do with such a child but marvel at him?

"My darling," I cried, "you must promise me to eat up all the nourishing food you are given. You must grow into a strong man. Your Papa was not strong as a boy, but look at him now."

"I want that," he told me.

"You should say we want, my darling . . . as the King does." I was trying to teach him to become a King for I always remembered his father's saying that he had been taught nothing.

"The King and I say 'we want' together, Maman. But I am right, for the King does not say we for himself."

He looked so grave and wise and I did not know what I wanted to do —weep or laugh.

And as I was beginning to hope, he became ill again. He awoke in the night suffering terrible convulsions. He suffered so, my dearest son; and I could do nothing for him. The doctors were always examining, always suggesting treatment. They tortured him with blisterings and they talked of cauterizing his spine. He bore all this with a sweetness which was amazing. He found it comforting to lie on a billiard table and I had a mattress placed on it for his greater comfort. He read a great deal—history mostly. I was there once when the Princesse de Lamballe asked him if he picked out the exciting parts of the book—it was a history of the reign of Charles VII—and he looked at my dear silly Lamballe almost reprovingly and replied: "I do not know enough about it to choose, Madame; and it is all so interesting."

As he grew weaker he did not want anyone with him but myself. His eyes would brighten as I came in. "Maman," he would say, "you are so beautiful. I feel happier when you are near me. Tell me of the olden days."

He meant by that those days when he was able to run about and play as his young brother loved to do. And Moufflet would curl up beside him and I would tell him of little incidents from the past such as the occasion at the Trianon theater when he had sat on Papa's knee and watched me on the stage.

"I remember, I remember," he would cry. "And what happened?"

He would nod as I told, knowing it word for word for indeed I had told him the story many times, of how I had forgotten my words and Monsieur Campan in the prompter's box, his large spectacles on his nose, had sought to find the place. My little son cried out in a dramatic tone which could be heard all over the theater, "Monsieur Campan, take off those big spectacles. Maman cannot hear you."

He laughed and I laughed with him but as always I was near to tears.

The air of Versailles was perhaps not pure enough for him. La Muette would perhaps be better suggested one of the doctors.

"It is unprotected from the cold winds," said another.

"Ah, but those winds sweep the air clear."

"Monseigneur's chamber at Versailles is damp," said Sabatier. "The windows look on the Swiss Lake which is stagnant."

"Nonsense," replied Lassone. "The air of Versailles is healthy."

My husband remembered that when he was a child he had been sent to Meudon and the air there was said to have made him stronger.

Louis had made the decision. The Dauphin was sent to Meudon.

The members of the States General were to assemble in Versailles. I was afraid of the States General because I was aware of an anxiety among those whom I considered to be my true friends. Axel on those occasions when we exchanged a word or two made me aware of his alarm. I knew that he considered the position very grave and that he was afraid for me.

"Louis," I said to my husband, "would it not be better to hold the Assembly some distance from Paris?"

"They must come to Versailles and the capital," my husband replied.

"They will rob you of your power and your dignity," I said. I was certain of it. They were elected from all classes of society. Members of the lower classes would have a say in the affairs of the Government. It was a state of affairs that neither Louis XIV nor Louis XV would have tolerated. But my husband assured me that it was necessary.

There were great preparations for the opening ceremony; hopes had risen in the country; it seemed as though everyone was hoping for a miracle from the States General.

When I went to Meudon to see my son I forgot all my anxieties about the coming ordeal—for I must take my place in the procession—because the Dauphin was clearly rapidly failing.

His face lit up when he saw me. "The best times," he said, "are when you are with me."

I sat by his billiard table holding his hand. What should I wear? he wanted to know.

I told him that my gown was to be of violet, white, and silver.

"That will be beautiful," he said. "If I were strong and well I should ride in the carriage with you."

"Yes, my darling. So you must get well quickly."

"I could not do it in time, Maman," he said gravely. And then: "Maman, I want to see the procession. Please, please let me see you ride by. I want to see you and dear Papa."

"It would tire you."

"It never tires me to see you. It makes me feel better. Please, Maman."

I knew that I could not deny him this and I told him that it should be arranged.

The bells were ringing and the sun shone brightly. This was the 4th of May in the year 1789—the year of the assembling of the States General. The streets of Versailles were colorful with decorations and everywhere the fleur-de-lis was fluttering in the light breeze. I had heard that there was not a single room to be found in Versailles.

There was optimism everywhere. I heard it whispered that the old methods were passing now that the people were to have a hand in managing the country's affairs. That was what the States General was all about. The King was a good man. He had invited the States General. Taxes were to be abolished—or equally shared. Bread would be cheap. France was to be a heaven on earth.

I remember that day clearly. I was so unhappy. I hated the warm sunshine, the faces of the people, their cheering voices (none of the cheers were for me). The bands were playing. There were the French and Swiss Guards. Six hundred men in black with white cravats and slouched hats marched in the procession. They were the Tiers Etat, deputies of the commoners from all over the country; there were three hundred and seventy-four lawyers among them. Following these men were the Princes and the most notable of these was the Duc d'Orléans who was already well known to the people as their friend. What a contrast the nobles made with those men in black—in lace and gold and enormous plumes waving in their hats. There were the Cardinals and Bishops in their rochets and violet robes—a magnificent sight. No wonder the people had waited for hours to see them pass. In that procession were men whose names were to haunt me in the years ahead—Mirabeau, Robespierre; and the Cardinal de Rohan was there too.

My carriage was next. I sat very still looking neither to right nor left. I was aware of the hostile silence. I caught whispers of "The Austrian Woman!" "Madame Déficit." "She is not wearing the necklace today." Then someone shouted *"Vive d'Orléans."* I knew what that meant. Long live my enemy. They were shouting for *him* as I rode by.

I tried not to think of them. I must smile. I must remember that my little son would be watching the procession from the veranda over the stables where I had ordered he should be taken.

I thought of him instead of these people who showed so clearly that they hated me. I said to myself: "What should I care for them. Only let him grow strong and well and I shall care for nothing else."

I could hear the crowd shouting for my husband as his carriage came along. They did not hate him. I was the foreigner, the author of all their misfortunes. They had chosen me for the scapegoat.

How glad I was to return to my apartments, the ordeal over.

I was sitting at my dressing table, my women about me. I was tired but I knew I should not sleep when I retired to bed. Madame Campan had placed four wax tapers on my *toilette* table and I watched her light them.

We talked of the Dauphin and his latest sayings and how he had enjoyed the procession; and suddenly the first of the candles went out of its own accord.

I said: "That is strange. There is no draft." And I signed to Madame to relight it.

This she did and no sooner had she done so than the second candle went out.

There was a shocked silence among the women. I gave a nervous laugh and said: "What candles are these, Madame Campan. Both to go out."

"It is a fault in the wick, Madame," she said. "I doubt not." Yet the manner in which she said it suggested that she did doubt her statement.

A few minutes after she had lighted the second candle the third went out.

Now I felt my hands trembling.

"There is no draft," I said. "Yet three of these candles have gone out . . . one after another."

"Madame," said my good Campan, "it is surely a fault."

"There have been so many misfortunes," I said. "Do you think, Madame Campan, that misfortune makes us superstitious?"

"I believe this could well be so, Madame," she answered.

"If the fourth taper goes out nothing can prevent my looking upon it as a fatal omen."

She was about to say something reassuring when the fourth taper went out.

I felt my heart heavy. I said: "I will go to bed now. I am very tired."

And I lay in bed, thinking of the hostile faces in the procession, the whispering voices; and of the little face which I had seen from the stable veranda.

And I could not sleep.

We were summoned to Meudon—Louis and I—and we set out with all speed.

I sat by my son's bed; he did not wish me to go. His hot little hand was in mine and he kept whispering, "Maman, my beautiful Maman."

I felt the tears running down my cheeks and I could not stop them.

"You are crying for me, Maman," he said, "because I am dying, but you must not be sad. We all have to die."

I begged him not to speak. He must save his breath.

"Papa will look after you," he said. "He is a good kind man."

Louis was deeply affected; I felt his hand on my shoulder, kind and tender. It was true he was a good man. I thought of how we had longed for children, how we had suffered because we could not have a son and now how we suffered because we had one.

Little Louis-Joseph was fighting for his life. I think he was trying to cling to it because he knew I so much wanted him to live. He was thinking of me even in those last moments.

I cried to myself: "Oh God, leave me my son. Take anything from me but leave me my son."

But one does not make bargains with God.

I felt a warm hand in mine and there was my youngest boy. Louis had sent for my daughter and son to remind me that they were left to me.

On one side of me my lovely ten-year-old daughter and on the other four-year-old Louis-Charles.

"You should comfort your mother," said the King gently.

And I held my children close to me and was, in some measure, comforted.

20

25th June 1789: "Nothing. The stag was hunted at Saint-Appoline and I was not there."

14th July 1789: "Nothing."

Louis XVI's Journal

"I have just come from Versailles. Monsieur Necker is dismissed. This is the signal for a St. Bartholomew's day of the patriots. This evening the Swiss and German battalions will slit our throats. We have but one resource: To Arms."

Camille Desmoulins at the Palais Royale

"Still the people spoke of the King with affection and appeared to think his character favorable to the desire of the nation for the reform of what was called abuses; but they imagined that he was restrained by the opinions and influence of the Comte d'Artois and the Queen; and those two august personages were therefore objects of hatred to the malcontents."

Madame Campan's Memoirs

THE FOURTEENTH OF JULY

The four candles had gone out and it seemed that the lights of my life were going out for me. Two children lost in less than two years. I turned to those left to me . . . my serene and lovely daughter, whom I called affectionately Mousseline, loving and calm, never causing me anxiety, and my dearest son. The new Dauphin was very different from his brother, willful yet lovable, and even more passionately devoted to me; he was by nature gay and one of the best tonics I could have during those days of mourning was to hear his merry laughter as he played his games. He was self-willed and showed temper if he could not have his own way—but what child of four does not? But he could always be brought to obedience when I showed that I wished it. He adored his sister and it was a pleasure to see them together for she liked to mother him and he wanted to share everything he had with her. Like most boys his great passion was for uniforms and soldiers; and he was a great favorite with the guards and would watch them from the windows or better still go out into the garden and march along beside them.

His charm endeared him to all. I called him my *chou d'amour.*

I did not wish him to be too much aware of his position; yet on the other hand I always remembered my husband's complaint that he had never been educated to understand statescraft. I had even wondered whether this neglect was in some way responsible for our present difficulties.

So I talked to my son about the change his brother's death had made in his future.

"So you see, my darling," I said, "you have now become the Dauphin."

He nodded while he traced a pattern with his fat little finger on my dress.

"Which means you will one day be the King of France. Think of that."

He looked at me gravely. "I'll tell you something better, Maman," he said. "Shall I?"

I lifted him on to my lap. "What could be better, dearest?"

He put his mouth close to my ear and whispered: "Moufflet is my dog now."

I held him to me too tightly apparently for he said: "Maman, it is good to be loved but sometimes it hurts."

I felt a rush of emotion. And I thought: Oh, my little one, how right you are!

Life was moving fast toward some fearful climax, and the death of my son had temporarily made me forget this, for during those first days of grief I did not care much what happened. But now I realized that I had others to consider.

The first meeting of the States General had been held in Salle des Menus and there the King, Baretin, the Keeper of the Seals, and Necker had spoken. Necker explained to the Assembly that they had been called together at the express wish of the King, whose chief point was that the two wealthy orders—the nobility and the clergy—were willing to make great sacrifices for the sake of the country. Something happened which was significant of the new mood of the people. Having uncovered his head while speaking, the King replaced his hat at which point the custom was that the nobles should remove theirs and the members of the Third Estate kneel. This the latter declined to do and put on their hats.

Indignation was expressed by the nobles and someone called out an order to the Third Estate to take off their hats. It was immediately apparent that they obstinately refused to do this; and what would have happened I cannot say if my husband with great presence of mind had not removed his own hat; which gesture meant that everyone else must do the same—even the churlish members of the Third Estate. Thus it seemed that an unpleasant contretemps was avoided. But this was symbolical of the struggle which was about to begin with the nobles and clergy on one side and the members of the Third Estate on the other.

The name which was on everyone's tongue was that of the Comte de Mirabeau. He was an aristocrat by birth but had been made to suffer greatly during his childhood by a sadistic father, who had beaten and tortured him and even sent him to prison. He was a brilliant man and by placing himself on the side of the Third Estate he had greatly strengthened that body and it very soon became apparent that there was to be a conflict between the Third Estate and the rest of the States General.

The Third Estate had set itself up as the National Assembly; for they declared they represented ninety-six percent of the nation. They began to make their rules and announced that they would draw up a Constitution setting out how much power belonged to the King.

The Duc de Luxembourg who was the President of the Nobility called on the King in company with the Duc de la Rochefoucauld-Liancourt and talked earnestly to him.

"The Monarchy will be lost if Your Majesty does not dissolve the States General," said de la Rochefoucauld-Liancourt.

The King was in a dilemma. He wished to please all, he said.

He summoned Necker who advised him to act in a conciliatory fashion. I was against this. Something told me that the States General was planning our destruction. I was on the side of the Duc de Luxembourg and the Duc de la Rochefoucauld-Liancourt, who were asking that the States General be disbanded. The Deputies, I said, were a pack of madmen. We must dismiss them.

Louis as usual could not make up his mind. I could see him swaying toward Necker's views and then to mine. He compromised. He would not, he said, treat with rebels.

It was on the 20th June when the King was out hunting at Le Butard and the Assembly wished to meet. The Salle des Menus Plaisirs was shut so they held their meeting in the tennis court and there they swore not to dissolve until they had fulfilled the wish of the people and a Constitution had been granted.

This was defying the King for it was the King's right to dissolve the Assembly when he so wished.

When Louis discovered that the oath had been taken in the tennis court he was as undecided as ever. On one side were those who declared that the men who were now called rebels should be driven away by the military; and on the other was Necker advising conciliatory methods. Mirabeau, the strength behind the Third Estate, then announced that the National Assembly would only give way at the point of the bayonet, while Jean Sylvain Bailly, the President of the National Assembly, added that the nation once assembled could be dismissed by no one.

And the nation had assembled. That was what we did not realize soon enough. The Duc d'Orléans, who had added his voice to that of the Third Estate, had been spreading sedition in the Palais Royale and was encouraging agitators. Each day there were meetings; new pamphlets were appearing several times a day.

The words Liberty and the People had a magic quality. There was an air of tension through Versailles and the whole of Paris. And there was fear everywhere. We could not guess what would happen next. Axel spoke to me; he said: "You know that I shall always be here if I am wanted." And I felt happier than I had for some time.

Perhaps he, as a foreigner, one who mingled with the people of Paris, understood the situation far more than we could. We did not believe that the Monarchy was tottering; we could not conceive it; but he had mingled with those crowds in the Palais Royale, he had heard the mutterings of the people.

It was necessary for Louis to go to Paris to attend a meeting of the States General and I was worried as to what would happen there. I could not forgive Necker for not accompanying him. The man was annoyed because the King would not take his advice and although I had asked him specially to be with the King he had failed to do so. Louis' great quality was his courage. I never saw fear in him as in most men. If he took the wrong action—which he did so often—it was never through fear. Now that he had decided to be firm I knew that if someone could put up a good argument in favor of changing that firmness he would waver again.

At the Assembly he made a firm declaration. He would not allow any changes of institutions by which he meant the Army. He would make taxation equal; the nobility and the clergy should resign their privileges. He wished advice as to how to abolish *lettres de cachet*.

When he left he ordered that the Assembly should be disbanded for the night but no one obeyed the order. And when the Master of the Ceremonies, the Marquis de Brézé announced the meeting closed and advised all to go home, Mirabeau stood up and shouted that they would go when they wished and as for Brézé he could go back to those who sent him; and he repeated that only by the use of bayonets could they be separated.

But how typical of Louis to lose his firmness as quickly as he had put it on. When Brézé reported to him he merely shrugged his shoulders and said: "Very well. Let them stay where they are."

Then he made a mistake. He dismissed Necker and called in de Breteuil to take his place.

I was with the children reading to them aloud from the fables of La Fontaine. My daughter leaned against my chair following the text as I read and my son sat in my lap watching my lips and every now and then he would shriek with laughter as some phase of the story struck him as particularly funny.

We were at the Trianon which seemed to have changed its character in the last year or so. The theater remained shut. I had no heart for it. Often I would wander through the gardens with Gabrielle and we would try not to speak of the fears that were in our hearts. I was no longer surrounded by gay young men. They had been robbed of those sinecures which they had all sought and which I had delighted to bestow upon them. They were a little sullen. "We shall all be bankrupt," was their cry.

I had stopped reading and closed the book.

"I wish to show you my flowers," said Louis-Charles. And so we went out into the garden to that little patch which I had given him all for his own for he delighted in flowers and already, with the help of the gardeners, was cultivating them. "Flowers and soldiers, Maman," he had said, "I do not know which I love the best."

And hand in hand we walked out into the gardens and my dear villagers of the Hameau came out to curtsey and adore my children with their eyes; and no one would have guessed what was happening in the outside world. And yet again the Trianon was my haven.

My son released my hand and ran on ahead.

He reached his garden and stood waiting for us. "I have been talking to a grasshopper," he said. "He's been laughing at an old ant. But he won't laugh, will he, Maman, when the winter comes."

"When did you speak to the grasshopper, my love?"

"Just now. You couldn't see him. He ran out of the book while you were reading."

He looked at me seriously.

"You are making that up," said his sister.

But he swore he wasn't. "I take my oath," he said.

I laughed. But his way of exaggerating did disturb me a little. It was not that he did not mean to be truthful; he had such a vivid imagination.

Then he was picking flowers and presenting them to me and his sister. "Maman," he said, "when you go to a ball I will make you a necklace of flowers."

"Will you, darling?"

"A beautiful, beautiful one. It'll be better than a diamond necklace."

Always close to me were the warning shadows.

I picked him up suddenly and kissed him fiercely.

"I'd far rather have the flowers," I said.

I heard news of what was happening in Paris. During those hot July days it seemed as though the city was preparing itself, waiting. I heard the names of dangerous men mentioned often. Mirabeau, Robespierre, Danton, and the biggest traitor of them all, Orléans—Prince of the Royal House—who was urging the country to rise against us.

"What does he hope for?" I demanded of Louis. "To step into your shoes?"

"It would be impossible," replied my husband.

But I heard that crowds were thronging to the gardens of the Palais Royale day and night and that Orléans was already king of this little territory. The journalist agitator Camille Desmoulins was in his pay, it was said. These men were working against us.

"They can never succeed against the throne," said Louis.

Madame Campan was quiet and more serious than ever.

"Tell me everything," I said. "Hold nothing back from me."

"There have been riots in Paris, Madame. Mobs are roaming the streets and the shopkeepers are barricading their shops."

"Violence!" I muttered. "How I hate it."

"Danton speaks in the Palais Royale gardens, so does Desmoulins. They have discarded the green cockade because those are the colors of the Comte d'Artois."

"I fear they hate Artois almost as much as they do me."

I was sad, remembering those extravagant adventures we had shared.

"They have chosen the colors of Monsieur d'Orléans, Madame—red, white, and blue, the tricolor. They are asking for the recall of Necker. They parade through the streets with busts of Necker and the Duc d'Orléans."

"So they are heroes now."

Louis had changed again. He now decided that firm action was needed. He would call out the military; he would send garrisons to the Bastille. The States General must be disbanded. And while garrisoning the Bastille the King gave orders that the guns were not to be used against the people.

I shall never forget that night of the fourteenth of July. The hot sultry day was over and we had retired to our apartments.

I was unable to sleep. How different from Louis. His rest seemed never to be disturbed. He had to be aroused when the messenger came.

It was the Duc de la Rochefoucauld-Liancourt riding in haste from Paris with a terrible tale to tell. His face was ashen, his voice trembled.

I heard him calling to be taken to the King and I rose and wrapped a gown about me.

The King's servants were arguing. The King was in bed. He could not be disturbed at this hour!

And Liancourt's terse answer: "Awaken the King. I must see the King."

The Duc was in the bedchamber.

"Sire," he cried. "The people have stormed the Bastille."

Louis sat up in bed rubbing the sleep from his eyes.

"The Bastille . . ." he murmured.

"They have taken the Bastille, Sire."

"But . . . the governor . . ."

"They have killed de Launay, Sire. They marched into the prison with his head on a pike."

"This would seem to be a revolt," said the King.

"No, Sire," answered the Duc gravely, "it is a revolution."

21

"Upon you I throw myself. It is my wish that I and the nation should be one, and in full reliance on the affection and fidelity of my subjects, I have given orders to the troops to remove from Paris and Versailles."

Louis XVI to the National Assembly

"The Queen then appeared on the balcony. 'Ah,' said the woman in the veil, 'the Duchess is not with her.' 'No,' replied the man, 'but she is still at Versailles. She is working underground like a mole, but we shall know how to dig her out.' . . . I thought it my duty to relate the dialogue of these two strangers to the Queen."

Madame Campan's Memoirs

"Goodbye, dearest of friends. It is a dreadful and necessary word: Goodbye."

Marie Antoinette to Madame de Polignac

FRIENDS LEAVE VERSAILLES

The Terror was upon us.

Artois, white-lipped, all his gaiety gone, came to the apartment where the King and I were together.

"They are murdering people all over Paris," he said. "I have just heard that my name is high on their list of victims."

I ran to him and threw my arms about him. There had been a coldness between us lately, but he was my brother-in-law; we had once been good friends and there were so many memories of shared follies from those days when neither of us allowed any cares to disturb us.

"You must go away," I cried. I had a horrible picture of his head on a pike as poor de Launay's had been.

"Yes," said the King calmly. He was the only one among us who was calm. "You must make your preparations to leave."

I wondered about myself. How high was I on the list? Surely at the top of it.

Then I thought of those dear friends of mine—Gabrielle who had been the subject of so much scandal; my dear Princesse de Lamballe.

I said: "And there will be others."

Artois read my thoughts as he used to in the old days.

"They are talking of the Polignacs," he said.

I turned away. I went to my private chamber and I sent Madame Campan to bring Gabrielle to me.

She came startled; I took her into my arms and embraced her warmly.

"My dearest friend," I said, "you will have to go away."

"You are *sending* me away?"

I nodded. "While there is time."

"And you?"

"I must be with the King."

"And you think . . ."

"I do not think, Gabrielle. I dare not."

"I could not go. I would not leave you. There are the children."

"Are you like these rebels then? Do you too forget that I am still the Queen? You will go, Gabrielle, because I say you shall."

"And leave you?"

"And leave me," I said turning away, "because that is my wish."

"No, no," she cried. "You cannot ask me to go. We have shared so much . . . we must stay together. You would be happier if I stayed than if I went."

"Happy! I sometimes think I shall never be happy again. But I could find more comfort in thinking of you safe far from here rather than to live in fear that they would do to you what they have done to de Launay. So begin to prepare at once. Artois is going. Everyone who can must go . . . and perhaps in time it will be our turn."

With that I ran out of the room, for I could bear no more.

I went back to the King. Messengers had come from Paris. The people were demanding the presence of the King there. If he did not come they would march to Versailles to fetch him. They wanted him in Paris; they wanted to take "good care" of him.

"If you go you may not return," I said.

"I shall come back," he answered, as calmly as though he were about to set out for a day's hunting.

The people demanded that his brothers accompany him. I trembled not only for my husband but for Artois. They said he was my lover; that was an old scandal, but the old scandals were resurrected now.

The coach was at the door and I accompanied Louis to it. "God guard you," I whispered; and he pressed my hand. His was firm. He was so sure that his people would do him no harm; but I could not share his optimism. I kept asking myself whether I should ever look on his face again.

I must occupy myself in some way. I dared not be alone to think. I kept visualizing the mob breaking into the Bastille and de Launay's head on the pike; but instead of the Bastille's governor I saw that of the King.

I would try to act normally. What should I do? My children were losing their governess. I must find a new one for them.

I thought awhile and decided on Madame de Tourzel—a widow, a serious-minded woman, and she had what was becoming one of the most prized qualities, loyalty.

I told her that she would be appointed and she understood why. She would have known that in the streets they were burning effigies of Gabrielle with me, that they were circulating obscene pictures and verses about us.

Oh yes, Madame de Tourzel understood and I wanted to tell her how I appreciated her for the calm manner in which she thanked me for the honor and swore to serve my children for as long as I should give her permission to do so.

I went to my apartments. I wanted to be alone. I was terribly afraid that I would show the anxiety I was feeling. What was happening to my husband in Paris? Had they gone so far that they would murder their King? What should I do? Should I prepare for flight with my children?

I would have clothes packed. I would order that the carriages should be equipped and ready.

I went to the children's apartment. I must stay with them for I was afraid of treachery.

My son brought the book of La Fontaine's Fables to me.

"Let's have the one about the fox, Maman . . . I saw a fox last night. The soldier brought him in . . ."

I let my hand rest on his head. "Not now, my darling."

He looked puzzled. "Where is Madame de Polignac?" he asked.

"She is in her apartments," replied his sister. "She is very busy."

"Everybody is different today," said my son. Then he brightened. "Maman, come and I will show you my garden."

"I think we will stay in today, my love. Yes . . . I will read to you after all."

So I sat there reading, my ears strained for the sounds of a messenger with what dread tidings I dared not contemplate.

It was eleven o'clock when the King returned. I was sitting in my apartment in an agony of fear, waiting. He had walked back surrounded by the Deputies of the National Assembly and followed by a rabble of men and women who carried cudgels and shouted as they came.

I heard the cry: "*Vive le Roi!*" and I felt my spirits lifted; then I ran down to greet him.

He looked very tired but as calm as ever. His coat was stained, his cravat awry and in his hat was the tricolor.

I was almost sobbing with relief and he was touched by emotion.

"You should have been in bed," he said. "Why, you are worn out with waiting."

As if we all found it as easy to sleep in face of such horror as he did!

But these people did not give us any peace. They were all crowding into the courtyards.

"The King!" they cried. And then: "The Queen! The Dauphin!"

I looked at my husband and he nodded. I turned to Madame Campan who was constantly beside me during these terrible days.

"Go to the Duchesse de Polignac and tell her that I want my son to be brought here immediately."

"And Your Majesty wishes Madame de Polignac to bring him?"

"No, no. Tell her not to come. These terrible people must not see her."

Madame Campan brought my son to me.

The King took him onto the balcony and the people roared: "*Vive le Roi! Vive le Dauphin!*" And my little son lifted his hand and waved to them which seemed to touch them.

"The Queen!" they shouted.

Madame Campan laid a hand on my arm. I saw the fear leap into her eyes. I knew she was wondering what they would do to me when I appeared.

But I must go out there onto the balcony. If I did not they would storm the palace. They had cheered my husband and my son. They bore no malice—at the moment—toward them. But what of me?

I stepped onto the balcony. I was murmuring a prayer under my breath and I was thinking of my mother and all the warnings she had sent me and I wondered if she was watching me in Heaven now. I had been guilty of great folly but at least I would not disgrace her now. If I was to die I would do it as a Hapsburg, as she would expect me to.

I stood there, my head high, determined to show no fear. There was a silence which seemed to go on for a long time . . . and then someone called: "*Vive la Reine.*"

The shouts were deafening. I felt dizzy but I stood there smiling.

Down there the people were shouting for me, for the King and the Dauphin. It seemed that they no longer hated us. They loved us.

But I was not the fool I had once been. I knew that the people's love one day was its hatred the next. Hosanna and crucify had not been far apart.

At length that interminable day was over and we sank exhausted into our beds. Louis was immediately asleep. But I lay wondering what new trials awaited us in the days ahead.

The next day the King told me what had happened in Paris. Refreshed after his sleep he gave no sign of the ordeal through which he had passed. I never knew a man who could face calamity with such indifference. It was almost as though Divine Providence had especially equipped him for the role he was to play.

When he had arrived in Paris, Bailly, the Mayor who had become President of the Third Estate, was waiting to receive him and to offer him the keys of the city. This return to an old custom aroused Louis' optimism, never far from the surface. Everything was going to be all right.

Bailly said: "I bring Your Majesty the keys of your good city of Paris. These were the words which were spoken to Henri Quatre. He reconquered the people; here the people have reconquered their King."

The words were less comforting; the contrast between him and the King whom the French had always considered their greatest was insulting; but Louis showed no rancor and calmly accepted the keys. I could well imagine his benign smiles on the menacing rabble which closed about his carriage. The fact that he would not appear to see their menaces would, I could well imagine, disconcert them.

Someone fired a shot at him in the Place Louis XV but it missed him and killed a woman; and in the general tumult the incident was scarcely noticed.

At the Hôtel de Ville, Louis descended from his carriage and men with pikes and swords made an avenue under which he passed. There he made his way to the throne while shouting men and women crowded into the hall. I could picture the scene which would have struck terror into any heart but his, yet he must see himself as the little father—sad because his children were behaving very badly, but ready to smile and forgive at the first sign of repentance.

There was no repentance. They were the masters now and although his demeanor bewildered them they were determined not to forget it—and that he should not either.

He was asked if he accepted the appointment of Jean Sylvain Bailly as Mayor of Paris and Marie Joseph Gilbert Motier de La Fayette as Commander of the National Guard. He agreed that he did.

He then took off his hat and standing bareheaded declared: "Upon you I throw myself. It is my wish that I and the nation should be one, and in full reliance on the affection and fidelity of my subjects, I have given orders to the troops to remove from Paris and Versailles."

There were cheers. He smiled benignly, refusing to believe that now he had given the rebels a free road to revolution.

When they gave him the tricolor to put into his hat he was not dismayed. How would his grandfather have reacted to such an insult? Who would have dared offer it to Louis XIV? But my Louis mildly took it, removed his hat and stuck in the symbol of the people. He, the King, was one of them. And what could they do? Even at such a time they must have been just a little overawed by royalty.

They cheered him. "Vive le Roi!" they cried.

Fortunately there were some men present who while they wished for reforms loathed violence and realized that the country could only be saved from disaster if they were brought about in an orderly and constitutional manner. One of these was the Comte de Lally-Tollendal.

He cried: "Citizens, rejoice in your King's presence and the benefits he will bestow." And to my husband: "There is not a man here, Sire, who is not ready to shed his blood for you. King and citizens, let us show the world a free and just nation under a cherished King who, owing nothing to force, will owe everything to his virtue and his love."

When I visualize this scene as Louis told it to me I believe even now that he could have saved France. His very courage demanded their respect; his good intentions were always present. If only he had been singleminded; if he had not seen every side; if he had pursued a straight course; if he had taken a decisive action. But then he would not have been Louis.

Then he stood before that crowd and with tears of emotion in his eyes he cried: "My people can always count on my love."

And so surrounded by his cheering subjects, the tricolor in his hat, he came back to Versailles.

The next morning we talked. I had been awake all night making my plans. We could not stay here. I knew we were in danger.

I had sent Madame Campan to mingle with the crowds in the court-yard so that she might report to me what she had heard and this had proved to be very revealing.

"It was easy to see, Madame," she had said, "that many of the people in the mob were disguised. They were not of the poor people, although their clothes might indicate this. Their manner of speaking betrayed them."

"Did you speak to any?"

"Some spoke to me, Madame. There was one with a black lace veil over her face. She seized my arm quite roughly and said: 'I know you very well, Madame Campan. You should tell your Queen not to meddle with government any longer. Let her leave her husband and our good States-General to arrange the happiness of the people.'"

I shivered. And I forced myself to say: "What else?"

"Then, Madame, a man dressed as a market-man approached me; he had his hat pulled low over his eyes; he seized my other arm and said: 'Yes, tell her over and over again that it will not be with these States as with the others, which brought no good to the people. Tell her that the nation is too enlightened in 1789 not to make something more of them and that there will not now be seen a deputy of the Tiers Etat making a speech with one knee on the ground. Tell her this, do you hear me?'"

"So that is what they are saying?"

"Yes, Madame, and when you appeared on the balcony . . . they talked across me to each other, but it was really to me."

"And they said?"

"The woman in the veil said: 'The Duchess is not with her.' And the man answered: 'No, but she is still at Versailles. She is working under-ground, molelike, but we shall know how to dig her out.'"

"And that was all, Madame Campan?"

"They moved away from me then, Madame, and I hurried into the palace."

"I am glad you told me. Please never fail to talk to me of these things."

"Madame, I should believe I had failed in my duty if I had not done so."

I pressed her hand. "At times like this," I said with some emotion, "it is good to have friends."

When I told the King what Madame Campan had heard he listened gravely.

"There will always be some to speak against us," he said.

"Perhaps we should be more surprised when we discover people who speak for us," I retorted bitterly. "We must leave, Louis. It is no longer safe for us to stay."

"How could we leave Versailles?"

"Easily. By slipping away with the children and those of our friends whom we trust."

"Artois should have left by now. I saw the hostile looks directed toward him. There were cries against him and I heard one cry of: 'The King forever, in spite of you and your opinions, Monseigneur.' And my brother looked haughtily indifferent and they did not like that. I was afraid for him. Yes, Artois must go quickly."

"Artois . . . and Gabrielle. They are not safe here. We are not safe here."

"I am the King, my dear. It is my duty to be with my people."

"And your children?"

"The people expect the Dauphin to remain at Versailles."

"I have seen murder in their faces; I have heard it in their voices."

"It will be a matter for the Council to decide."

"Then call the Council. There can be no delay."

"I believe we should stay."

I talked to him of the dangers which beset us and our children. We should not stay if we valued our lives. I had everything packed. My jewels particularly; they were worth a fortune.

"To where should we fly?"

"To Metz. I have thought of nothing else for days. We could go to Metz and then there would be a civil war in which we should subdue these rebels."

"It is for the Council to decide," insisted Louis.

And the Council met and they talked through the day and night. I paced up and down my apartment. I had told my husband that we must leave. There should be no delay. I had ordered my friends to leave as soon as it was dark because I knew it was unsafe to stay. Unsafe for us, more so than for them.

And Louis was listening to the Council. They would decide. But I had impressed on him the need for flight. He could not ignore my pleadings. He always longed to please me.

At length he came out of the council room. I ran to him and looked up into his face.

He smiled gently: "The King," he said, "must stay with his people."

I turned angrily away, tears of frustration filling my eyes. But his mind was made up. Whatever else happened. He and I must stay and so must our Dauphin.

Night had come. There were sounds of muffled activity in the courtyard—low voices; the impatient pawing of a horse's hoof.

They were about to go—all those gay friends who had been the companions of my carefree days. I had been alarmed for the Abbé Vermond who had aroused the anger of the people because he had lived close to me. I had told him that he must go back to Austria and not return to France until things were happier.

He was an old man, the Abbé. He would have liked to tell me that he would never leave me. But the terror was creeping closer and it was reflected in the faces of them all.

So he too would leave and make his way to Austria.

I had said my last farewell to them all, those of our family and household whom we had ordered to save themselves by leaving Versailles and Paris behind them.

Gabrielle and her family were among them. Dear Gabrielle, who was so loathe to go, who had been my constant companion for so long, who had loved me wholeheartedly and had been my true friend; she had suffered with me on the death of my children; she had helped me nurse them, had rejoiced in their childish triumphs, mourned their childish sorrows.

I could not bear to lose her. An impulse came to rush down to that courtyard to implore her not to leave me. But how could I bring her back to danger. I must not see her, not tempt her to remain, not tempt myself. I loved this woman. All I could do for her now was to pray that she might reach safety.

The tears were streaming down my cheeks. I picked up a paper and wrote to her.

"Goodbye, dearest of friends. It is a dreadful and necessary word: Goodbye."

I laughed bitterly; I had blotted the lines as I always did. But although the handwriting was uneven and shaky, she would understand with what sincerity, what deep and abiding love they had been written.

I sent a page down with the letter which he was to give to Madame de Polignac in the last seconds before she drove away.

Then I threw myself heavily upon my bed and turned my face away from the light.

I lay listening; and at length I heard the carriages leave.

The great halls were filled with emptiness; silence in the Galerie de Glaces; deathly quiet in the *oeil de boeuf*; not a sound in the Salon de la Paix. In the mornings we heard Mass accompanied by a few of our attendants such as Madame Campan and Madame de Tourzel; no *fêtes*, no cards, no banquets. Nothing but this dreary waiting for something more terrible than we could even imagine.

Every day news brought to us of the riots in Paris, and not only in Paris; it was throughout the country. Mobs were raiding the châteaux, burning and looting; no one was working, and so no bread was brought into Paris. The bakers' shops were shuttered and bands of hungry people collected outside and tore down the shutters invading the shops, searching for bread and when they could not find it setting fire to buildings and murdering any whom they considered their enemies.

The agitators were busy. Men like Desmoulins were still producing their news-sheets inflaming the people with revolutionary ideas, urging them to revolt against the aristocracy. Copies of the *Courrier de Paris et de Versailles* and the *Patriote Française* were smuggled in to us. We were dismayed and horrified to read what Marat was writing about us and our kind.

Every day I would wake and wonder whether it would be my last. Each night when I lay down and tried to rest I wondered whether the mob would come that night, drag me from my bed and murder me in the most horrible manner it could contrive. In all these sheets my name was prominent. They did not hate the King. They despised him as a weakling ruled by me. I was the harpy, the greatest criminal in this fearful melodrama of Revolution.

Foulon, one of the Ministers of Finance, who had been generally hated for his callous attitude toward the people was brutally murdered. He had once said that if the people were hungry they should eat hay. They found him at Viry, dragged him through the streets, stuffed his mouth with hay, hung him on the *lanterne* and then cut off his head and paraded it through the streets.

His son-in-law Monsieur Berthier was treated in the same way at Compiègne.

I knew that the fate of these two men was due to the fact that Foulon had advised the King to make himself master of the Revolution before the Revolution mastered him.

It was terrible to contemplate the fate of men one had known. I trembled for my dear Gabrielle who was on her way to the frontier, for I heard that coaches and carriages were being stopped throughout the country, that their occupants were being dragged out and forced to give an account of their identity, and if they were proved aristocrats their throats were cut . . . or worse. What would happen to Gabrielle if she were discovered, for her name had been coupled so often with mine.

I dreamed of poor Monsieur Foulon and wondered how his remark about hay had been distorted. They were saying of me that when I had heard the people were demanding bread I had asked "Why don't they eat cake?" This was absurd. I had said no such thing.

Madame Sophie had remarked that the people would have to eat pastry crust if they could not get bread. Poor Sophie was always vague and a little odd; she loathed pastry crust; and when she was getting old and ill and near to death, she had made this remark which was reported, and like so many others put into my mouth. Nothing was too trivial to bring against me; and nothing too wild. I was, according to the people, capable of the utmost frivolity and folly and yet I was represented as the clever scheming woman.

There was no fighting these libels. The people wanted to believe them.

So passed the days of that fearful hot summer. I was trying hard to act normally; to fight the fear which was so often with me.

I tried repeatedly to urge the King to flight. I kept my jewels packed ready. I was certain that we should attempt to escape as our friends had done. I had heard no news of Gabrielle and Artois and I presumed they had reached safety for if they had been murdered I should have known.

There were four people of whom I was growing fonder because I realized that their friendship to me was real; and it is at such times that one understands and values such devotion. My dear simple Lamballe, my pious Elisabeth, my children's devoted governess, Madame de Tourzel and my practical and serious Madame Campan. I was constantly in their company. They risked death, even as I did, but I could not persuade them to leave me.

I think what helped me most was the practical manner in which Madame de Tourzel and Madame Campan went about their duties as though there had been no change in our fortunes.

I liked to talk to the former about the children and between us we could bring an atmosphere that was almost peaceful into the room.

I talked to the governess of my little anxieties about the Dauphin. "I have seen him start at a sudden noise . . . the bark of a dog, for instance."

"He is very sensitive, Madame."

"He is a little violent when angry . . . and quick to anger."

"Like all healthy children. But he is good-natured, Madame. And generous."

"Bless him. When I gave him a present he asked for one for his sister. He has a very generous heart. But I am a little worried about his habit of exaggerating."

"The sign of a fertile imagination, Madame."

"I don't really think he has any notion of his position as Dauphin. But perhaps that is as well. Our children learn all too quickly . . ."

We were silent. She must have been wondering as I was, how quickly he would learn what was happening about us.

A page was at the door.

A visitor to see me. My heart leaped and fluttered uncomfortably. How could I know who was without? How could I know when those people with the faces of bloodthirsty maniacs would be bursting upon me.

I did not ask the name of the visitor. I rose, composing myself.

He was at the door and when I saw him, the reversal of feeling was so overwhelming that I thought I should faint.

He came into the room and took my hands; he kissed them. What did Madame de Tourzel think as she stood there? She bowed and, turning, left us together.

He was looking at me in silence as though he were reminding himself of every detail of my face.

I heard myself say foolishly: "You . . . you have come . . ."

He did not answer. Why should he? Was it not obvious that he had come?

Then I remembered the horrible cries of the mob, what they had done to friends of the Queen.

"It is not the time to come," I said. "There is great danger here. Everyone is leaving . . ."

"That is why I have come," answered Axel.

22

"I am beginning to be a little happier for I can from time to time see my friend freely, which consoles us a little for all the troubles she had to bear, poor woman. She is an angel in her conduct, her courage and her tenderness. No one has ever known how to love as she does."

Axel de Fersen to his sister Sophie

"I shudder even now at the recollection of the *poissardes*, or rather furies who wore white aprons which, they screamed out, were to receive the bowels of Marie Antoinette, and that they would make cockades of them."

"It is true that the assassins penetrated to the Queen's bedchamber and pierced the bed with their swords."

"The *poissardes* went before and around the carriage of their Majesties crying, 'We shall no longer want bread—we have the baker, the baker's wife and the baker's boy with us.' In the midst of this troop of cannibals the heads of two murdered bodyguards were carried on poles."

Madame Campan's Memoirs

THE TRAGIC OCTOBER

The Petit Trianon had been my refuge in the past. It now became my escape from the horrors of reality. In past years in that little paradise I had shut myself away, refusing to take heed of the lessons my mother thrust at me, never listening to the warnings of Mercy and Vermond. Now I would go there and try to forget the rumbling of disaster. I would try to recapture that dream world which I had endeavored to make years ago and in which I still believed that I could have been happy had I achieved it. It was not that I asked a great deal. I told myself that I did not really care for the extravagance, the fine clothes, the diamonds. Had not Rose Bertin been at my elbow to urge me to extravagant follies, had not the court jewelers been so insistent, I should never have thought of buying their goods. No, what I longed for was a happy home with children to care for—above all children—and a husband whom I could love. I loved Louis, in my way; perhaps I should say I had a great affection for him. But just as he was not fitted for the role of King, he was not fitted for that of husband.

The kindest most self-effacing man in the world, his weaknesses were so obvious to me; even when he granted my wishes I might have respected him more if he had not. He was a man of whom one could be fond but could not entirely respect. He lacked that strength which every woman asks of a man. His people asked it too and he failed to give it to them as he failed to give it to me.

Am I excusing myself for those fevered weeks at the Trianon—those waiting weeks between that fateful fourteenth of July and the tragic October day which more than any other was a turning point in our lives?

Perhaps I am, but even now, remembering soberly with my life behind me and death so close, looking over my shoulder, I believe I should have acted exactly the same way.

I loved the Trianon more than any place in the world; and the world was crashing about my shoulders—I was soon to lose the Trianon . . . my children . . . my life . . . So I snatched at that brief idyll. I must fulfill my life. I felt the urgency, the passionate need as I never had before.

Axel had left Versailles previously because he had feared the consequences if he stayed at Court; he told me now how he had longed to stay, but that he knew his name was even then being coupled with mine and he knew what harm could befall me if he stayed.

And now? It was different now. The entire picture had changed. I needed him now. I needed every friend I could find; and he assured me that never in my life would I find a friend such as he was.

"You risk your life staying here," I told him.

"My life is at your service," he answered. "To be risked and lost if need be."

I wept in his arms and said I could not allow it.

He answered that I could not prevent it. I could command him to go but he would not listen. He had come to stay close to me, closer even than danger.

He had mingled with the people; he had read what was circulated about me; he had heard threats against me which he did not repeat to me but which had decided him that he must remain at my side.

And while I urged him to go, I longed for him to stay and our passion was too strong to be resisted.

The Trianon was the perfect setting for lovers, and there we could meet unobserved.

I do not think I could ever have deceived my husband. I was not the kind of woman who could have pretended to love him and to have a secret lover. Louis knew of my relationship with Axel de Fersen; he understood full well that my feelings for the Swedish Count were such as I had felt for no one else. There had been scandals about other men, Luzan, Coigny, Artois . . . and many others, but they had been meaningless. Axel de Fersen was different. He had known that long ago.

There had been a time when papers had been written about myself and Axel and these had been shown to the King. I remembered how distressed I had been at the time.

He had guessed then my feelings for Axel, but I had shown him clearly that I would never take him as my lover while I had been bearing my husband's children, *les enfants de France*. I was well aware of that duty.

Louis understood. In his kindly way he made me see that he understood, that he appreciated my actions while he knew that I had been unable to prevent my feelings. Axel went away and I had more children. Louis could never make up to me for all the humiliation of those first years of marriage.

Now there was no physical relationship between us. That had stopped after the birth of Sophie Béatrix. We had believed then that we had our four children—two boys and two girls. How were we to know that we were to lose two of them and that perhaps it would have been better if we had never given the children to France? Neither of us was a slave of sexual passion. But my love for Axel was different from everything that had ever gone before. Our physical union was an outward manifestation of a spiritual bond. It would never have happened but for the fevered atmosphere about us, the sense of living from day to day, from hour to hour because we could not know what the next would bring.

And Louis wished it to be so. That kind man, that tender man wanted me to live as fully as I could during those terrible days.

So I existed between the love of these two men, with my children never far from my side. Perhaps I was wrong; perhaps I was foolish; but I had often been so and it seemed to me then the only way I could live through these fearful days.

August came—overpoweringly hot. And I seemed to be leading two lives—one in the empty palace of Versailles, alive only with echoes of the past and forebodings of the terrifying future, and another at the Trianon, my happy home, an escape to another world, where my rosy-cheeked respectable tenants lived on in their Hameau, so different from those terrifying people who carried sticks and cudgels and cried out for bread and blood.

We met at dusk. I would wander out to the Temple of Love—so aptly named; and there we would sit and dream and talk and, although we would not mention this, each time we wondered whether this was the last we should lie in each other's arms.

The guards had deserted. I awoke one morning in Versailles to find that there were none to defend us.

On August 4th the King was obliged to give his consent to the abolition of feudalism; and to agree to his statue being set up on the site of the Bastille to be inscribed: "To the Restorer of Liberty to France." This has never been erected and never will be now. Louis declared that while he was ready to give up all his own rights he was not prepared to give up those of others. Then there were cries that the King should be brought from Versailles to Paris and we wondered what this would mean.

A few weeks later La Fayette was drawing up a Declaration of the Rights of Man in the American style; this was the beginning of that decree which was to end all hereditary titles and declare all men equal.

La Fayette was, I believed, at times a little disturbed by the violence of the mob and sought to keep them in order; but there were occasions when he found this an impossibility yet I believe that during the months of August and September he did prevent them forcibly removing the King to the Louvre.

Mercy came to see me. How grave he was these days. And how avidly I listened to every word he uttered. He told me that he believed it was folly for the King to stay at Versailles. Axel was telling me this too every time we met. He wanted us to escape. He assured me that we were living in perpetual danger.

"On the eastern frontier at Metz," said Mercy, "the Marquis de Bouillé has twenty-five to thirty thousand men. They are loyalists whom he has taught to despise the *canaille*. They would fight for their King and their Queen. The King should be persuaded to leave for Metz without delay."

I told Mercy that I agreed with this and . . . others . . . had warned me of the need.

Mercy looked at me severely. He knew whom I meant by others. He, who had observed me so closely all the time I had been in France, first for my mother and then for my brother—though never so assiduously for the latter as the former—must know of my love for Axel. I looked at him defiantly; if he had dared to criticize me I should have reminded him that I was well aware of his own liaison of long standing with Mademoiselle Rosalie Levasseur. But he did not reproach me. Perhaps he too understood my need at this time; perhaps he felt that in my own interests it was good to have a friend so close that I could rely on completely.

He said: "I am glad that you have wise friends."

And I knew what he meant.

But I still could not persuade Louis to leave. He could not run away, he said. No matter how his people behaved toward him he must always do his duty to them.

We were very unsure of La Fayette's attitude toward us. He had sent National Guards to be on duty at the palace and Mercy told me that he no doubt had had information of our efforts to persuade the King to escape to Metz.

In September the Régiment de Flandre came to Versailles and the officers of this regiment and those of the Body Guards decided to show their friendship for each other by dining together; and in view of the feelings of the day some of the *sous-officiers* and the soldiers were invited to join.

Louis offered them the theater at Versailles for the occasion; tables were set upon the stage and members of the diminishing Court were invited to occupy the boxes.

I was afraid that the banquet would end in some disaster, which I was now expecting from all quarters, and I decided that Madame Campan should go for I could always rely on her to give me a faithful account of what had happened.

Some of the Council had said that it would be good for the King and myself to be present, but I was against this for I was so unpopular that I was afraid my appearance would be the sign for violence of some sort.

"Madame Campan," I said, "I have been advised to attend this dinner but I feel it would be unwise to do so. I wish you to occupy one of the boxes and report to me what happens."

She said she would take her niece and give me an accurate account of everything.

My husband went off hunting. It was astonishing how in the face of everything that happened he persisted in behaving as though life was going on normally. I sat in my children's nursery for I never liked to be far from them when danger seemed a little closer than usual.

It was while I was there that one of my women came to me and told me that the soldiers were behaving in a most loyal manner, and that the Duc de Villeroi who was Captain of the first company of Guards, had invited all present to drink four toasts—to the King, the Queen, the Dauphin and the royal family; and that this had been done and although someone had proposed the toast of the Nation, little attention had been paid to this.

While she was talking to me, my husband returned from the hunt and I asked my woman to tell the King what she had told me.

"It might be well if we showed ourselves," I said. "If we do not, they will think we are afraid, and perhaps that would be worse than anything."

He agreed with me for in all our troubles I never saw Louis show the slightest fear for his own safety. I sent for Madame de Tourzel and asked her to bring the two children to me.

The Dauphin was very excited.

"We are going to see the soldiers," I told him.

Nothing could have pleased him more; he was all ready to see the soldiers. He thought Moufflet would like to see them; but I told him Moufflet could not come on this occasion.

We went to the theater and showed ourselves in the railed-in box which faced the stage. There was a hushed silence and then the cheering broke out.

"*Vive le Roi! Vive la Reine!*" Yes, even *Vive la Reine*. My spirits lifted as they had not for a long time.

There in the theater I felt that our cause was not hopeless, that we had some friends and that I had allowed myself to be unduly alarmed by those people with the savage faces.

The tables had been set in the shape of a horseshoe and two hundred and ten places had been laid; and there sat those soldiers . . . those loyal soldiers whose cries of friendship drowned the few dissenting voices.

"They want us to go down to the stage," said my husband, tears in his eyes; he was always deeply moved by his subjects' displays of affection.

I picked up my son in my arms and carried him. I did not want him to be too far from me, and we went down on to the stage.

The Dauphin's gaiety and delight charmed the soldiers and I stood him on the table while they drank his health. Then he walked over the tables being very careful not to tread on the glasses and he told the men how he liked soldiers better than anything . . . better even than dogs; he thought he was going to be a soldier when he grew up.

They were enchanted. Who could help being? And there was lovely Mousseline so happy because she believed that everything was coming right for us and the anxiety of the last months was over.

They began to sing one of the popular songs of the day by the musician Grétry—a good and *loyal* song:

"*O Richard, ô mon Roi,*
L'univers t'abandonne
Sur la terre il n'est donc que moi
Qui m'intéresse à ta personne."

It was wonderful to stand there, to see the triumph of my little son, the admiration these good men felt for my daughter; to see their loyalty to the King and their affection for me.

How I had missed it! I prayed then for another chance. Let everything be as it used to be and I would work with my husband for the good of the people of France.

That night I slept more peacefully than I had for a long time.

But in the morning I summoned Madame Campan and asked for her account of the affair.

She said she had been surprised when she saw us appear and she had been deeply moved by the singing of *O Richard ô mon Roi* and *Peut on affliger ce qu'on aime?* which had followed it.

"But," I asked, "you were not entirely happy?"

"Though many shouted for Your Majesties," she told me, "there were some who did not; and there was one in the next box to that which I occupied with my niece who reproved us for shouting *Vive le Roi*. He said that American women would be contemptuous of us, screaming as we were for the life of one man. It was shocking he said to see handsome Frenchwomen brought up in such servile habits. To which, Madame, my niece replied that we had all lived close to the King and to do so was to love him and he had better save his breath, for his disloyalty to a good King did not affect us one jot."

I laughed. "But was it not wonderful? They were so enthusiastic. They loved us and they wanted us to know it. We have seen so much of our enemies that we have forgotten our friends."

She was less complacent than I. Dear Campan, she was always so much wiser.

The affair caused some consternation in Paris. The pamphleteers, fearing that more might wish to show their friendship, were feverishly printing their sheets. Marat and Desmoulins wrote of that evening as though it were an obscene orgy. They declared that we had all trampled the tricolor underfoot. Was it not time that someone slit the throat of the Austrian woman?

Bread had become more and more scarce in the capital. There was no flour to be had. "They are hoarding the people's flour at Versailles!" was the cry which was echoing through the streets of Paris.

The winter lay ahead—the cold and hungry winter—for October was with us.

It was the afternoon of the fifth of October, a dull day with an overcast sky and intermittent showers. I decided that I would go to the Trianon. Perhaps I would sketch a little. Perhaps Axel would come to see me. If we could be together for even a little while I would find the courage to go on. I now realized that the banquet had not been the wonderful turn of the tide which I had made myself believe. I knew of the riots that were continuing and becoming more and more violent every day. There was no end to the terrible tales of atrocities. We were less safe than we had been a week ago for with every hour our danger increased.

Why would Louis not leave for Metz? Surely he could see it was the wise thing to do. At times I was sure he agreed but always he would waver.

So I would go to Trianon and perhaps between the showers walk out to the Hameau. Perhaps I would drink a glass of milk fresh from my cows or sit in the Temple of Love and dream of Axel.

The Petit Trianon! Even on a gray day it was beautiful. I sat in the white and gold room and looked out on my gardens. Did I have a premonition then that I would never see it again?

I walked through the house; I touched the carved and gilded wooden panelling; I went to my bedroom which had been so entirely my own and I remembered how when I entertained friends there and my husband had come as a guest—for he always respected my desire for privacy—and we had put the clock on an hour to make him leave earlier so that we could enjoy ourselves without restraint.

So many memories of the past . . . and the present.

I longed to hear Axel's voice on this day—more, I told myself, than ever before. I wanted to see him walking across the garden to the house. But he did not come.

The rain had stopped and I took my sketching pad and walked out to the grotto, and I sat there not sketching but thinking. I looked over the grounds at the changing leaves. There were few flowers left. The winter was very close. How beautiful! Those gentle hillocks, the pond, Cupid's Temple, the meadows, the charming little houses of the Hameau . . . my own little village which was so natural and yet was in fact the height of artificiality.

How I loved it!

There was no need to hurry. I would stay here until it was almost dark. Perhaps I would stay the night here. I could send for the children. How pleasant it would be . . . not to sleep in the palace, to pretend Versailles was miles away.

I heard the sound of footsteps. My heart leaped in anticipation. Could it be Axel who had come in the hope of finding me here. The thought drove away my morbid reflections and temporarily I was as lighthearted as that young woman who had once held her Sunday balls on the lawns here, who had milked her own ribbon-decorated cows into Sèvres pails.

Then I saw not Axel but one of the pages from the palace. His hair was awry; he was hot and breathless but there was no mistaking his relief when he saw me.

"Madame . . . Madame . . ." he cried. "I have here a note from the Comte de Saint-Priest." The Comte was one of those ministers resident at Versailles.

"You have hurried," I began, but he interrupted without ceremony, "Monsieur de Saint-Priest says the matter is most urgent. Your Majesty must return at once to the palace."

I opened the note and read: "*Return to the Palace immediately. The mob is marching on Versailles.*"

I felt the horror grip me. I rose and picked up my hat.

"I will walk back through the woods at once," I said.

"Monsieur de Saint-Priest commanded me to bring the carriage, Madame. Some of the mob may already be in Versailles. The danger is great."

"Take me to the carriage," I said.

In silence I rode back to the palace.

No sooner had I arrived at the château than the King came back. He was mud-spattered from the hunt but as calm as ever.

The Comte de Saint-Priest was waiting impatiently.

He said: "There is little time. The women of Paris are marching. They are on the outskirts of Versailles."

The Captain of the Guards came in and saluting the King asked what his orders were.

"Orders," cried Louis. "For a crowd of women? You must be joking."

Saint-Priest said: "Sire, these are no ordinary women. There may be men disguised as women amongst them. They come with weapons . . . knives and cudgels. They are in an ugly mood."

"We cannot use soldiers against women, my dear Comte," said the King.

The Comte de Saint-Priest raised his eyebrows and then I heard the clatter of boots on the staircase and into the room burst Axel. His eyes at once sought me and his relief was obvious.

He cried: "The mob is on the march. They're . . . murderous. The Queen and the children must leave at once."

Louis smiled at him as though he understood the concern of a lover. "Monsieur de Saint-Priest wishes to discuss this matter," he said. "You should join us, my dear Comte."

I could sense Axel's impatience. After all he had seen those women. He knew their mood; he had heard their comments; he knew they were after blood . . . my blood. He knew too that the march of the women was a clever ruse on the part of the revolutionaries. If men had come the soldiers would have fired on them but the chivalrous King would never allow them to fire on women. The revolutionary leaders had planned this well. They had inflamed the women of Paris; they had held up bread supplies so that the scarcity seemed even worse than it was; they had circulated their pamphlets more assiduously than ever—and they were more scurrilous against me.

I was the reason for the women's march on Versailles; they wanted my head; they wanted to march back to Paris with the King and my children . . . and myself. But it was to be my mutilated body carried in pieces by a mob of women as wild as savages with the blood lust in their hearts.

I could read this in Axel's face. I had never seen him so afraid before and never did I see him afraid for his own safety—only for mine.

Saint-Priest was aware of the relationship between Axel and myself but his one idea was to preserve the Monarchy and he knew that Axel was a good friend, a reliable friend. He could be of service and who more loyal than a lover?

Saint-Priest immediately called a conference of the loyal ministers who remained. Immediate action was needed, he said. The bridges of the Seine should be guarded by the Flanders regiment; Saint-Cloud and Neuilly should be held. The Queen and the royal family should be sent to Rambouillet, and the King with a strong force of Guards should ride out to meet the marchers. With a thousand horse and armed soldiers he could order the mob to retire, and if they refused there would be no alternative but to open fire.

"And if this did not succeed, if there were armed men and women in the mob, if fighting broke out?" asked the King.

"Then, Sire, at the head of the troops you would march to Rambouillet. There you would make plans to join the forces at Metz."

"Civil war?" asked the King.

"Preferable to revolution, Sire," replied Axel.

"It means that the King would face danger," I said.

"Madame," answered Axel, "you are facing danger at this moment."

The King was wavering. I knew what would happen. He would ride out there but he would never give permission for women to be fired on. Saint-Priest's excellent plan would founder because my husband would never stand firm.

I must be with him. I believed it was imperative that I remain at his side. Moreover, I did not wish him to face a danger which I did not share.

I turned to him and said: "I believe we should be together. You should leave with me and all the family now for Rambouillet."

The King hesitated. Then he decided that he could not run away. He must face these people. And so we talked and Axel grew more and more alarmed and news was brought to us that the marchers were almost on the palace. Some carried knives; they were shouting threats; they wanted my blood. They wanted to take the King to Paris.

"Sire," said Saint-Priest, "if you let the people take you to Paris you have lost your crown."

Necker, who was afraid of losing his popularity with the people, advised against the Rambouillet scheme. And Louis oscillated between the two—at one moment turning to Saint-Priest. "Yes, yes, my dear Comte, you are right. We must do this . . ." and to Necker, "You are right. I must stand my ground." And to me: "We must be together. We must not be separated."

And meanwhile the decisive moments were ticking by. This I suspected was what Louis wished. He would not be forced to make the choice. Circumstances should do it for him. This was how he had always been. This was why we now teetered on the edge of revolution. I can see it so clearly now . . . all the steps which had led to our downfall, the many chances which fate had offered us and at each one Louis had hesitated until it was too late and the decision was no longer his.

Down in the courtyards the horses were pawing impatiently; the servants were awaiting orders. They went on waiting. The rain was teeming down and the women of Paris put their skirts over their heads to protect them while they shouted obscene remarks to each other—and they were about the Queen.

They were in Versailles . . . cold, wet, and angry—and intoxicated, for they had raided the wine shops on the way.

Behind the mob rode La Fayette and the National Guard. Whether he intended to curb them we were not sure. We were never sure of La Fayette, except that his actions were always too late to be effective and we suspected that he was not entirely enamored of this revolution which he had done his best to bring about. He was imbued with American ideas and ideals. He doubtless visualized a speedy conflict and then a new nation built on the remains of the old, in which liberty, fraternity, and equality flourished. But he was not dealing with a band of colonists who fought for an ideal of freedom; his army was made up of agitators and prostitutes, men and women who were fed on envy, who demanded blood all the time not because they wished for freedom, not because they wished to build a new way of life—but because they wanted revenge. La Fayette was a man of honor. He must have realized this. He knew that he had aroused a fury of lust, greed, envy, sloth, covetousness, wrath, and pride . . . all the seven deadliest sins. And I believe he was an uneasy man.

But the very fact that the National Guard was there with its commander showed that this was no ordinary assault. There was purpose behind it; and if the purpose of the women was to kill me, that of the Guards was to take the King to Paris.

Mist had fallen over the town; it seeped into the château; it hung in patches like gray ghosts. The marchers now surrounded us. I could hear their chanting: *"Du pain. Du pain."*

Then I heard my name. They wanted the Queen. They wanted her head on a pike. They were going to fight over my body. They would make cockades of my entrails. They would tear out my heart and carry it to Paris. They would slit my throat with their butchers' knives; they would ram the moldy bread they had been forced to eat down my throat and make me eat it before they strangled me.

I tried to think of my mother who had always told me that I must never be afraid of death. When it came I must welcome it for it was the end of all earthly sorrows. Oh my mother, I thought, how I rejoice that you did not live to see this day.

I thought of my children. They would surely not harm them. Oh God, what would become of us?

The King's calmness was a help to us all. He refused to believe that his good people would harm any of us. They would not even harm me for they would know how that would grieve him. And when they said they would send a deputation of women to parley with him he declared himself very happy to receive them.

Five of the women were chosen to speak to the King and tell him of their grievances. This cheered us greatly for it seemed a reasonable arrangement.

The women were brought to the King and they chose for their spokeswoman Louison Chabry, a flower girl of outstanding beauty, who certainly looked well nourished, so it was evident that all the people of Paris were not starving.

I guessed her to be a bold creature, but brought face to face with the courteous manners of the King she was bewildered and tongue-tied. Even Louis, who was so unlike his grandfather, had inherited a little of that aura which surrounded his ancestors, and bold Louison suddenly realized that she was in the presence of royalty and could only goggle with amazement and murmured: *"Du pain, Sire."* Perhaps the march in the rain had been too much for her; perhaps she was overcome by excitement but she fainted and would have fallen if the King had not caught her.

The King called his doctor and the girl was revived. Then he talked to her of her troubles and all she could do was look at him with round eyes of wonder and murmur: "Yes, Sire. No, Sire."

If only they had all been as easy to handle as Louison!

He told her that he regarded himself as the little father of his people and that his one desire was to make them happy and see them well fed. Clearly she believed him and was ready to change her revolutionary ideas and become a loyal subject without more ado. And when she left Louis kissed her with fervor. It was the first time I ever saw him kiss a woman with relish. He even joked and said that the kiss made it well worth the trouble. Well worth the trouble! I thought. Of having a howling mob at our gates! Of losing the crown? There were times when I believed his lethargy was a physical disability. Could any normal man be so calm in the face of such unprecedented disaster?

Louison returned to her friends. How her account of her interview was received no one can imagine. Meanwhile night was falling and the women took off their skirts as they said to dry them and mingled with the soldiers who were supposed to be guarding the château.

The uneasy day had passed into uneasy night.

Saint-Priest and Axel wanted immediate action. As they saw it, it was folly to stay.

Louis began to see that we should leave for Rambouillet—not only myself and the children but himself and the rest of the family.

He took my hand and said: "You are right that we should not be parted. We will go together."

I hurried into the children's apartments.

"We are leaving in half an hour," I told Madame de Tourzel. "Get the children ready."

But even as I spoke one of the King's servants came to tell me that the escape was now impossible, for the crowds were in the stables and they would not allow the carriages to leave.

I could have wept. Once more we had hesitated and lost.

I told Madame de Tourzel not to disturb the children and I went back to my husband's apartments. Axel was beside me; he could no longer restrain himself; he gripped my hand and said: "You must give me an order that I may take horses from the stables. I may need them to defend you."

I shook my head. "You must not risk your life for me," I told him.

"For what else?"

"For the King," I suggested. And I added trying to soothe the anguish he showed so clearly he was feeling: "I am not afraid. My mother taught me not to fear death. If it has come for me I will accept it with fortitude I believe."

He turned away. He was determined to save me. But how could one man's love save me from those howling men and women who were bent on my destruction?

De La Fayette arrived at Versailles about midnight, and stationing his men in the Place d'Armes he came to the palace to see the King.

He entered in a theatrical way. I often wondered whether Monsieur de La Fayette saw himself as the hero of the Revolution who would bring about the reforms he believed the country needed with the minimum of violence. He made a grandiloquent speech about serving the King and bringing his own head to save that of His Majesty, whereupon Louis replied that the General must never doubt that he was always pleased to see him and his good people of Paris. He begged the General would tell them this.

The General asked that those guards who had deserted their posts and gone to the National Guard a few weeks before should be allowed to resume their old duties. It would be a gesture of trust.

What were gestures of trust with those people down there? Yet I believed that both Louis and de La Fayette believed in it.

The King took my hand and kissed it.

"You are exhausted. It has been a tiring day. Go to bed and get some sleep now. Our good Monsieur de La Fayette will see that all is well."

La Fayette bowed. "Your Majesties need have no anxiety," he said. "The people have promised that they will remain calm throughout the night."

I went to my bedchamber and sank onto my bed. It was true. The events of this day had left me exhausted.

I was awakened just before dawn by unfamiliar sounds. I started up in bed and peered into the darkness. I heard the voices again . . . coarse, crude voices. Whence did they come? I rang the bell and one of my women came in. She must have been near, which surprised me, for I told them not to sleep in my room but to go to their own beds.

"Whose voices are those?" I asked.

"The women of Paris, Madame. They are wandering about on the terrace. There is nothing to fear. Monsieur de La Fayette has given his word."

I nodded and went back to sleep. It seemed a short while afterward when I was awakened by the same woman and another standing by my bedside. The room seemed full of shouting voices.

"Madame . . . quickly. You must dress. They are invading the château. They are close . . ."

I leaped out of bed. Madame Thiébaut, Madame Campan's sister, was there. She was thrusting shoes on my feet and trying to wrap a robe about me. Then I heard the voices close:

"This way. We'll get her. This is her apartment. I'll cut her heart out myself."

"No . . . No, that honor's for me."

"Come quickly," cried Madame Thiébaut. "There is no time to dress. They are almost upon us."

"The King's apartment . . ." I stammered. "The children . . ."

They were dragging me through the narrow corridor toward the *oeil de boeuf*. The door was locked. It was the first time I had ever known it locked and I was seized with a violent horror because I knew from the nearness of voices that the intruders were already in my bedroom.

Madame Thiébaut was banging on the door. "Open . . . Open for God's sake. For the Queen's sake . . . open . . ."

I heard the shouts. "She's fooled us. She's gone. Where is she? We'll find her."

"Oh God," I prayed. "Help me to be brave. This is the moment. This is death . . . horrible death."

I was hammering on the door and suddenly it was opened and we fell into the *oeil de boeuf*. The page who had opened it locked it again and we sped across to the King's apartments. I was sobbing with terror. Death I could face, but not violent, obscene death at the hands of those savages.

"The King," I cried.

"He is going to your bedchamber to find you," I was told.

"But they are there!"

"He has gone by means of the secret corridor under the *oeil de boeuf*." It was the secret way he had come when people used to watch his visits to my bedchamber and snigger over them. How fortunate that I had had that secret way made!

But what would happen to him? Would he be safe? They were crying for my blood not his.

"The children . . ." I began. And then Madame de Tourzel came in leading them, hastily snatched from their beds, robes over their sleeping clothes.

They ran to me and I embraced them; I held them to me as though I would never let them go. Then the King came in—calm, almost unhurried.

"They are in your bedroom," he said, "despoiling the room."

I had a horrible vision of them slashing the bed which was still warm, pulling down the hangings, snatching up my treasures. I thought strangely enough of the little clock which my son so loved and which played a tune. I heard the tinkling sound quite clearly.

> "*Il pleut, il pleut bergère,*
> *Presse tes blancs moutons . . .*"

"Listen," I said. "What is that?"

It was the sound of blows on the door of the *oeil de boeuf*.

We waited. I think even Louis believed then that our last hour had come.

Then . . . the blows ceased. One of the pages came running in to tell us that the Guards were driving the mob out of the château.

I sat down and covered my face with my hands.

My son was pulling at my skirt. "Maman, what are they all doing?"

I just held him against me. I could not speak. My daughter took her brother's hand and said: "You must not worry Maman now."

"Why?" he wanted to know.

"Because there are so many things to think of."

I thought: They will kill my son. He smiled at me and whispered: "It's all right, Maman, Moufflet is here."

"Then," I whispered back, "it is all right."

He nodded.

In the Cour Royale and the Cour de Marbre they were shouting for Orléans. I shivered. How deeply was the Duc d'Orléans involved in this?

Elisabeth had taken the Dauphin onto her knee; I felt comforted to have Elisabeth with us.

"Maman," said my son, "Chou d'amour is hungry."

I kissed him. "In a little while you shall eat."

He nodded. "Moufflet too," he reminded me; and we all smiled.

The crowds outside the château were shouting for the King.

"The King on the balcony."

I looked at Louis. He stepped out. They must admire him surely. He showed not a vestige of fear. They were not to know that he felt none.

La Fayette had arrived in the apartment. He was clearly amazed that the mob had broken into the palace. He had had their word.

I was not surprised that he was nicknamed General Morphée; he would have been fast asleep in his bed while the assassins were breaking into the château.

Provence arrived with the Duc d'Orléans, both well shaven and powdered. Provence looked cold as usual and Orléans sly. Madame Campan told me afterward that there were many who swore they had seen him disguised among the rioters in the early morning and that he was the one who had shown the mob the way to my apartments.

La Fayette made his way to the balcony.

"The King," roared the crowd.

La Fayette bowing, presented the King. The General lifted his hand and told them that the King had now consented to the Declaration of the Rights of Man. Much had been achieved and now he knew they would wish to go home. He, the Commander of the National Guard, requested them to.

Did he expect them to obey him? He could not have been such a fool. He was a man playing a part—the part of hero of the hour.

Of course the crowd did not move. They were going to have what they had come for.

Then a voice shouted: "The Queen. The Queen on the balcony."

The cry was taken up. Now it was a deafening roar.

"No," said the King. "You must not . . ."

Axel was there. He made a step toward me but I ordered him with my eyes to keep away. He must not betray our love before all these people. That could only add to our troubles.

I stepped toward the balcony.

My daughter began to cry and I said: "It's all right, darling. Don't be frightened, little Mousseline. The people only want to see me."

It was Axel who thrust my daughter's hand in mine and lifting my son put him in my arms.

"No!" I cried.

But he was pushing me onto the balcony. He believed that the people would not harm the children.

There was silence as I stood there. Then they cried: "No children. Send the children back."

I was sure then that they were going to kill me. I turned and handed the Dauphin to Madame de Tourzel. My daughter tried to cling to my robe but I pushed her back.

Then alone I stepped onto the balcony. There was buzzing in my head but perhaps it was the whispering below me. It seemed to take me minutes to make that one short step. It was as though time itself had stopped and that the whole world was waiting for me to cross the threshold between life and death.

I was alone and defenseless facing those people who had come to Versailles to kill me. I had folded my hands across my gold and white striped robe into which I had been hastily put when I was aroused from my bed; my hair fell about my shoulders.

I heard a voice cry: "Now, there she is. The Austrian Woman. Shoot her."

I bowed my head as though to greet them; and the silence went on and on.

What happened in those seconds I do not know—except that the French are the most emotional people in the world. They love and hate with more vehemence than others. All their feelings are intense and the more so perhaps for being transient.

My apparent lack of fear, my extreme femininity perhaps, my cool indifference to death touched them momentarily.

Someone shouted: "Vive la Reine." And others took it up. I looked down on that sea of faces—on those disreputable people with their knives and cudgels and their cruel faces. And I was not afraid.

I bowed once more and stepped into the room.

There I was received by a few seconds of bewildered silence. Then the

King was embracing me with tears in his eyes and my children clinging to my skirts were crying with him.

But this was a momentary respite.

The crowd was shouting again; "To Paris. The King to Paris."

The King said this matter must be discussed with the National Assembly. They should be invited to come to the palace.

But the people outside were growing restive.

"To Paris," they chanted. "The King to Paris."

Saint-Priest was gloomy. So was Axel. "They will break into the château," he said. "It is clear, Monsieur de La Fayette, that you have no power to restrain them."

La Fayette could not deny this.

"I must save further bloodshed," said the King. "I will go peaceably to Paris." He turned to me and said quickly: "We must be together . . . all of us."

Then he stepped onto the balcony and said: "My friends, I shall go to Paris with my wife and children. I shall trust what is most precious to me to the love of my good and faithful subjects."

There were shouts of joy. The journey had been a success. The mission carried out.

La Fayette stepped from the balcony into the room.

"Madame," he said gravely, "you must consider this."

"I have considered," I answered. "I know that those people hate me. I know they are intent on murdering me. But if that is my fate I must accept it. My place is with my husband."

It was one o'clock when we left Versailles. Yesterday's rain had given place to sunshine and it was a lovely autumn day, but the weather could not lift our spirits.

In the carriage in which I rode with the King were my children and Madame de Tourzel, with the Comte and Comtesse de Provence and Elisabeth.

I shall never forget that drive and although I was to experience greater humiliations, greater tragedies, it stands out in my mind. The smell of the people; their leering faces beside our carriage; the murderous looks which came my way; the long slow drive which took six hours. I could smell blood in the air. Some of these savages had murdered guards and carried their heads before us on pikes—a grim warning, I suppose, of what they would do with us. They had even forced a hairdresser to dress the hair on these heads; the poor man, revolted and nauseated, had been obliged to do so at the point of a knife.

Astride the cannon were drunken women who shrieked obscenities to each other. My name was mentioned often; I was too sickened to care very much what they said of me. Some of the women, half naked for they had not bothered to replace their skirts, went arm in arm with the soldiers. They had robbed the royal granaries, and carriages had been loaded with sacks of flour which were well guarded by the soldiers. The *poissardes* danced about the carriage crying: "We shall no longer lack bread. We are bringing the baker, the baker's wife, and the baker's boy to Paris."

My little son was whimpering: "I'm so hungry, Maman. Chou d'amour has had no breakfast, no dinner . . ."

I comforted him as best I could.

And at last we came to Paris. Bailly, the mayor, welcomed us by the light of torches.

"What a splendid day," said the mayor, "when Parisians are at last able to have His Majesty and his family in their city."

"I hope," replied Louis with dignity, "that my stay in Paris will bring peace, harmony, and obedience to the laws."

Tired out as we were we must drive to the Hôtel de Ville.

There we sat on the throne where the Kings and Queens of France had sat before us. The King told Bailly that he should tell the people that it was always with pleasure and confidence that he found himself among the inhabitants of his good city of Paris.

Bailly when repeating this left out the word confidence and I noticed this at once and reminded Bailly of his omission.

"You hear, gentlemen," said Bailly. "This is even better than if my memory had not betrayed me."

They were mocking us. They were pretending to treat us as King and Queen when we were merely their prisoners.

And then we were offered a brief respite. We were allowed to drive from the Hôtel de Ville to the Tuileries—that gloomy, deserted palace which they had chosen for us.

23

"No one would believe all that has happened in the last twenty-four hours and yet whatever one imagined would be less than what we have had to endure."

Marie Antoinette to Mercy

"When one undertakes to direct a revolution, the difficulty is not to spur it on but to restrain it."

"Oh excellent but weak King. Oh, most unfortunate of Queens! Your vacillation has swept you into a terrible abyss. If you renounce my advice, or if I should fail, a funeral pall will cover this realm."

Mirabeau

"He (Fersen) has established himself at the village of Auteuil . . . and so goes to Saint-Cloud under cover of darkness. A discharged soldier of the guard met him leaving the castle at three in the morning. I thought it my duty to speak of this to the Queen. 'Do you not think,' I said to her, 'that the presence of the Comte de Fersen and his visits to the château may be a source of danger?' She looked at me with that disdainful air which you know. 'Tell him so yourself, if you think it right to do so . . .'"

Saint-Priest

"I thank you indeed for all that you say concerning my Friend (Marie Antoinette). Believe me, my dear Sophie, she deserves all the feeling you can have for her. She is the most perfect being I have ever known or could know . . ."

Axel de Fersen to his sister Sophie

TUILERIES AND SAINT-CLOUD

With what a horrible feeling of doom I entered the Tuileries. It was long since the place had been inhabited; it was damp and cold. The passages were so dark that even by day they had to be lighted by oil lamps which smoked. We were so exhausted that all we wanted to do was sleep. The Dauphin had given up declaring that he was hungry; his eyelids were drooping but he said: "This is an ugly place, Maman. Let us go home now."

"Why, mon Chou d'amour, Louis Quatorze lived here and liked it. So you must like it, too."

"Why did he like it?"

"Perhaps you will find out."

He was too sleepy for more questions and I was glad of that.

I tried to sleep on the hastily improvised bed; but I kept waking, startled and fancying I could feel the movement of the coach, hear the shouts of the people and see those bloody heads held aloft on pikes.

What will become of us now? I wondered.

The King slept heavily.

In the morning my spirits were lifted a little. The sun showed up the decrepit appearance of the palace but at least the daylight was comforting; and I felt that to have lived safely through the night was somehow a triumph.

The King was full of optimism. "We will have furniture brought here from Versailles," he said. "I am sure my people will wish to see us properly housed."

It seemed incredible that he could still believe in the love of his people.

Our faithful servants found some food for us and we were able to explore the palace. The only part that seemed in order was that which looked on the gardens. On the first floor were several rooms which could be lived in and these became the King's bedroom, Elisabeth's bedroom, one bedroom each for the Dauphin and his sister, a drawing room and a few reception rooms; on the ground floor was my bedroom with four more rooms; a flight of stairs connected the apartments so that in any emergency we could very quickly all be together.

But it seemed we were to have little peace for with the coming of the morning the people were assembling again. My son heard them and came running to me.

"*Mon Dieu*, Maman," he cried, "is it yesterday again?"

I tried to comfort him but the women were already shrieking for me to appear on the balcony. I stepped out, believing as I had yesterday that I could well be stepping out to death; but this was a different crowd, I saw at once, a more sober crowd. These were the citizens of Paris; they stood firmly behind the revolution but they were not the criminals and prostitutes who had marched on Versailles. I sensed at once the difference and I believed that I could speak to them.

There was a silence as I stood there. I knew that they respected my courage in showing no fear in facing them.

I said: "My friends, you should know that I love my good city of Paris."

"Oh yes," cried a voice, "so much so that on the fourteenth of July you wanted to besiege it and on the fifth of October you were about to flee to the frontier."

There were cheers and laughter; but how different it was from yesterday.

"We must stop hating each other," I said; and there was again that silence. Then someone said: "She has courage, this Austrian woman." Another silence and then: "*Vive la Reine.*"

When I stepped into the room, I felt greatly comforted, but I knew nothing would ever be as it had in the past.

I sat down and wrote to Mercy, whom I had told to keep away from the Court for a while because I feared that the Austrian Ambassador would be considered an enemy and would doubtless be in danger:

> "If we forget where we are and how we came here, we should be pleased with the people's mood, particularly this morning. I hope that if there is no lack of bread a great many things will settle down . . . No one would believe all that has happened in the last twenty-four hours and yet whatever one imagined would be less than what we have had to endure."

The King came into my room and he said: "I heard the people applauding you. This is the end of the revolution. Now we will work out a new order . . . the best for us all."

I embraced him but I did not really agree with him. I could not forget that however mild the mood of the people today, we were prisoners; and as I said to Madame Campan when I knew that they were going to force us to leave Versailles for the Tuileries: "When Kings become prisoners, they have not long to live."

The mood of the people certainly had changed for within the next few days furniture began to arrive from Versailles. Carpenters and upholsterers were in the palace all through the day and in a very short time those apartments we had chosen began to look more suitable for a royal residence. Our royal bodyguards, chosen from noble families, had of course been dismissed and replaced by members of La Fayette's National Guard and we found this tiresome for these men were curious and ill-bred and showed little restraint in invading our privacy.

I was terrified that my son would offend these guards and I impressed on him the need to be friendly with them. This he did not find difficult; he would question them and talk to them in a way which they could not fail to find charming.

He was old enough to be puzzled by what was happening, to compare the present life with that of the past; all of us attempted to hide our apprehension in his presence and to try to lead him to the belief that everything that was happening was perfectly natural.

But he was too bright to be taken in.

One day he ran to the King and said: "Papa, I have something very serious to say to you."

His father smiled and said he would be glad to hear more of this serious matter.

"What I do not understand, Papa," said the Dauphin, "is why the people who used to love you so much, are all at once angry with you. What have you done to make them so cross?"

The King took the boy on his knee and said: "I wanted to make the people happier than they were but I want money to pay for the cost of wars, so I asked the people for money as all Kings must do. But the Magistrates who make up the Parlement opposed this and said that only the people had the right to consent to it. I asked the principal inhabitants of all the towns, whether distinguished by birth, fortune, or talent to come to Versailles. That is called a States General. When they came they asked concessions of me which I could not make either with respect to myself or in justice to you who will one day be their King. Wicked men, who urged the people to rise, have been responsible for what has happened during the last few days. You must not think the people are to be blamed for this."

I do not know whether he understood it all, but the boy nodded gravely; and after that conversation he seemed to lose a great many of his childish ways.

The dreary winter progressed. We had settled down to routine which was very different from the old life. Versailles and the Petit Trianon seemed years away. But I had changed too.

I was thirty-four years old and I had learned a terrible lesson. I was beginning to see that if I had behaved differently I should not have been reviled as I was by the people. They did not hate the King as they hated me.

I had changed so much that I chose those apartments on the ground floor so that I could be apart from my family, so that I could be alone to contemplate. How strange that I who had never been able to concentrate for a few seconds or so on any subject which did not interest me should now seek to know myself.

I would spend hours in writing, setting down what had happened in the past, which I have continued to do, and which is the only way I can know myself and follow each step to the place which I have now reached.

I had become changed. I had grown from a frivolous girl into a woman. The change had been sudden—but only as sudden as the change in my fortunes. I felt as though I had lived through a lifetime of suffering and fear in twenty-four hours. That must have its effect on anyone.

When I remember the letters I wrote to Mercy I know how great the change was.

"The more unfortunate I am," I wrote, "the stronger grows my affection for my true friends. I am looking forward so much to the moment when I shall be able to see you freely and to assure you of the feelings which you have every right to expect from me—feelings which will last to the end of my life."

At last I realized the worth of Mercy, for now I saw how different everything might have been if I had paid attention to his warnings and those of my mother.

But I took courage from the fact that now I could see that I was wrong— a fact of which I had been ignorant until great suffering opened my eyes.

During that dreary winter the days seemed long and monotonous. My great comforts were my children and Axel, who was able to visit me frequently. I would sit in the schoolroom while the Abbé Davout was teaching my son and I saw how difficult he found it to concentrate which reminded me so much of my own childhood that I warned him against this.

"But, Maman," he said gravely, "there are so many soldiers here, and they are so much more interesting than lessons."

Great soldiers, I reminded him, had to learn their lessons too.

We all attended Mass each day and took our meals together. We were more intimate than we had ever been before, for we lived like a bourgeois family sitting at table with the children who joined in the conversation. Poor Adelaide and Victoire had changed very much. Sophie had died and they were always saying: "Lucky Sophie. To have been spared this."

But they were no longer my enemies; this misfortune had changed them too. They had enough sense to realize that the scandals they had spread about me in the past had played a strong part in bringing us all to the state in which we now found each other, and they were contrite. I think they were astonished too that I bore them no malice. I had no time to be vindictive; I could take no pleasure in reminding them of all the harm they had done me. I could only be sorry for them who had lived so long in a state of society which was now cracking under their feet and leaving them defenseless.

Their attitude toward me had taken a complete turnabout; they were affectionate and devoted—perhaps even adoring, for Adelaide could never do anything by halves and Victoire, of course, followed her sister.

Elisabeth's natural saintliness was increased. She was always with me and the children. Together we set about making a tapestry rug which filled long hours of that winter as pleasantly as could be expected.

After dinner the King would slump in his chair and sleep, or go to his apartment to do so. He was gentle with the whole family and could always soothe the hysterical outbursts of the aunts which they could not help letting escape from time to time. They longed so much for a return of the old days; they, more than any of us, found it hard to adjust themselves to the new *régime*.

I lived for Axel's visits. We could not be alone together but we held many whispered conversations. He told me he could not rest while I was here in Paris. He thought continually of that terrible drive from Versailles to Paris.

"Those *canaille* . . . How I loathe them! How I despise them! God knows what harm they might have done you. How can I tell you of the agonies I suffered when I knew you were in their midst? I tell you I will never rest until you are out of this city. I want you right away . . . where I know you shall be safe."

I smiled and listened. His love for me, my children's affection for me and my husband's tenderness were all I cared to live for.

And during that long winter the theme of my lover's discourse was Escape.

After a while my fears were lulled a little. We were in a sense prisoners but at least at the Tuileries we had a semblance of a court. La Fayette was a constant visitor and he assured the King that he was his servant. La Fayette was a man of good intention, and in this respect he was not unlike Louis. He failed to be on the spot at the important moment; he was always too late when the decision should be made promptly and too quick when it needed a great deal of consideration. But we were glad of his friendship.

He had evidence that Orléans had helped to arrange the march on Versailles and was certain that those people who swore they had seen the Duc disguised in a slouch hat had not been mistaken and for this reason he believed that Orléans should be sent where he could do no more harm.

The King could not believe that his own cousin could be such a traitor. But La Fayette cried: "Sire, his plan is to dethrone you and be Regent of France. The very fact of his birth makes this possible."

"What proof have you!" asked the King dismayed.

"Plenty, Sire. And I can get more. The rabble which marched on Versailles was strongly augmented by men in women's clothes. They were not the women of Paris as we were meant to believe. They were paid agitators many of them and one of those who organized the march was Monsieur d'Orléans."

"It is incredible," insisted the King; but I pointed out to him that it was not incredible at all. Orléans had been my enemy from the days when I had first come to France; and I could well believe this of him.

The King looked at me helplessly but La Fayette, sure now of my support, went on: "Sire, some heard the cry 'Vive Orléans, notre roi d'Orléans!' I think that makes it clear. He plans to destroy you and the Queen and set himself up in your place. He should be sent out of the country."

"Let him go to England," said the King. "But I think it should be said that he goes on a mission for me. I would not wish publicly to accuse my cousin of treachery."

So to London went Orléans; and there he met Madame de la Motte and together they planned what further calumnies they could pile upon me.

Those long winter days! Those drafty corridors! Those smoking lamps! And our privacy continually disturbed by the guards!

I do not think I could have endured that winter but for Axel's presence. I missed Gabrielle sadly. The Princesse de Lamballe was a goood friend and I loved her dearly but she had never had the place in my feelings which I gave to Gabrielle. Elisabeth was a constant consolation—and of course the children. My daughter was growing into a sweet-natured girl. She was resigned and accepted hardship without complaint. She was greatly influenced by the attitude of her Aunt Elisabeth and the two were always together. Sometimes when I was particularly sad I would send for my little Chou d'amour and he would enliven me with his precocious sayings. Like the child he was he had quickly adapted himself to the life at the Tuileries and I sometimes thought that he had forgotten the splendors of the Trianon and Versailles.

"We must be careful not to spoil him," I told Madame de Tourzel, "but he is such a darling, it is difficult. We must remember, though, that we should bring him up to be a King."

She agreed with me, and I often thought how fortunate I was to be surrounded by so many true friends; and that it could only be in times of misfortune that we could discover them.

The King was relying more and more on my judgment. He seemed aware of the change in me and I remembered how in the beginning he had declared he would never allow a woman to advise him. We had both changed.

But there was one quality in him which never altered—that unnatural calm. It almost seemed that he lacked interest in his own affairs.

I heard one of his ministers say that to discuss affairs with him made him feel that he was discussing matters concerning the Emperor of China instead of the King of France.

For this reason I found myself being drawn more and more into affairs. I had tried to keep out of them but Mercy had warned me that if I did not play a part in them no one would. Someone must be at the helm of a ship which was being buffeted by a fierce storm. This was said by Mirabeau, who now that Orléans was no longer in France, was the one man who could hold back the Revolution.

That man was right. He was brilliant I knew. Mercy wrote of him often; Axel spoke of him. He was a rascal, said Axel, and we should not trust him; but at this time he was the most important man in France and we should not ignore him.

It was noticed that I was taking a part in affairs. The King would never agree to anything without as he openly said "consulting the Queen." The new person I had become, although ignorant of much, at least had a firm opinion on what should be done and this was better than the attitude of the King which was never the same for two days running. I was for standing firm against the revolutionaries. We had conceded enough, I declared. We should concede no more. Axel confirmed me in my opinions.

Perhaps I drew on him for them. He was not only my lover; he was my adviser; and the fact that he and Mercy were in agreement on so many points pleased me.

Mirabeau began to change his mind. He now remarked: "The King has only one man with him—his wife."

And this meant that Mirabeau considered me a greater power in France than the King.

"When one undertakes to direct a revolution," Mirabeau was reported to me as having said, "the difficulty is not to spur it on but restrain it."

I gathered from that remark that he wished to restrain it.

In February my brother Joseph died. I felt numbed when I read the letter from Leopold who had succeeded him. There had been a bond between Joseph and myself although his criticism had irritated me; but I realized now that he had meant to help me and how much wisdom there had been behind his comments. Leopold and I had never been so close, so now I felt even the links with Vienna slipping away from me.

We were all suffering from colds; the King had put on more weight for he missed the violent exercise he had been accustomed to take, and an occasional game of billiards could not make up for it. I myself was far from well and I could not contemplate a long summer in the unhealthy atmosphere of the Tuileries. When I suggested that we go to Saint-Cloud for the summer there was only the mildest dissension. I felt very relieved and in lighter spirits than I had been for a long time, because when we got into our carriages in order to make the journey only a small hostile crowd tried to stop us and a much bigger crowd shouted that we needed the more salubrious air and called out: "*Bon voyage au bon Papa!*" which delighted the King and raised my spirits even higher.

I really believed that the Revolution was over and that in time we should be allowed to return to Versailles—to a different life, it was true, but a dignified one.

What a joy to be at Saint-Cloud! The air was invigorating and how beautiful it seemed compared with gloomy Tuileries which I hated. I felt the old days were almost back. It was not the Trianon of course, but it was the next best thing.

Mercy, who was in Brussels, was writing to me urging me not to ignore the advances of Mirabeau who was eager to bring about a *rapprochement* and was the one man in the whole of France who could end the Revolution and put the King back on the throne.

I considered the man—an aristocrat by birth who had not been received well by the nobility and had no doubt for this reason allied himself with the Third Estate. He had given his talents to Orléans, but Orléans was now an exile; and Mirabeau wished to turn around and end the Revolution which he had helped to start. Perhaps he had not intended it should go the way it did. Perhaps he had really wished to make changes constitutionally. In any case that was what he apparently wished now.

He had written letters to the King who had not answered them. I had read these letters and had not persuaded my husband to pay attention to them for I believed that any man who could have been responsible for setting the whole tragedy in motion should be shunned for ever more.

"I shall henceforth be what I have always been," he wrote, "the defender of monarchical power regulated by the laws, and the champion of liberty as guaranteed by monarchical authority. My heart will follow the road which reason has already pointed out to me."

I heard a great deal of this man. Axel talked of him continuously. He was too important to be ignored, he said. We could use him. He had led the people once; he would lead them again. He, and he alone, was able to put an end to this intolerable situation.

"And you suggest that we should make terms with such a man?" I asked.

"I do," answered Axel.

"Why does he wish to join with us now?" I demanded. "Only because he will want to be the President of the National Assembly, at the King's right hand, the first minister. In truth he wishes to be the ruler of France."

Axel smiled at me tenderly. "When he has restored the Monarchy the King and the Queen will be in a strong enough position to deal with him, perhaps."

"I see how your mind works."

And because Axel was in favor of employing this man, he was gradually making me realize that it would be an excellent idea. Perhaps Mirabeau himself touched my vanity for it was to me he wished to make known his plan . . . not to the King.

I wanted that summer to go on and on. I dreaded our return to the Tuileries. Axel was staying nearby in the village of Auteuil and after dark he would slip into the château and would stay with me until just before dawn. We were reckless but these were reckless times. Our passion had reached a fervor no doubt because we did not know which would be the last night we should ever spend together.

One of those who had been sent to guard us saw him one early morning and watched to see him again. Then he thought fit to report the matter to Saint-Priest.

Saint-Priest spoke to me when we were alone one day and said: "Do you not think that the visits of the Comte de Fersen to the château might be a source of danger?"

I felt my face stiffen. I hated this perpetual spying.

I said haughtily: "If you think it right to do so, you should tell the Comte."

Saint-Priest said nothing to Axel but I told him of this. He was disturbed and said he must not come so often and for a few nights he did not; but he could not stay away and I could not bear to be without him, so the visits continued.

Meanwhile he was persuading me to see Mirabeau and I agreed to meet the man in the park at Saint-Cloud so that our meeting could appear casual. This must be arranged with secrecy, of course, and I was reminded of that other meeting which was supposed to have taken place in a park, between the Cardinal de Rohan and myself. This meeting should be in daylight. Mercy who knew of the plan and supported it wholeheartedly wrote expressing pleasure that I had listened to the advice of my good friends. Like Axel he was eager to see the Monarchy restored and since these two were so wholeheartedly in favor of the rendezvous with Mirabeau I could only believe that it was the best thing possible so I threw myself into the scheme with enthusiasm.

I wrote to Mercy:

> "I have found a place which, though not as convenient as it might be, is suitable for the proposed meeting and free from the inconvenience of the gardens and the château."

I chose Sunday morning at eight when the Court would be asleep and the grounds therefore deserted, and I went out to meet this man.

I had heard a great deal about him but I was yet unprepared for his ugliness. His skin was deeply pitted with smallpox and his hair stood up like an untidy mat about his head; this was a brutal face suggesting great strength and vitality. I had heard too that at the first meeting women shuddered and in time grew to love him passionately. This was the man of a hundred seductions, who had spent years in a French prison; who had written many pamphlets; who was in fact the most vital, the most powerful man in the country.

When he spoke I thought his voice one of the most beautiful I had ever heard but perhaps this was in contrast to his replusive appearance. His manners were gracious and he treated me as though I were indeed the Queen and with a respect which I so often missed during these days.

He told me that he had passed the night at his sister's house in order to be in time for the appointment and that I need have no fear that any of those who spied on me should know of the meeting as he had taken the precaution of diguising his nephew as a coachman in order to drive his carriage here.

He then began to explain how he wished to serve us. He could do this. He would bend the people to his will. What he needed me to do was persuade the King to receive him that he might lay his plans before us both.

I listened to him. I was excited by his enthusiasm which was in such contrast to my husband's lethargy. He reminded me of Axel who was so eager to save me—except that Axel was beautiful, and this man so ugly.

I believed him capable of doing all he said and I told him so.

For his part I am sure he was sincere when he laid his hand on his heart and said that in the future it would be his greatest desire in life to serve me. From now on I could count him as my champion.

I told him that he had given me fresh hope and he replied that I might well hope for soon all the humiliations I had suffered would be behind me.

There was such a sense of power in the man that I could not fail to believe him.

I left him feeling that the interview had been one of marked success. Axel was delighted; so was Mercy. I felt all we had to do now was wait for Mirabeau to act.

When I heard that he had written to the Comte de la Marck, who was one of the go-betweens in the affair: "Nothing shall stop me. I would die rather than fail to fulfill my promises!" I was exultant.

The autumn had come and we must leave Saint-Cloud and return to the Tuileries. It was with great sadness that we returned to our dank dark home.

The aunts were wretched. They could only vaguely understand what had happened and they hated the crowds who were always watching us and treating us with no respect; they loathed the guards who spied on us so insolently.

They were constantly in tears and their health was failing. They envied poor Sophie more than ever. Anyone who had died before this terrible thing had happened was to be envied, declared Adelaide.

Mirabeau was in touch with us and the King was receiving him. I pointed out that if some plan was formed which might involve our leaving Paris it would be as well to have the aunts safely out of the way. Louis agreed with us but in his usual way did nothing about it, so I consulted Axel, who said that we should arrange for them to slip away. They must cross the frontier and perhaps go to Naples where my sister would undoubtedly receive them.

I shall never forget the day they left. They were desolate, like two lost children. They embraced me fondly and Adelaide cried that she wanted me to come with them . . . myself, dear Louis, and the darling children. I said we could not and she looked at me mutely and I knew she was asking my forgiveness for all the spiteful malice of the past. I wanted her to understand that I bore no malice. In the past I had been too careless to do so; now I realized that there was too much hatred in the world for me to wish to add to it.

I kissed them. I said, without believing it for one moment, that perhaps soon we should all be together. And they went out into the courtyard where the carriages were waiting. I was horrified to see that a crowd had gathered and some effort was made to prevent their leaving.

I heard a voice shout: "Shall we let them go?" And I listened, my heart beating wildly for the answer.

There was a pause but when during it the coachmen had whipped up the horses and the carriage moved off, no one attempted to follow them.

It was only Mesdames—the mad old ladies.

I stood at the window looking out without seeing anything.

They had gone now . . . another phase was over.

It was a long time before I heard from them. Their carriage had been stopped on the way; ugly faces had peered at them. As they could not be the Queen disguised they were allowed to pass on and eventually they reached Naples where my sister Caroline welcomed them.

I heard that they spoke of me with something like reverence. So they must have been truly sorry.

Orléans had returned to Paris. Why should he stay away? Because the King had sent him into exile? But what power had the King? The people of Paris welcomed him back. And with him came Jeanne de la Motte. Why should she stay away? There was no danger now of her being asked to pay the penalty for her part in the diamond necklace fraud. Everyone believed that she had been the scapegoat and that I had had the necklace. She set herself up in the Place Vendôme and devoted her time to the writing of fiction in which I was always the central character. She wrote her newest version of the Diamond Necklace scandal. Her works were received with enthusiasm for their purpose was to revile me.

Meanwhile Mirabeau was bringing all his energy to the problem of restoring the Monarchy. I believe now that he could have done it. He was working with the National Assembly and with the King and we were closer now to reconciliation than we had been for a long time. Mirabeau could have saved us. I realize that now.

He was not entirely altruistic. He wanted power for himself and he wanted riches too. His debts were enormous. The King must provide a million livres which would pass into Mirabeau's possession when he had brought the Revolution to an end and the King was firmly back on the throne. His, Mirabeau's, debts would be naturally settled and he would earn the undying gratitude of the King.

With his golden voice and his mastery of words he could sway the assembly. Marat, Robespierre, and Danton were watchful. So was Orléans. It must have seemed to them that Mirabeau was planning to destroy all they had agitated for.

He talked fiercely to the King.

"Four enemies," he said, "are marching upon us: taxation, bankruptcy, the army, and the winter. We could prepare to deal with these enemies by guiding them. Civil war is not certain but it could be expedient."

Louis was horrified.

"Civil war. I could never agree to that."

"Law and order would merely be arms to fight the mob. And does Your Majesty doubt which would win?"

The King looked at me. "The King would never agree to civil war," I told him.

Mirabeau was exasperated.

"Oh excellent but weak King!" he thundered. "Oh, most unfortunate of Queens! Your vacillation has swept you into a terrible abyss. If you renounce my advice, or if it should fail, a funeral pall will cover this realm. But should I escape the general shipwreck, I shall be able to say to myself with pride, 'I exposed myself to danger in the hope of saving them, but they did not want to be saved.'"

And with that he left us. How right he was. How foolish we were.

But the King would only say: "I would never agree to civil war."

I, too, was afraid of it—too much afraid to attempt to persuade him, which no doubt I could have done.

Mirabeau was not the man to give up because we had rejected his first plan. He knew of Axel's devotion to me and they talked together of the necessity of getting us out of Paris. Mirabeau believed this to be a good plan and suggested that Axel should go at once to Metz near the frontier where the Marquis de Bouillé was stationed with the loyal troops. Axel was to discover the position there, explain the plan to Bouillé and then return to Paris with all speed so that the arrangements could begin.

Axel came to say goodbye to me and I was terrified.

"Do you realize," I asked him, "what these *canaille* would do to you if they knew you were working for us?"

He knew, he replied. But they were not going to discover. The plan was going through. He was going to transport me to safety.

"They would not care that you were a foreigner," I cried. "Oh, Axel, go away from France. Stay away . . . until all this is over."

He merely smiled and took me into his arms. He said that he would soon be back from Metz and then there should be no delay. He would be leaving Paris . . . and I should be with him.

So he went to Metz and I tried to settle into the routine of the new life—so monotonous, but like a smoldering fire which will at any moment burst into a wild conflagration.

It was wonderful to see Axel safely back but the news he brought was not good. Bouillé was growing anxious, for the troops were becoming restive. News of what was happening in Paris was coming to them—often highly exaggerated, and he was less sure of their loyalty than he had been. Bouillé believed that inactivity was responsible. If decisive action was to be taken, there should be no delay.

Axel agreed wholeheartedly; so did Mirabeau.

"You should begin making plans for the escape," Mirabeau told Axel. "As a Swede you are less suspect than a Frenchman would be." In the meantime he still clung to his first plan. He wanted boldness on the part of the King; he wanted him to behave as though he were a King, to go into the streets, to show himself. He was not disliked, the people showed their affection for him by calling him their little papa.

"I think it would be unwise for the Queen to appear in the streets," said Axel.

Mirabeau lifted his shoulders. "In an affair of this nature, certain risks must be taken. The mood of the people at this moment is such that I do not think the Queen would be harmed. That mood can, of course, change suddenly."

"I do not care for the Queen to expose herself to the rabble," said Axel fiercely.

So even between these two there was disagreement.

But there was new hope in the Tuileries. Axel was working for us as only a fervent lover could; Mirabeau was using all the fierce determination of an ambitious man for the same purpose. I believed that this could not fail.

Fate was against us, for ill fortune always seemed close behind ready to catch up with us.

I could not believe it when I was told that Mirabeau was dead. The day before he had appeared to be in perfect health, his vitality astonishing everyone. By day he was haranguing the National Assembly, formulating plans with the King and at the same time working with the Assembly. By night he continued to indulge in the pleasures of the flesh. I heard that the night before he died he slept with two opera singers.

We did not know exactly how he died. All we knew was that he was no longer with us.

The verdict was death from natural causes; but we shall never know what killed Mirabeau. He was a man who no doubt suffered from certain ailments. The life he had been leading for so long may have made them inevitable; but there were many who said that the Orléanists had determined to be rid of a man who was trying to run with the Monarchy and hunt with the National Assembly. It would not be difficult to find someone ready to slip a little something into his food or wine.

The fact remained that we had lost Mirabeau and with him our best hope of restoring the Monarchy to France.

And so we were back to the routine of the Tuileries. I spent a great deal of time in my room, writing. I was learning now where I had taken my most fatal steps and how I might have acted. If I ever had a chance, I decided, I would not make the same mistakes again.

I was embroidering my tapestry rug with Elisabeth and we spent long hours together talking of the children; sometimes I played a game of billiards with the King. For exercise we walked in the Bois de Boulogne but we were always uneasy when out of doors. Our experiences at Versailles had taught us that walls could not protect us from the fury of the mob, but there was a certain sense of security within walls. My son remained very friendly with the soldiers and I encouraged this because I thought that he must inspire some affection in them and if the mob ever broke in on us as they had at Versailles these soldier friends of his would protect him.

I was longing for the summer and the comparative freedom of Saint-Cloud. It seemed far away and I suggested to the King that we slip away to Saint-Cloud for Easter. He agreed to this and I said we would make ready.

Remembering how, when the aunts had left, the mob had surrounded their carriage and had debated whether or not to let them go, I said that we must not let it be generally known that we were going. All the same certain preparations had to be made and the members of my intimate circle knew of them.

I trusted them absolutely, although there was a newcomer named Madame Rochereuil of whom I knew very little, but she had been well recommended and it never occurred to me to doubt that she was not to be relied on.

Preparations were complete; Easter was almost on us; the carriages were in the courtyard and we were ready to leave. But as we began the drive we found ourselves surrounded by the rabble; this was the same kind of mob which had brought us from Versailles to Paris. I felt sick with horror; my son turned his face from the window of the carriage and I put my arm about him to comfort him.

The insults came—the crude obscenities.

"Little Papa must stay with his children," cried the crowd.

La Fayette came up with his soldiers and ordered the mob to retire and let the royal carriages pass but he was jeered at, and mud was flung at him. I knew instinctively that this was another organized revolt.

"You are behaving as enemies of the Constitution," cried La Fayette. "In preventing the King from leaving you make him a prisoner and you annul the decrees he has sanctioned."

But they would not listen to reason. What had reason to do with them? They had been gathered together for this purpose; they had been *paid* to do what they did.

They leered in at the carriage windows. When the King tried to speak, they shouted "Fat pig!" at him.

I could not help showing my disdain for them. It was something I could never hide. My looks betrayed the contempt I felt for these people.

"Look at her," they cried. "Shall we let this *putain* dictate to us."

La Fayette rode to the carriage.

"Sire," he said, "have I your orders to fire on the mob?"

"I could never permit it," cried Louis. "I do not want one drop of blood to be shed for me. We will return to the Tuileries."

So the carriages were turned and amid shouting and jeers we rode back.

As he alighted Louis said with a sigh: "You will bear witness that henceforward we are not free."

I was desolate. I said to my husband as we entered that palace of doom: "We are indeed prisoners. They are determined that we shall never leave the Tuileries."

24

"Are you imbeciles that you take no steps to prevent the flight of the royal family. Parisians, fools that you are, I am weary of saying to you over and over again that you should have the King and the Dauphin in safe keeping, that you should lock up the Austrian woman . . ."

Marat in L'Ami du Peuple

June 11th. "La Fayette has ordered that the sentinels be doubled and that all carriages be searched."

June 18th. "With the Queen from 2:30 till 6."

June 19th. "With the King . . . Stayed at the château from eleven till midnight."

June 20th. "On taking leave of me the King said: 'Monsieur de Fersen, whatever may happen, I shall never forget all you have done for me.' The Queen wept a great deal. At six I left her . . . Returned home. At eight I wrote to the Queen to change the meeting place of the waiting women and to tell them to let me know the exact time by the body-guards . . ."

Comte de Fersen's Journal

"Louis has abdicated from the Monarchy. Henceforth Louis is nothing to us. We are now free and without a King. It remains to be seen whether it is worth while appointing another."

Resolution passed by the Jacobin Club after the flight of the Royal Family

"Sire, Your Majesty knows my attachment to you, but I did not leave you unaware that if you separated your cause from that of the people I would remain on the side of the people."

La Fayette to Louis XVI

TO VARENNES

When Axel heard that we had been turned back to the Tuileries he came straight to Paris from Auteuil, the little village near Saint-Cloud where he had arrived intending to stay there while we were at the château. He was deeply disturbed, convinced that we were in acute danger.

I took him to my husband who listened to what he had to say, and prodded by the memory of the mob's insolence, he was ready to agree that we must consider flight.

Artois and the Prince de Condé who had safely reached the frontier were aggravating the situation by talking too freely of their attempts to bring an army against the revolutionaries. They were traveling from foreign court to foreign court trying to urge rulers to make war on the French people and force them to restore the Monarchy.

My brother Leopold was aware of this; he wrote to Mercy:

> "The Comte d'Artois has little concern for his brother and my sister. He ignores the dangers to which his projects and his attempts expose them."

Mercy was urging me to persuade the King to consider flight also. We must escape from Paris; the King must raise a loyal army and take by force or menaces that which had been snatched from him. Louis was beginning to realize that this was necessary—but it was too late now that Mirabeau was dead, for Mirabeau was the man who could have managed it.

However, we still had friends and at length we had persuaded Louis that flight was essential.

Axel begged to be in charge of the preparations. He would start preparations immediately and the first was to have a carriage—a berlin—made which would be suitable for the escape.

He was a constant caller at the Tuileries and lest this should attract too much attention sometimes came disguised; I could never be sure whether he would come as a lackey, a coachman or stooping a little as an aging nobleman.

This lent excitement to the days. I had not felt so alive for a long time, and Axel was possessed with a furious determination to make the plan succeed.

"I shall carry you off to safety," he told me.

He would talk of the berlin which was to be a very luxurious affair. "Nothing but the best will do," he had declared; he had mortgaged some estates in Sweden to provide the money. It was wonderful to be so loved. His plan was that we should leave with as few people as possible. Madame de Tourzel must come with us because the children would need her to look after them, so Axel's plan was that Madame de Tourzel would be a Russian lady, Madame de Korff, traveling with her children, their governess and one lackey; and three women servants one of whom should be Madame Elisabeth. I was to be the governess, Madame Rochet. He had acquired a passport in the name of Madame de Korff and we knew we could trust Madame de Tourzel to play her part.

The days were flying past; we were so excited; even Louis was caught up in it and eager to begin our flight. But, said Axel, there must be no hitches; everything must be planned down to the last detail and we must not slip up. The most difficult part would be to get out of Paris. That was the danger spot. Axel himself was going to take the part of coachman and would drive the berlin. Everything depended, he said, on our putting as great a distance between ourselves and Paris before our escape was noticed.

Provence, who was to escape with us, pointed out that the berlin was so magnificent that it might attract attention, but Axel reminded him that we had to travel many miles in it. It would be an uncomfortable journey and the Queen could not endure hours in a badly sprung vehicle.

Provence shrugged his shoulders and said that he would provide his own conveyance for himself and his wife, and decided on one of the shabbiest carriages that he could find.

Meanwhile Louis made a stipulation. Axel naturally wished to drive us to the frontier but the King said he should do so only to the first halt which would be Bondy.

Axel was dismayed. This was his plan. He was in charge; and how could he be if he were to leave us at Bondy! But Louis for once was stubborn. I wondered whether he was comparing himself with Axel and realizing why I could love this man as I never could himself. I could not believe Louis was jealous; I knew that he loved me in his way but it was an affection without passion. Yet he was adamant and would not allow Axel to come beyond Bondy; so there was nothing we could do but accept his decision. The sixth of June was the day which we settled on to begin our escape.

I was absorbed in my preparations. Madame Campan was with me; she knew of the plan for I could trust her absolutely. I told her that when I arrived at Montmédy I should not want to appear as a governess but as a Queen and how could I take all I would need with me? Madame Campan must make the preparations for me. She must order chemises and gowns. She must also buy for my son and daughter. She had a son of her own who could act as model for the Dauphin, I told her.

I knew Madame Campan would carry out these commands although from her expression she was against my ordering clothes.

She was always frank and said: "Madame, the Queen of France will find gowns and linen wherever she goes. This buying may well attract attention which is what we wish to avoid."

I was lighthearted and growing as careless as I used to be, so I smiled at her. But she was disturbed.

I told her about the berlin, which I couldn't help boasting of because Axel had designed it. "It is painted green and yellow," I said, "and upholstered in white Utrecht velvet."

"Madame," she answered, "such a vehicle will never pass unnoticed." She added with that touch of asperity which she did not hide even from me that the berlin would be very different from the carriage in which Monsieur and Madame traveled.

"Oh very different," I agreed. Theirs had not been designed by Axel.

I was to realize later how firmly planted in our minds were those rules of etiquette at which I had laughed so much when I had first come to France. We could not even attempt to escape except in the royal manner even though what we must disguise was our royalty. There were to be six of us in the berlin—myself, the King, the children, Elisabeth, and Madame de Tourzel. This was a large number and would slow down the speed, but we must all be together and naturally Madame de Tourzel as Madame de Korff must be with us. I had never dressed myself so I must have two ladies-in-waiting who were to follow the berlin in a cabriolet. Then of course we must have outriders and lackeys so that the party was brought up to more than a dozen; and of course Axel and his coachman would be with us. Our clothes packed in new cases had to be carried too; which would make the berlin very cumbersome and cut down speed even more.

But it was such a wonderful vehicle. It filled me with pleasure merely to look at it. Axel had thought of everything; there was even a silver dinner service, a canteen to contain bottles of wine, a cupboard, and even two *pots de chambre* in tanned leather.

It was too much to hope that our plan would go through without hitches, and there were hitches in plenty.

The first came through the wardrobe woman, Madame Rochereuil. I had become suspicious of her soon after we were turned back to the Tuileries when we had planned to go to Saint-Cloud for I had learned that she had a lover, Gouvion, who was a fierce revolutionary and had in fact arranged that she should have the post in my household that she might spy on me. She had warned Gouvion of our intention to go to Saint-Cloud at Easter and in consequence the Orléanists had had time to inflame the mob and prevent our going.

How I longed to rid myself of that woman but of course we were in truth prisoners and unable to choose those whom we wished to serve us.

I told Axel that we could not go on the ninth for the woman had seen me packing and may even have overheard the date mentioned. If we attempted to leave then we should most certainly find ourselves stopped. What we must do was go on with our preparations, let the woman think we were leaving on the ninth and then stay at the Tuileries as though it were all a mistake. When we had lulled her suspicions we could leave swiftly, without her having an inkling we were going.

Axel saw the reason in this but was dismayed for he said the longer we delayed the more dangerous it was becoming, but we fixed a secret date for the nineteenth which was long enough to allow Madame Rochereuil to become convinced that she had been mistaken.

This was the first set back, but, we all agreed, inevitable.

As the nineteenth came nearer the tension was almost unbearable. How grateful I was for Louis' calm; he at least had no difficulty in showing a placid face to all. I tried to too, but I dared not look at Elisabeth for fear I should betray by a look that there was a secret between us. We had not of course told the children.

The nineteenth was almost upon us. All was ready.

It became very clear that something had leaked out because an article by Marat appeared in *L'Ami du Peuple*, in which he expressed his suspicions that there was a plot afoot.

"The idea is to remove the King forcibly to the Low Countries on the pretext that his cause is that of the Kings of Europe. Are you imbeciles that you take no steps to prevent the flight of the royal family? Parisians, fools that you are, I am weary of saying to you over and over again that you should have the King and the Dauphin in safe keeping; that you should lock up the Austrian woman, her brother-in-law, and the rest of the family. The loss of one day might be disastrous to the nation, might dig the graves of three million Frenchmen."

Axel was frantic with anxiety. "It is too coincidental," he said.

"I know it is that Rochereuil woman," I cried. "She is aware of something, though I do not believe she is sure what."

"Yet we must leave on the nineteenth," insisted Axel. "We *dare* not wait longer."

It was the eighteenth and we were prepared to begin the escape next day. Then Madame de Tourzel came to me in some excitement and lowering her voice told me that Madame Rochereuil had asked leave of absence for the twentieth.

"I have ascertained," added Madame de Tourzel, "that she wishes to visit a sick friend. Gouvion is unwell, so it seems obvious whom she will visit."

"We must postpone our departure until the twentieth," I said, and I sent a messenger at once to Axel. He was disturbed at the postponement for everyone involved throughout the journey had had their instructions; but we arranged that Léonard, the hairdresser, whom I knew I could trust, should take my jewels to Brussels and at the same time he could meet the cavalry on the road with a note explaining that we should be a day late.

This was settled; Léonard left with the jewels. And now we were breathlessly awaiting the twentieth.

The important day had arrived. The sun was shining brilliantly and this seemed a good omen. There would be few people in the city, I whispered to Elisabeth; they would be out in the country on such a day. Madame Rochereuil had gone off to visit her sick friend; and the day passed very slowly so that I thought it would never end. But outwardly it appeared to be an ordinary day which was as we wanted it.

At last it was suppertime; we lingered as usual but naturally there was not the same ceremony as we had had to endure at Versailles. At least we could be thankful for this. I went to my bedroom and from there hurried to my daughter's on the first floor. The waiting woman, Madame Brunier, opened the door. I told her she must dress Madame Royale as quickly as possible and be prepared to slip out of the château with Madame Neuville, the Dauphin's waiting woman. A cabriolet was waiting for them at the Pont-Royal; they were to leave Paris at once and wait for us at Claye.

My daughter was old enough to guess what this meant. She did not ask questions. Poor child, she was being brought up in an odd world. She looked a little surprised at the simple dress we had made for her; it was cotton with little blue flowers on a gosling green background—pretty enough for the daughter of a Russian lady; scarcely a Princesse's gown.

I kissed her and held her against me for a few seconds. "My darling Mousseline," I whispered. "You will obey . . . quickly."

And she nodded and said, "Yes, Maman," almost reproachfully as though she was surprised I should ask.

Then to my son's room. He was already awake and gave a cry of delight when he saw me.

"Maman," he cried. "Where are we going?"

"We're going where there are a lot of soldiers."

"May I take my sword. Quick, bring me my sword, Madame. And my boots. I'm going to be a soldier."

He was dismayed when he saw what he was to wear: a girl's dress! "Oh . . . is it a play then?" he asked. "So we are going to be disguised." He began to laugh. He loved playacting. "And at night too," he added. "That is the best time for plays."

"Now, my little Chou d'amour, you must be quiet and quick and do what you're told. Everything depends on that."

He nodded conspiratorially. "Trust Chou d'amour, Maman."

"I do, my darling," I said kissing him.

It was a quarter to eleven. Axel had worked out times very carefully and we should be on our way. The plan was that the children with Madame de Tourzel should leave first. I had been against this for I could not bear to think of the children's beginning the perilous journey without me but Axel would be with them until I joined them and that had to be my consolation.

Madame de Tourzel picked up the Dauphin and, taking my daughter's hand, I led the way to the apartments of one of the gentlemen of the bedchamber who had left Paris only the day before; consequently his apartments were empty. I had the key to these apartments and we went in. From there we stepped into the Cour des Princes through a door which was unguarded. Waiting there was Axel. I scarcely recognized him in his coachman's uniform.

In the middle of the courtyard was the *citadine* which was to take them to the rendezvous in the Rue de l'Echelle at the corner of the Place du Petit-Carrousel.

Axel lifted the Dauphin into the carriage; Marie Thérèse followed with Madame de Tourzel and Axel shut the door. He looked at me for a brief second and although he dared not speak he was telling me that he would defend them with his life if need be. Then he leaped into the coachman's seat, cracked his whip and the *citadine* moved off.

I felt sick with apprehension. What if my children should be recognized? What if my son in his excitement at the adventure should betray them? What if they should be attacked? Memories of faces I had seen in the mob kept coming into my mind; I kept thinking of those dirty bloodstained hands touching my darlings.

But Axel was there to defend them. His love for me would give him the strength of ten men and the cunning to outwit a mob of savages.

But I must not stand here in the Cour des Princes. If I were recognized the whole plan would fail. I was courting disaster; I went quickly back into the palace through the empty apartments to the drawing room, where Provence and his wife were saying goodbye. I embraced them and wished them good fortune. He and his wife had never been friends to me but misfortune had softened resentments. Provence was more of a realist than Louis. Perhaps had he been the King . . . But who could say? Now, though, rivalry had gone. The only goal of us all was to preserve the Monarchy.

I heard them leave through those empty apartments. In their shabby carriage they left the Tuileries and were on their way.

I left the King in conference with de La Fayette and went to my room. My women undressed me; the servants fastened the shutters and I was alone. I looked at the clock. It was eleven fifteen—the longest half hour I had ever known.

Madame Thiébaut came into the room. I was out of bed in a second and she was helping me to put on the gray gown and black mantle. There was a large hat with a veil falling from it to shade my face. I looked unlike myself—but I was ready.

Madame Thiébaut slipped back the bolt on the door and I started out. I jumped back in terror. There was a sentry outside my door. I shut the door quietly and looked at Madame Thiébaut. What now? They had heard. They were waiting for me to go and then . . . they would stop me. Had they already stopped the *citadine?* What was happening to my children, to my lover?

Madame Thiébaut said she would slip out and that might engage the sentry's attention; when his back was turned I must somehow cross the corridor and reach those empty apartments. It was a desperate plan; but it had to be.

And we did it. I had been always light on my feet and spurred on by the thought of the children, I dashed across the corridor to the staircase and flew down; I stood for a second listening; there was no sound of commotion. I had succeeded.

Outside the unguarded door of the empty apartment the loyal guard who was to conduct me to the rendezvous in the Rue de l'Echelle was waiting. He was disguised as a courier and I scarcely recognized him.

"Madame," he whispered; and I could sense his agitation. The affair of the sentry had delayed me almost ten minutes. "You should take my arm."

I did so and we walked across the Cour des Princes in the manner, I hoped, of a courier and his wife or mistress.

No one looked at us. It is succeeding, I thought. Soon I shall be with the children.

It was fantastic. Here I was walking through the streets of Paris on the arm of a courier, brushing shoulders with men and women who did not give me a second glance . . . fortunately. I wondered what they would say, what they would do if someone suddenly recognized the Queen. But it was something I dared not think of.

How little I knew of our capital city! The alleys and byways were new to me. All I knew of it were the palaces, the Opera House, the theaters . . .

My companion drew up suddenly with a start for a coach was coming toward us and before it walked the torchbearers in the livery of La Fayette. I was quickly drawn into the dark shadow; I lowered my head, but through my veil I saw the General. There was one second when had he looked into my face, he who knew me so well, would have recognized me and that would have been the end of everything.

But luck at that moment was with me. He did not glance at the woman on the pavement and his coach went rattling on. I felt dizzy with the shock and I heard the man beside me whisper: "Thank God, Madame! A lucky escape."

"Perhaps," I murmured, "he would not have recognized me in this."

He answered: "Madame, it is not easy for you to disguise yourself. I am going to take a slightly longer route to the Rue de l'Echelle. We cannot risk meeting any more carriages."

"I think that would be best."

"We must hurry because it will take a little longer and we are already late."

So instead of taking the planned route through the main streets we went through the byways and alleys and when we had gone a little way my guide stopped and declared himself lost.

I was conscious of the time, which had seemed so slow during that first half hour, and now was maliciously rushing by. My companion was mortified, myself in a panic. I pictured Axel's anxiety. Even my husband must be there by now for we had seen La Fayette leaving the palace and as soon as he was rid of him Louis would have prepared himself to leave.

For half an hour we wandered through those alleys—afraid to ask the way—and then at last my guide gave a cry of triumph. We had reached the Rue de l'Echelle.

They were all there, Axel, pacing the pavement; Elisabeth as pale as a ghost; the King roused from his usual placidity; my daughter calming my son who was plaintively asking when I was coming.

"We lost our way," I said; and Axel helped me into the *citadine*.

In the coach everyone was trying to embrace me at once. I felt so relieved I was almost in tears. I took my son onto my knee while my husband told me how easily he had affected his escape.

We must have been an hour late.

The King looked out on his city as we rode through it. He was feeling very sad, I knew, because he had stood out for so long against running away; it seemed to him unworthy of his ancestors. I took his hand and pressed it and he returned the pressure.

He whispered to me: "This is not the quickest way to the Saint Martin Barrier."

"The . . . the coachman will know the way," I answered.

"It is not the quickest way," he said; and I wondered whether he was stirred to some resentment because the hero of this adventure was my lover and not himself. He had seemed to understand my need of Axel so well; but perhaps there were some depths which I had not yet probed in this unusual man who was my husband.

The carriage drew up in the Rue de Clichy where the berlin had been kept. Axel leapt down and knocked on the door. The porter told him that the berlin had left at the appointed time. Satisfied, Axel jumped into the driver's seat and we were off.

It was half-past one when we went through the Barrier. On for a little and then we stopped. There was consternation for the berlin was not where it had been arranged it should be.

Axel was nonplused. He dismounted and I could hear him calling. We sat there while time began its trick of racing on. How much time had we lost so? How late were we so far?

It was half an hour before Axel found the berlin. The coachman whom

Axel had employed had grown anxious because we were so late and had thought he had better hide the berlin in a less prominent position. This he had done with the consequence that we lost half an hour looking for it.

It was now two o'clock; this was the height of summer and the nights were the shortest. In an hour or so dawn would be on us. We should have been much farther on our journey by now.

Axel drove the *citadine* to the side of the berlin so that we could get into the latter without leaving the former. We settled in and were away and in half an hour we had reached Bondy, the place where the King had decreed that Axel was to leave us.

I almost thought he would refuse to leave us; but Axel was a born royalist; he would accept the orders of the King.

Bondy! The place of separation. We had drawn up. The carriage door opened and there was our coachman.

"Adieu, Madame de Korff," he said. And he was looking at me.

The King said in moving tones that he would never forget the service Axel had done to him and his family.

Axel bowed and replied it had been his duty and his pleasure. He leaned toward me and said: "Your Majesty should not forget that for the journey you are Madame Rochet the governess." And in those words he managed to convey a world of tenderness and devotion.

Axel mounted the horse which he had arranged should take him back to Le Bourget; then he left us. And as I listened to his horse's hoofs on the road I tried to still the foreboding in my heart and to tell myself that in two days' time we should meet at Montmédy.

Then we resumed our journey.

We were two hours behind schedule.

The children slept and I was glad of this. So did the King. Would anything disturb his slumbers? Elisabeth, Madame de Tourzel and I closed our eyes. I doubt if those two slept; I know I did not.

The Dauphin woke. He was hungry.

I told him we would have a picnic. He had always loved them. He began to chatter. We would find a spot. A shady spot perhaps. It would be a breakfast picnic. I told him it would be a carriage picnic; and I showed him the cupboard in the coach and the food and wine it contained. He was delighted and we all declared that he made such an odd little girl in his frock and bonnet that we were soon laughing as we discovered how hungry we all were.

How different, I thought, everything is by daylight. It is at night that the fears come. Yet it was the cover of darkness we needed badly. The bright sunshine could serve to betray us. I remembered those words: "It is difficult for you to disguise yourself, Madame." They were true. My picture had been painted many times. It had hung in the *salons*; crude drawings of me had been circulated daily about the city and although, I trust, these were ill representations, they bore some resemblance of likeness, for the people had to know whom the picture was meant to portray.

Still for the time being I laughed with the children as we devoured the delicacies which Axel had provided as being fit for a royal party.

And I tried not to think of what would be happening back at the Tuileries where our escape would very soon be discovered if it had not been already.

Louis took a map and followed the route we were to take . . . after Bondy, Claye, where we pick up the two ladies who had gone on ahead, and then La Ferté and on to Châlons-sur-Marne.

Châlons-sur-Marne! How I longed to be there, for there we should meet the cavalry under the young Duc de Choiseul, nephew of my old friend, and outside that town, Bouillé would be waiting to conduct us to Montmédy . . . and at Montmédy . . . safety . . . and Axel.

How much happier I should have felt if Axel had been driving us now!

The Dauphin whimpered that he was hot. It was certainly stifling in the berlin which labored painfully up the hills overloaded as it was. Madame de Tourzel suggested that she get out and walk up the hill with the children which would lighten the load and give them a little fresh air and the opportunity to stretch their legs.

This seemed a good idea but the Dauphin wanted to stay in the fields awhile and he ran away and Madame de Tourzel and his sister had to catch him. The sound of his merry shrieks was like a tonic, but the minutes were slipping by.

In the afternoon we stopped at Petit Chaintry, the small village near Chaintry, for Axel had wisely said that we should change horses at the smaller rather than the larger places.

At the inn a young man came out to look at the berlin. He was talkative; I heard him chatting to the coachman. He had never seen such a magnificent carriage. The occupants must be very rich and important people. His name he said was Vallet . . . Gabriel Vallet and he was the postmaster's son-in-law. He was an innkeeper himself and he often went to Paris.

He passed the window of the coach, I was sure to see what manner of people traveled in such style. And as he looked in at us he knew.

I glanced uneasily at Louis. His wig was the rough wig of the lackey he was supposed to be but those heavy Bourbon features had been well known in France for centuries. Then his eyes went to me. Did I look like a governess? I felt the haughty look coming into my face which always seemed now to be there much as I tried to suppress it when I came into contact with the people.

He moved away and went to the postmaster; I saw them whispering together. Then the postmaster approached the carriage.

He bowed and his words sent shivers through me.

"Your Majesties, this is a great honor. And we shall remember it as long as we live. We are humble but all we have is at your service."

Louis, who had always been moved by any affection displayed by his subjects, was even more so now. Tears came into his eyes and he said that it made him very happy to be with friends.

The postmaster signed to his wife and children who all came to the berlin and were presented; then Vallet's wife came and she too mumbled her awareness of the honor.

"Your Majesties, we have a goose cooked already to be eaten. If you would honor us by eating it we should be deeply honored."

Louis was the King immediately. To refuse such an invitation would be churlish. Therefore we must all descend and eat goose with the postmaster. The children were delighted. It was such a pleasure to get out of the stuffy berlin. And it was quite clear that this loyal family were aware that we were escaping from Paris.

When we had eaten and the King explained that it was imperative he must say goodbye although he would have wished to spend more time with such kind, good people, Vallet asked a favor. Could he act as postilion on the berlin as far as Châlons-sur-Marne?

How could the King refuse such an offer of loyal service? We would have an extra passenger but there was no help for it and so we set off. And to show his zeal Vallet tried to drive the berlin beyond its capabilities with the result that two of the horses fell and there was damage to the traces. Repairs took further time and when we arrived at Châlons we were even farther behind the arranged time.

Châlons was a larger town but the people were more interested in wine growing than the Revolution; the berlin attracted attention but the people shrugged their shoulders. Some rich *émigrés*. There were too many of such people to cause a great deal of comment.

It had been a mistake to bring Vallet, I began to realize, for although he was the most loyal of subjects he could not hide his awareness of the honor that had been done to him. While the horses were being changed one or two people spoke to him and he betrayed the fact that he was on no ordinary mission. People were already looking askance at the magnificent vehicle. Two children! That in itself was suspicious.

I was very glad when we left Châlons although the King had noticed nothing. As we rode out of the town he settled down to a nap.

We were near Pont de Somme-Vesle; at that town according to the plan we should meet the Duc de Choiseul's cavalry; he would then join us and remain with us until we reached Bouillé's loyal troops.

The worst was over. We could all settle down secure in the thought that we were really at the end of our journey.

The heat grew intense. My son wanted to get out and pick some flowers. He loved flowers and he had missed his little garden at Trianon sadly.

"Please, Madame Rochet," he said mischievously for I had warned him that part of the play was that I was his governess and he must not forget it.

The King woke up and said that he believed Monsieur le Dauphin should have his wish and that it would do us all good to stop for a while.

So the cumbersome vehicle pulled up at the side of the road and Madame de Tourzel and Elisabeth got out with the children.

The Dauphin was picking the flowers and bringing them to me.

I was longing to move on but the King said a few minutes more could do no harm and he sat benignly smiling at the children through the open door.

And while we sat there we heard the sound of galloping hoofs, and soon a rider came into view. He was coming straight toward us and as he approached the berlin he did not stop although he slackened his pace. As he came level with us he shouted: "Take care. Your plan is known. You will be stopped."

Before we could question him he had ridden on.

We summoned the others back to the berlin and the King gave orders for us to proceed at once with all speed.

Into Pont de Somme-Vesle where the cavalry should be waiting. The place was deserted. While the horses were being changed a cavalryman rode up.

"Where is the Duc de Choiseul?" asked the King.

"He has left, Sire," was the answer.

"Left! But he had orders to meet us here."

"You did not arrive at the appointed time, Sire. He could not understand the confused message of Monsieur Léonard and Monsieur de

Choiseul presumed that you had not left Paris and the plan was called off."

"He had orders to wait."

"Yes, Sire, but he feared trouble. People were asking why there were troops on the road and there were rumors that a magnificent berlin grand enough for royalty alone was on the road. There has been trouble between the peasants and soldiers so Monsieur de Choiseul has gone to Clermont and has sent Monsieur Léonard with a message to the Marquis de Bouillé explaining this."

Now I was frightened. I saw the chain of misfortunes which had led us to this—the sentry, the immense ill-luck of meeting La Fayette's carriage which had made us change our route; that was the beginning. Then the inability to find the berlin . . . but one misfortune had grown out of another. We should not have stayed to eat the goose. We should not have allowed the children those rests by the roadside. I can see that it was not only fate which was to blame and I wondered vaguely whether it ever is.

"But we must go on," I said. "We must go without our escort. We have missed the support of Choiseul's hussars but the dragoons will be at Sainte-Menehould and we must join up with them as soon as possible."

Uneasily we rode on.

When we came into Sainte-Menehould I knew that something was wrong. This was not as Axel had planned. Oh, why had he not come with us? That seemed to me the greatest misfortune of all. The town was full of soldiers and this naturally aroused the curiosity of the people. Something very extraordinary was about to happen in their town. What?

And into this town of suspicion rolled the most elaborate berlin which had ever been created and its passengers were two children, a lackey who looked astonishingly like the King and a governess who had an uncontrollably haughty air, and a Russian lady who could not somehow hide her deference toward her lackey and governess; and a quiet woman who was supposed to be a maid of some sort yet who had the air of a Princesse.

Who were these travelers? Rich émigrés, yes, but very special émigrés and they had a striking resemblance to a very celebrated family.

I did not know then, but I was to learn later that the son of the postmaster was an ardent revolutionary, a certain Jean-Baptiste Drouet. He had looked at us sullenly and not recognized us; but rumor was in the air.

It must have been after the horses were changed and we were on our way to Varennes that someone told Drouet the news. The King and

Queen had escaped from Paris and were traveling along this road toward Montmédy.

It was ten o'clock when we came into Varennes. The King was sleeping, but I felt I should never sleep easily until I was in Montmédy. It was dark.

We were passing under an archway and there was just room for the berlin when we were suddenly called to a halt.

A voice said: "Passports."

Madame de Tourzel produced the forged document with which Axel had provided her and which announced that she was Madame de Korff from Russia traveling with her children and servants.

I did not recognize the man who took the passport as Jean-Baptiste Drouet who had been at the posting station at Sainte-Menehould; but I did realize that he was trembling with excitement.

"This passport is not in order," he said, and although he spoke to Madame de Tourzel he was studying me intently.

"I assure you it is in order," protested Madame de Tourzel.

"I am sorry but I must take it to the town's solicitor, and I must ask you to accompany me to his house."

"What!" cried Madame de Tourzel in dismay. "All of us!"

"Yes, Madame, all of you. You will be led to the house of Monsieur Sausse."

I looked out of the window and saw that the berlin was surrounded by young men and that all wore the badge of the Revolution.

The berlin moved slowly on and drew up before a house. The King showed no sign of alarm. He whispered: "It is nothing. Merely a check on the passport. It is in order. Fersen will have seen to that."

Monsieur Sausse was not only the solicitor but a keeper of a shop and mayor of Varennes. A mild comfortable man, I recognized him at once as one who would want to keep out of trouble.

He examined the passport and proclaimed it to be in order. We had his permission to leave at once.

But Drouet was a fierce revolutionary. He cried out: "This is the King and Queen. Are you going to be a traitor, Monsieur Sausse, and let them slip through the people's fingers?"

Monsieur Sausse was alarmed, for even now the crowds were gathering outside his door.

He looked at us apologetically and I recognized that respect in his eyes. He knew us . . . even as Drouet did.

"I must regret," he said, "that you cannot leave Varennes tonight. I offer you what hospitality I have."

It was over, I knew. Desperation overwhelmed me. People were gathering about the house. I could hear the shouts. It was going to be that terrible October all over again.

I could hear the mob screaming. From the window I could see their scythes and pitchforks.

Not that again! I thought. Why did we attempt this? Why did we not know that God was against us.

Not God, I thought, we have brought this on ourselves.

The Sausses were our friends, however. They had prepared a good meal for us, and that made it clear that they wished us nothing but good luck. If they could have prevented our detention, they would. As it was, in their humble home they treated us as their sovereigns. They dared not help us escape, though. That would have been more than their lives were worth. And what would be the use of attempting escape when the mob surrounded the house?

Throughout Varennes Drouet was gathering his revolutionaries together. He was doubtless visualizing the great honor which would come to him. The man who prevented the escape of the King and Queen!

I was surprised how the King could eat in the face of all this. Appetite in such circumstances astonished me. While he was eating, two soldiers fought their way into the house and when I saw them my spirits rose for they were the loyal dragoons.

Their names were de Damas and Goguelat and they told us they had brought a company of soldiers with them to the town but when their men had seen the revolutionaries gathering and knew that the King and I were prisoners they deserted. They had no wish to anger the leaders of the Revolution by helping the King and Queen escape.

It was not long after when Choiseul himself arrived; he had a small company of men with him and had also had to fight his way to us.

He told us that the battle had been fierce and that he had been obliged to inflict wounds on some of those who sought to deter him.

The plan had gone awry he said and now they must plan afresh from here.

"I have sent warning to Bouillé and it cannot be long before he joins us. I suggest, Sire, that we fight our way out of Varennes and take the road to Montmédy, we cannot then fail to meet Bouillé. He will have his loyal troops and none will dare attack us then. We can carry Your Majesties to safety."

"This is an excellent idea," I cried. "We must do it."

But the King shook his head. "I have said all along that I will not be responsible for shedding the blood of my people. If we tried to fight our way out of here many would be killed. Those people out there are determined not to let us go."

"They are the mob," said Choiseul. "They have their pitchforks but pitchforks are no use against our weapons."

"As I said there would be slaughter. Who knows, the Queen or the Dauphin might be hurt."

"We could protect the child," I said. "I am ready to take a chance."

"I would never permit it," said the King. "For even though we were all safe some of my people would surely be killed. No, no. We must wait for Bouillé to come. When the people see him they will realize that it is no use to fight against him and his army. They will go back to their homes and allow us to depart peacefully."

"It is possible, Sire, that the revolutionaries may decide to take Your Majesties back to Paris before Bouillé gets here."

"It is a chance we must take. I will not have bloodshed on my account."

I saw the stubborn look in his face and I knew he meant it.

I knew too that everything depended on Bouillé's reaching Varennes in time.

I did not sleep through that terrible night. I was aware of the voices outside the house, of the light of torches.

I was praying silently. Not that again! It is more than I can endure. Let Bouillé come . . . or let death come quickly, but not that. The horror of it came back to me . . . that ride from Versailles to Paris . . . the crowd . . . the unclean crowd . . . the smell of blood, the horrible leering savage faces, the obscene words on vile lips. I hated them, God help me; they were *canaille*; it was not love of country that prompted them; it was love of cruelty. I thought: I would rather die now than suffer it again. And the children, those innocent children to be submitted to this humiliation, this fearful knowledge of all that was bestial in the world to be thrust under the innocent eyes. Oh God spare us.

Louis slept. I could almost hate him. Was he a man . . . to sleep while we were all in such danger? He must not have bloodshed . . . he must not harm his dear children . . . his *children* . . . those screaming beasts out there; he called them his children. Why was not Axel with us? Axel would have fought his way through them.

How I lived through that fearful night I do not know. But the dawn came and with the daylight the noise outside the house increased.

I tried to close my eyes; I tried to sleep. If only I could sleep for a few minutes as Louis had all through the night.

A hammering on the door startled me; I heard heavy feet on the stairs, and two men burst in upon us.

I recognized one of them as a man named Romeuf who had guarded us in the Tuileries. The other was a man named Bayon.

They explained that they came on orders from the National Assembly. One of them handed a document to the King. I read it with him. His rights were suspended and these two men had been sent to prevent his continuing on his journey.

I screwed it up and threw it into a corner of the room.

The men looked on helplessly. At least they had some shame.

The King said gently: "The Marquis de Bouillé is on his way to Varennes. If you try to force us to return to Paris there could be bloodshed."

"On the Orders of Monsieur de La Fayette we are to take you back to Paris, Sire."

"And what of the orders of your King?" I asked indignantly.

"We are obliged to obey the Assembly, Madame."

"I wish to avoid bloodshed," said Louis gently. "I do not wish to fight my people. When the Marquis de Bouillé arrives I shall leave here and, from a place to which we shall go, come to an understanding with those who are making this Revolution."

Romeuf looked at his companion. "We could wait for the Marquis to arrive," he suggested, "since we were given no orders as to when we were to return to Paris."

Bayon did not possess his loyalty. "Are you a fool?" he demanded. "Bouillé is armed. What have the people but their pitchforks and a few knives? We must set out for Paris *before* Bouillé arrives."

"We are exhausted," I said. "There are the children to consider."

Bayon did not answer. He left us and I heard him go out of the house and talk to the crowds.

Romeuf looked at us apologetically and said: "You must think of anything, Your Majesties, which will delay the departure. Once Bouillé arrives you are safe."

"Thank you," I said quietly.

Bayon came back. Already I heard the shouts of "À *Paris*" outside the house.

"Prepare to leave at once," said Bayon.

"The children must not be frightened," I told him. "They are exhausted. They must finish their sleep."

"Arouse them at once, Madame."

Madame de Tourzel and Madame Neuville awoke them. The Dauphin looked at Bayon and Romeuf and shrieked with pleasure.

"Now we have soldiers!" he cried. "Are you coming with us?"

"Yes, Monsieur le Dauphin," said Bayon.

Even the soldiers agreed that we must eat before we left and Madame Sausse was told to prepare food. I saw the determination in her face to take as long as she possibly could doing so.

Bayon was impatient. He warned her that the people would not feel very kindly toward a dilatory housewife who was responsible for holding up their orders. Poor Madame Sausse, she did everything she could to help us. Such people as herself and Romeuf brought great hope to us in our difficulties.

I tried to eat but could not. In fact the only ones who could do justice to the food Madame Sausse had been so long preparing were the King and the children.

"Come now," said Bayon.

And there was no sign of Bouillé.

It is all over, I thought. We can find no excuse to stay longer. Oh God, send Bouillé. Please give us this.

"Come," said Bayon roughly. "There has been enough delay."

He was hustling us to the door when Madame Neuville gave a little cry and slipped to the floor; she started to throw her arms about and made strange noises as though in a fit.

I knelt beside her. I knew she was acting. I cried: "Fetch a doctor."

Bayon, cursing, gave the order; but everyone outside was determined that the doctor should be brought in record time.

All the time I watched Madame Neuville lying there on the floor I was praying: "Oh God, send Bouillé."

But it was the doctor who came not Bouillé and Madame Neuville could no longer keep up her pretense. She was given a potion and helped to her feet. She swayed and would have fallen again but Bayon supported her and with the help of the doctor dragged her out to the cabriolet.

No sign of Bouillé.

"À *Paris!*" shouted the mob. No more waiting.

There was no help for it. We must all follow Madame Neuville out of the house. A shout went up when we appeared. I held the Dauphin's hand tightly, too frightened for him to fear for myself.

It was coming again . . . I knew so well. I should never forget. The humiliating ride . . . a longer one this time, not merely from Versailles but from Varennes to Paris.

The journey to Paris lasted three days. I thought when we had come from Versailles that I had reached the nadir of humiliation, horror, discomfort, and misery; I was to learn that I had not done so.

The heat was intense; we could not wash or change our clothes, and all along the route were those shrieking screaming savages. I cannot call them people—for all semblance of human kindness and dignity seemed to have left them. They hurled insults at us—mostly at me. I was the scapegoat as I had become accustomed to being.

"À bas Antoinette," they screamed. "Antoinette à la lanterne."

Very well then, I thought, but quickly . . . quickly. Gladly I will go rather than submit to life in these circumstances. Only let my children go freely. Let them live the lives of ordinary gentlefolk . . . but let me die if that is what you want.

They had set two men of the National Assembly to guard us—Pétion and Barnave. I suppose they were not bad fellows; I know they were not now. There was a difference between the rabble and those who believed that the Revolution must come about for the good of France, whose creed was liberty, equality, fraternity; they would have been ready to bargain for it around a conference table and Louis would have been eager to grant them what they wished. Men such as these were far removed from those animals outside who shrieked obscenities at us, who demanded our heads . . . and other parts of our bodies . . . who wanted blood and who laughed with demoniacal joy at the thought of shedding it. Oh yes, these men were different. They talked to us, as they thought reasonably. We were only people, they told us. We did not deserve to be privileged because we were born in a different stratum of society than they were. The King listened gravely, inclined to agree with them. They talked of the Revolution and what they wanted from life, and the inequalities of it; it was not reasonable to suppose that a people would go on indefinitely in want while a certain section of society spent on a gown what would keep a family in food for a year.

The Dauphin took a fancy to the two men and they to him. He read the words on the buttons of their uniforms. "Vivre libre ou mourir."

"Will you live freely or die?" he asked them gravely; and they assured him they would.

I felt that Elisabeth and Madame de Tourzel were near breaking point. I knew that it was for me to keep them sane. My way of doing it was to attempt a lofty indifference. It did not please the mob but it forced some respect from them. When we were obliged to draw up the blinds of the berlin, which they demanded now and then, and Barnave or Pétion would declare we had better do so as this mob was getting violent, I would sit staring straight ahead. They would come up to the window and call obscenities at me and I would look straight ahead as though they were not there.

"Whore!" they shouted and I would not seem to hear.

They jeered, but it had its effect on them.

Food was brought to the berlin for us; the people shouted that they wanted to see us eat.

Elisabeth was terrified and thought we should pull up the blinds as the crowd demanded, but I refused to do so.

"We must keep our dignity," I told her.

"Madame, they will smash the berlin," said Barnave.

But I knew that to draw up those blinds was to degrade ourselves and refused to do so until I wished to throw out my chicken bones and this I did into the crowd as though they did not exist for me.

Pétion was the fiercer of the two; I detected in Barnave an admiration for me. He admired my manner with the mob and I could see that he was changing his ideas of us. He had thought arrogant aristocrats were unlike human beings, but I noticed how astonished he seemed when I spoke to Elisabeth and called her "little sister," or she addressed the King as "brother." These men were astonished at the way we talked to the children and impressed by the obvious affection between me and my family.

They must have been fed for years on those absurd scandalous sheets which had circulated through the capital. They thought I was some sort of monster incapable of any tender feelings—a Messalina, a Catherine de Medicis.

Pétion tried in the beginning to speak insolently of Axel. There had been many rumors about our relationship.

"We know that your family left the Tuileries in an ordinary fiacre and that this was driven by a man of Swedish nationality," he said.

I was terrified. They knew then that Axel had driven us!

"We should like you to tell us the name of this Swede," went on Pétion, and I could see by the gleam in his eye that he enjoyed talking about my lover before my husband.

"Do you think I would know the name of a hackney coachman?" I demanded scornfully.

And the haughty look I gave him so subdued him that he did not broach the subject again.

Pétion was a fool. When Elisabeth slept—she was next to him—her head fell on his shoulder and I could see by the smug manner in which he sat still that he believed she had laid it there purposely. As for Barnave his manner was becoming more and more respectful toward me with the passing of every hour. I believed that given the opportunity we could have turned these two men from their revolutionary ideas and that they would have been our loyal servants.

These were the lighter moments of that nightmare journey. It lives with me now; in so much horror it still haunts me.

We were approaching Paris and there, of course, we knew the worst awaited us.

We were exhausted, dirty, unkempt; the heat seemed more unbearable than ever; the crowds more dense and hostile.

When someone in the crowd called "*Vive le Roi*," the mob turned on him and cut his throat. I saw the blood before I could stop myself looking.

This was Paris—that same city in which I had once been told—a lifetime away—that two hundred thousand of its people had fallen in love with me.

They were all round the berlin now.

A face looked in at me, lips drawn back in a snarl, lips I realized I had once kissed.

"*Antoinette à la lanterne.*"

It was Jacques Armand, that little boy whom I had found on the road and brought up as my own until my children had arrived and made me forget him.

Were all my past sins and careless frivolities coming home to roost like so many vultures watching for the end?

I held my son against me; I did not wish him to see.

He was whimpering. He did not like it. He wanted to see the soldiers, he said. He did not like these people.

"We shall soon be home," I told him.

Home—that dark dank prison from which a few days ago we had escaped.

I do not want to write of it; I cannot bear to think of it. None who have not lived through it could realize its horror.

I was almost glad when we arrived at the Tuileries and to the jeers and bloodthirsty threats stumbled out of the berlin.

We were ingloriously home.

Exhausted, desolate, we made our way to our old apartments.

"It is over," I said. "We are where we were before we attempted to escape."

But of course that was not true. We had gone forward toward disaster.

There was no longer a King and Queen of France. I knew it; although no one had told me yet.

I took off my hat and shook out my hair.

It was a long time since I had looked at myself in a mirror. I stared for a few seconds without recognizing the woman with the red-rimmed eyes, the face covered with the dust of the roads, the torn gown. But it was not these things which startled me.

My hair which my brothers and Madame du Barry had referred to as "carrots" and which the dressmakers of Paris had called the "color of gold" was completely white.

25

"I exist . . . nothing more. How anxious I have been for you and all you must have suffered in having no news of us . . . On no account think of returning. It is known that it is you who have helped us to get away and all would be lost if you should show yourself."

"I can tell you that I love you and have only time for that. Do not be troubled about me. I am well . . . I long to know the same of you . . . Tell me where I should address my letters so that I may be able to write to you, for I cannot live without that. Farewell, most loved and loving of men."

Marie Antoinette to the Comte de Fersen

"Tribulation first makes one realize what one is. My blood courses through my son's veins and I hope that a day will come when he will show himself worthy to be the grandson of Maria Theresa."

Marie Antoinette to Mercy

Feb. 13th 1792: "Went to see her. Made very anxious because of the National Guards."

Feb. 14th: "Saw the King at six o'clock. Louis is, in truth, a man of honor."

Fersen's Journal

"The *Marseillaise* was the greatest General of the Republic."

Napoleon

THE FAUBOURGS ON THE MARCH

During those first day in the Tuileries I existed in a state of numbness. I would start up in my sleep imagining filthy hands on me, foul wine-sodden breath in my face. I lived again a thousand times the horror of that ride back to Paris. La Fayette had saved us from the fury of the mob with men such as the Duc d'Aiguillon and the Vicomte de Noailles who had never been friends of mine; but they had been disgusted by the tornado which was raging all about us.

Everywhere we looked there were guards. We were prisoners as we had not been before. They were determined that we should never have an opportunity of escaping again.

We heard that Provence and Marie Josèphe had safely crossed the frontier. Their shabby carriage had got by whereas our luxurious berlin had failed. I refused to remember that it was Axel's berlin which had delayed and betrayed us. He had wanted the best for me but fugitives of course should give up luxury for a chance of freedom.

I wept when I heard that Bouillé had arrived at Varennes with his troops only half an hour after we left; and when he realized that we had gone he had disbanded his troops, for there was no point in making war on the revolutionaries then. Half an hour between us and freedom! Had we not stopped to gather flowers on the roadside, had we traveled more simply we could have traveled at greater speed. Freedom was within our reach and we had lost it. Not through ill luck. I must be reasonable and see this. It was not in our stars but in ourselves that we had failed.

I was desperate during those long winter months. I even attempted to intrigue through Barnave who had shown his admiration for me during that terrible journey in the berlin. I wrote letters which were smuggled out to him in which I flattered him, telling him that his intelligence had so impressed me that I was asking for his co-operation. I told him that I was ready to compromise if it were necessary and that I believed in his good intentions. Would he be prepared to help me? Barnave was flattered and delighted, although naturally apprehensive. He showed my letters to some of his trusted friends and wrote to me that they were interested and would prefer to deal with me than with the King.

I must, they told me, do all I could to bring my brothers-in-law back to France and try to persuade my brother, the Emperor Leopold, to recognize the French Constitution. They drafted the letter which I was to send—and this I did, although I had no intention of submitting to the new Constitution and immediately wrote secretly to my brother to tell him in what circumstances I had written the first letter.

I was in fact involved in a dangerous and double game for which I was ill equipped, intellectually and emotionally. I was deceiving these men who were ready to be my friends, but I could not lightly give up what I believed to be my birthright. I must make some effort to regain what we had lost, since my husband would not do so. But how I hated the deception! To lie and deceive was not one of my faults.

I wrote to Axel:

> "I cannot understand myself and have to ask myself again and again whether it is really I who am acting in this way. Yet what can I do? It has become necessary to do these things and our position would be worse if I did not act. We can gain time in this way and time is what we need. What a joyful day it will be to me when I can tell the truth and show these men that I never intended to work with them."

I continued to be very unhappy because of this role into which I had fallen.

Worse still, there was no news from Axel. Where was he? Why did he not get in touch? I heard that he was in Vienna trying to interest my brother in our cause, trying to urge him to send an army to France with whom our loyal soldiers could link up and so restore law and order—and the Monarchy—to our tortured country.

When I heard that Comte d'Esterhazy was going to Vienna I asked him to take a ring to the Comte de Fersen. It was engraved with three fleurs-de-lis and inside the inscription *Lâche qui les abandonne* was engraved.

I wrote to Esterhazy when I sent the ring.

> "If you write to him," I wrote, "tell him that many miles and many countries can never separate hearts. This ring is just his size. Ask him to wear it for me. I wore it for two days before wrapping it. Tell him it comes from me. I do not know where he is. It is torture to have no news and not even to know where the people one loves are living."

No sooner had I sent that letter to Esterhazy, who I knew was my good friend and would do as I asked, than I was terrified that Axel would see it as a reproach and return to danger. I immediately wrote to him:

> "I exist . . . nothing more. How anxious I have been for you and all you must have suffered in having no news of us. Heaven grant that this reaches you . . . On no account think of returning. It is known that it is you who helped us to get away, and all will be lost if you should show yourself. We are guarded and watched

night and day . . . Be at rest. Nothing will happen to me. Farewell. I shall not be able to write to you any more . . ."

But I had to write to him. I could not have gone on living during those dreary days if I had not.

Soon I was writing again:

"I can tell you that I love you and have only time for that. Do not be troubled about me. I am well. I long to know the same of you. Write to me in cipher by the post and address it to Monsieur de Browne and in a second envelope for Monsieur de Gougens. Tell me where I should address my letters so that I may be able to write to you, for I cannot live without that. Farewell, most loved and loving of men. I embrace you with my whole heart . . ."

I was deeply resentful of the manner in which we were treated. The doors of my apartments were barred at night; and the door of my room had to remain open. I felt reckless at times, resigned at others. But I continued in correspondence with Barnave.

At last there was news from Axel. He wanted to come to Paris and I was delighted at the prospect of seeing him, but at the same time terrified.

"It would endanger our happiness," I wrote, "and you can truly believe I mean that, for I have the keenest desire to see you."

I was staying in my rooms all day. I no longer cared to go out. I spent my time writing.

My children were constantly with me. They provided my only joy, my only reason for wanting to stay alive.

I wrote to Axel:

"They are the only happiness left to me. When I am most sad I take my little son in my arms and hold him against my heart. That consoles me."

The National Assembly had prepared its draft of a Constitution and had laid it before the King for his acceptance. To ask for it was a meaningless gesture. The King was their prisoner. He had no alternative but to agree.

"It is a moral death," I said to him, "worse than bodily death which frees us of our troubles."

He agreed, knowing that his acceptance of the constitution was a sacrifice of all he stood for.

Louis was obliged to attend the Assembly; I went to watch him make his speech and it filled me with indignation and sorrow to see that the Assembly remained seated while he made his oath.

When he returned to the Tuileries he was so dispirited that he sank into a chair and wept. I put my arms about him to comfort him and wept with him for although I now believed that had he acted with resolve and determination we might have escaped this dire misfortune, I could not help remembering his kindness and tenderness and it occurred to me that it was his very goodness of heart which had added to our troubles.

I wrote to Mercy:

> "As regards the acceptance of the constitution it is impossible that any thinking person can fail to see that whatever we may do we are not free. But it is essential that we should give these monsters who surround us no cause for suspicion. However things turn out, only the foreign powers can save us. We have lost the army; we have lost money; there exists within this realm no power to restrain the armed populace. The very chiefs of the revolution are no longer listened to when they try to talk about order. Such is the deplorable position in which we find ourselves. Add to this that we have not a single friend, that all the world is betraying us; some because of hatred and others because of weakness and ambition. I myself am reduced to such a pitch that I have come to dread the days when we shall be given a semblance of freedom. At least in view of the impotence to which we have been condemned, we have no reason to reproach ourselves. You will find my whole soul in this letter . . ."

Later I wrote:

> "Tribulation first makes one realize what one is. My blood courses through my son's veins and I hope that a day will come when he will show himself worthy to be the grandson of Maria Theresa."

The fact was, I was ashamed for having had to negotiate with Barnave. I was not clever. I had no wish to live other than in a straightforward manner.

To Axel I wrote:

> "It would have been nobler to refuse to accept the constitution but refusal was impossible . . . Let me advise you that the scheme which has been adopted is the least undesirable of many. The follies of the *émigrés* has forced us to this; and in accepting

it it was necessary to leave no doubt that the acceptance was made in good faith."

I was very unhappy in this. I believed that my mother would not have approved of the manner in which I had acted. But then she had never been in the position in which I now found myself. She had never ridden from Versailles to Paris, from Varennes to Paris surrounded by a howling bloodthirsty mob.

The result of the King's acceptance of the Constitution was immediate. The rigorous guard was removed from the Tuileries. I no longer had a guard outside my apartments; I was allowed to shut my bedroom door and sleep in peace.

We had accepted the Revolution and were no longer reviled; when we went out I even heard people shout "Vive le Roi!" and most unusual of all "Vive la Reine!"

It was February, the height of the cold cruel winter. I was alone in my bedroom on the ground floor when I heard a footstep. I started up in terror for in spite of the changed attitude toward us, I could never be sure when one of those figures which played such a prominent part in my nightmares might appear in reality, bloodstained knife in hand to do to me what I had heard threatened so many times.

The door of my room was opened and I stared for I believed I was dreaming. It was impossible.

I recognized him at once in spite of his disguise. He could never deceive me. And for the moment I was only conscious of joy—sheer unadulterated joy—an emotion I had believed I should never feel again.

"Axel!" I cried. "It is not possible!"

He laughed and said: "Can you not believe your own eyes?"

"But to come here . . . ! Oh . . . it is dangerous. You must go at once."

"A good welcome," he said laughing, and embracing me in such a manner which told me he had no intention of leaving me.

I could only cling to him for the moment not caring what had brought him, how he had come, only that he was here.

I was dazed. One cannot easily leap from the depth of despair to the heights of happiness. I told him this. I wept and I laughed and we clung together and for a time shut out the whole world of sorrow and terror. This was the power of our love.

Later I heard of his fantastic adventure. He had written: "I live only to serve you," and he meant it.

He had procured a false passport, on which he had forged the signature of the King of Sweden, the bearer of which was supposed to be on a diplomatic visit to Lisbon. The passport was made out for his valet who took the part of the gentleman on the mission to Lisbon while Axel was posing as his servant. The papers had not been closely examined and they had had no difficulty in reaching Paris. He was staying with a friend in Paris who was ready to take the risk of helping him.

"As soon as it was dark," he said, "I came to the palace. I still had the key and found the door unguarded so I came to you."

"They know you helped us to escape. This is madness."

It was—a divine sort of madness; and I could not help but rejoice that he had come.

Axel stayed with me all that night and the next day. On the evening of that day I asked Louis to come to my apartment as an old friend wished to see him.

When Louis arrived Axel eagerly told him of plans he had made for another escape.

"We should learn by the mistakes of the last," he said. "This time we should succeed."

Louis shook his head. "It is impossible."

"Perhaps we should try," I suggested.

But I saw the stubborn look in my husband's face.

"We can speak frankly," he said. "I am accused of weakness and irresolution, but as no one else has ever been in my position they cannot say how they would have acted in my place. I missed the right moment to leave which was earlier than we did. That was the moment to act. Since then I have never found another. I have been deserted by everyone."

"Not by the Comte de Fersen," I reminded him.

He smiled sadly. "That's true. And I shall never forget what you have done for us. My friend, the National Guard is stationed round the château. It would be a hopeless endeavor and just as the position was worsened by our first attempt so would it be by yet another."

Axel was still convinced that we could succeed; and the King at last explained his true reason for refusing the aid which was offered. He had given his word not to attempt to leave again.

I was exasperated but as Axel said to me: "The King is an honest man."

Honest, yes. But of what use was honesty when dealing with our enemies?

Still Axel was certain that he could persuade King Gustavus of Sweden to come to our aid. He would return at once to his native country and work for us there.

We parted and he left. I was desolate to say farewell, yet his visit had stimulated me to such an extent that I felt hope returning. Axel would never cease to work for us. When I thought of that, I could believe that one day all would be well.

How ill luck pursued us. Axel had not been long in Sweden where he arrived without mishap when news of the death of King Gustavus came to us.

He was thinking of us at the end because the last words he spoke were: "My death will make the Jacobins in Paris rejoice."

How right he was. And another avenue was closed to us.

We could only hope for help from Austria and Prussia now.

Madame Campan came back to me. I was very pleased to see her because I had always been fond of her and I liked her sound good sense. I remembered now how discreetly she had disapproved of the magnificent berlin which Axel had had made with such pride.

She was startled when she saw me. I saw her glance at my hair.

"It has turned white, Madame Campan," I said sadly.

"It is still beautiful, Madame," she answered.

I showed her a ring I had had mounted with a lock of hair. I intended to send it to the Princesse de Lamballe whom I had commanded to go to London. She had left reluctantly and I wanted her to know how it pleased me to think of her in safety. I had the words *Bleached by sorrow*" inscribed on the ring. It would be a warning to her not to return, for she had written to me telling me that she could not bear to stay away from me and that she believed that if I were in peril so should she be.

"She was always a little stupid," I said to Madame Campan, "but the kindest and most affectionate of souls. I rejoice that she is not here."

My brother Leopold had died and his son Francis was now Emperor. He was twenty-four and I had never really known him; he showed little sympathy for my plight. He did not encourage those *émigrés* who in his country were agitating against the revolutionaries of France; nor did he banish them.

The situation between France and Austria had become tense and eventually Louis was prevailed upon to declare war. It seemed like a nightmare to me. I remembered how my mother had worked to foster the alliance between France and Austria—and now here they were at war.

I was not dismayed. I could not become any more unpopular than I already was. And if my countrymen beat the French, their first task would be to restore the Monarchy.

I was exultant. I wrote to Axel:

> "God grant that vengeance will at length be taken for the provocations we have received from this country. Never have I been more proud than at this moment to have been born a German."

I was foolish perhaps. In truth I had long forgotten that I was a German. I could scarcely speak the language. My husband was French; my children were French; and for years I had called this my country.

It was the French themselves who had refused to receive me. All I wanted was to go back to the old days; to be given another chance. I had learned bitter lessons and I now had the sense to apply them. I wanted to be left in peace to bring up my son to be a good King of France. That was all I asked.

The Princesse de Lamballe returned to Paris. While I embraced her I chided her.

"You were always a little fool," I told her.

"Yes, I know," she answered; and she laughed, and flung her arms about me and demanded to know how I thought she could be far away from me when she had to listen to all the terrible tales of what was happening in Paris.

June had come again. It was a year since we had attempted to escape. The summer weeks were the weeks of danger; then people congregated in the streets, in the Palais Royale; then it was easier to spread sedition.

Every effort seemed to be made to humiliate the King; he was asked to sanction two decrees ordaining the deportation of priests and a formation of a camp of twenty thousand men outside Paris. Louis would have given way but I urged him to apply the veto. This enraged the revolutionaries and I was to regret it afterwards but I could not help deploring my husband's weakness.

The people had a new name for me: Madame Veto. They reminded themselves that I was the Austrian Woman and that they were at war with Austria. The members of the National Assembly now believed that they would never conquer their enemies abroad until they had first dealt with those at home. I was the enemy—not the King.

Vergniaud, one of the leaders, was thundering warnings to the Assembly.

"From where I speak," he declared, "I can see the dwelling place in which false counsellors lead astray and deceive the King who has given us the Constitution . . . I see the windows of the palace where they are hatching counter-revolutions and where they are contriving ways of sending us back to slavery. Let those who dwell in the aforementioned palace realize that our Constitution guarantees inviolability to the King alone. Let them know that our laws will run there without distinction among the guilty, and that there is not any head proved to be criminal which can hope to escape passing beneath the ax."

This was a direct attack on me. I was accustomed to them from the rabble; it was different when they came from the leaders of the Revolution

It was the 20th June—the anniversary of our flight when the mob gathered about the Tuileries. They were shouting: "Down with the veto. The nation forever."

From the window I saw them—their filthy red caps on their heads; their knives and cudgels in their hands. These were the *sans culottes* . . . the bloodthirsty mob, and they were already in the palace. My first thought was for the children. I ran upstairs where they were with Madame de Tourzel and the Princesse de Lamballe.

"They have the King," said the Princesse.

"I must go to him," I cried. "If he is in danger, I must be there." I turned to Madame de Tourzel. "Guard the children . . ."

But one of the guards had come in and he barred the way. He said, "Madame, they are calling for you. It would madden them to see you. Stay here. Stay with the Dauphin and the Princesse."

My son was clutching at my skirts.

"Maman, stay with us. Stay with us," he cried. And the guard bade me stand by the wall with my children and Madame de Tourzel and the Princesse de Lamballe and some of the other women who had come running to join us. He put a table before us as a sort of barrier.

Elisabeth said: "They have come for you. I will go. They will think I am you . . . and that will give you a chance to get away with the children."

I protested and the guards would not let her go. "There is nothing to be done, Madame, but stay here. The mob is all over the palace. They are surrounding it. There is no way out. To move from here would endanger yourself and do no good to anyone."

She reluctantly came back to stand behind the table. The National Guard, I realized, had come to protect us. One of them put a red cap on my head and another on the Dauphin which was so large that it covered his face.

We could hear the shouts coming from the room in which they held the King.

I was struck with terror wondering what was happening to my husband. I learned later how once more he won their respect. It is difficult to understand how a man who could not make up his mind, who was laughed at for a fool, could so quell a mob determined to kill him.

It was that extraordinary calm, that ability to look death in the face with indifference. They were never allowed to see my fear but I showed it in my contempt for them. Louis never lost his tenderness for them. However vile they were, they were his children. His was the true courage.

The guards called out that it was their duty to defend the King with their lives and they intended to do their duty.

But what were a few guards against such a mob?

"À bas le veto!" they cried.

But the guards reminded them that the King's person should not be harmed. It was in the Constitution.

"I cannot discuss the veto with you," said Louis calmly, "though I shall do what the Constitution demands."

One of the mob strode forward, his knife in his hand.

"Have no fear, Sire," said one of the guards. "We will defend you with our lives."

The King smiled gently. "Put your hand on my heart," he said. "Then you will perceive whether I am afraid or not."

The man did so and cried that he was astonished that any man could be so calm at such a time.

None of them could doubt that the King's pulse was absolutely normal and they could not fail to be astonished.

Disconcerted in the face of such extraordinary courage they did not know what to do, so one of them held out his red cap on the edge of his pike and with a natural gesture, which could only have been inspired, Louis took it and put it on his head.

The mob was silent for a while. Then they cried: "Vive le Roi!"

The danger was over for the King.

But they had never felt much rancor against the King. They rushed from the room and came to the Council Chamber where I stood behind the table holding my children close to me.

A group of guards immediately placed themselves about the table.

They stared at me.

"That's the one. That's the Austrian woman."

The Dauphin was whimpering; the red cap was suffocating him. One of the guards saw my look and took the cap off the child's head. The women protested but the soldier cried: "Would you suffocate a harmless child?"

And the women . . . for they were mostly women . . . were ashamed and did not answer. I felt relieved then. I could feel my son clutching my skirt hiding his face against me to shut out the horror of all this.

It was so hot; the crowded room was stifling. "Oh God," I prayed. "Let death come quickly."

I would welcome it, for if we all died together there could be no more suffering like this.

The soldiers had unsheathed their bayonets; the mob eyed them warily; but they were shouting obscenities about me; and I prayed again: "Oh God, close my children's ears." I could only hope that they did not understand.

A man who was carrying a toy gibbet from which hung a female doll approached the table. He chanted: "*Antoinette à la lanterne.*"

I held my head high and pretended not to see him.

One woman tried to spit at me. "Whore!" she cried. "Vile woman."

My daughter moved closer to me as though to protect me from this creature. My son clung tighter.

I looked into the woman's face and said: "Have I ever done you any harm?"

"You have brought misery to the nation."

"You have been told so, but you have been deceived. As the wife of the King of France and the mother of the Dauphin I am a Frenchwoman. I shall never see my own country again. I can be happy or unhappy only in France. I was happy when you loved me."

She was silent and I saw her lips moving; there were tears in her eyes.

I was aware too of the stillness about us. Everyone was quiet, listening to me as I spoke.

The woman looked at my child and lifted her eyes to me and said: "I ask pardon, Madame. I did not know you. But I see you are a good woman."

Then she turned away weeping.

That incident gave me courage. The people must be made aware that they had been fed on lies, for when they came face to face with me they knew they were false.

Another woman said: "She's only a woman . . . with children."

That provoked ribald comments; but something had happened. The woman's tears had driven murder out of the room. They wanted to get away.

We stood behind the table for a long time and it was eight o'clock before the guards cleared the palace and we made our way over the debris of broken doors and furniture to our apartments.

I guessed that Axel would hear of this new assault and be anxious so I sat down to write to him at once.

"I am still alive, though by a miracle. The twentieth was a terrible ordeal.

But do not be anxious about me. Have faith in my courage."

Now we were living in a damaged palace and I felt we were on the edge of disaster. As the weather grew hotter I was aware of the rising tension. The assault on the Tuileries would not be an isolated attack, I was sure of that.

I ordered Madame Campan to have a padded under-waistcoat made for the King so that if he should be attacked at any time there might be time for the guards to rescue him. It was made of fifteen folds of Italian taffeta —and comprised a waistcoat and a wide belt. I had had it tested; it re-sisted ordinary dagger thrusts and even shots fired at it were turned off.

I was afraid that someone would discover it and I wore it myself for three days before I had an opportunity of getting the King to try it on. I was in bed when he did so and I heard him whisper something to Madame Campan. It fitted him and he wore it, and when he had gone I asked Cam-pan what he had said.

She was reluctant but I said: "You had better tell me. You should un-derstand that it is as well for me to know everything."

She answered: "His Majesty said: 'It is only to satisfy the Queen that I submit to this inconvenience. They will not assassinate me. Their schemes have changed. They will put me to death in another way.'"

"I think he is right, Madame Campan," I said. "He has told me that he believes that what is happening here is an imitation of what once hap-pened in England. The English cut off the head of their King Charles I. I fear they will bring him to trial. But I am a foreigner, my dear Madame Campan, not one of them. Perhaps they will have less scruples where I am concerned. They will very likely assassinate me. If it were not for the children . . . I should not care. But the children, my dear Campan, what will become of them?"

Dear Campan was too full of sense to deny what I said. She was so practical that she immediately set about making me a corselet similar to the King's waistcoat.

I thanked her but I would not wear it.

"If they kill me, Madame Campan, it will be fortunate for me. It will at least deliver me from this painful existence. Only the children worry me. But there are you and kind Tourzel and I do not believe that even those people would be cruel to little children. I remember how moved that woman was. It was because of the children. No, even they would not harm them. So . . . when they kill me do not mourn for me. Remember I shall go to a happier life than I suffer here."

Madame Campan was alarmed. All during that sultry July she refused to go to bed. She would sit in my apartment dozing ready to leap up at the first sound. I believe she saved my life on one occasion.

It was one o'clock in the morning when I started out of a doze to find Madame Campan bending over me.

"Madame!" she whispered. "Listen. There is someone creeping along the corridor."

I sat up in bed startled. The corridor passed along the whole line of my apartments and was locked at each end.

Madame Campan dashed into the anteroom where the *valet de chambre* was sleeping. He too had heard the footsteps and was ready to rush out. In a few seconds Madame Campan and I heard the sounds of scuffling.

"Oh, Campan, Campan!" I said and I put my arms about the dear faithful creature. "What should I do without friends such as you? Insults by day and assassins by night. Where will it end?"

"You have good servants, Madame," she said quietly.

And it was true for the *valet de chambre* at that moment came into the bedroom dragging a man with him.

"I know the wretch, Madame," he said. "He is a servant of the King's *toilette*. He admits taking the key from His Majesty's pocket when the King was in bed."

He was a small man and the *valet de chambre* was both tall and strong and for this I had to be grateful, otherwise it would have been the end of me that night. The miserable wretch no doubt thought to earn the praise of the mob for doing something which they were constantly screaming should be done.

"I will lock him up, Madame," said the *valet de chambre*.

"No," I said. "Let him go. Open the door for him and send him away from the palace. He came to murder me and if he had succeeded the people would be carrying him about in triumph tomorrow."

The *valet* obeyed me and when he returned I thanked him and told him that I was grieved that he should be exposed to danger on my account. To this he replied that he feared nothing and that he had a pair of very excellent pistols which he carried always with him for no other purpose but to defend me.

Such incidents always moved me deeply and I said to Madame Campan as we returned to my bedroom that the goodness of people such as herself and the *valet* would never have been appreciated by me but for the fact that these terrible times brought it home to me.

She was touched but she was already making plans to have all the locks changed the next day and she saw that the King's were too.

Now the great Terror was upon us. It was as though a new race of men had filtered into the capital—small, very dark, lithe, fierce, and bloodthirsty—the men of the south, the men of Marseilles.

With them they brought the song which had been composed by Rouget de Lisle, one of their officers. We were soon to hear it sung all over Paris and it was called the *Marseillaise*. Bloodthirsty words set to a rousing tune; it could not fail to win popularity. It replaced the until now favorite *Ça Ira* and every time I heard it it made me shiver. It haunted me. I would fancy I heard it when during the night I woke from an uneasy doze for I was scarcely sleeping during these nights.

> "Allons, enfants de la patrie,
> Le jour de gloire est arrivé.
> Contre nous de la tyrannie
> Le couteau sanglant est levé
> Le couteau sanglant est levé
> Entendez-vous dans ces campagnes
> Mugir ces féroces soldats?
> Ils viennent jusque dans nos bras
> Égorger nos fils, nos compagnes.
> Aux armes, citoyens!
> Formez vos bataillons!
> Marchons! Marchons! Qu'un sang impur
> Abreuve nos sillons."

The gardens outside the apartments were always crowded. People looked in at the windows. At any moment one little spark would set alight the conflagration. How did we know from one hour to another what atrocities would be committed. Hawkers called their wares under my window. "*La Vie Scandaleuse de Marie Antoinette,*" they shrieked. They sold figures representing me in various indecent positions with men and women.

"Why should I want to live?" I asked Madame Campan. "Why should these precautions be taken to save a life which is not worth having?"

I wrote to Axel of the terror of our lives. I said that unless our friends issued a manifesto that Paris would be attacked if we were harmed, we should very soon be murdered.

Axel, I knew, was doing everything possible. No one ever worked more indefatigably in any cause.

If only the King had had half Axel's energy. I tried to rouse him to action. Outside our windows the guards were drawn up. If he showed them he was a leader they would respect him. I had seen how even the most crude of the revolutionaries could be overawed by a little royal dignity. I begged him to go to the guards to make some show of reviewing them.

He nodded. I was right, he was sure. He went out and it was heartbreaking to see him ambling between the lines of soldiers. He had grown so fat and unwieldy now that he was never allowed to hunt.

"I trust you," he told them. "I have every confidence in my guard."

I heard the snigger. I saw one man break from the ranks and walk behind him imitating his ponderous walk. Dignity was what was needed. I was a fool to have expected Louis to show that.

I was relieved when he came in. I looked away for I did not wish to see the humiliation on his face.

"La Fayette will save us from the fanatics," he said heavily. "You should not despair."

"I wonder," I retorted bitterly, "who will save us from Monsieur de La Fayette?"

The climax arrived when the Duke of Brunswick issued the Manifesto at Coblenz. Military force would be used on Paris if the least violence or outrage was committed against the King and the Queen.

It was the signal for which they had been waiting. The agitators were working harder than ever. All over Paris men were marching in groups . . . the *sans culottes* and the ragged men of the south; they sang as they went:

"*Allons, enfants de la patrie . . .*"

They were saying that we were preparing a counter-revolution at the Tuileries.

On the tenth of August the *faubourgs* were on the march and their objective was the Tuileries.

We were aware of the rising storm. All through the night of the ninth and the early morning of the tenth I had not taken off my clothes. I had wandered through the corridors accompanied by Madame Campan and the Princesse de Lamballe. The King was sleeping, though fully dressed. The tocsins had started to ring all over the city and Elisabeth came to join us.

Together we watched the dawn come. That was about four o'clock and the sky was blood-red.

I said to her: "Paris must have seen something like this at the Massacre of the Saint Bartholomew."

She took my hand and clung to it. "We will keep together."

I replied: "If my time should come and you survive me . . ."

She nodded. "The children, of course. They shall be as my own."

The silence occasioned by the cessation of the bells seemed even more alarming than they had been. The Marquis de Mandat, Commander of the National Guard, who had many times saved us from death received a summons to the Hôtel de Ville. We watched him go with misgivings and when shortly afterward a messenger arrived at the Tuileries to tell us that he had been brutally murdered on his way to the Hôtel de Ville and his body thrown into the Seine, I knew that disaster was very close.

The Attorney General of Paris came riding in haste.

He asked for the King. Louis arose from his bed, his clothes awry, his wig flattened, his eyes heavy with sleep.

"The *faubourgs* are on the march," said the Attorney General. "They are coming to the palace. And their intention is massacre."

The King declared his belief in the National Guard.

Oh God, I thought, his sentimentality will get us all murdered!

The Guard was all about the palace but I had seen the sullen looks on some faces; I remembered how they had sneered at Louis when he had made an attempt to review them; I remembered the man who had broken the line and mocked him from behind.

"All Paris is on the march," warned the Attorney General. "Your Majesties' only safe place is in the National Assembly. We must take you there and there is not a minute to be lost. Action would not help us against so many. You see that resistance is impossible."

"Then let us go," said the King. "Call the household."

"Only you and your family, Sire."

"But we cannot abandon all the brave people who have been with us here," I protested. "Should we leave them to the fury of the mob?"

"Madame, if you oppose this move, you will be responsible for the deaths of the King and your children."

What could I do? I thought of dear Campan, Lamballe, Tourzel . . . all those who were almost as dear to me as my own family.

But I saw that I could do nothing and the Dauphin was beside me.

We left the palace. Already some of the people were looking at us through the railings and others had come into the grounds, but they made no attempt to stop us. The leaves were thick on the ground although it was only August. The Dauphin kicked through them almost joyously. Poor child, he was so accustomed to alarms like this that he found them part of his life and as long as we were together he seemed indifferent to them. That was something to rejoice about. In the distance I could hear the shouts and screams. The mob was very close. I could hear raucous: "*Allons, enfants de la patrie . . .*"

The King said calmly: "The leaves have fallen early this year."

As we approached the Assembly Hall a tall man picked up the Dauphin in his arms. I screamed in terror, but he looked at me kindly and said: "Have no fear, Madame. I mean him no harm. But there is not a minute to be lost." I could not take my eyes from my child. I was terrified but the Dauphin was smiling and saying something in his precocious way to his captor.

And as we came to the Assembly Hall my son was given back to me. I thanked the man and grasped the boy's hand so fiercely that he reminded me I was hurting him.

But we had reached the Assembly Hall and there we were placed in the reporter's box while the President declared that the Assembly had sworn to stand by the Constitution and that they would protect the King.

During the walk from the Tuileries my watch and my purse had been stolen. I laughed at myself for the momentary concern I felt for these worthless objects. For in the Assembly Hall I could hear the shouts of the mob as they reached the Tuileries, and I wondered what was happening to those faithful friends. I thought in particular of the Princesse de Lamballe who might have been safe in England but who had come back for love of me.

I wept silently; and I wondered what would happen next for we could not return to the ruin which those people would have made of the Tuileries.

But what did it matter? Why fight to preserve an existence which was not worth the effort.

26

"When it is necessary, I shall know how to die."

Louis XVI

"Frenchmen, I die innocent of the crimes imputed to me. I forgive the authors of my death, and I pray that my blood may not fall upon France."

Louis XVI on the scaffold

PRISONERS IN THE TEMPLE

We were lodged in the Temple—not that palace which had been the castle of the Knights Templar and in which Artois had once lived and where I remembered driving in my gay sleigh one winter's day to dine with him—but to the fortress which adjoined it, the grim prison, not unlike the Bastille with its round towers, slits of windows and courtyards from which the sun was excluded. Here we were kept as prisoners.

The Deputy Public Prosecutor Jacques René Hébert was in charge of the Temple; he was a man whom the more idealistic leaders such as Desmoulins and Robespierre despised. He was cruel and unscrupulous, delighting in the Revolution not because he truly believed it could bring a better life to the poor but because it gave him an opportunity of behaving brutally. He had become powerful through his newspaper *Père Duchesne* in which he had done as much as many men to inflame the mob.

My dismay was great when I learned that we were in the charge of this man. Whenever I saw him he regarded me with insolence and I knew that he was thinking of the scandalous things which had been written of me. I read his evil thoughts and in my fear I endeavored to appear indifferent to him which had the effect of making me seem haughtier than ever.

But there were men in the Commune whose desire was to show us and the world that cruelty was not in their program. They it was who controlled the mob, who had plucked us only recently from its blood-hungry hands. These were the men who wanted reforms—liberty, fraternity, equality—through constitutional methods and at the time they were in control.

Therefore life was not as uncomfortable for us as I am sure Hébert would have liked it to be. The great tower of the Temple had been fitted out for us and four rooms were given to the King and four for Elisabeth, myself and the children. We were allowed to walk in the grounds—always closely guarded it was true, but we were not to be denied that exercise considered necessary to our health. There was plenty to eat and drink; there were clothes and books.

I was astonished how Louis and Elisabeth settled into this life. How different I was! It seemed to me that they had no spirit. Elisabeth was so meek, and accepted the misfortune which had fallen on us as the will of God. Perhaps that was the difference between us—she had a belief which I lacked. I envied them in a way—both Louis and Elisabeth. They were so passive, never wishing to fight, always accepting. Elisabeth had her religion and she told me that she had always thought the life of a nun would be one she would like to adopt, and life at the Temple was like living in a nunnery. Louis had his religion too; he had his food and his drink; he slept a great deal of the day and the night; and as long as he was not called upon to shed the blood of his people he was resigned.

They exasperated me, yet I admired and—in a way—envied them.

Sometimes I would sit at my window and watch Louis showing the Dauphin how to fly his kite in the gardens. Always kind and patient he had none of the bearing of a King.

I heard many of the simple people who were brought in to guard us and who had read accounts of myself and the King in *Père Duchesne* express surprise to find the King such a simple man, who played with his son in the courtyard, measuring how many square feet there were, for the child's amusement; sometimes they saw him dozing after a meal or reading quietly. They saw me, at my needlework, reading to the children, looking after them; and I sensed they were astonished. I was haughty, it was true, but how could such an arrogant woman have indulged in those obscene adventures they had heard about? How could such a Jezebel care so much for her family?

I used to think that if we could have known the people and the people could have known us, there need never have been a revolution.

September came. The weather was still warm. News had come to Paris that the Prussians and Austrians were advancing. The mob came into the street. They were shouting that soon my relations would be in Paris, and they would murder the people whom they would say had ill-treated the Queen.

I heard shouts of "*L'Autrichienne à la lanterne!*"

The short lull was over. What now?

The tocsins were ringing.

We kept in one room, the whole family. Our great desire was to be together in disaster.

"It may be," said the King, "that the Duke of Brunswick has already reached Paris. In which case we can expect to be free very shortly."

If only that were so! I had no optimism left with which to delude myself.

The crowds were about our window. I could hear them shouting: "Antoinette to the window. Come and see what we have brought you, Antoinette."

The King went to the window and at once called to me to keep away.

But he was too late. I had seen it. I had seen the pike on the top of which was the head of my dear friend, the Princesse de Lamballe.

In that second I knew that as long as I lived I should never banish it from my mind. That once lovely face now set, in staring horror, the still beautiful hair falling about it . . . and the horrible horrible blood.

I felt unconsciousness enveloping me and I was glad to escape, if only temporarily.

How could they comfort me?

"Why did she come?" I demanded. "Did I not tell her. She could have been safe in England. What did she ever do . . . but love me?"

I thought of a hundred incidents from the past. How she had welcomed me when I had first come to France . . . so much more warm, so much more friendly than the rest of the family. "She is stupid," Vermond had said. Oh, my dearest and most stupid Lamballe! Why did you come from safety . . . to be with me, to comfort me, to share my misfortune? And to end like this!

How I hated them, those howling savages out there. I flayed my hatred of them into a fury; it was the only way to forget my grief.

Later they brought the ring to me . . . the ring I had so recently given her. She had been wearing it when the mob had dragged her from the prison to which they had taken her when they had brought us to the Temple.

This was the result of what was called the September Massacres when permission had been granted to murder any prisoners who might be regarded with suspicion.

What an opportunity for the mob when men like Danton approved these murders! And how many of my friends had suffered in these massacres? Surely these were the darkest days in the history of France.

Three weeks after that dreadful day we heard the sounds of shouting in the streets again. We gathered together as we had before and waited. What terrible event was to overtake us now?

The guards told us that the people were not angry today. They were rejoicing. They were dancing in the streets. We should hear soon enough.

France no longer had a King. The Monarchy was at an end.

The attitude was changed toward us. No one called the King "Sire" any more. To say Your Majesty would be considered a slight to the nation. Heaven knew what penalties that would provoke.

We were no longer the King and Queen but Louis and Antoinette Capet.

Louis' comment was: "That is not my name. It is the name of some of my ancestors but it is not mine."

No one took any notice of that. From then on we were the Capet family—no different from any other, except, of course, that a close watch was kept on us and the people continued to revile us and threaten our lives.

Hébert delighted in insulting us. He called Louis "Capet" with great relish. He encouraged the guards to do the same. They would yawn in our faces, sit sprawled out before us, spit on our floors, do anything they could to remind us that we had been robbed of our royalty.

But even this did not last. The King still remained a symbol. There were still some to remember and secretly to show us that respect which they could not throw aside merely because they were told we were no longer King and Queen.

We now had only two servants, Tison and Cléry. Tison was an evil old man who bullied his wife and forced her to spy on us. The two of them slept in a room next to that one which I occupied with the Dauphin for I had moved his bed into my room—my daughter slept in the same room as Elisabeth; but a glass partition enabled these two to see everything and we did not feel safe to move without the knowledge that we were being closely watched.

The King would leave his bed at six o'clock; then Cléry would come to my room and dress my hair and that of Elisabeth and my daughter, and we would all go and have breakfast with the King.

Louis and I gave our son his lessons for Louis was eager that he should not grow up ignorant; he often said sadly that he had no intention of allowing his son's education to be neglected as his had been. He was particularly keen that the Dauphin should study literature and would make him learn passages from Racine and Corneille, to which the boy took with enthusiasm. But all the time we were watched. I remember one occasion when I was teaching little Louis-Charles his tables, the guard who could not read snatched the book from my hands and accused me of teaching him to write in ciphers.

Thus we passed our days. Had it not been for the gloom of our surroundings, for the continual surveillance, I think I could have been moderately happy in this simple life. I saw more of my children than I should have done had I been living in state at Versailles; and the affection between us grew. If I do not write so much of my daughter as I do of my son it is not because I loved her less. She was gentle and sweet natured; she lacked the more violent temperament of her little brother; she was very like Elisabeth and one of the greatest comforts of my life. But because Louis-Charles was the Dauphin I was in a continuous state of anxiety about him; I must be thinking of his welfare continually and thus he was more often in my thoughts.

When we had taken our meals like any simple family, the King would doze as any father might; I would sometimes read aloud, usually history; and Elisabeth and Marie Thérèse would take it in turns to read from lighter works such as "*The Thousand and One Nights*" or Miss Burney's *Evelina*. The King would awake and ask riddles from the *Mercure de France*. At least we had each other.

There was always needlework to be done, for Elisabeth and I had to mend our clothes.

But every day we had to endure humiliations, to be reminded that we were prisoners, that we were no different from anyone else now—in fact we were not so important, for our jailers were at least free men. We had friends though. Turgy, one of our servingmen, who had been with us at Versailles (he it was who had opened the door of the *oeil de boeuf* for me when the mob had been at my heels) was constantly keeping us informed of what was going on outside. Madame Cléry used to stand outside the walls of the Temple and shout out the latest news so that we could know what was happening. I discovered that some of those guards who arrived full of hatred were won over when they saw us all together acting in such a manner as to belie all the gossip they heard. I used to show them cuttings of the children's hair and tell them at what age they had been when I had cut off all these locks. I had tied them with scented ribbon and I used to cry over them a little. I often saw some of those grim faced men turn away more than a little moved.

But nothing remained static; and Louis had been right when he had said that they did not wish to assassinate him, but they had some other plan for removing him.

We heard that Louis was to be tried for treason.

The first move was to rob us of all cutting instruments—scissors, knives and even forks, although we were allowed forks for meals but they were taken from us as soon as we had eaten. One evening Louis was told that he was to be removed from us.

This was a bitter blow. We had come to believe that we could endure anything as long as we were all together. We wept bitterly but it was of no avail. Louis was taken from us.

Then followed the weeks of waiting. What was happening? I had little idea. All we knew was that the King was no longer merely a prisoner under observation; he was a doomed man.

All through those cold days I waited for news. Sometimes I would hear my husband walking up and down in his apartment for he was imprisoned on the floor below the one in which we lived.

It was the 20th of January when a member of the Commune called on me and told me that I, with my children and sister-in-law, might visit my husband.

A terrible sense of foreboding filled me when I heard this for I guessed what it meant.

They had sentenced my husband to death.

I cannot shut from my mind the picture of the room with its glass door. Four of the guards stood by the stove. The light of one oil lamp gave a feeble glow to the room but as I entered holding the Dauphin by the hand the King rose from the rush-seated chair on which he was sitting and coming to me embraced me.

I clung to him, mutely. What could words say now even if I could have uttered them?

I saw that Elisabeth was crying quietly and my daughter with her. The

Dauphin broke into loud sobbing and I found that I could no longer hold back my tears.

Louis tried to calm us all. He himself showed little emotion; his great grief was to see our distress.

"It sometimes happens," he said, "that a King is asked to pay the penalty for the wrongdoings of his ancestors."

I cannot shut out the sight of him in his brown coat and white waistcoat, his hair lightly powdered, his expression almost apologetic. He was going and leaving us alone in this terrible world—that was his concern.

To try to calm our grief, he told of his trial, how he had been asked questions he had not been able to answer. He had never meant any harm to anyone, he had told them. He loved his people as a father loves his children.

He was deeply moved when he told us that among his judges had been his cousin Orléans.

"But for my cousin," he said, "I should not have been condemned to die. His was the casting vote." He was puzzled, unable to understand why the cousin who had been brought up close to him should suddenly hate him so much that he wanted him to die.

"I always hated him," I said. "I knew he was an enemy from the first."

But my husband laid his hand gently over mine and he was imploring me not to hate, to try to resign myself. He knew well my proud spirit but there was one thing I had learned: if when my time came I could face death as courageously as he was facing his I should be blessed.

Poor little Louis-Charles understood that his father was to die and he was giving way to a passion of grief. "Why? Why?" he demanded angrily. "You are a *good* man, Papa. Who would want to kill you? I will kill them . . . I will . . ."

My husband took the boy between his knees and said seriously: "My son, promise me that you will never think of avenging my death."

My son's lips were set in the stubborn line I knew so well. But the King lifted him onto his knee and said: "Come now. I want you to lift your hand and swear that you will fulfill your father's last wish."

So the little boy lifted his hand and swore to love his father's murderers.

The time had come for the King to leave us. I clung to him and said: "We shall see you tomorrow?"

"At eight o'clock," said my husband quietly.

"At seven! Please let it be seven."

He nodded and bade me look to our daughter who had fainted. My son ran to the guards and begged them to take him to the gentlemen of Paris so that he could ask them not to let his Papa die.

I could only lift him in my arms and try to comfort him and I threw myself onto my bed and lay there with a child on either side of me and Elisabeth kneeling by my bed in prayer.

All through the night I lay sleepless, shivering on my bed.

I was up in the early morning waiting for him; but he did not come.

Cléry came to us.

"He feared it would distress you too much," he said.

I sat and waited, thinking of my husband, of our first meeting and what I knew now would be our last.

I did not know how time was passing. I was numb with misery; and suddenly I heard the roll of drums; I heard the shouts of the people.

Underneath my window the sentry cried: "Long live the Republic."

And I knew that I was a widow.

27

"*Veuille Dieu tout-puissant sauver une tête si chère. J'aurais trop perdu si je la perds.*"

Axel de Fersen

"My dear Sophie, you have no doubt learned by now about the terrible disaster of the removal of the Queen to the Conciergerie and about the decree of that despicable Convention which delivers her to the Revolutionary Tribunal for judgment. Since I heard of this I have no longer been alive for it is not truly life to exist as I do and to suffer the pains I now endure. If I could but do something to bring about her liberation, I think the agony would be less, but I find it terrible that my only resource is to ask others to help her . . . I would give my life to save her and cannot; and my greatest happiness would be to die for her in order to save her . . ."

Axel de Fersen to his sister Sophie

"*Non, jamais il n'y aura plus pour moi de beaux jours, mon bonheur est passé, et je suis condamné à d'éternels regrets et à trainer une vie triste et languissante.*"

Fersen's Journal

IN THE ANTEROOM

They gave me mourning clothes; I had a black dress and petticoat, black silk gloves, two head scarves of black taffeta and a black cloak.

I looked at them with indifference. I told myself that it could not be long now until the end.

I never went down to the courtyard because I could not bear to go past those rooms which the King had occupied; but with Elisabeth and the children I went to the top of the tower for fresh air; there was a gallery there surrounded by a parapet and there we would walk during those winter afternoons.

Toulan, one of the guards, had brought to me a ring and a seal and a lock of Louis' hair. These had been confiscated by the Commune but Toulan had stolen them and brought them to me because he believed they would comfort me. Toulan! A man who had been at the storming of the Tuileries; who had determined on our destruction. He had been set in charge of us because of his fierce revolutionary views; because he was trustworthy and reliable. They had forgotten that he also had a heart. I had seen the tears in his eyes; I had seen his admiration of our fortitude. He was a brave man. There was another too named Lepitre who had been won over to our side.

I still had Cléry, the King's Valet, and Turgy, who had been in the kitchen of Versailles; he was a bold and brazen fellow and very brave for he had managed by fabricating stories about his revolutionary zeal to become one of my guards.

I am thankful to these loyal people; it was they who gave me hope during those dark days. For the first weeks after Louis' death I would sit listless thinking of the past, full of remorse, accusing myself of a hundred follies.

I would talk to my friends sadly of the loss of the King. It was Toulan who said: "Madame, there is still a King of France."

This was true. My little boy was now Louis XVII. If I could get him out of this prison . . . if I could join my friends . . .

I was suddenly alive again. I had a purpose.

My little circle was delighted in the change in me. I realized that I was the center of that little circle for Elisabeth was too passive to be, the children too young. Toulan and Lepitre thought of all kinds of ways of smuggling news into me. Turgy, who served meals, would wrap notes round the corks of bottles so that it would appear that the paper had been put there to make them fit more securely; and although the Tisons would examine the bread to see if notes were in it and peer under the cover of dishes, they never discovered this ruse. Turgy sometimes would carry notes in his pockets and at an arranged signal one of us would lift them out as he brushed past us when serving us. From Madame Cléry shouting the news outside our windows I learned that the whole of Europe was shocked by the execution of Louis; even in Philadelphia and Virginia murder was shuddered at. All very well to depose of a tyrannical Monarchy, but not ruthlessly to kill its figurehead who could scarcely be entirely responsible.

Sensing the disapproval did nothing to make the Republic more lenient toward us; in fact it increased their severity.

But the thought that I had friends had given me a reason for living: Escape.

And when I heard that Axel was trying to rouse Mercy to action, that he had prevailed upon him to ask the Prince of Cobourg to send a regiment of picked men to march on Paris and pluck me from the Temple—wild as it was, rejected as it was—it put new heart in me. It was the plan of a lover rather than a strategist, just as the flight to Varennes had been. I saw now that it indicated a frantic desire for my safety which was too passionate in its intensity to be practical. And I loved him all the more because of this.

One piece of news which was brought to me was that Jacques Armand had died at the battle of Jemappes. I thought sadly of the lovely little boy whom I had picked up on the road when I so longed for children. He had been my substitute until I had my own. He had never forgiven me for that . . . and now, poor boy, he was dead.

I spoke to Elisabeth of the sadness of this and she tried to comfort me, pointing out the different life he had had because of what I had done for him; but I only replied: "I used him, Elisabeth. I used him as a toy with which to amuse myself for a while. One cannot use people in that way. I see it now. There is so much I see now that I did not see then. But one thing I believe, Elisabeth. No woman ever paid more highly for her follies than I have done. If I am given another chance . . ."

"You will be," she told me in her placid way. But I was not sure. I lacked her faith.

Each evening the *illuminateur* came to light the lamps. I welcomed his coming because he had two little boys and I had always loved children. They were rather dirty, their clothes clothes stained by the oil used in the lamps for they helped their father. The *illuminateur* never looked in my direction. There were so many like him who were afraid of appearing royalist. This dreadful Revolution was not called the Terror for nothing. Countless numbers of its supporters went in terror of their lives never knowing when the great monster they had created would snap at them.

Sometimes the children would look wistfully at the food on the table and I liked to give them some of it. This they ate greedily; and I would find their eyes under their floppy hats regarding me intently. I wondered what tales they had heard of the Queen.

Madame Tison would come hustling in frowning at them, searching them, looking to see whether I had given them some message to take out.

The visits of the *illuminateur* were one of the pleasant interludes of the day because of the children.

Toulan spoke to the lamplighter and asked him whether the boys were learning the trade. The lamplighter nodded.

Toulan saw the boys regarding me with awe. "At what are you looking?" he demanded. "The woman? No need to blush, boy. We're all equal now."

The *illuminateur* gave his agreement by spitting on the floor.

I was accustomed to this; I wondered whether Toulan had scented something suspicious in the *illuminateur's* attitude and that was why he had mentioned we were all equal.

We all had to be very careful.

I was disappointed when the *illuminateur* came alone. I sat, my eyes on my book.

"Your Majesty . . ."

I started. The *illuminateur* was filling the lamp in a not very skillful way and I realized that it was not the same man who had come with the children.

"I'm Jarjayes, Madame. General Jarjayes."

"Why yes . . ."

"Toulan bribed the *illuminateur* and got him the worse for drink in a tavern. I am in touch with the Comte de Fersen . . ."

At the mention of that name I could have fainted with happiness.

"The Comte is determined to free you. He has sent a message to say he will not rest until you are free."

"I knew he would do this . . . I *knew* . . ."

"We have to plan carefully. But Madame, be ready. Toulan is our good friend. Lepitre too . . . but we must be sure of him."

I saw Madame Tison hovering in the doorway and I tried to convey by my expression that we were spied on.

The General went away; and I felt a wild hope surging within me.

Axel had not forgotten me. He had not given up hope.

From Toulan I heard how the plan was progressing. He was to smuggle clothes into the prison which when they put them on would make the

Dauphin and his sister look like the lamplighter's boys. Elisabeth and I were to be disguised as municipal councilors. It would not be difficult to obtain the hats, cloaks and boots, and of course the tricolore sashes which would be required.

The Tisons who were never far from us would be our great difficulty. We could never escape while they were watching over us.

But Toulan was a man of imagination. "We will drug them," he said.

They had a fondness for Spanish tobacco. Why should not Toulan present them with some? It would be heavily drugged and make them unconscious for several hours. When they were under its influence we would hastily dress in our clothes and pass out of the prison in the company of Toulan. It was a bold but not impossible plan.

"I should need a passport," I told him; but he had thought of that.

Lepitre could provide it.

By the time the flight was discovered we could all be in England.

We were all ready, waiting.

But Lepitre was not a brave man. Perhaps it was too much to ask of him. He had prepared the passport, but a chance remark of Madame Tison's made him wonder whether she knew that something was brewing.

Lepitre could not bring himself to go on with it. It was too risky, he said. We must make another plan in which I alone should escape.

This I would not do. I would not consent to be parted from the children and Elisabeth.

I wrote to Jarjayes:

> "We have had a beautiful dream and that is all. But we have gained much in finding again on this new occasion a further proof of your wholehearted devotion to me. My trust in you is limitless. You will always find I have some courage, but the interests of my son are my sole care, and whatsoever happiness I may be able to win, I can never consent to leave him. I could do nothing without my children and the failure of any such idea is something I do not even regret."

I sent him my husband's ring and lock of hair that he might take them to the Comtes de Provence or Artois for I feared they would be taken from me; and I had a wax impression made of a ring Axel had given me on which was inscribed: "*All leads me to thee.*"

I sent this impression to Jarjayes with a note which said:

> "I wish you to give this wax impression to one you know of, who came to see me from Brussels last year. Tell him at the same time that the device has never been more true."

There was another attempt, but I believe I expected failure from the start. I had begun to believe that I was doomed and nothing could save me.

Baron de Batz, a royalist adventurer, formulated a plan in which Elisabeth, Marie Thérèse, and I were to walk out of the prison in the uniform of soldiers with members of the loyal guard; the Dauphin was to be hidden under the cloak of one of the officers.

Everything was prepared but the Tisons had grown suspicious and the day before that fixed for the escape Madame declared that she suspected Toulan and Lepitre of being too friendly with me.

As a result they were removed and that plan collapsed for it could not be carried out without their help.

I can scarcely write of this scene. It fills me with emotion and a sorrow so acute that my hand grows limp with agony. They could not have thought of a more exquisite torture. During these days of gloom and horror my great solace had been my children. They had enabled me to feign a haughty indifference to insolence and cruelty. Now they saw the way to pierce that armor of indifference and disdain.

It was July—hot, turgid—and we were in our room together—Elisabeth, Marie Thérèse, my boy and I. I was mending my son's coat and Elisabeth was reading aloud to us.

We looked up startled for this was no ordinary visit. Six members of the Municipaux had come into the room.

I rose to my feet.

"Messieurs," I began.

One of them spoke and his words struck me like the funeral knell for a loved one.

"We have come to take Louis-Charles Capet to his new prison."

I gave a cry; I reached for my son; he ran to me, his eyes wide with terror.

"You cannot . . ."

"The Commune believes it is time he was put into the care of a tutor. Citizen Simon will care for him."

Simon! I knew this man. A cobbler of the lowest, coarsest, crudest type.

"No, no, *no!*" I cried.

"We're in a hurry," said one of the men roughly. "Come on, Capet. You're moving from here."

I could feel my son clutching my skirts. But rough hands were on him; they were dragging him away.

I ran after them but they threw me off. Elisabeth and my daughter caught me as I fell.

They had gone. They had taken my boy with them.

I could think of nothing but that. My sister-in-law and my daughter tried to comfort me.

There was no comfort. I shall never forget the cries of my son as they carried him away. I could hear him screaming for me.

"Maman . . . Maman . . . don't let them."

It haunts my dreams. Never never can I forget. Never never can I forgive them for doing this to me.

This was depth of sorrow; there could be nothing more terrible . . .

I was wrong. These fiends had found they could plunge me into even further despair.

So I was without him.

Life had no meaning now. He was lost to me . . . my beloved son, my baby.

How could they do this to a woman? Was it because they knew that while I had him with me I could go on living, I could hope, I could even believe that there was some happiness left to me.

I lay on my bed. My daughter sat beside me holding my hand as though to remind me that she still remained. How I could have lived through those days without her and Elisabeth I cannot imagine.

Madame Tison was acting strangely. Perhaps she had been doing so for some time. I was scarcely aware of her. I could think only of my son in the hands of that brutal cobbler. What were they doing to him? Was he crying for me now! I almost wished that he had died as his brother had rather than that he should have come to this pass.

Sometimes I heard as though from a long way off Madame Tison storming at her husband; sometimes I heard her giving way to wild crying.

And one day she came into my room and threw herself at my feet.

"Madame," she cried, "forgive me. I am going mad because I have brought these troubles on you. I have spied on you . . . They are going to murder you as they murdered the King . . . and I am responsible. I see him at night . . . I see his head all bloody . . . it rolls off, Madame, on to my bed. I must have your pardon, Madame. I am going mad . . . mad . . ."

I tried to calm her.

"You have done as you were bidden. Don't blame yourself. I understand."

"It's dreams . . . dreams . . . nightmares. They won't go . . . They are after me . . . even by day. They won't go. I murdered the King . . . I . . . I . . ."

The guards rushed in and carried her away.

Madame Tison had gone mad.

From one of the window slits on the spiral staircase I could see the courtyard where my son was sent out for fresh air.

What joy it seemed when I saw him after all those days.

He no longer looked like my son. His hair was unkempt; his clothes were dirty and he wore the greasy red cap.

I did not call him, I feared it would distress him; but at least I could stand there and watch. Each day at the same hour he came there; so here was something to live for. I should not speak to him, but I should see him.

He did not seem unhappy, for which I was grateful. Children are adaptable. Let me be grateful for that. I saw what they were doing. They were making him one of them, teaching him crudities . . . making him a son of the Revolution. This I realized was the duty of the tutor, to make him forget that the blood of kings ran in his veins, to rob him of dignity, to prove that there was no difference between the sons of kings and the sons of the people.

I shuddered as I heard his shouts.

I listened to his singing. Should I not rejoice that he could sing?

"*Allons, enfants de la patrie . . .*"

The song of the bloodthirsty revolution. Had he forgotten the men who had murdered his father?

I listened to the voice I knew so well:

> "*Ah, ça ira, ça ira, ça ira,*
> *En dépit des aristocrates et de la pluie,*
> *Nous nous mouillerons, mais ça finira*
> *Ça ira, ça ira, ça ira.*

Oh, my son, I thought, they have taught you to betray us.

And I lived for those moments when I could stay at the slit in the wall and watch him at play.

It was only a few weeks after they had taken my son from me when at one o'clock in the morning I heard a knocking at the door.

The Commissaries had come to see me. The Convention had decreed that the Widow Capet was to stand trial. She would therefore be removed from the Temple to the Conciergerie.

I knew that I had received my death sentence. They would try me as they had tried Louis.

There was to be no delay. I was to make ready to go at once.

They allowed me to say goodbye to my daughter and my sister-in-law.

I begged them not to weep for me and I turned away from their sad stunned looks.

"I am ready," I said.

I felt almost eager because I knew this meant death.

Down the stairs, past the slit in the window—no use to look out now. Never . . . never to see him again. I faltered and struck my head against a stone archway.

"Have you hurt yourself?" asked one of the guards, moved as sometimes these brutal men were by a flash of kindness.

"No," I answered. "Nothing can hurt me now."

So I am here . . . the prisoner in the Conciergerie.

This is the grimmest of all the prisons in France. It has become known during this reign of Terror as the anteroom of death. I am waiting to be called in to death as so many waited to be called to see me in my state apartments of Versailles.

I know now that I am here that there are not many days left to me.

Strangely enough I found kindness here. Madame Richard was my jailer —a very different woman from Madame Tison. I saw her compassion from the first. Her first act of kindness was to tell her husband to fix a piece of carpet over the ceiling from which water dripped onto my bed. She told me that when she had whispered to the market woman that the chicken she was buying was for me she had surreptitiously picked out the most plump.

She implied in a hundred ways that I had my friends.

Madame Richard had a boy of the same age as the Dauphin.

"I do not bring Fanfan to see you, Madame," she told me, "because I feared it might remind you of your son and make you sadder."

But I said I would like to meet Fanfan and she brought him. It was true I wept over him for his hair was as fair as the Dauphin's, but I loved to listen to his talk and I looked forward to his visits.

My health was beginning to fail; the damp caused pains in my limbs and I suffered frequent hemorrhages. My room was small and bare; the walls were damp and the paper, stamped with the fleur-de-lis, was peeling off in many places. There was herringbone pattern on the stone floor which I stared at so much that I knew every mark. The bed and the screen were the only furniture. I was glad of the screen for I was under constant supervision and it afforded me the little privacy I had. There was a small barred window which looked onto the paved prison yard for my room was a semi-basement.

Madame Richard had given me the services of one of her servant girls, Rosalie Lamorlière, a kind and gentle creature like her mistress and these two did everything they could to make my life more bearable.

It was Madame Richard who prevailed on Michonis, the chief inspector of the prison, to bring me news of Elisabeth and Marie Thérèse.

"What harm to the Republic could that do?" demanded the good woman.

And Michonis who was a tender-hearted man could see no harm either. He even had clothes brought for me from the Temple and he told me that Madame Elisabeth had said they were what I should need. I was pleased because in spite of my despair I had always been conscious of my appearance and more able to bear my misfortunes if I were suitably dressed. So it was with a mild pleasure that I discarded the long black dress which was frayed at the hem and the white fischu which never seemed white enough, for something which I thought more fitting. My eyes were constantly watering. I had shed so many tears. I missed the little porcelain eye bath I had used in the Temple but Rosalie brought a mirror for me which she told me was a bargain. She had paid twenty-five sous for it on the quais. I felt I had never possessed such a charming mirror. It had a red border with little figures round it.

The length of the days! There is nothing I can do. I write a little but they are watchful and suspicious. There is always a guard sitting in the corner of my room. Sometimes there are two. I watch them playing cards. Madame Richard brought me books and I read a great deal. I have kept a little leather glove which my son used to wear when he was very small. It is one of my greatest treasures—in a locket I have a picture of Louis-Charles. I often kiss it when the guards are not looking.

The nights are so long. I am not allowed a lamp or even a candle. The changing of the guard always awakens me if I am dozing. I sleep very little.

Michonis came into my cell today. With him was a stranger. He dismissed the guards for a few moments. He said he would guard me. With him was a stranger who was looking at prisons. I asked the usual questions about my family and looking closer at the stranger I recognized him as a Colonel of the Grenadiers, a man of great loyalty and courage, the Chevalier de Rougeville. He saw that I recognized him and with a quick gesture he threw something into the stove.

When he and Michonis had left I went to the stove and found a carnation. I was disappointed and then examining it closer I discovered a thin paper among the petals.

On it I read:

"I shall never forget you. If you have need of three or four hundred livres for those who surround you I will bring them next Friday."

The note continued to tell me that he had a plan for my escape. Would I agree to this?

I felt my hopes rising. This I believed was another of Axel's attempts. He would never tire of making them, I knew. The money would be brought for me to bribe my guards . . . a means would be found for taking me out of the place. And when I was out we would bring out my children and my sister-in-law, and we should join Axel. We would work to bring back the Monarchy to end this reign of Terror. I believed we could do it. People like the Richards, Rosalie, Michonis upheld me in this belief.

But how to smuggle out a note?

I tore up the fragments of his and wrote:

"I depend on you. I will come."

I must get the note to Rougeville. Rosalie would take it. But what if she were discovered? That would be a poor way to repay her for all she had done.

No, I would not involve her or Madame Richard, so I asked one of the guards, Gilbert, to give it to the stranger when he next came to the Conciergerie which he would most certainly do. The stranger would reward him with four hundred louis.

Gilbert took the note and then was terrified so he showed it to Madame Richard. She was sympathetic but she did not wish to risk her head so she showed it to Michonis. Both these people were good; they were sorry for me; but they were servants of the Republic. They did not wish to betray me so Michonis advised Madame Richard to warn me of the dangers of such actions to all of us.

Had Gilbert said nothing all would have been well and it would have been just another attempt that failed. In any case it was too vague to have come to anything and I wondered afterward how I could have been so foolish as to have hoped it could.

Gilbert told his superior officer and as a result Michonis was dismissed and so were the Richards.

I now have new jailers. They are not unkind but in view of what happened to the Richards they will run no risks.

I miss that kind woman; I miss little Fanfan.

And slowly the days and nights pass.

Soon they will bring me to stand my trial.

The time has come. This morning the door of my cell was opened and an usher and four gendarmes entered. They had come to conduct me to the old Grand Chambre which was now called the Hall of Liberty.

It is the seat of the Revolutionary Tribunal: the tapestries decorated with fleurs-de-lis which I had known had been removed and the picture of the Crucifixion replaced by another representing the Rights of Man. I was given a seat on a bench in front of Fouquier-Tinville, the Public Prosecutor. The room was dim for it was lighted only by two candles.

They asked me my name and I replied calmly: "Marie Antoinette of Lorraine and Austria."

"Before the Revolution you carried on political relations with foreign powers and these were contrary to the interests of France from which you drew many advantages."

"This is not true."

"You have squandered the finances of France, the fruit of the people's sweat for your pleasure and intrigues."

"No," I said, but inwardly I felt sick. I thought of my extravagances: The Petit Trianon, Madame Bertin's bills, Monsieur Léonard's services. I was guilty . . . deeply guilty.

"Since the Revolution you have never ceased to intrigue with foreign powers and at home against liberty . . ."

"Since the Revolution I have forbidden myself any correspondence abroad and I have never meddled at home."

But it was not true. I was lying. I had sent out my appeals to Axel. I had written to Barnave and Mercy.

Oh yes, they would prove me guilty for I was guilty in their eyes.

"It was you who taught Louis Capet the art of profound dissimulation by which he so long deceived the good French people."

I closed my eyes and shook my head.

"When you left Paris in June 1791 you opened the doors and made everyone leave. There is no doubt that it was you who ruled the actions of Louis Capet and persuaded him to flight."

"I do not think that an open door proves that one is constantly ruling a person's actions."

"Never for one moment have you ceased wanting to destory liberty. You wanted to reign at any price and reascend the throne over the bodies of patriots."

"We had no need to reascend the throne. We were already there. We have never wished for anything but France's happiness. As long as she was happy, as long as she is so, we shall always be satisfied."

"Do you think a King necessary for a people's happiness?"

"An individual cannot decide such matters."

"No doubt you regret that your son has lost a throne to which he might have mounted if the people, finally conscious of their rights, had not destroyed the throne?"

"I shall never regret anything for my son when his country is happy."

The questions continued. They asked about the Trianon. Who had paid for the Trianon?

"There was a special fund for the Trianon. I hope that everything connected with it will be made public for I believe it to be greatly exaggerated."

"It was at the Petit Trianon that you first met Madame de la Motte."

"I never met her."

"But did you not make her your scapegoat in the fraud of the Diamond Necklace?"

"I never met her."

It was then I believed I was living in a nightmare . . . that I had died and gone to hell. I could not believe that I heard correct.

What were these monsters saying about my son? They were accusing us of incest. My own child! A boy of eight! I could not believe it. This Hébert . . . this monster . . . this crude man of the streets was telling this court that I had taught my son immoral practices . . . that I had . . . But I cannot write it. It is too painful; too horrible . . . too fantastically absurd!

My son had admitted it, they said. We had indulged in these practices . . . he and I and Elisabeth . . . His saintly Aunt Elisabeth and I his mother!

I was staring ahead of me. I saw the boy playing in the yard . . . my boy who was in the hands of these wicked men. I saw the dirty red cap on his head; I heard the coarse words in his mouth; I heard him singing the Ça Ira in his childish voice.

They had forced this confession from him. They had taught him what to say. They had ill-treated him, made him agree to what he could not understand. He was eight years old and I was his mother. I loved him. I had lost my lover and my husband—and my boy was my life. Yet they had taught him to say these things of me . . . and his aunt who had taught him to say his prayers.

I heard only snatches of the report. I heard them say that they had confronted him with his sister, with his aunt and that naturally these two had denied the accusations. It was natural, they said, that these people who were capable of such unnatural actions should.

His Aunt Elisabeth had called him a monster.

Oh Elisabeth, I thought, my dear Elisabeth, what did you think of my boy?

I had believed when they took him from me that I had touched the depth of despair. Now I knew that I had not done so then. There was more to be suffered. This!

Horror possessed me. What had they done to my child to make him say this? They had ill-treated him . . . starved him, beaten him. He, the King of France, my love, my darling!

Hébert—surely these people only had to look at him to understand that he was a degraded creature—was looking at me slyly. How he hated me! I remembered how he had regarded me when we had first come into his power. Devil! I thought. You are not fit to live on this earth. Oh God, save my child from such men.

I felt that I was going to faint. I fixed my eyes on the candles trying to steady myself. And then I was conscious of what I so often encountered in my prisons . . . the sympathy of women. There were mothers in this courtroom and they would understand how I was feeling. I was an enemy of the state, they believed; I was haughty, arrogant, and I had frittered away the finances of France . . . but I was a mother and they knew I loved my son. I felt those women in the courtroom would vindicate me.

Even Hébert was aware. He was growing a little uneasy.

He did not believe that this disgustingly immoral conduct was indulged in for the sake of immorality. It was solely for the purpose of weakening my son's health so that when he became King I should govern him, that I should be able to dominate him and rule through him.

I could only look at this man with the contempt and loathing I felt. I could not see those women in the court but I knew they were there and I felt that they were with me. Perhaps they were those who had cried *Antoinette à la lanterne,* but I was not a Queen now I was a mother, accused by a man with brutality written all over his face. And they did not believe him.

They believed the stories of my lovers; but they would not believe this.

I heard someone say: "The prisoner makes no comment on this accusation."

I heard my voice loud and clear echoing through the court.

"If I have made no reply it is because nature refuses to answer such a charge brought against a mother. I appeal to all the mothers present in this court."

I sensed the excitement, the murmurs of anger.

"Take the prisoner away," was the order.

Back to my cell.

Rosalie was waiting for me. She tried to make me eat but I could not. She made me lie down.

She told me later that she had heard Robespierre was furious with Hébert for bringing the charge against me. It was false. Everyone knew it was false. No one doubted my love for my son. Robespierre was afraid that had I stayed in that courtroom the women would have risen against my judges and demanded my freedom, that my son be given back to me.

"Oh, Madame, Madame," sobbed Rosalie and she knelt by my bed and wept bitterly.

I was taken back to the court. I listened to an account of my sins. I had plotted with foreign powers; I had led my husband into wrong doing; I had squandered the country's money on Trianon and my favorites; the Polignacs were mentioned; but nothing was said of that other vile charge.

Then the questions were put to the jurors:

Was it established that there were intrigues and secret dealings with foreign powers and other external enemies of the Republic, which intrigues and secret dealings aimed at giving them momentary assistance enabling them to enter French territory and facilitating the progress of their armies there?

Was I convicted of having co-operated in these intrigues?

Was it established that there was a plot and a conspiracy to start civil war with the Republic?

Was Marie Antoinette, widow of Louis Capet, convicted of taking part in this plot and conspiracy?

I was taken to a small room close to the Grande Chambre while the jury decided, but the verdict was a foregone conclusion.

At length, it came. I was guilty and I should be punished by death.

I sit in my room writing. There is little more to be said.

First I must write to Elisabeth. I think of what my son has said of her and knowing her chaste mind I understand well how shocked she will be. I must make her try to understand.

I take up my pen.

"It is to you, sister, that I write for the last time. I have just been condemned, not to a shameful death, for it is shameful only for criminals, but to rejoin your brother. Like him, innocent, I hope to display the same firmness as he did in his last moments. I am calm as one is when one's conscience holds no reproach. I deeply regret having to abandon my poor children. You know that I lived only for them and for you, my good sister. In what a situation do I leave you, who for your affection sacrificed everything to be with us . . ."

I went on to write of my dear daughter whom I had heard had been separated from her. I wanted her to help her brother if that were possible . . . And I must write of my son to Elisabeth. I must try to make her understand.

". . . I have to mention something which pains my heart. I know how much distress this child must have caused you. Forgive him, my dear sister. Remember his age and how easy it is to make a child say anything you want, even something he does not understand. The day will come, I hope, when he will be the more conscious of the worth of your goodness and tenderness . . ."

The tears were blinding me and I could write no more, but later I would take up my pen and finish.

The time is almost upon me.

The cart will come for me. They will cut my hair; they will tie my hands behind my back; and I shall ride through the streets along the well-known route which so many of my friends of the old days have traveled . . . as Louis went before me, through streets where I once rode in my carriage drawn by white horses, where Monsieur de Brissac had told me two hun-

dred thousand Frenchmen were in love with me . . . through the Rue
Saint-Honoré where Madame Bertin might be watching, to the Place de
la Revolution and the monster guillotine.

They will shout at me as they have so many times before, and I shall be
thinking of my life as I ride. I shall not see the streets with those shouting
gesticulating crowds all calling for my blood. I shall think of Louis gone
before me, of Axel, grieving somewhere . . . oh but do not mourn too
bitterly, my love, for I shall be past my pains. I shall be thinking of my
boy and praying that he will not suffer too great a remorse. My darling
. . . it is nothing. I forgive you . . . You did not know what you said.

So now I wait and pray that during this last ride I shall be a true
daughter of my mother. I shall face death with the courage she would
have wished.

There is no time to write more. They are coming.

A great calm has descended on me. There is one thing of which I am
certain. The worst is over; I have suffered the greatest pain. What remains is the last sharp stroke which will bring deliverance.

I am ready. And I am not afraid. It is to live that requires courage—
not to die.

BIBLIOGRAPHY

Abbott, John Stevens Cabot. *History of Marie Antoinette.*
Albini, F. D. *Marie Antoinette and the Diamond Necklace.*
Anthony, Katharine. *Marie Antoinette.*
Arneth, Alfred Ritter von and Geffroy, M. A. *Correspondance secrète entre Marie Thérèse et Mercy-Argenteau et Marie Antoinette.*
Aulard, A. Translated by B. Miall. *The French Revolution.*
Barbey, Frédéric. *A Friend of Marie Antoinette.*
Batiffol, Louis. Translated by Elsie Finnimore Buckley. *National History of France.*
Baumann, Emile. *Marie Antoinette et Fersen.*
Belloc, Hilaire. *Marie Antoinette.*
Bicknell, Anna L. *The Story of Marie Antoinette.*
Bidou. *Paris.*
Bishop, M. C. *The Prison Life of Marie Antoinette.*
Campan, Madame. *Mémoires.*
—— *Memoirs of the Court of Marie Antoinette and Anecdotes of her Private Life.*
Carlyle, Thomas. *The French Revolution.*
Castelot, André. *Marie Antoinette.*
Coryn, M. *Marie Antoinette and Axel de Fersen.*
Dumas, Alexandre. *La Route de Varennes.*
Dunlop, Ian. *Versailles.*
Funck-Bretano, Franz. Translated by Sutherland Edwards. *The Diamond Necklace.*
Gaxotte, Pierre. Translated by J. Lewis May. *Louis the Fifteenth and His Times.*
Gooch, G. P. *Louis Fifteenth, the Monarchy in Decline.*
Guizot, M. Translated by Robert Black. *History of France.*
Haggard, Lieut. Colonel Andrew, C. P. *The Real Louis XV.*
—— *Louis XVI and Marie Antoinette.*
—— *Women of the Revolutionary Era.*
Heidenstamm, O. G. de. *The Letters of Marie Antoinette, Fersen and Barnave.*
Hudson, William Henry. *France.*

Kunstler, Charles. Translated by Margot Robert Adam. *Personal Life of Marie Antoinette.*
Lenôtre, G. Translated by Frederick Lees. *The Dauphin (Louis XVII).*
Lenôtre, G. Translated by H. Noel Williams. *Paris in the Revolution.*
Mairobert, Pidansat de. *Memoirs of Madame du Barry.*
Mathiez, Albert. *The French Revolution.*
Mercier, Louis Sébastien. *Le Tableau de Paris.*
Michelet, Jules. *Histoire de France.*
—— *Louis XV et Louis XVI.*
Montague, Violette. *The Celebrated Madame Campan.*
Morris, C. L. *Maria Theresa.*
Morton, J. B. *The Bastille Falls.*
—— *The Dauphin.*
Pilkington, Iain, D. B. *The King's Pleasure, The Story of Louis XV.*
—— *Queen of the Trianon.*
Rochéterie, Maxime de et le Marquis de Beaucourt (Editées par). *Lettres de Marie Antoinette.*
Rothschild, Baron Ferdinand. *Personal Characters from French History.*
Saint-Amand, Imbert de. Translated by Thomas Sergeant Perry. *Marie Antoinette, The End of the Old Régime.*
Saint-Armand, Imbert de. *La Dernière Année de Marie Antoinette.*
Sainte-Beuve, C. A. Translated by Katharine P. Wormeley. *Portraits of the Eighteenth Century.*
Schumacher, Karl von. Translated by Dorothy M. Richardson. *The Du Barry.*
Stryienski, Casimir. Translated by H. N. Dickinson. *The National History of France.*
Thiers, Louis Adolphe. Translated by Frederick Shoberl. *History of the French Revolution.*
Webster, Nesta H. *The French Revolution.*
—— *Louis XVI and Marie Antoinette. Before the Revolution.*
Yonge, Charles Duke. *The Life of Marie Antoinette.*
Younghusband, H. A. *Marie Antoinette, Her Early Youth.*
Zweig, Stefan. *Marie Antoinette.*